Jean Watt.

KT-584-511

A WOMAN IN SUNSHINE

A WOMAN IN SUNSHINE

FRANK SWINNERTON

'He that has light within his own clear breast
May sit i' the centre, and enjoy bright day:
But he that hides a dark soul and foul thoughts
Benighted walks under the mid-day sun;
Himself is his own dungeon.'

JOHN MILTON: *Comus.*

HUTCHINSON & CO. (*Publishers*) LTD.
LONDON : NEW YORK : MELBOURNE

MADE AND PRINTED IN GREAT BRITAIN AT
ST. ALBANS BY *The Mayflower Press (of
Plymouth)*, WILLIAM BRENDON & SON, LTD.

CONTENTS

Part One

THE OCTOBER SUN

Part Two

THE CLOUDS GATHER

Part Three

TEMPTATIONS

CONTENTS

Part Four

AFTERPIECE

THE OCTOBER SUN

One

THE GLIMPSE

ALTHOUGH THE AUTUMN day was as mild as late Spring, Letitia, entering the tall house in Kensington, slightly shivered. She was pale; the hand holding her doorkey had hesitated. She closed the door behind her as if she had escaped a pursuing ghost.

A moment later, soothed by the familiar warm silence of her home, she was normal again; smilingly unreadable, a dark-haired woman of the middle height, with unlined brow and wise eyes, obviously good-natured, and quite sure of herself. One would never have guessed at that shiver, that hesitation, that over-quick closing of the door.

It was then that Letitia saw always-attentive Ruth, who came with a whisper of silk from the shadowed corner beyond Monty's study door. Ruth waited, as if with a watch in her hand, until it was almost intolerably the last instant to speak. Just so, Letitia thought, knowing well that Ruth suffered from a nervous catch in her breath, might a pedantic producer time the entrance of a messenger. Ruth was the messenger. She would announce death or her own marriage with the same outward serenity. Wonderful Ruth! She shrank mysteriously to diminished plumpness when she spoke; there came from a small circle between her rosy cheeks a low and beautiful voice. Above both the circle and the cheeks her chocolate brown eyes glowed, like those of an affectionate horse, in a funless smile of adoration.

'Mrs. Wilton is here, Madame,' she murmured.

Oh, heavens! Constance! Letitia, no longer amused by Ruth, exclaimed at her own forgetfulness. She alone knew how clearly it betrayed the disturbance of her mind.

'Very long?'

'Not ten minutes, Madame. She said she was quite happy.'

They exchanged smiles at this discreet echo of a heartier speech. In turning, Letitia said quickly:

'Thank you, Ruth. We'd better have tea at once.'

'Yes, Madame.'

Ruth moved away with stiff shoulders. But Letitia knew that she would patter at full speed, like a little dog, down the kitchen stairs, probably jumping the last two of them with a flying skirt. Ruth was at least half-a-dozen people, from unspoiled country kid to parlourmaid; perhaps, for a young man, an elusive, maddeningly unreadable torment, playing with her lover until, in desperation, he struck her. How strange, thought Letitia, that would be! Not impossible. Nothing in human affairs was impossible . . .

Then: Dear Constance! Always impatiently patient. Always, restlessly, quite happy!

She hurried to the first floor, unfastening as she went the top button of her short coat of grey Persian lamb. And as she swept impulsively into the blue and yellow room, contrite, but sure of pardon, she cried:

'Constance! Unforgivable! I put myself upon God and my country——'

Her face was flushed with recent haste, not with shame. She could never keep out of her smile the natural merriment which gave her the vivacity of a girl. Yet she was fifty-three, and, by the standards of the era in which she had been born, an elderly woman. At a similar age her grandmother had folded idle hands and worn a white cap. Her mother, had she been a different kind of woman, might have done the same without anachronism.

Constance sat in front of the fire, a thin creature with a very white face and frighteningly yellow hair, dressed in a silk of brilliant green which made her resemble a gigantic parakeet. There was no shadow between herself and Letitia. This room was her ideal resting-place. She liked to sit in it, to move here and there about its ample space, and to wonder gapingly why, like a stage, it always moved her to thrilling elation.

Like a stage. The audience was there at the window, or by the chimney-piece; and she herself was imaginarily eloquent in a part of her own choosing which could never, by any miracle of authorship, be written. It passed at lightning speed from 'No, no, Sir Jasper; unhand me this instant!' to 'Ah, moi dear-r-r little gairl, listen to an ould woo-oo-man who's seen the wurruld's wickudness . . .' And from a child's innocence to a wanton's shrill laughter and the mockery of one who recognised *all* the shams of the theatre and hugged them to her heart. Every melodramatic tag of the Victorian stage had its place in Constance's dream-part. She was as quick and skittish and firm as a mother-cat playing with a kitten.

And she could not isolate this room's secret; perhaps because it was the product of height and shape and character. She knew only that it was like a stage; that, for London, it was astonishingly lucent; and that it offered her—besides its sunny breadth, fine open fire, full length mirror, recently published books, bold, almost modern but still comprehensible pictures of town and country scenes, and unceasing memory of its mistress—an absorbing puzzle for the mind and heart.

There was always more to think about this room. Always more to think about Letitia and her family . . .

Constance, who had been stretching one foot towards the fire, in order to admire her own instep (for self-admiration was so natural to her that it was woven into her deepest concerns with love, friendship and meta-physics), instantly felt, as always, that she had been interrupted just as she was on the point of solving the mystery. She leapt up to meet her friend's embrace.

'I'd wait a hollow week,' she declared, in her over-emphatic way. What a deep voice she had! It filled the room. 'I'd wait a month. Without a whinny of protest.'

'Hollow but heroic!' agreed Letitia, laughing.

'One feasts on beauty and hope.' Constance peeped at Letitia, her comedienne's white face droll under the genuinely curly but artificially yellow hair. Thirty years earlier she had been a bizarre beauty; now she wore an indiarubber mask which could be endlessly distorted, as a rule into expressions of arch wickedness. When, at this moment, she looked away, and upwards, the flick of those long-lashed big green eyes, which were catlike in their power to be suddenly and purposefully intent, was of irrepressible, intimidating slyness. 'Why, you might be a child again! It's the hat, of course. No, the complexion. No, the—oh, my dear, how you *manage* it!'

She groaned. The twisted mouth opened. One saw her raised tongue, which was pretty and mocking and sharp-pointed. At a glimpse of it, any determined bachelor would have seized his hat and bolted to China, Labrador, or Llandudno; any domineering wife would have gathered her strength for battle in the last ditch of possession; any priggish maiden lady would have shivered with hope for the worst. But Letitia had no qualm. They had been friends for nearly forty years, bound together by common love of the theatre and by mutual respect and affection; and the dangerous insincerity of Constance's manner never stirred a doubt in her breast. We all have a technique in speechless communication, and each of these women was mistress of her own.

So it was that, this afternoon, Constance told Letitia, without words, that before they turned to less attractive matters she wished an eye to be given to her slimness and satisfactory chic, and to the fact that she was well and in funds. Letitia, who was so much more moderate in all things that she always rested Constance's ego, similarly told her friend that everything had been observed and admired, that she, for her part, was healthy, and that she would be glad if Constance would not at this moment try to discover why she had been late.

Both, drawing apart, smiled in pleasure. Each felt that the other kept almost no unimportant secrets from her, and that their mutual understanding was entirely feminine. Then, with her hat and coat removed, Letitia looked as if she had been present all the afternoon; and Constance looked as if she did not know that Letitia had just had a painful shock.

Constance, boisterously tactful, exclaimed:

'I adore this room! You never leave me here long enough. A day, two days . . . I shouldn't notice. "I try door after door." I'd even wait —firm as a mountain—not a tremor—to hear the result of an X-Ray.'

'Oh, dear!' cried Letitia, gaily. 'My dream to bring Harley Street into the home!'

Constance's eyes rolled. That large mouth opened again, lengthening her chin to extraordinary depth. A notable shrug twisted not only her expressive shoulders but her whole person.

'Absurd! Only the stillness. The clock. How I looked at *that* when Ruth said you weren't back. I said "Good heavens! Not back? Something's happened!" ' She imitated her terrible cry with relish. ' "Something awful!" ' The lashes flickered at Letitia; a sign of great danger, often the prelude to a pouncing question that left one breathless. Letitia felt her heart stop beating. Then a slight thudding flurry was followed once more by the dull ache of shock which she had had for the past half-hour.

Danger passed. She did not exclaim. And although she could not have said whether she smiled, and in smiling refused to betray the smallest sign of anguish, she knew that Constance was reluctantly obeying her demand for peace. Constance said:

'*No* waiting-room has a full length mirror.'

Letitia smiled in relief.

'Yes, the mirror's good,' she calmly observed. 'A great success with judges.'

'To see if their wigs——. No, naturally not . . . You astonish me, Letitia!' Constance, contorting her face into a look of surprise at the vanity of grave old men, could not keep it up. She laughed ringingly, a good hearty laugh that hit every projecting angle in the room. 'How I'd love to see one of them!'

She became a judge, catching unexpected sight of herself in the mirror, posing severely, less severely, tolerantly, and with gradually triumphing benevolence, until the mimicry ended in a stage chambermaid's backward kick of glee . . .

Ruth, demurely rustling, and wearing her set little smile, entered with the tea-wagon. She moved deftly about the room, gathered Letitia's hat and coat from a chair, disappeared behind the silently closed door. Constance, watching with greedy professional eyes, said when Ruth had gone:

'The French say we over-act. It's true. Ruth's perfection shames me!'

As if to prove her shame, she grinned maliciously at Letitia, who was pouring out tea—as they both perceived—with the quite comparable perfection of the perfect hostess.

ii

'Now that we're alone, darling,' Constance presently began. Letitia felt alarm. 'And you're refreshed by a cup of tea——'

'You're going to relieve your conscience?' asked Letitia.

'No, no. I'm serious. I want to tell you *my* troubles.'

Letitia, sitting quite still, could think again. Her fingers rested against the cold tray; she saw the sunlight pass from the room. '*My* troubles!' They were at cross purposes.

'*Have* you got troubles?' she breathlessly said. 'Oh, Constance, I'm ashamed to have teased——'

'Not in *that* sense.' Constance was merciful; it was too much to hope that she had noticed nothing. 'No, I'm all poshed up, as you see—a little vulgar, I grant; but it's what I like. I *am* vulgar. And I'm in a vulgar show that's opening at the end of the month. No, *my* trouble's old Gabriel's trouble.'

'Poor Gabriel! Is he unhappy?'

'Unhappy!' snapped Constance. 'When was he anything else?' The lively face was full of shadows. 'He's ill.'

'He's never quite well.'

'Malingering. This is different. That's what I meant about the X-Ray!'

'Constance!' Letitia was overwhelmed by a sense of her own egotism, her levity. 'Are you sure?'

'I'm sure, all right. He's like a death's head.'

Letitia pictured the bony little face of Gabriel, which was that of an ascetic whose fasting had turned his blood to gall. Constance's description would have been apt at any time.

'That might be something constitutional. One builds a panic very easily.'

'I know. But he's riding me off. Pretending he's never been heartier. Actually *singing*. It's grotesque.'

'Good heavens!'

'Loathsome. Uncanny. Because of course Gabriel's no stoic, wearing the old school upper lip. He's as terrified as I am.'

'Poor Gabriel!' This news was disturbing, for Gabriel was the kind of man who spreads his discomforts to as wide a circle as possible. Letitia had always seen him as a creaking door; one who, living in sickness for a century, would at last, with impunity, and to the maddened annoyance of their offspring, write pungent memoirs of his defunct friends. 'Will he see a doctor?'

'He's done it. I'm *sure*. But who? If I knew, I'd find out everything.'

'Yes. Could you? Isn't it like the confessional?'

'It wouldn't be.' Constance grimly smiled. 'They're only men. I'd go as a patient. "Oh, doctor, I could get better if only children believed in fairies—if I knew what's the matter with my husband——" Yes, but I can't find anything! It's extraordinary. I've ransacked his desk. Nothing about this. Several other curious things that would amuse us if I weren't so worried. I'll tell you, some time . . . I've unlocked his locked cupboard where he kept the prussic acid——'

'Constance!'

'Oh, that was long ago. I substituted oil of almonds. You *have* to do these things. Not you; but then Monty's sane. Not a wild-headed idiot——'

'But prussic acid!'

'Oh, some idiotic notion.'

'It was daring of you——'

Constance allowed herself a sudden grin.

'I've wondered if he ever took it. After one of our rows, when he's ready to cut off his nose to spite my face. "I'm done with her!" *Takes poison, and waits.* Frightful anticlimax. Rather a relief, I expect, when nothing happens.'

'Unbearable humiliation,' objected Letitia, seriously.

'Who cares?' Constance was defiant in face of possible criticism. 'What about the public humiliation of his wife?' She did not pause for any comment; but continued: 'I've checked the stubs in his cheque books.

He doesn't know I know about his second account; but I do. It's in the name of Marmaduke Stacey. How ridiculous! Childish! I've been through his telephone calls. Oh, he's a devil! Fiendish at covering his tracks, if it's only been half-an-hour alone in a news theatre.'

Sympathetic as she was, Letitia could not help smiling at these motherly disclosures. Her friend was without pride. But what an uneasy marriage in which one rummaged a husband's desk! Thank God for Monty! She had long known the secretiveness of little Gabriel, the hollow-eyed, round-shouldered, dramatist who tenderly pressed one's fingers as he whispered imaginary sorrows and symptoms; but Gabriel, for all his naughty pen, was innocent, and if he were frightened about himself it was with reason. The smile passed.

'What shall we do?' she asked. 'D'you think Monty as Sherlock Holmes——'

'Oh, nothing so archaic! Hopeless. Gabriel's quite *smart*, Letitia!'

'I'm sure he is,' agreed Letitia, unruffled. 'You love him.'

'I'm his *slave*!' A famous squeak came into Constance's voice. On the stage it always brought a laugh. But though it was now meant equally to amuse—and to expunge the insult to Letitia's husband—it held affecting pathos. The slave Constance had no disguise left.

There was a little emotion-filled pause, in which with every dropping of the eyelids a change occurred in their mutual understanding. At last Letitia realised that Constance had lost her first instinctive resistance to Monty as intermediary.

'Monty's really rather adroit.'

'I'm sure of it. Sure.' Constance slipped into wariness. 'But isn't he too much the tactician? Gabriel's as quick as a monkey—almost before you've thought the thing yourself.'

Letitia spiritedly retorted:

'Well, Monty's no remainder biscuit. I've known him quicker than light.'

It all seemed new to Constance. She no longer denied; but she said, as if meditating aloud:

'Isn't it funny how you can know people a lifetime and sort of *not* know them. I'm devoted to Monty—that's obvious. I'm carried away when he flatters me. He's the nicest man I know. Far nicer of course, than Gabriel, who's like an old witch. But I never quite do myself justice with Monty. It's that awful wig, you know.'

'But dearest, he doesn't wear wigs at home. You've got wigs——'

'I know. On the green. But I *see* it all the time. Like the sword of Damocles. I should be terrified of him in Court. "What were you doing at six o'clock on the twenty-sixth of February, nineteen hundred and ten?" Of course, not the faintest notion. Something wrong, I've no doubt; but *what*? Myself stuttering; and all those furious men in wigs, shouting "Answer the question! Answer the question!"'

Letitia, laughing, cried:

'You eat hearty suppers!' Poor Monty, the mildest man who ever scuttled a battleship——'

'Don't ever tell him this, Letitia! I should faint if I thought——'

'You don't definitely refuse his help over Gabriel?'

'No, no! I only—forgive me, darling; we have no reserves—I only doubt if he's got the rather . . . hectic pace——'

'This is where pride in our greyhounds clashes!' declared Letitia. 'But I really don't depend on Monty's speed. Rather, on his embracing heart. And of course on Gabriel's *need*. Look here, let me *tell* Monty. If he thinks he can help, we'll get him to work. He'd say "no" at once if he thought it. Bring Gabriel to dinner. Tell him he needs some legal jargon for his play. Tell him Monty's bursting with material for a great Court scene.'

'But is he?' Constance ruefully pursed her lips.

'He will be.'

Constance said at length: 'Well, you know him to the heart. I don't. I always respect him too much to think he's clever.'

'That's his cleverness,' Letitia asserted.

'Yes, yes, I see that. Gabriel says I'm superficial. You won't think I've been beastly, will you? One's so self-centred. When shall we come?'

'I'll ask Monty this evening. He's in London.'

Constance looked at her friend with lightning quickness; to be satisfied that it was not over Monty that she had been alarmed this afternoon. No discovery, for example, that Monty had a mistress . . . Or that he'd murdered, embezzled, turned over some new horrible leaf . . . Evidently not Monty. Who? What? Well, it had been a bargain that the confessions that day should be her own . . .

'And ring me? Thank you, darling. Now we'll forget it.'

'Tell me about the new part. You're pleased with it?'

'Well——' Constance would be *pleased* with nothing short of Lady Macbeth. 'It's passable. The usual henlike old mother with three brilliant young Left Wing cygnets. A sort of fussy up-to-date Malaprop, spiced with politics. Rather clever; but nothing in it. I wonder young dramatists don't tire of guying their parents.'

'This one's young, is he?'

'He'd be adolescent at any age. And the children get all the fat. Talking about children, how are *your* three?'

Letitia thought: That was premeditated! At the Bar she'd make witnesses jump like parched peas. She said:

'Much as usual, I think. Christine still at the School of Economics; settling everything with a high voice. Often at her least likeable; charming when she's not crushing. Mark's talking to magistrates——'

'Does he still talk to his wife?'

'Why not?'

'I only wondered. I shouldn't think she was easy.'

'No.' Letitia seemed to consider. In reality, she was noticing that her heartbeat was certainly less steady. 'No, she's not easy. I think she's kind and intelligent, though. And Mark's a better talker than you think. Like Monty.'

'You're a tease, Letitia. I love them all. I won't let you suggest that I undervalue them.'

'Far from it. But you *must* let me tease you. And Mark does seem to get some acquittals. He and Monty are very legal when they're together. Monty thinks well of him.'

'Of course he does; they're exactly alike.'

Letitia smiled, seeing in fancy the two long heads close together, and the lines of their minds extending, without contact, to infinity. She didn't think them at all alike.

'In sincerity, at least,' she mildly answered.

There was a short pause, by which Constance indicated that she thought her friend fondly self-deceived. Such a pity, when she'd so excellently brought up three of them. Constance, to her grief, was childless. She remembered that; supposing Letitia also to remember it when, as now, it was inconvenient.

'And I assume Julian's still in America?'

Letitia had been long prepared.

'I haven't heard from him for a month,' she blandly replied. 'He's almost as mysterious as Gabriel.'

'Oh, Gabriel——' began Constance, completely deflected. 'It's a sort of *meanness* in Gabriel. He's like a *miser*. But what he hoards is just nothing. A scrap of something you wouldn't want to see, even if he showed it to you.'

'Maddening. Like a boy's pockets!'

In spite of her hearty agreement, Letitia thought, but did not say: In this case probably a doctor's temporising prescription. They wouldn't tell him. Or you, whatever you think. Only each other, in the way doctors do —whisper, whisper behind their hands; much more terrifying than the flat truth. No wonder you're frightened, poor lamb! In your place I should be out of my wits! Oh dear, that's crazy! Am I *in* them?

iii

Constance had gone when Monty returned home. Letitia, having had time only to remount the stairs, saw him from the drawing-room window, coming along the road in the twilight, a very tall top-hatted figure with rather stooping broad shoulders, carrying his umbrella in hands which were bunched behind his back.

He walked slowly, all elasticity lost. With a pang, she understood that, when alone, he was melancholy, and that he was ageing. The vivacious kindness which he showed in company was no longer active. Now, supposing himself unobserved, an anonymous creature in a London street, he yielded wholly to sadness. Letitia moved impulsively to the window, other thoughts pushed away by this realisation. Monty was tired now; perhaps depressed. Should she run downstairs to meet him, or leave him to himself? Oh, *go*. *Always* go. You could withdraw at a glance, and no harm done; but to refrain from going was cowardice. A silent house, underlining loneliness or failure or disappointment, might carry a sensitive man to the depths.

She went slowly down the broad staircase, reaching the middle of the lower flight just as Monty, having admitted himself, turned, breathing audibly, to hang up his hat and coat. What did that breathing indicate?

Letitia was thankful, then, that she had come; for his face, which had been drawn with weariness, lighted in a smile which none but Christine and herself could evoke. It was a good face, long-chinned, clean-lipped, and not too narrow at the cheekbones; very broad above the temples. Though Monty's hair was thinning, he had still, when he smiled and straightened his shoulders, a youthful distinction.

'Hullo, Pet!' he cried. 'I hope this means you're alone. How are you?'

'I'm alone; and everything's all right. Do you want a drink?'

'No, I don't think so. I'd rather sit quietly. Have we to go out tonight?'

'No. We're alone. Not even Christine.'

'Glorious. A quiet evening—my dream.'

It did no harm to think that. It wasn't true. He needed sharp distractions.

'Well, come into the study. There's a fire there, I know.' She found that his hands were rather cold; he had been walking slowly, and the warmth of the day had gone. She knew him to be a man of moods, and this was the mood of lowered hope. Its visits were becoming too frequent. And, much as she herself—having a merry heart which relished its own inventions—enjoyed solitude, Letitia wondered whether, in Monty, that expressed desire for it might not be a sign of darker moods to come. Like an animal going away to die. 'I've had Constance to tea. She's to be in a new show.'

'But not tonight,' he benignly observed. 'So long as it's deferred, nothing's lost.'

'That's true,' said Letitia. 'I promised to ask her to dinner soon, though.'

Monty was warming his hands at the open fire. When he rubbed them together they chafed like two parchment sheets. It was a dark room now that illumination came only from a table lamp and the fire; and while his chin and the tip of his nose caught the light of a flickering coal the rest of his face was in shadow.

'I don't mind. I like Constance. I like her better than she likes me.'

'No, not as much as she likes you. But you disconcert her, Monty. She imagines you in a wig.'

The flicker revealed his smile. He murmured:

'It's probably a complex. I expect she's buried babies at the bottom of the garden. She sees me as justice. But it won't be I who'll judge her.'

Letitia sat down in an armchair.

'Evidently you *do* judge her,' she said. 'You realise that Gabriel will come, too.'

'I can bear it. However, poor fellow, this is no time to speak harshly of him.'

Letitia was startled.

'You *know* he's ill?'

'Bless me, yes. He's got a stone; or so they suppose. It's painful and it's alarming—at his age, *very* alarming;—and he feels very ill; and he needs sympathy. So he came round to tell me about it.'

'Monty, do you realise that Constance is worrying herself to death because she guesses all this, and he hasn't told her a word?'

Monty took the armchair opposite. He was again smiling. He said: 'Why doesn't she ask him pointblank? Don't tell me she enjoys being on tenterhooks. I shall think her a really morbid subject. Tell her to ask him at once. He's longing for sympathy. A few wifely words would make him skip. Surely Constance can speak them? Not that she's the wife I've got. If I'd been Gabriel, I should have blurted it out to you days ago.'

'I wonder,' mused Letitia. 'I haven't noticed you blurting out much lately.'

'But then I'm not ill.'

'No.'

There was a pause. Not impulsively, but with slow candour, Monty said:

'What's troubling *me* is something I can hardly express.'

'Make an effort,' she suggested, from the grave darkness across the hearthrug. 'I should prefer that to my own inventions.'

For this, Monty had to stand. He was used to standing when he spoke. His hands were behind his back; and his back was to the fire.

'Well, old Littler is seriously ill. He may recover. If he doesn't, the consequences to us may be important. I've had a great deal of work from him in the past. It might stop, as the work I had from Faradays stopped— more or less—when Thomas had his stroke. You see, these old solicitors are very steady employers; but, when they go, their places are taken by younger men. And the younger men have their own favourites. There are two young silks on our Circuit who've been getting a lot of the work in the last two years. They're both able chaps. If I were to have only what they couldn't handle, I should be rather far down the slippery slope.'

Letitia felt her heart swell. He had spoken patiently and with great sincerity. She understood why his walk this evening had been meditative. But it was not of himself that he had been thinking.

'You like Littler, don't you?' she asked.

'Very much. As well as anybody I know. His illness is a shock. I've been to his house today, of course; but he's too ill to be seen.'

'You're not an old man.'

'I don't feel old. I'm not *less* competent. But the barrister's professional life is one of the shortest there is. He doesn't earn a living at the Bar much before forty. And if he hasn't an immense practice—there have always been bigger, more ambitious men than myself to take the London plums—he begins to peter out after, say, fifty-five. Then, failing a Judgeship, he has to do what *we* may have to do. A cottage in the country; for me a little cheap golf and the shopping basket; for you——' he broke off. She saw him smiling again. 'Perhaps pottering in a garden with leather gloves and round shoulders. Both in very shabby tweeds, and given to the naïvest of good works.'

'Do you want a Judgeship?' asked Letitia.

'I shouldn't mind; but I shouldn't get one. Not through lack of capacity; on other grounds.'

'Such as?'

'My own fault. No politician. Don't know the nobs. Can't pull strings. And I've never been a pusher.'

'And you haven't had a wife who pushed you?'

'I've had thirty years of happiness.'

'So have I. I wonder whether, in a professional man, happiness is the highest good?'

'It leaves him free to do his best. I've done my best.'

'And now you've a declining practice?'

'As we're swopping candours, an almost moribund practice.'

There was a moment's silence. My fault. My fault, thought Letitia. He should have been assured of a Judgeship. Otherwise his wisdom and experience is wasted. When I've thought myself a success, I've been a great failure as a wife. Yes; if domestic happiness, which we've both set before his career, represents failure. Domestic happiness must have become a sin; so the world does move. What's the real purpose of life?

'Well, to me it seems to promise the ideal old age,' said she, with reassuring stoutness.

'If the children were self-supporting, yes,' agreed Monty.

It was of the children that they had both all the time been thinking. But while Monty saw that problem as one of responsibility and economics; for Letitia it was composed of responsibility and emotion. Her eyelids dropped and remained still for several seconds. Mark, Christine, and Julian; especially Julian. Not because Julian was better loved than the others; but because . . . because . . .

She was tempted to tell Monty of all that weighed upon her heart. She did not tell him. The instinct to bear all troubles, including their own, is in some natures too strong to be gainsaid. Her excuse was that Monty had burdens enough; but the reality lay very far below her excuse.

'By the way,' she heard his voice saying from some distance. 'Where's Christine?'

iv

'Hullo. What are you sitting in the dark for?' Christine's brisk voice heralded the snapping on of much painful light. It blazed over the thoughtful husband and wife, blinding them, blasting their contentment, and disturbing all the subtleties of unspoken sympathy. 'Good heavens; fast asleep!'

'Switch off the light, darling!' begged Monty. 'Quickly, my pet.'

Christine had always obeyed that tone; and they were at once in darkness again. But not before Letitia had seen their daughter in all her young arrogance, flushed, with her pointed nose high in the air and her eyes bright under fashionable brows, looking down upon two fogeys with the amused, insensitive contempt of a stranger. Contempt for age, inaction. domesticity, silence, and morbid preference for semi-darkness. As if the words had been spoken, she heard Christine think: 'They're half-dead; pretending to re-live Love's young Victorian dream. Thank God I'm different.——'

B

If this Pharisaic expression had been all there was in her daughter, Letitia might in self-defence have been irritated. But she understood that Christine, having almost danced home, glowing, in the twilight, full perhaps of good news or somebody's unexpected praise, had plunged into the first probable room in search of her best-loved, and, because the glow was still upon her, had obeyed a thoughtless impulse. Regretting the impulse as soon as she saw what she had done, and feeling gauche and callow, she was now defiant. Defiant and resentful. Whatever the fathers might have done, it was certain that, in these nineteen-thirties, the children's teeth were set on edge.

'The truth is, you took us by surprise, Chris.'

A partial softening occurred.

'Sorry, Mother. I'm in a frightful hurry.' The crestfallen figure was stiffly retreating.

'Don't go!' cried Monty. 'I haven't seen you.'

But his rebuke had been unforgivable.

'I must.'

'Want any help?' This was from Letitia.

'No thanks.' The figure was almost gone. Not quite. Not *too* far. 'I expect Ruth's put out my things.'

The door closed. A little deadness remained in the atmosphere.

'She gets more like a draught every day!' grumbled Monty, mildly. 'An icier draught.'

'Only icier because it blows cold on herself,' said Letitia. She smiled, thinking with comprehension of that lovely, active young body and restless mind and ghastly over-sensitiveness. 'I must go and de-snub her.'

'Stay, rather, and de-snub *me*——'

'I'll give my evening to that——'

She followed Christine up the shallow stairs of this elderly house, loitering a little in its silence, so as not to appear too officious.

Christine, having guessed—or hoped, or feared—that she would come, was already, with her clothes flicked off, hurrying to the bath in a flimsy robe.

'I've got twenty minutes,' she said, over her shoulder.

'Hurry up, then.'

They probably would not refer to the scene downstairs, and the moment for any wholehearted communication of passing good news was gone; but Letitia knew that by coming upstairs she had lessened Christine's embarrassment. She moved about the bedroom, collecting the hastily discarded clothes and draping a frock upon its hanger in the wardrobe. Then she saw that the dress which was to be worn that evening was lying ready upon Christine's Spartan bed, and glanced round the treasure-filled room to make sure that everything else was ready. She was leaving when Christine returned, and she felt her daughter's arm pressed about her for an instant. That was the only caress she was ever given, nowadays; and, even so, it was an event.

'Daddy in the dumps?' came a low, preoccupied voice.

'Contemplating our latter end,' said Letitia.

'Oh, well, it's dire for all of us.'

'You think so?'

'Everything's bloody.' As she spoke, Christine lost not an instant. She was as deft as a rackets-player, unashamed that anything she did should be seen by her mother.

'Yes, I suppose it's worse for you than for us.'

It made Christine look sharply at her mother.

'Immeasurably,' she replied, with the utmost cheek.

'Well, make the most of your evening. Any mitigations?'

There was a slight pause. Then:

'Oh, nothing. I was just rather pleased at something.'

'Some triumph?'

Carefully casual, Christine began to make up her face.

'Taylor was pleased with me.'

'Splendid. He's not too free with praise.'

'Well, of course, he thinks we're all pigmies. As we are.'

'All the better to be told you're life-size.'

'So I thought. Pigmy life-size.'

'What did he say?'

'Oh, nothing much. His best student.'

'Not bad,' agreed Letitia, with such laughter within her that only a cretin could have missed the warmth of her voice. 'I've often wondered.'

Christine, being no cretin, shook slightly in sympathy (perhaps also in triumph); but remembered quickly that an elderly person's laughter could not be other than disrespectful. She looked at Letitia in the mirror, found that she was grave, loved her anew with a child's love, and said:

'Hm. I'm sorry I barged in just now.'

Letitia replied:

'The barge was nothing. The light was an outrage.'

'I know.' At first Christine thought she felt snubbed anew; but after one frowning moment she saw that it was not so. 'I did know.'

'Don't remember it against us.'

'I suppose I'd better say good-night to Daddy before I go?'

'Would you? He'd be tremendously relieved.'

'Sez you. All right; I'll attend to it.'

Smiling, Letitia left her daughter.

v

She was alone at last, in the bedroom which Julian used when he was at home. It was at the back of the house, on the second floor, and it was remote enough from noise to give her the sense of solitude which she needed. But she had come to this room for another reason; because it was of Julian that she must think. And here, where his books were, and the relics of his discarded enthusiasms, such as a box of water-colours, some skates, a cricket bat, and three or four framed pictures of actors and actresses in costume parts, she was as near to him as she felt she ever would be. There

was no picture of Julian himself in the room; the only portrait of a member
of the family was the enlarged snapshot of Christine as a schoolgirl which
stood upon the mantelpiece. But, wherever the eye rested, a memory,
poignant and unblurred, had its symbol. Julian seemed to stand before
her, outwardly languid, but inwardly as quick, as uncertain, as fire; hardly
as tall as herself, slim and dark and sharp-tongued; an unmatured schoolboy
who tired soon of his enthusiasms and found no rest or satisfaction in any
of them.

Letitia loved all her children, of whom Julian was the second; and she
knew them to be good and honourable. With Mark, the serious eldest,
she had never had a misunderstanding. He had been altogether normal,
as a boy a keen footballer and a good scholar, the very type—but of course
never strictly in accord with that type—from which England derived her
great name and her spiritual strength. In his present manhood there was
one complication—his young wife, Stephanie. Otherwise everything was
clear. She could not imagine Mark's courage or his honour, which is
simply moral courage, failing.

With Christine, the understanding of childhood had not been spoiled.
No jealousy or resentment upon either side had carried them apart. But
with Julian all was different. This relation had been the least easy of all
for Letitia. It had grown more and more difficult as Julian passed from
boyhood to adolescence and manhood. Coat after coat of polish had hidden
his immediate secrets from everybody; but the secrets had belonged
inescapably to a character already known to his mother. Julian could be,
she well knew, the truest friend; he could be wholly selfish and completely
self-forgetful; he could be charming, hard, sophisticated, immature, wise,
and shockingly unreasonable within a quarter of an hour.

Could not Letitia herself be all these things? Why should it be assumed
that each human being, because in retrospect his actions, 'mood after mood
of the one mind within,' look consistent, has not a multitude of desperately
opposed personalities?

But Julian must not be base.

Letitia's head drooped. For the second time that afternoon she shivered.

Two years before, Mark had met and fallen in love with a girl of whom
Letitia had never heard until he announced that they were going to be
married. A girl belonging to a family which apparently had brought artistic
talent into business, had not found it particularly suitable for the job, but
had kept it there for want of any skill in living. An untidy family, shabby,
now uncreative, but still potentially gifted and never at any time conventional. To Letitia they seemed like anachronisms who belonged rightly to a
novel by George du Maurier. Of course they had no notion of this, or that
Letitia thought it. They felt baffled superiority to the rest of their species.

Stephanie, very impulsive and high-spirited, had caught hard at Mark
as a stable character, and had married him in feverish impatience. She had
been surprised to meet with no opposition from his family. She had made
sure that they would be odious, strait-laced snobs, her natural enemies,
people who would need to be forced into unwilling recognition of her brilliant
indifference to their dusty standards. Finding them, on the contrary,

much more sophisticated than herself, and most warmly ready to accept her as she was, she had been at first puzzled and then disarmed. She was still puzzled. And, having planned to flout Letitia, she had tried hard, with a little flamboyance and much more pathos, to justify herself. Letitia had never met such assurance joined to such self-defensiveness. But, although such contradictions made her quake for Mark's happiness, she felt great affection for Stephanie, and much respect for her private determination to discipline an ill-trained character.

The young people had been married a year. It had not been a simple year. Two strong wills had met and struggled, as it were, in front of Letitia, whose sympathies had been first with one and then with the other. In both, will had been tempered by love and good faith, which had created a wish to do right. But will had led to obvious conflict.

What had happened in the last three months, Letitia did not know. They had seemed quieter; she had seen Stephanie less often, and Mark only because he had several times come to discuss with his father some question of law. There had been no suggestion of estrangement or stress. Her mind had been—if only hesitantly, tentatively—easy about them.

She had not realised until now, when fresh knowledge brought every old alarm back at the gallop, that one cause of her greater ease had been Julian's absence in the United States. The discovery was frightful. How *could* she have so resolutely suppressed every intuition of danger? That had been the crassest folly.

But the boy, whose interest in the newer arts excused what might otherwise have seemed a rudderless experimentalism, was not easily calculable. Suspicion of him would have been cruel. She had had no suspicion. Nevertheless she had been thankful when he was offered, and had taken, a learner's job in a New York film studio. It had promised to teach him much that he really wanted to know about film-making; and as the term of his contract, which was subject to renewal, had been six months, it had offered a long enough stay in that most stimulating atmosphere to allow, if not a great maturing of character, at least a myriad chances of diversion. Of this term of six months, Julian had been away for two.

That afternoon, as she walked easily in Kensington Gardens, enjoying the lovely Autumn day and measuring the time which she could spare before returning to greet Constance, Letitia had been the witness of a most unexpected scene, which had left her deeply agitated. A short distance ahead, where the leaves had swirled into what looked like a golden beach, another path crossed the one she trod. It was evergreen-shaded; and, without warning, she saw two figures pass at considerable speed. The first of them, who led by perhaps two yards, was a tall young woman, fierily red, striding with her head high in the air. She looked angry, but alarmed; alarmed but ear-strained, as one exultant, who, against her passionate inclination, *would* not stay. The second, following, entreating, stumbling with weariness and extreme excitement, was a hatless young man, haggard but determined. He called something hoarsely to the young woman, demanding that she should stop. Letitia thought the words were 'Don't be a fool! Stop! Listen! . . .' Both pursued and pursuer were gone as soon as they had been seen.

They left her stricken and incapable of movement. For these were not figures from the ballet 'Carnaval.' The young woman was Mark's wife, Stephanie; the young man was Julian, who should have been three thousand miles away.

What, in such circumstances, did a mother do? Letitia, for whom presence in this room quickened every emotion, until the scene was enacted a second time before her eyes, could no longer stand. She was forced to sit upon Julian's bed. That evening she had heard Constance's fears for Gabriel, Monty's for their material future, Christine's joy at some important praise. But her sympathy with these dreads and this joy, although great, was trivial in comparison with the anguish she felt at a glimpse which might foretell the ruin of three young lives.

What should she do? What was there she *could* do?

Two

F. R. AND HIS WIFE

i

AT THAT SAME moment, in another part of London, from which the trees of Regent's Park could just be seen above the roofs of some intervening houses, a middle-aged man sat alone in a rather shabby room. The street below him was quiet, and although the room was darkened by those other houses he had not turned on a light because he could still see to read by the blue and yellow glow of a gas-fire. The man, who was heavily bearded and bushy-browed, was huddled in an armchair, his skinny knees as high as his shoulders. He was smoking a strong pipe. In the hearthstoned fireplace were several matches and the ash and tiny dottles from an almost equal number of previously smoked pipes.

At last he could see no longer. The dusk came between his eyes and the printed page; and he let the book drop slowly to his knees. From under heavy lids he looked at the greying wall. But he was by no means drowsy; he was continuing to think of the criminal mystery about which the book had been written, and, insensibly turning from one theme to another, about the chances and absurdities of his own life. That was a never-ending entertainment. He sometimes believed that his reverie approached the profundity of pure contemplation; but in this he was self-deceived. It was the wearied inactivity of an otherwise restless mind, a state of inertia which had often preceded the swift strokes of planning upon which the more advantageous of his uncertain adventures were founded.

This man, whose name was Farringdon Reynolds, enjoyed the sensation of resting in his chair, away from his wife, who was childless (he thought this description of her very explanatory, and it absolved himself), and allowing a quick mind to dart through the presumed darkness of semi-slumber. He imagined that great statesmen, great generals, great financiers must all work in the same way; wholly relaxed in their bodies, but unsleeping in their schemes. Mighty men; he was of their company, destined even yet to great fortune. True, his schemes had always fallen short of perfection—perfection being outstanding profit—but that was because Thelma, his wife, had far too often jockeyed him into premature effort. It was the worst habit of women. They wanted rapid and tangible results. Usually they got, as a consequence, nothing. F. R. smiled to himself, a sardonic smile. Women! He considered his wife.

He considered her slowly, with malicious boredom. Her respectability, the poor quality of her shallow mind, her stupid longing to be thought 'somebody', or the wife of 'somebody'; a sure sign of inferior character. He remembered how early she had lost her colour and charm. Drained out of her, like wine from a white glass. He realised what a millstone she had been to him for the last dozen years. Of course, she had been fascinated; it went without saying. In such a tedious place as that suburb of Cape Town, where she saw only dumb bipeds and her father's antediluvian cronies, he must have seemed positively lustrous. A young god. Fairly young. You had to allow for the attractiveness, to women, of the hard-bitten man. They knew all evil, intuitively, and despised milksops. He hadn't been at all fascinated by Thelma.

No, he hadn't been fascinated; he'd been tired, and damned hard up. And he'd believed the old man was warm. He wasn't. He was stone cold; on an annuity or some sort of pension, and thankful, as time showed, to have found a kind gentleman ready to support his only child. When the plot had been carried to success he was quickly dead. 'Now lettest thou thy servant depart in peace.' Very well, F. R. had made nothing on the deal. He'd merely added to his luggage something less portable than a hand-grip. A mistake. The greatest mistake he'd ever made. Thinking of it now, he felt his neck glow.

He'd behaved well. Instead of clearing out, as he might have done, he'd had a plain-spoken row with Thelma and shrugged his shoulders. She'd wept; but as she wept she'd—in effect—as a precaution hidden his trousers. Thoughtful girl! A strong sense of her own bread and butter. They'd moved on. And on. And on. Now they were in London; and Thelma, probably deceived by his old South African stories of grand friends there, which he had told in order to play her, expected him to land a job. 'But, my dear girl, men don't land jobs—at my age—in London in nineteen thirty-two. There's a depression on!' 'What about your splendid friends?' 'I've been away too long.' 'Have they forgotten you?' 'I've forgotten *them*.' 'What then? Do we starve? Or do you expect *me* to find a job?' Blandly, he'd replied: 'Of course that would be ideal.' Oh, his front teeth could still make a good show as he smiled. He knew it. Like this. No actress was better aware of what could be done with a smile of that sort . . .

'Dammit!' thought F. R. A quizzical nick appeared between the bushy brows. 'I'm a heartless devil!'

Yes, he was a heartless devil; but unless something was put into the gas meter p.d.q. he'd be as cold as Mount Everest.

'A peak among men. A blizzard. A polar circumference . . .' No, a peak was best. It combined superior height with unscalability. He had superior height. He was six feet two inches; he was as slim now as he'd been at five-and-twenty. And—under the rose—he wasn't by any means broke. Not by any means. Thelma didn't guess it; but he'd got a couple of hundred pounds over and above what she knew about. Call it four hundred, all told.

F. R. began to plan. His plan was taking shape. It involved the exploitation of Thelma, who could cook. She could *cook*. The thing to do was to start a boarding-house. A private hotel. Some girls could no doubt be found to do the housework (but Thelma, bless her simple heart! would take care that they were plain girls); and every day, at the right moment, just as the meals were ready, he would stroll into the dining-room, take his place at the head of the table, and lead the conversation. Well, he'd knocked about, travelled, seen odd things, met odd people. He could *talk*. They'd hang on his words. Tell their friends. Absorbing entertainment. Afterwards the men apart, cards, drinks, stories; especially cards . . . There ought to be money in it. Money and fun and freedom.

Now, where should they set up house? London, or the country, or by the sea?

There were pros and cons. Pros and cons. At the seaside, windows rattled damnably, and you could never get any fish. Besides, with the wrong place, Winter might be a dead season. In central London rents were too high and clients too facile in movement. Many of them would bilk. In the suburbs, everybody knew too much about you; tradesmen could make themselves damned unpleasant. No, no, no; a slip at cards or with a cheque or a woman, and ill-repute crept in. Fini. Well, it would need careful thought.

Getting dark. He was cramped. F. R. struggled out of the chair, and as he moved away from it the flames of the gas fire sank gently and sweetly out of sight. There was a very faint sound; no more than a breath. He heard it, recognised it, and did not turn. Instead, he walked stiff-legged to the window, and looked at the grey, lamp-twinkling street.

Opposite, the window of another room was bright; and he could see into the room, where a mother and two children were gathered about a white tablecloth, having a meal. One of the children was a fair-haired boy of perhaps thirteen; the other a still fairer-haired girl several years younger. The mother was dark, not beautiful, but comely; not an easy woman; very strong-willed and unadventurous. To F. R. uninteresting. But the room struck him as obviously comfortable; there were plenty of dishes on the white tablecloth; and mother and children were all talking and laughing (the children using their hands to indicate things of various sizes), as if they re-lived their delight in a couple of excited hours at the circus.

F. R's bushy brows came down, and the nick showed once again over his quizzical eyes. He wasn't really amused. He tried, by concentration of will, to make the laughing family self-conscious, aware of their own tawdry silliness in feeling happy. But he could not persuade himself that they had grown less cheerful; and after a few moments of effort he found that the table from which they ate with such gusto was making him feel ravenous. So he turned away from the window, back into the room; noticing for the first time, as he did so, a smell of gas.

He smiled, and fumbled for matches. Ha! Thelma could always find a shilling to ensure her own comfort. Unless she hoped he was sleep, with every breathing space in the room closed except his mouth. Of course he was joking . . .

He would draw the curtains now, and shut out those futile people across the street. Ph! The bad taste of that ostentatious meal, and the sentimentality of their fond merriment, were disgusting. A last glimpse, an arm raised to the curtains upon their heavy rings, and the picture was gone. Now he could begin again to read his excellently baffling detective story—the investigation of a subtle murder by poison. And, as he read, he would reflect, at another level of consciousness, on his plan for running a boarding-house; and somewhere, below even this level, he would return to that theme which was his incessant preoccupation—his precious and terrible superiority to other men.

ii

F. R. was wide awake. He clearly heard the steps in the passage. He settled himself more comfortably in the chair. When she walked at this rate, stamping, Thelma was usually short of temper . . . She had worked herself up into a female tantrum. And in tantrum she cast off the sluggishness of her late father, Dr. Bauer, which F. R. had once, long, long ago, when he associated it with what had proved to be illusory wealth, imagined to be, in Thelma, restful submissiveness. She became a stupid virago.

Oh, yes, decidedly that door-handle clicked in the grasp of an angry woman. Under his bushy eyebrows and his big beard, F. R. was smiling. This was to be an entertainment, of which he was the master. He had no fear whatever of Thelma. He was fully her equal in sexual vigour; greatly her superior in finesse; a much cooler mind. He felt complete disregard of what anybody else might think of the rows which she began. And so his air of languor grew more noticeable; a lustre was added to his calm. When Thelma, plunging drably into the room in a shapeless home-made dress of thick cloth which left her no grace, allowed many words to burst from her lips, he looked up as if he had been taken by surprise. Then, as her tirade developed, he carefully put a marker in his book and gazed at her, trying apparently to collect thoughts from deeper concerns and to understand somebody primitive and childish, who spoke too loudly in a foreign tongue which she had not quite properly learned. It was quite true that she had an un-English accent. Her phrases were sometimes un-English . . .

Thelma, whose throat swelled so much when she was in fury that she choked easily, was screaming in a thin voice:

'Idling here; reading books; not even troubling to move when the gas goes out. Lazy. Crass. Selfish. I don't know what use you are. I don't

B*

know why I stay with you. I'm in the midst of ironing, and the gas goes out. Goes out! But you—you do nothing. Above it. Superior. Pretend you don't know. But I know very well that you *do*. I know very well. *I know very well——*'

'I'm sure you do,' replied F. R., smiling kindly at her. 'Three times over. One better than the thrush. Nobody could——'

'Idling here; reading books—*reading*!'

'You *did* say that,' remarked F. R. 'Excuse me for mentioning it.'

'Excuse you! You've been excusing yourself all your life. You've done it to *me* for twelve years. Twelve! It's like fifty! While I struggle to keep the place as it should be, you idle. You read, you smoke. You litter the hearth with matches and read books. Read books——'

'Yes, you're no reader.' He was regretful.

'No time! I have no time! I work from morning to night. But I won't stand it. I'll leave you. I'll——'

F. R. began to look long-suffering. Her voice jarred upon his delicate ear. He hissingly drew his breath in distaste. He said fastidiously:

'Careful; careful, my darling. You're screaming yourself hoarse. You'll end by hurting your throat.'

The warning was a goad. It was meant to be a goad. Her father had died of cancer of the throat. But it was meant also as an intimation that she could do nothing but amuse and bore him by screaming. More furious still, she cried:

'Yes, I *will* scream. I won't hurt myself. You wish I would. You wish——'

'Now you're quite ridiculous.'

'Warning me! How absurd! But I'll warn *you*——'

'That's unnecessary. Now don't stand there jerking your arms about and screaming. You look silly, darling. Silly and clumsy and impotent.'

'I warn you——'

'Silly and clumsy and downright *ugly*——'

The outcry ceased. Thelma had at all times a dead white face. Even now, although it was swollen, it was without colour. But her eyes, which did not open very wide, glowed with venom, reminding him of the eyes of a snake. She was stouter than she had been as a younger woman, and by no means tall; and she knew that when she was in a rage her rotund smallness caused F. R. only cruel sport. His shoulders, even now, were jumping slightly in real or pretended amusement.

He had told her twelve years ago that only a tall woman can storm with effect. She remembered it. He had told her that, in temper, because her long, descending, thin lips could not form themselves into an oval, she looked like a white toad gaping at a fly. She remembered that, too. He had told her other wounding and dreadful things, the memory of all of which now rushed into her mind as she saw him sniggering behind his beard. She could have killed him. But she had no weapon, and, for that shocking deed, no courage. Made speechless by humiliation, therefore, she turned and rushed from the room, making as much wind in slamming the door as she had raised in entering.

F. R., seeing her go, re-opened his book, and wriggled himself into a more comfortable position.

'Slightly deflated,' he thought. 'I hope to God this doesn't make supper late.'

He then became absorbed again in the mystery story; while Thelma, back in the small putty-coloured kitchen, stood sobbing palely under the gaslight. The tears swelled her angry eyes and rolled down her cheeks. Her heart pounded. As so often before, black imaginings of revenge darted in her mind, mingling there with all the love and hate she bore her husband. But at last the tears were dry. Her fists unclenched. Still sobbing, she took the old flat-iron from its place upon the gas stove and in a trembling hand held it to her face to test its warmth.

iii

Now that night had come, a cold wind stirred about the streets and rattled at any open windows, whistling its way down the chimneys and causing dawdlers to hasten their steps or turn up the collars of their coats. It whirled the leaves of trees in the London parks, catching them up from the ground where they had fallen and carrying them waist-high for many yards until at last it flung them into fantastic piles. It caught those who trudged up stairways from the underground railways, and made them gasp for breath. And in the deserted main streets it made the tall lamps shine like beacons in a world of storm, while the streets themselves were very nearly as clear as they would have been in moonlight. But the smaller, darker streets were darker still.

At home, Monty and Letitia sat upon either side of the fire in Monty's study, holding books which they were not reading. Letitia, having twice telephoned in vain to Mark's flat, listened for the ringing of a bell in the house; Monty listened to the wind, which was not more uneasy than his thoughts. Neither confessed to gravity; neither knew how much the other realised of what was happening to their three greatly-loved children. The only sound in the room was that husky whispering which came from the glowing coals as they perpetually rearranged themselves in the very process of consumption.

In that flat near Regent's Park, F. R. and Thelma behaved as if there had been no one-sided quarrel between them, a behaviour made easy by F. R.'s indifference to any but inward excitement and by Thelma's power to swallow—although not to forget—the persisting indignation with which she awoke, as with a toothache, every morning. Thelma all the time almost knew, but could not bring herself to believe, that F. R. disliked her, and that each outburst of rage weakened any attraction which she might have had for him before marriage. She desperately missed the warmth and sunshine amid which she had grown up. She regretted her youth, the mistake she had made in marrying F. R., and the fiendish coolness of her one link with humankind.

F. R., finishing his book, tossed it aside as something of no importance. He had solved the mystery sixty pages before the author saw fit to do so. His bearded chin was dropped to his hands. He began to scheme. He schemed to make much money, to show his cleverness, to escape from the need to scheme, to be free once more to wander, unencumbered, over oceans and continents, to leave Thelma here, where in spirit she belonged. He would never return. But before he left her he would skilfully use her. That thick white skin, those raisin eyes, the heavy hands, all alike hateful to him, should be turned to account. He pictured himself using men and women everywhere; always for his own ends, and for the sake of his need for freedom.

Thelma guessed some of his schemes. As she surreptitiously watched him she saw his eyes moving in time with his quick thoughts. He was too vain of his quickness to keep the eyes still. And, sardonically, she discounted his other vanities and accepted the unlikeliness of any golden future. She knew he had never had any real friends. She knew he would never stick to one of his schemes until it succeeded. As he tired of it he moved on to another; always as if the new one were grander and simpler and more certain. He forgot every scheme as quickly as a puppy forgets its brothers. Thelma saw nothing behind him but pretence and waste. Ahead lay—what? Probably, unless she saved him, more and more pretence and waste. He would scheme as he died, probably to defraud the undertaker.

She was mending one of his shirts. She was always industriously and with mediocre talent mending or making something with her slow, thick, yellow hands; and it was her object to send F. R. from the flat looking like a respectable shopkeeper having an afternoon away from his work. She had never realised that his height and beard, his lean wrists and his loose-limbed carriage, now marked him as an adventurer. She thought she had learned all about him by secret experience, and was blind to all the accumulated outward signs of it. And so she pursued her own dream, which was of security and part-proprietorship in a money-making F. R. She thought it a more possible dream than his, and believed that because she could keep her eyelids down she was cleverer than he.

At last, seeing from his idle yawn that F. R. had reached the end of his newest considerations, Thelma put away her mending, and, looking directly at him, said:

'Couldn't your sisters help you?'

F. R., who had turned that idea in his mind long before he and Thelma reached England, pretended not to understand what she meant.

'Help? Sisters?'

'Well, aren't they both in good positions?' demanded Thelma, in a hard tone of resentment.

'My dear woman, my elder sister's a lickspittling slave to my mother; and my mother's a tiresome old fiend. Her one idea, if she saw me, would be to sponge on me.'

'But you have no money, you say.'

'She's a leech. She'd use my credit and get me into a mess. Probably into gaol. No, I left England to get away from being strangled by her. You won't catch me going back to her abominable arms.'

Thelma was by no means discouraged. This was quite a long and pleasant conversation for her. She said:

'That was a considerable time ago.'

'It was twenty years ago,' replied F. R. 'She wasn't as old then. She's now twenty years worse.'

'Weaker. She may be a dear old lady.'

'My foot! A dear old octopus. And I'll keep out of her clutches. As to my sister Muriel, she's only got what she pilfers. She's been a slave all her life, for the sake of what she can pick up when the old girl dies. She's got even fewer brains than you have. But she's more artful. And she sticks. If she once planted her toes in this place, she'd be all over us with a spate and splutter of rubbish, her fingers in your purse, her tongue dripping devotion and scandal until we bolted to Australia. Or the Argentine.'

'She might be very friendly. And there's nothing *in* my purse, I'm sorry to say.'

F. R.'s nose wrinkled. Thelma could not see the grimace upon his hidden lips.

'She'd have the lining. She'd steal the clothes off your back. She's a limpet, a sponge, and a chatterbox. No, my good creature. Make friends with the charwoman, if you must; I draw the line at Muriel.'

'You draw it everywhere.'

'By no means. When I've hatched out my plan——'

'By reading detective stories?'

'There are worse relaxations for a busy brain.'

'I hope you don't get wicked ideas from them. I think you do. Besides, I think you *ought* to see your relations.'

F. R. scowled. But he knew that she had no notion of the circumstances in which he had left England twenty years earlier. He therefore continued—amazedly observing his patience with a stupid questioner—to put her off with jaunty indifference.

'I should be delighted for you to see your *own* relations,' he sneered. 'At any time.'

'You know I haven't got any, even in South Africa. I'd love to see them if I had. I'm very lonely. And I think you *ought* to introduce me to yours.'

'I don't agree.'

'You mean you're ashamed of me.'

'I've other reasons.'

'And even if you think Muriel would be a nuisance there's always the *other* one.' He took no notice. 'You don't say *she's* a limpet and a chatterbox.'

F. R. shrugged unexpectedly rigid shoulders.

'Didn't I? She's worse. She's a prig.'

'I don't believe she is. And I don't believe you *think* she is. I put two and two together, my dear husband; and I think you have some other reason——'

'That's enough! That's enough,' interrupted F. R. testily. 'Both my sisters are bores. My mother's a positive bore. I want nothing to do with any of them.'

For a moment, Thelma, surprised and pleased to have pierced his nonchalance, was silent. But she did not resume the work she had been doing. Instead, she remarked:

'She's got a pretty name. And she was a pretty girl——'

'God!' swore F. R. 'You've been at my wallet!' He jumped forward in his chair, clapping his hands fiercely upon his high, bony knees. 'I might have known you left nothing of mine unmauled!'

Thelma's long lips were parted in an ugly but not a disagreeable smile.

'Well, I *suppose* it was your sister. Not an early wife.'

'I don't know.'

'The name was "Letitia," ' said Thelma. 'I know the other name too; her married name. It wouldn't be hard to find out where she lives. I might write to her. Or even call . . .'

F. R. made no reply. He was no longer listening. He had thrown himself back in his chair in an attitude signifying disregard of all that Thelma had suggested. But in spite of this disregard he looked secretly alert, as though he had received an inspiration; as though the name of Letitia had started unexpectedly in his mind a new, splendid, triumphant plan.

Three

DAY OF ORDEALS

i

LETITIA AWOKE IN a fright and deeply confused, hearing her own voice cry in a desperate tone: 'I can't bear any more!'

Though she had always, hitherto, kept the childish habit of springing instantly from sleep to full awareness, often smiling with expectation of the day's delights, she now wondered thickly where she was, and how she had come there; a frail being without resources in an atmosphere of alarm.

'This is old age!' she thought. ' "One day the lady saw her youth depart"!'

The morning was dull. Last night's high wind still rustled in the garden and thudded against the wall of the house; and it was so early that Monty lay as quiet as a dead body, hardly to be seen among the room's other shadows. *Was* he dead? 'If so, I shall die, too.' She held her breath, listening, praying for reassurance.

Thank God he was with her. She was not alone.

Sense returned. The beating of her heart grew less violent, less and less violent, until languor caused it to become imperceptible. As she lay relaxed, still in the disturbed posture of nightmare awakening, she wearily yawned. The night had been broken by long fits of thought which had exhausted her mind, coming again and again and bringing no solution with them. These thoughts returned, like a gramophone record of cacophonous music.

Should I have run after Julian, catching at his arm? Ridiculous! He'd have thrust me aside; perhaps disliked me for ever. That would have been the end of all influence—for good or ill. Perhaps I imagined everything? No, I imagined nothing. I *saw* . . . What am I afraid of? Surely not treachery in Stephanie? Stephanie flew along, scarlet. Outraged. It seemed so. Poor child! But then, didn't she *want* to listen? To Julian? Wouldn't she, in the end, listen? *Any* woman? . . . If she's always been steadfast, how can she have let him pass from amusement at her untidy emotions into this terrible infatuation?

Had Julian's amusement always been a disguise? Wasn't that what, in my bones, I feared from the first? Wasn't I afraid it hid some hot temptation? I've seen men watching, and women *knowing* they watched . . .

Stephanie loved Mark. She'd been mad for him. If she now played with Julian, what was the cause? Wantonness? Vanity? Resentment at believing herself unprized by him? Fascination? A first inevitable reaction against engrossed happiness in another man, her first lover? It was useless to say that the younger generation had no moral values. One spoke, not vaguely of a generation which was as loose in morals as the flies, but of Stephanie, of Julian . . .

But if one spoke of those one loved it was not necessary to be hypocritical about human nature.

Besides, the clue to the present—to her alarm, to Julian's character, to the need for a plan to save all three—lay, not in post-war morals, whatever they might have been, but in old intuitions about her mother and father, and Muriel, and Farringdon.

They were not only intuitions. There was a strain of the over-emotional, even of the bogus, in her own family; instability without genius. Not instability in the sense of violent swaying of inclination; but appalling irresponsibility. Julian had this instability. He was not evil. But he could do wrong, realising clearly that he did wrong, and not troubling to defend or deceive himself; and in this characteristic lay the present danger *to Mark*. Was it the same with her own brother and sister? She did not think so. Muriel had no evil. Muriel had not even Julian's capacity for evil. She was nothing. An unintentional liar, who was the first, and perhaps the only, person to be misled by her own preposterous lies. What of Farringdon, who hadn't been seen for twenty years, and who probably, owing to the circumstances of his departure, would never be seen again? He could do wrong, and had done wrong. But although he had had capacity for doing great evil he had not the determination to persist in it. He was a clown.

Mother represented the family capacity for evil, *dramatised*. She was so busy seeing herself in the melodramatic part of a sorceress that she had no time or energy to spare for action. Therefore, though inconvenient, she was harmless. Poor Father, representing respectability, had been long dead; and with his death the Devil had departed from Mother, only returning at intervals when he wanted a snack at her poorly spread table. The Devil had no pride; he fed where he would, mumbling a crust with very small sinners when he thought fit. Did Muriel remember those odd, terrible scenes? Muriel was a natural whitewasher. She pretended that there had been only what she called 'Those little rubs of temperament that all families have'. 'Little rubs!'

Letitia, as a girl, had run away from home. She had been forbidden to return. But by her wicked mother, not by her respectable father. He, poor man, had clung to her. He had loved her. She had loved him, too; but less desperately. He had seen her as *his* child (the others, with horror, as his wife's abominable spawn), and he had more than once tried to make her his conspiratorial confidante. Never with success. *He* had been undignified; *she* had been too young to curb her pride; both had been bitterly embarrassed. The memory of common failure reddened her cheeks, even now.

Father had been what was called, in documents, a Gentleman (with a secured income of five hundred pounds a year); and it had been a supposed punishment for Letitia that when she ran away her name was ostentatiously cut out of his will. She was 'disinherited', as Farringdon had been; and everything—she and Farringdon having had their non-existence declared—was left to his wife, with reversion, if she approved, to Muriel. Muriel, hanging on to the reversion, had lived as a toady ever since. Lamentable Muriel!

As if it had mattered to Letitia! The solemn disinheritance had been to her a cause of laughter, ridicule, further rebelliousness. How rebellious she had been! Silly with vain pride. As hard and self-willed as the jade they had pretended she must be. But, she thanked God, also self-reliant, even aware of good, and the need for good, in her own faulty character. This had been her salvation.

Father, creeping unbeknown to the Islington lodging, and finding her defiant amid the squalor of liberty, had given her a hundred pound note in an envelope. A priceless balm to his own wounded love, which she was to use if her need ever grew desperate. It had been kindly meant, and she had known that; but it hadn't quickened a wearied love for him. Nothing could have done that then. In her young cruelty she had only seen how unctuously the gift would soothe his conscience. She had not used the note; would never have used it; and when he died four years later she gave it impatiently away. Hard, hard creature! Without pity, because love had been dried by all she had observed and heard and suffered at home before she was fifteen. Those had been years of a persisting black mood, in which but for the grace of God she would, as a soul, have perished. The rest had been different, because she had fallen in love with Monty, and the rind about her heart had been broken for ever.

Now she realised that her father, besides bribing his conscience with the hundred pounds, and getting pleasure from his own artful theft of the money for a generous act, had been terrified lest, in becoming an actress, she should as it were re-cast herself in her mother's mould. He had detested her mother, whom he had taken from the stage, and whose nature he had discovered with nausea as soon as it was too late. If Letitia had known this at the time, could she have given him the warmth of love he craved? She saw the little man standing by her bed in this dusky light, frock-coated and top-hatted, as always, with long black whiskers that looked inkily false. He was shaking his head. She heard his affected speech—'vewy', and 'people of our clawse'—as if he rebuked her in faded clichés. She recalled the frightful violences of abuse and accusation which he had been used to exchange with his lazily malignant wife. Great remembered misery shook her anew.

And so, looking quickly into past eccentricities, and not able to clothe herself in the weeds of remorse or the flannel of subsequent good deeds, Letitia took much blame to herself and her family for all that Julian might ever do that was cruel or idiotic. But whereas she and Muriel and Farringdon had had nothing but poor models to follow, Julian had been more fortunate. Besides being the descendant of Sebastian and Lorna Reynolds he was the son of Monty . . .

Monty lay sleeping within a few yards of her. When she thought of him, everything, from the rapture of being in his arms in the first weeks of marriage, to the sight of him coming home the evening before, a stooped, reflective, ageing man, was clearly involved. His body, his mind, his fun, their always shared happiness of thirty years, were implicit in her consciousness of him, the one person in the world for whom, while giving everything she had to give, she had taken with insatiable pleasure. Julian was Monty's child. Again, again and again, he must not act basely.

I couldn't bear it.

This, *this* temptation, thank God! I was spared.

But we set a higher standard for our children. Rightly so. The highest of all.

The light was stronger now, although still grey. There were darker objects in the room, and the lines of the curtains could be distinguished. So, too, the line of the foot of her bed. A first car or cart could be heard whirring in the road below. A milkman. Then there was silence again, apart from the rustling of leaves in the wind and the sound of the wind's more distant roar, and the far, embracing murmur of London. Letitia turned her head upon the pillow, and moved it further, until coolness stung her cheek.

I must see Julian.

Stephanie is the only person who will know where he is.

Letitia lay very still, rigid with repugnance. She did not want to see Stephanie. Instinct, at this moment, which defended her son, was too strong. She could not bring it to the challenge of justice.

But as courage revived she felt new hope. She would see Stephanie. And once this resolve had been made the rigidity passed.

ii

Moments fled, while Letitia felt a headache rising and clamping its weight upon her. How artful her body was! It was always alert to provide her with excuses for doing nothing! In spite of its artfulness she must be vigorous; for she had much to plan this day.

And first, since Constance and Gabriel were coming to dinner in the evening, the meal and its after-arrangements must be considered in detail. She and Monty and their guests would be alone, because otherwise there could be no frankness between them. Wasn't it always so? Each of Letitia's responsibilities had to be taken separately, like wine-stains in a table-cloth; and she was always, for this reason, in debt to time. Duty was her bugbear.

What misery the sense of it could cause! Only young people, who were not yet burdened as she was, had freedom. They alone could fall in love, and out of it, and play havoc with each other's lives, and heedlessly go their ways.

Oh, folly! what bitter prating this was; as false to herself as it was to truth. She felt compassion for all who newly faced the disheartened, apprehensive world of after-war terror. Formerly the young, upon an ever-descending scale of hope, could look forward to Paradise, to Utopia, to Eldorado, to what was called a modest competence or a safe job. Now, nothing lay before them but the darkling unknown, which was cynically foreseen as dusty failure.

Too easily did journalists—she remembered how much too easily in the last months of mountingly shirked responsibility—rejoice because in Germany Chancellor von Papen intended nothing but peace, because Fascist and road-making Italy intended nothing but peace, because the close of Gandhi's latest fast unto death promised in India nothing but peace, because the Lytton report on Japan's invasion of China could cheerfully be smothered in the interests of peace, and because one day—one day, when a miracle happened—the terrible unemployment figures would improve and there would be peace at home. Peace was everywhere, declared the wiseacres, like old ladies who said 'That horrible man's following us, swinging his cudgel; but perhaps, if we don't look round, he'll go away!'

And these were but public aspects of a Life that came crowding horribly upon innocent boys and girls who had not shared in making society what it was. The boys and girls might have done no better than their seniors; they *could* have done no worse. No wonder they chattered and gesticulated, roared their contempt and intolerance. They were without hope.

So was she . . .

The boys and girls who chattered were those who, like her own, had been protected in childhood. As they tried to carry into an ignoring world the privileged freedoms of such shielded youth, they realised their own impotence; the spirit and courage of youth were frustrated. Like the hero of 'The Pit and the Pendulum', they saw horrible, irresistible death descending upon them.

Meanwhile Gabriel might be dying; and she must remember that everything she ordered for dinner must tempt his ravaged appetite. Meanwhile Christine's immediate happiness depended upon the success of her birthday party next week, and Letitia must be sure that all the arrangements were made in good time and order. Meanwhile Monty's father and mother were coming to stay—two very antique lovers, of incredible placidity;—and they must be entertained, dined, wined, placated, taken to the theatre and to concerts of semi-modern music which they would only pretend to understand for fear of being thought antediluvian. Meanwhile——

'Oh, Golly!' exclaimed Letitia, starting up in bed. 'I believe it's raining!'

Sure enough, a horrid spattering upon the window-panes announced that the day had begun as badly as possible.

iii

By lunch-time the rain had passed; and the town was refreshed by its drenching. Leaves and small twigs lay untidily about the lesser roads and beside the Park. Nobody could have denied that the Autumn was well advanced and that a new chill had settled upon the atmosphere. Letitia trudged along from the Marble Arch feeling as wintry as the afternoon.

But as she rang the door-bell of the flat near Baker Street station her look gave no hint to the world of her load of trouble. And although she was thinking all the time of what she must say to her lovely daughter-in-law she had not failed—such is the subtlety of the human mind, even in hours of deepest preoccupation—to notice brilliant chrysanthemums on show in the flower-shop window, and a newsbill held by a shabby old bookie's tout at the corner, and the jubilant prattlings of a rosy child in a scarlet beret, whose nurse chatted with a policeman. These were surface impressions, to be caught and remembered by the temperamental artist. Reality lay deeper, in that confused turmoil of anxiety and delight over the strongest personal concerns which—being life itself—continued ceaselessly by day and night.

There was no answer to her ring.

Listening hard to the silence which followed, and hearing that silence in the dark lobby as a long, throbbing echo of doubt, Letitia trembled. Why were these blocks of modern flats so cavernously deserted, as if nobody living in them was ever at home? Perhaps this *was* just that nobody was ever at home in them.

She thought: But Stephanie's not out; she's hiding; perhaps they're both there, the bell cutting into their conspiracy, making them shiver, draw apart, and stand quite stricken. Horrible! Horrible! I don't believe it. Yes, but I can't go until I *know* it's not so.

So she rang again, a little ring such as she and her family had always used when they were in haste or burdened with tidings. It was used now unconsciously, perhaps to show only that the ringer was a friend and no enemy. She thought suddenly of Mark and Stephanie, who in their early days had constantly exchanged merry glances of sympathy, as if everything must be shared between them for ever. She did not now think of Julian at all. In this relationship, Julian was the intruder. Did her mind, being stale, cling sentimentally to the stabilities? Was she wrong? Was she prurient? She listened again, ardently praying: 'Do, do answer, darling. You must. You *must* . . .' Every nerve and muscle seemed to be clenched in that urgent entreaty.

For a very long time there was nothing but silence. But as Letitia's fears grew big she thought she heard a rustle. Some small sound. She could imagine that a door within had been quietly opened, that somebody, standing as rigid as herself, strained acutest sensitiveness to identify the person standing without. She said in a whisper to the high letter-box: 'Stephanie, it's I . . . Letitia. Letitia, do you hear!'

Seconds passed. And then, as if a leaf had turned in her thoughts, she knew that the door was to be opened, and was forced to rest a steadying hand upon the neighbouring wall. It was like ice. Her lips parted, trembling, in a smile. But it seemed an hour before the sound, and the certainty, were followed by an abrupt click of the lock and the sight of a narrow, darker bar of darkness at the door's edge.

Stephanie. Stephanie quite tranquil? Or unsmiling and suspicious; and then coolly, repressively self-possessed? Or Stephanie falsely explanatory? Or Stephanie dark-eyed and upon edge? All, in view of Stephanie's character, were possible variations in demeanour. But, to Letitia's unspeakable relief, none of these Stephanies greeted her. The young woman who widened the bar of darkness was evidently overjoyed. Thank God! Every doubt raced to oblivion; this was a Stephanie understood, loved and trusted. She lightened the spirit; because, whatever her faults, they were those of high and natural temper.

'What a worthless hag I am!' thought Letitia in self-reproach. 'I swim in evil!'

'Hullo!' cried Stephanie, in the hushed voice of a nurse whose patient is asleep. 'I'm sorry I didn't answer the door at once. I'm alone, and thought you were somebody else. In the end I found I couldn't resist a bell. Like people on the stage, who drop everything to answer the 'phone. How *are* you?'

'People off the stage are just the same,' replied Letitia, with the gaiety of release, as she entered the flat. 'They're thankful for any diversion. But a door-bell's not as bad as the telephone. Callers soon go away.'

Stephanie grimaced, protesting:

'You might have done so yourself.'

'I always ring three times, like a drowning man.'

'Beggars ring twice. Canvassers endlessly—a dozen times. It's one's friends who soon go.'

'Only the chicken-hearted, who aren't sure of you. But it's true that every door should have its judas window.'

They had reached Stephanie's sparsely furnished and always untidy sitting-room, where books were pitched headlong, and an empty cup and saucer stood upon a chair, and fragments of torn letters littered the floor about a small bureau. Letitia thought: No lunch, tea and a biscuit; a difficult letter; she's distracted; poor kid!

As if she realised what Letitia must be thinking, Stephanie ceased to talk. Instead, apparently for the first time seeing her room as it must strike somebody who entered it, she bent down to pick up the little fragments of paper. And in so doing she looked so adorably like a child at play that her visitor's breast swelled with pity. Such reluctant grace, clearly emphasising

Stephanie's unfinished youth, was a reminder that this girl was little older than Christine.

And yet how different they were! Christine, outwardly self-possessed but inwardly a child, both simple and calculable, a darling in her directness. Stephanie, in body more generously built, much more haphazard in movement, with a range of mood and emotion which Christine would never equal. Stephanie was taller, richly dark, with hair that was almost black. She did not paint her lips; her hands were large, her movements so free that—compared with Christine—she was like a handwriting profuse in loops beside an original but rather constrained script. And in thus, for Letitia, personifying immaturity she always recalled the truism that growth ends for most human beings long before they are thirty, when they can do nothing but repeat themselves with ever-increasing virtuosity. Luckily the moribund state, which ends only in the grave, has so many compensations that Letitia never envied her daughter-in-law. On the contrary, she remembered youth as a time of agonising ill-adjustment.

'You always make me feel a sloven,' said Stephanie, looking up from her task. She was smiling shyly; her hair was becomingly disordered; the dark green serge dress she wore, which was very plain, and which did not suit her, showed a rent under the outstretched arm.

'We aren't indifferent to one another,' responded Letitia, also smiling. 'We never have been.'

'Oh! I thought it was one-sided. Do I *affect* you?'

'Certainly. I warm my heart at you.'

'At *me*? When I'm——' Stephanie sat back upon her heels, thoughtfully, as if she cast her mind back over the last eighteen months. 'I'm so raw. When I first saw you, I expected you to hate me,' she frankly said. 'Even now, I feel that, one day, you'll know devastatingly too much about me. Perhaps you do already; but you're so polite that you'd never suggest it. Not polite: kind. A terrific number of people *pretend* to be kind: it's a favourite hypocrisy. They're only inquisitive. But I don't feel you pretend at all. You're just naturally kind.'

'No.' Letitia was brushed by depression. 'I'm not. But I love my children very much. *All* my children.'

'You mean me?' asked Stephanie, breathlessly. The ready colour came into her cheeks. Her eyes looked as if they had filled with tears. Then, in a low voice: 'How kind you are to me.'

'I wonder,' said Letitia, in grave doubt. 'Sometimes I think I'm horrid to you.'

'You're never that! Disheartening in contrast to my crudity, perhaps.'

'In any case a few scraps of paper don't worry me, so come and sit down. I feel I ought to be helping you; but I'm too old to crawl.'

Still with fragments of paper in her hands, Stephanie took a chair at the other side of the small room. Distance was necessary to her; perhaps also the stable backing of a wall. She looked thoughtful, rather ill. Her attention was not really given to what she was doing. Nevertheless when she at last spoke it was to refer to the room.

'Nothing I could do would make this place fit to be seen,' she remarked, earnestly.

Letitia pretended to think that this was what Stephanie had been thinking of. She said:

'Forget about it. Or move.'

'No, I mean at any time. I'm no housewife. Sometimes I wonder what I *am*.'

'Don't we all?' asked Letitia. 'About ourselves?'

She could tell that this question bewildered Stephanie, who, being self-engrossed, could not imagine the perplexities of another mind.

'You mean I'm not as novel as I think myself? Or just that I'm not as hopeless?'

'Hopeless.'

'Ah!' With a lovely gesture of relief, the girl flung all her fragments of paper into the air, and they fluttered apart, coming down again like a shower of snowflakes.

Letitia, enchanted by the movement, and touched by Stephanie's innocent egotism, would have kissed her if they had not been so far apart. But as she was moved to this warm affection she had an unexpected memory of that scene of the previous day, and was puzzled anew. Was Stephanie so naïve that she had forgotten it in twenty-four hours? Or—cruelties dart among the fondest thoughts and this possibility rose like an adder's tongue—was she an actress in the rôle of ingenue? She had those blue eyes which rarely go with a dark complexion; and her eyes were always serious, even when she laughed. Now they were dark, not at all to be read.

'I shan't bother to tidy the room,' Stephanie declared. 'I'd meant to. If you'd been Mark you'd have picked up every scrap of this paper. I should have watched you, choking with rage.'

'And admiration,' said Letitia, demurely. 'Mark's father once did that very thing. So I know what you mean.'

Again she had astonished Stephanie. Had old people, then, the child obviously thought, at one time been very young? Arrogant incredulousness was followed by a flash of affectionate esteem. Then by gravity, even misery.

'But you were *born* to be married,' said Stephanie, in a low tone.

'You too, I think,' answered Letitia, her heart beating more quickly although her smile held nothing but love. 'Don't *you*?'

She saw one quick glance, which was so hard, so little ingenuous, that it sent a chill through her blood. The smile which followed that glance held as much disregard as doubt; a petrifying smile, which startled Letitia and revived all her overnight fears. Evidently in at least one mood Stephanie considered herself quite unfettered by marriage.

At this moment the front door-bell rang again. Stephanie, as if she were dreaming, made no effort to rise and answer the ring. She was staring at the floor, so fixedly that one might have imagined the fragments of paper which lay about her feet to have come startlingly and amusingly alive. Letitia saw that her breast was rising and falling very quickly. The expression upon her face was obstinate, stupid, half-smiling, almost malignant; as if

several impulses simultaneously beset her and she took a dark pleasure in
their conflict.

iv

A second impatient ring immediately followed, and a third; until the
flat echoed as it would have done under a series of blows upon the door.
Unspeaking, with the noise rushing through her head like that of some
dreadful tocsin, Letitia leaned back in the chair, her hands at first resting
and then pressing hard upon the carved knobs at the ends of its arms. She
was appalled by her insight into Stephanie's emotions; recognising without
mercy the sensual core of that richness to which she had paid tribute, and
at the same time not wavering in her love for one who—she thought—
stood in need now, as never before, of love. She could not know that
her own glance, grown aquiline, struck terror by its revelation of searing
knowledge.

There could be no doubt that it was Julian who rang.

At length Stephanie stood upright, making herself menacingly tall.
From this height she stared down in an excitement of fear and power and
uncertainty, quite incapable of using her power. Though she opened her
mouth, no sound came from it. She was really frightened of Letitia. Only
when, by turning her back, she escaped from terror of those hooded eyes,
could she speak. Then, with great impudence, she drawled:

'Evidently, from the persistence, a canvasser. Excuse me.'

She was gone. She had closed the door behind her.

Letitia, left by herself in the square, colourless, untidy room, at first
uselessly strained her ears to catch the first note of Julian's voice. She
was in a tumult of imperfect knowledge, alarm, barely controllable anger.
But there came through the confusion several quick perceptions of the causes
of Stephanie's unease. She thought: 'She'll try and make him go. If she
succeeds, she'll pretend it was some other caller. But she won't succeed.
If, for her sake, or mine, or Mark's, he goes, she'll pretend no longer. The
fight will have shattered her. She's afraid. Not brazen at all. A tempted
child . . . She's not serious about it. She feels guilty, yes; with silly
excitement at being pursued; not because she means to desert Mark . . .'

She swept a glance about the room. It passed the green walls and bare
furniture and the tumbled books, and came to rest near her feet, upon two
or three remaining scraps of paper. She started, clenching her hands upon
the chair-arms. She would not pry. She would not seek to pierce those
scraps with her passionate curiosity. But as her eyes fell upon the nearest
of them she read in Stephanie's writing the words 'Dear Mark——'

A sudden shudder ran through Letitia. Mark could have left the flat
no more than six hours earlier. He would be home again in another few
hours. That Stephanie should have written to him, after yesterday, and
with Julian at the door, was overwhelmingly strange.

Yes, but don't forget, said a quieter voice within Letitia's breast; she
very nearly didn't come to the door when you rang, because she thought

you were somebody else. The letter's been destroyed. I believe she needs help. At this instant!

Upon uncontrollable impulse, she went directly to the door and drew it open. She could see nothing but darkness; but from beyond that darkness she heard a savage whisper of accusing entreaty.

Calm came to Letitia. She was mistress of herself.

'Julian!' she called, in a voice of smiling confidence. It was the voice, the natural, cheerful, loving voice with which, long ago, she had persuaded him to do something which he had refused in obstinacy to do for others. It had never failed, because it truthfully represented her attitude towards him. It would not now fail. 'Julian! Won't you come in here?'

V

The whisper stopped. She could imagine almost gaily the paralysing effect upon him of that hail. But although she loved him she felt stern towards him. In the following silence she pictured his angry 'What have you told her? You *have*! You *must* have!' and then sweeping memory of his whole life's love and fear of her. It had been Mark who, at sixteen, said 'I never tell Mother a lie; she'd be so offended.' But it had been Julian who added 'Worst of it is, she'd see through it before you began.' This Julian now stood without, faced with the knowledge that he hadn't a single secret from her.

He came at last, as white as he had been upon the previous day, sullen and heavy-eyed. There was no employment, now, of his famous lounging walk, which had indicated from schooldays that what other fellows did with pains he could do with a fairy touch. There was no rather cynical smile, the prerogative of those who have reached the sixth form at school and realised the need for protective armour. On the contrary, he stepped quickly, desperately, from the darkness to the light, with his thin lips firmly together and his dark brows drawn so close that they seemed almost to join in the middle. He had no greeting for her.

'Hullo, Julian,' said Letitia. She saw that he was trembling with agitation, and that there was perspiration round his eyes; and she was swept by a tide of love and pity. This was not a wicked Julian, but a boy, her own boy, racked with suffering. He was in agony. She put her arms about him, her cheek against his hair; felt him start and quiver as if he suspected cajolery; and at once withdrew herself. He had not yielded by so much as a softened muscle; but had darkened still further at sudden conviction that her presence there was part of a plot. At last he said with great quietness, as if he sought to pretend that he had not been driven three thousand miles by uncontrollable desire for Stephanie:

'This is a . . . surprise. Not to you, I suppose.'

His eyes moved quickly about, like those of a man whose life depends upon his alertness in dealing with an attack from two sides. His tone was bitter.

'A complete surprise,' said Letitia. 'If Mark were here it would be a reunion.'

Julian's lips were dry.

'I'm not afraid of Mark,' he cried, looking quickly at her.

'Why should you be? Or he of you?'

'That's as may be.'

Knowing that she must make this one thing clear immediately, she said:

'Julian, I knew you were in London. I . . . caught sight of you. When you didn't come home I felt I must try and find you. That's why I'm here. I didn't expect to *meet* you.'

It seemed as though he could not at first understand what she said; but as the words filtered through his defiance he stirred. He looked at her again, with diminished suspicion.

'Well, *that's* something,' he exclaimed. 'I'm glad you told me.' For the first time he glanced over his shoulder, to realise that Stephanie was not there, and that the door was closed. Fresh uneasiness caught him. When he grew paler yet, Letitia knew that he had read a cruel message to himself in Stephanie's absence. As if he thought aloud, he muttered: 'That's odd. Where's she gone?' Then he made as if to go to the door, shrugged, and stood irresolute.

At last it was Letitia who could bear the silence no longer. She said, coolly enough to deceive any casual ear:

'Are you staying long?'

He was trying to catch some sound from outside the room.

'What? Mother, I'm sorry to seem stupid. I'm very tired.'

'I can tell that. Why not come home with me now?'

'And leave this unsettled? Don't pretend you don't understand why I'm here.'

'No, I understand very well.'

'You're shocked. You think I'm very much to blame. As if I cared!' Julian grew scornful.

But Letitia was not affected by the easy scorns of anger.

'I expect you really know what I think,' she said. 'Don't you?'

He said stubbornly:

'This is nothing to do with you.'

'Only because I love you all.'

Julian tried to show disdain in a smile. His teeth gleamed. His hands, momentarily free, clenched again as he took a couple of steps away.

'Oh, God!' he cried. 'If you knew how you suffocate me with your *love*. You've been doing it for years. I'm free now——'

Letitia did not answer. Later she would recall and be tortured by that accusation. It was now an irrelevance. She saw him look at the scraps of torn paper, and to the writing desk. But although he did this he was unaware of them. Through all the excitement and chagrin of this moment he was hearing Letitia's voice again as she said she loved him, and in the confusion of anger and fear and weariness was remembering a lifetime that disproved his outburst. Some of the emotion, because she was his mother, Letitia shared; but she could only guess at what was in his heart of baffled passion, and despair at sight of that closed door.

At last he pointed to the door.

'Do you know what that means?' he asked in a low voice.

'I think so.'

'You're wrong.'

'I hope I'm right.'

'I won't believe it.' He went to the door. 'You can't stop me.'

'No, I can't stop you,' said Letitia, almost crying.

She heard him, after he had wrenched the door open, going wildly from room to room—it took but an instant—calling to Stephanie. There was no response. He went beyond the open front door, and he must have run up the stairs to the top of the building and then down again to the street, always with the same impetuosity. But, standing as she had stood when he went, as if transfixed in that very posture, Letitia heard him returning, panting as he came. He went back to the other rooms, and came again to the doorway, pitiable in his exhausted despair.

'She's gone,' he said, breathlessly. 'I don't understand this.' There was no accusation; no hatred of Letitia. He was like one lost. 'I really don't know what to do.'

'Will you come home with me now?' she asked. 'It would be a good thing to do.'

Julian shook his head.

'No, I must find her. That's what's so strange: I came to take her away.'

'I don't think you'll ever do that, now.'

He had realised it. His white lips were twisted in such an expression of grief that she knew he was at the end of his endurance. For one instant it seemed to Letitia that he was going to raise his arms and come to her breast as he had done when a child; and she drew a quick breath as her own arms made ready to hold him. But he then turned his head away, went out of the room, and disappeared. With aching heart she believed that she heard a sob burst from his lips; but all sound died with that of his running steps, and she was alone.

vi

It was some time before she moved, and when at last she relaxed she nearly fell, so great had been the strain of standing so long in one tense position. Her body felt bruised. Her mind, following Julian, and suffering with him, was altogether wearied. She groped her way to a chair, and sat down in it, blind, almost fainting. Ten minutes, a quarter of an hour, perhaps longer, passed as she sat alone, blaming herself, imagining Julian running through the streets, thinking of what this must mean to Mark and Stephanie . . . But at last, with a heavy sigh, she rose unsteadily to her feet. She must go. She had lost a son.

But before going, she was impelled to do more methodically what Julian had done in fevered haste. After first, so as to assure herself against interruption, shutting the front door and drawing its bolt—wasn't it possible that the first sound she had heard in the flat had really been the cautious withdrawing of that bolt?—she went into the other rooms and looked there for any clue to the immediate mystery of Stephanie's disappearance. Surely she would at least find some hurried note to herself?

There was nothing in the little kitchen—a box with a dresser, refrigerator, electric stove, and enamelled table. An open tea-caddy sprawled upon the dresser, with a cold teapot and a broken packet of biscuits. Letitia shut the caddy and put away the biscuits. The teapot she left after glancing into it in case it had been used for the note. There was nothing in the narrow dressing-room, where some of Mark's possessions hung as if they had been a great while forgotten, or in the bathroom, which was all of white china and chromium. And so it was to the blue and grey bedroom that she gave her waning hope.

Here Letitia half expected to see a disorder of hastily gathered or abandoned clothes; but the reflector-lighted room, which, it was clear, never knew direct sunshine, was as empty as the rest. It had been swept and dusted, presumably by Stephanie's morning help, and there was not a chair or a cushion out of place. Untidy Stephanie, who never put anything back where it belonged, and who disarranged at a touch, had not been in the room for hours. The pretty enamelled dressing-table set which had been part of Letitia's wedding-present to her was laid out barely, as usual, before a partially-dusted mirror. No message was to be seen beside it.

Letitia remained just inside the doorway of this room, slowly looking from the bed and chairs to the walls, upon which hung reproductions of three good modern paintings of women; and from the walls to the closed built-in wardrobe which was so meagre that one wondered how even present-day clothing could be kept within it. She knew ever-deepening perplexity.

'Stephanie! Are you hiding? I'm alone. Julian's gone!'

Her voice echoed. There was no answer. The flat was empty.

She returned to the sitting-room, and to the torn pieces of paper which, although greatly tempted, she could not bring herself to touch. Its state was completely baffling. Indeed, the whole flat in its nakedness and absence of comfort was so dire a comment upon at least one modern marriage that it depressed her to the verge of tears. Only tranquil and clear-headed spinsters, nowadays, made good homes for themselves. They had changed places with the bachelors of Queen Victoria's day, the clubmen; and were independent. How could marriages be permanent when they began so crudely? Here was a no-home which was as inhospitable as a railway station, a nest as roughly fashioned as that of a pair of doves. They were not ready to build or settle; they were forever in transit. More, they scouted the thought of permanence, which for them was like a life sentence . . .

Well, Stephanie was not here. In chasing sensation, however sincerely and with whatever self-dissatisfaction, she preserved no refuge for herself. Where would she have gone? Where would Julian seek her? Not her own mother's; for the mother, who was to blame for every incapacity of Stephanie's, disliked Julian as much as she disliked Mark. Where, then?

Stephanie had had friends, to whom the liaisons of others were an amusement; third-rate sophisticates; and it was to these that Julian would go.
Would he find her? If he did, it *could* only be because Stephanie had all along
desired his pursuit. She had not desired it. She would avoid them.

'I shall hear from her,' thought Letitia, aloud.

It was upon this confident note that she left the flat, her light shoes
making no more than a heart's-beat upon the stairs. But she had not gone
far away when she found herself shaking with humiliation at the thought
that Julian should carry betrayal of his own folly to such lascivious ears
as she had imagined. Nor did the homeward journey do anything to lift
the load from her heart.

As others have done before her, Letitia drew many inferences from the
faces and dress of fellow-travellers in train or omnibus; and, whether truly
or not, it seemed to her that in this bus all the faces were either sad or morose.
The conductor—it was an exceptional experience with a London conductor
—was ungracious. Opposite to her an old man who wore somebody else's
discarded bowler hat scowled at his fidgeting hands; a highly rouged and
lipstick-plastered girl with dirty shoes crushed in her hand a wet handkerchief which she often carried to her eyes; and two glum sisters, who only
peeped at each other with mean enjoyment and unkind interpretation when
they spied misfortune or unhappiness or any small defect in those about
them. These were Letitia's immediate neighbours; these sent her already
heavy heart lower and lower in distrust of that human nature which
ordinarily she accepted as comedy.

No doubt there must be for each of them a melancholy story to explain
and justify all they now were and all they now did; but she was not a realistic
novelist, to whom every living creature is an instance and a cause of interest.
She was a woman who, through the heightened sensitiveness created by
love and fear, was at the mercy of her own moods. She was soon forced,
in self-defence, to get out of the bus and walk. When she did so, she knew
that the others turned their heads to get the last miserable, envious, or
malicious glimpse of her, to soil her alarms with the stupid guesses of groping
and censorious minds.

At length, tired and deeply dispirited, Letitia reached home. And as
she went into the house she heard that silken rustle which she knew so well.
For once, it made her flinch. But she forced herself to smile at sight of the
rosy cheeks and adoring eyes and bud-like mouth of Ruth.

'Well, Ruth,' said she, very frankly. 'I hope nobody's waiting *this*
time.'

'No, Madame,' whispered Ruth.

'Some bad news?'

'No, Madame,' whispered Ruth. 'A gentleman called.'

'A stranger?'

'Yes, Madame. He wouldn't tell me his business. He wasn't a canvasser, Madame. He wouldn't leave any message. He said just to tell
you "Mr Farringdon" had called.'

'Farringdon?' For a moment Letitia could not bring herself to understand that her brother was in London. Her mind leapt, instead, to the

thought that this must be a name chosen by some friend as a facetious disguise. When the truth reached her she was aware of a slight chill.

'Unnatural creature that I am,' she thought; 'I don't like it. I feel as though a raven had come in at my window.' Only when that gloom was expressed did she feel the deeper excitement of old, unaccountable, sisterly affection. To Ruth she said: 'How did he look?'

The question nonplussed Ruth.

'He had a beard, Madame. He was very tall. He looked . . .' Ruth faltered and grew smaller; her glance softened appealingly; she crept so close to Letitia as almost to touch her.

'A beard? Like a sailor? A fossicker?'

'I beg pardon, Madame?'

'Was it a large beard?' Letitia held her hands at a distance of several inches from her chin. 'Did he seem well? As if he owned a gold-mine? No, I see he didn't. I think he *may* be my brother.'

The possibility quite paralysed Ruth. And from her paralysis Letitia gathered a number of instantaneous impressions. Chief among them was the certainty that Ruth had not approved of Mr Farringdon. Had he been shady, cheeky, threatening? Probably shabby, perhaps ironic, possibly piratical. In fact, Farringdon. Yes, that first apprehensiveness had been justified; a raven was at her window, and half within it. To the sense of failure with Julian and Stephanie, and Mark—because, although it was clearer, this affair was in one respect a stage worse than it had been at daybreak—was added a further and ominous cause for discomposure.

Oh, well . . . 'Thank you, Ruth . . .' 'Thank you, Madame.' In twenty-four hours the even tenour of her life, whatever that might be, had been interrupted. It was always being interrupted. Never as alarmingly as now. Oh, dear! How skeletons rattled in an adverse wind! But one must go on. One *did* go on. Only the dead sleep well; and one didn't envy *them*. . . . Now for Gabriel and Constance. They at least, if they were skeletons, had a little mercy!

vii

Darkness was upon London, which, in the West End, refused to admit darkness, and crackled with childish illuminations. But Kensington, always discreet, remained a land of broad streets in which residents drew their heavy curtains and sat apart from mankind. These residents might go abroad by day, and do good or evil; after dark their lives were their own. Even the silent-footed policeman who made necessary patrols and thought unutterable things between street lamp and street lamp did not know what was afoot behind the curtains. It was the English extended hour of privacy.

Every now and again there would be a stir in this night peace, as a taxi turned some distant corner and came nearer; and then echoes roused themselves from sleep and escorted visitors to one or other of the tall houses. The taxi-door would be slammed; the meter would give a ting; and muffled figures would slip inside a gate and mount broad steps to a heavy porch. Light would start out upon them; in a moment the darkness and silence would fall again. One might speculate delightedly upon all that would follow indoors—the distant maid, the welcoming host and hostess, the open fires, the sherry, and the very slow warming of stilted talk into animation; —but one could never be sure that it would be as it was pictured, or if all could really be as smug and dull as the derision of youth supposed.

From such a taxi came Gabriel and Constance, she jumping out first, he stepping more slowly and with carefully bent shoulders as he fumbled in his right-hand trousers pocket. It was always Constance who jumped, always Gabriel who followed. She was up the steps and at the bell before he turned away from the cab; and he, walking like a hunchback or an old man with stiff neck, reached the top step just in time to go straight into the house without a pause.

It gratified Gabriel to do this. Down in that packet of vanity which he called his heart lurked the phrase 'all doors fly open at his approach.' His craving was no longer for the personal popularity enjoyed by charmers; it was for mystery and precision. His favourite fairy story—and he knew all the fairy stories—was 'The White Cat.' He had a copy of it, translated into German (a language of which Constance knew nothing), upon his book-shelves, in the binding of an old school primer; and in moments of lost hope he read it. Unfortunately he was beginning to forget the simple German he had learned secretly as a youngish man; so that much of the old delight was in jeopardy. He no longer expected ever to enjoy the wonderful silent service of invisible hands, or indeed any adventure.

They were soon within doors, Gabriel darting his apparently poisoned glances in search of a stranger's hat, or a shifted picture, or a hole in the carpet; Constance mounting as one upon wings to the beloved room in which she would become a mixture of Mrs Siddons, Ellen Terry, and Marie Tempest, checked only by fear of Monty's invisible wig and the certainty that he would one day ask that ruthless question about a better-forgotten episode in her past. And when they had been greeted by Monty and Letitia, and were satisfied that no other guests were due, they both sighed with relief at having escaped an evening alone together.

How much of this fantasy of boredom was true, and how much she had invented for her own amusement, Letitia could never be sure. She loved Constance; and if she had not, so far, been able to love Gabriel so cordially she nevertheless felt that at any moment her kindness might quicken to affection. She had no fear of him, as some women had; but she was always disagreeably aware of an element in his blood which metallically darkened his flesh and gave him the spiteful tongue of an Alexander Pope. She could understand and be amused by his secretiveness. It didn't trouble her. She could even see how his cultivation of it had been provoked by Constance's over-eager interest. Constance was as curious and pressing as a fond child; she had no power of silence. If she had had children she would have been a possessive, exasperating mother. But with children to badger she would have spared Gabriel, and Gabriel would not have had to be the curmudgeon he was. Alack and alas that love should kill love!

'I hear you've got a trial scene in your mind, Monty,' snarled Gabriel, accepting sherry from his host. 'This is poison to me, of course.' His lips were twisted; he looked as if he disliked everything and everybody. 'Yet I drink it.'

To Letitia's relief, Monty did not falter. Smiling, he said:

'A whole play, Gabriel. Trial, judgment, and confession. Most dramatic. I'll describe it afterwards.'

Gabriel, always costive in invention, betrayed his jealousy.

'Stolen from one of the "Famous Trials", I suppose. You're turning dramatist, eh? You'll regret it.'

'It's for *you*,' Monty reassured him. 'And it's not a "Famous Trial".' There were no thanks.

'I never knew a suggestion that was any good,' said Gabriel.

'I've given him dozens,' exploded Constance.

All laughed, as perhaps she had hoped they would do; and Monty answered:

'Like the notes a prisoner sends counsel. They're always too ingenious.'

'Constance's aren't,' said Gabriel.

He sniffed his sherry, as a cat guardedly sniffs the food placed under its nose. Constance's amused, wounded expression showed that she knew she was always made smaller and more blundering in the eyes of others by her husband's tongue.

'You'd think he owed me nothing,' she nevertheless obstinately scoffed.

'Many a headache,' said Gabriel. 'Don't remind me. By Jove, what a world we live in! I'm going to write my autobiography. I shall call it "The Masquerade", and put on the title-page a quotation from Lever's "Cornelius O'Dowd". "You ask me if I am going to 'The Masquerade'. I am at it: Circumspice!" '

'You're not *really* going to write your autobiography?' demanded Constance, in a flutter of terror. 'My God! How awful!'

Gabriel for answer, pointed at her white face, and cackled.

'I mind the masquerade less than the mess,' said Monty. 'What a mess it is!'

'And *I* mind the mess less than the unhappiness,' added Letitia. 'Because nobody can deny that the general sense of unhappiness nowadays is appalling.'

Gabriel smacked his lips with relish as he answered:

'It's a dying world. Victorian empires disintegrating; Chicago gangsters the models for world politics; young people in the saddle abroad, swaggering, bullying, bawling threats, and our own young people so decadent——'

'No,' said Letitia. 'You oughtn't to say that. It's wicked. Young chivalry *perverted* abroad, and our own so shocked by the awful darkness of materialism that it's lost hope.'

'Ah!' said Gabriel, turning upon her in triumph. 'You think something, do you, Letitia? That's new. False, but new. You're only thinking adhesively of your own three. Why not be candid?'

'I am candid. But I find I speak and think differently in different companies,' explained Letitia. 'I'm so obliging.'

'All things to all men!' cried Constance. 'I thought that was *my* part.'

'No, you're just a parrot that fluffs its cues,' said Gabriel. He grinned at Letitia, showing long yellowish teeth with sharp points. It was not an unpleasant grin. 'Letitia's an original phenomenon.'

'I've lost confidence in myself,' admitted Letitia.'

'Oh, haven't we all! We lose it in the cradle! This new damned nursing doctrine, that a baby's to bellow its bowels out, is meant to kill *all* confidence; but it wasn't needed. The latest medical sadism.'

'We've been told for a quarter of a century that only the young matter,' said Letitia. 'And we almost believe it. It's made us cowards. So we try to protect our own young from the horrors of life. We've swallowed the horrible slogan "Safety first." '

'They'll accuse us, when the war comes, of hotting it up for them,' added Gabriel. 'What gratitude we shall get for our forethought!'

War! They all grew still.

Gabriel alone had not winced at the pronunciation of that word. He seemed to have been struck by a secret joy; for he became smilingly silent. He was thinking that a crying baby who was being brought up on the Spartan principle should be effective as chorus as an anti-Pacificist play. What a jumble of modern humbug could there be arraigned! Of course he could never bring himself to use anything so obvious; but an anti-Pacificist play, if he could find a producer brave enough to counter the 'compact liberal majority', would rile everybody very much, and so was to be attentively considered.

'Yes . . . Yes . . .' he hissed, in a malicious dream. 'Yessss.'

'Dinner is served, Madame,' whispered Ruth, who had waited, unseen by everybody, for this pause.

They momentarily forgot the nightmare word 'War', and the crying child, their own children (born and unborn), and everything grave, as they moved towards the pleasures of the evening.

viii

It was not until after dinner that Letitia sought Gabriel's aid. Then, while Constance played the minx-ingénue or gruff middle-aged coquette with Monty, who always mildly indulged her, she took the chance afforded by Gabriel's idle examination of books upon the neighbouring table to make him sit down beside her coffee tray.

'Gabriel, I want your advice,' said she, as she poured the coffee. She had not realised until that moment how brimming he was with goodwill towards her; but the light in his face left no doubt of his most disinterested wish to please.

'Mine?' he demanded, eagerly. 'But that's wonderful!'

'And help, too,' she warned him. 'If that's a part of your advice.'

'You enchant me!' cried Gabriel, taking his coffee from her hand. 'I shall begin to confess to you that——'

'You confess to everybody, Gabriel!' said Letitia, reproachfully. 'It's too bad of you!'

'How? Do they compare notes? What frightfully bad form!'

'No. They see you whispering to others. Their pride's alarmed. They perhaps hear from newer friends echoes of something *they* whispered to *you* long ago. I wonder if you're always discreet——'

'My tongue! A traitor!' His glee turned to seriousness. 'But you're different, Letitia dear. With you I should be discretion itself. If *you'll* trust me——'

Indeed, Letitia thought she could trust him. He crouched close to her, like a dog, holding his coffee-cup to his breast, his iron-dark face grimacing involuntarily at what—although this was good coffee—he always considered a noisome brew. Coffee and marmalade were his twin hatreds. He quickly emptied his cup and put it away, shuddering. Fearful stuff! Loathsome to take, costive in effect, and conducive to rotting of the intestines . . .

She did not know what reflections passed through Gabriel's mind. But as an introduction to her real purpose she told him of Farringdon's call and by a stiffening of the shoulders and indrawing of the lips, indicated Ruth's disapproval. The miming was so delicious that he forgot the coffee, exclaiming in a whisper:

'Marvellous actress! I wish I could get you back to the stage. Yes, I see the good Ruth; pitilessly conventional. And so *right*. But we——'

'What should I do with such a caller?'

'Hm. You realise that there's a play in this, Letitia? You give me a thousand ideas!'

'They're your own. You're not to be professional *now*.'

'I'm never that. I'm an artist. That means my inspiration's gone. In this case I promise absolute discretion. But I must admit that the mind races on to the second and third acts——. He *is* your brother, I assume? No Jacob and Esau stuff about the man? You'd know him by the mole on his left shoulder blade?'

'I know nothing but what I've told you. He may be an impostor. I daren't think so; the reality would threaten so much more trouble. But think it over. Now, I haven't finished. There's something else——'

'Of course. I wonder what it is.'

'How does one—out of the blue—get one's husband the offer of a Judgeship?'

He drew back with a breathless, mischievous 'O-o-oh!' and slapped both his knees with his fiddler's hands. His arms were very long, and this was why, in some respects, he reminded one of an ape. But there was nothing ape-like now in his demeanour. On the contrary, old lines had fallen from his face and he looked boyish. Letitia saw for the first time how almost noble the line of his brow was, and how—when for once he laughed without malice—the sneer he often assumed represented only the false sophistication of a spirit too timid for great deeds.

'I can't answer your question,' he admitted, gleefully. 'Of course, *you* know so much better than I how to get *anything* you want. As now, from me. But *do* you want this? Does *he*?'

'I want him at any rate to have the chance of not wanting it,' said Letitia, who, now that she had said the difficult words, could be light-hearted again.

C

'Most of our misery's caused by never having that chance to say "No".
Don't you agree?'

She was amused to feel about her head the full lightning of Constance's
scandalised reproachfulness. Wasn't this baffled desire of the power to
refuse just Constance's everlasting problem with Gabriel? How bitter,
indeed, to Constance, her husband's happy laughter must be. Poor
Constance! It wasn't fair to her to make him laugh. It was such an
impudent turning of the tables.

'The eternal aspiration. Feminine. Well, I'll make enquiries. I promise
every discretion,' grinned Gabriel. His glance slipped very fast to Constance
and away again. Yes, he too knew what she would be feeling; he was
diabolical in reading every sign of her discontent. 'You've surprised me.
I thought you'd got everything you wanted. I despaired——'

'Of what?' asked Letitia, still thinking of Constance, and wondering if
her friend would have been happy with a stupid, ultra-male husband.

'Of ever being your servant. Let me see you again about it. Ah—was
there *more* advice you needed?' He was so shrewd, so feminine, that there
could, after this, be no limit to his curiosity. It was almost frightening to
feel his thoughts flowing warmly about one's reserve, like a sensualist's
calculations of weakening resistance, seeking answers to thoughts of which
one was hardly aware oneself.

'There was. There is,' frankly declared Letitia. 'But I shan't ask it
tonight. Perhaps I shan't ask it at all.'

'I wish you would. You'd make me so happy,' urged Gabriel. ' "Half
mad for joy, James Lee." ' She saw his long hands trembling. 'Can't you
. . . stretch a point? Give me a clue. Christine? One of the boys?' His
expression was one of great sweetness, comprehension, urgent entreaty.
To laughter had succeeded what was obviously profound emotion.

But, although she unconsciously observed and would later remember
this, her real mind was now lost to him. It was back in that little bare flat
near Baker Street station, hearing strained young voices, condemning her
own failure, and trying in vain to imagine what would happen to the three
whose happiness was threatened with chaos. There had been no message;
the telephone had remained unanswered; even Mark had been unreachable.
But it was not for Mark, who had strength to bear all, that she would thankfully have obtained advice from a detached critic of unruly lives. It was for
tormented Julian. And Julian, whether in joy or torment, was beyond reach
of present succour.

Part Two

THE CLOUDS GATHER

Four

MORNINGS

i

MORNINGS AT BELLA VISTA were never tranquil. They began at odd hours, from seven to eleven o'clock or so; and they were governed by The Old Lady's temper. This might be savage or it might be pathetic, or it might even be of singing cheerfulness. She would awaken as herself, as a Billingsgate porter, as a negro slave, as a pair of cats, or a tormented begging soul for whom nobody in the world would do anything; and as all these beings had their own voices the neighbours upon either side of Bella Vista—at Littleholme or Stranraer—were never sure how many people really lived in the house.

These neighbours, and others, saw The Daughter go out shopping by herself; that was normal. And they saw The Old Lady taking a stately promenade alone—very much the Duchess; or leaning, very feeble, upon The Daughter's arm. So far all was clear. There were two; and if both were out the house was deserted. No negroes, cats, porters, or tormented souls bobbed up their heads as anybody passed. Once the Two Women returned, however, sounds arose which could not possibly have been produced by such obviously respectable people. Wild sounds. Sounds which suggested that the most dreadful orgies or séances were in progress. It was no wonder that as dusk fell upon Willowhaven some little girls who lived farther up the Meadowside Road ran as fast as they could past Bella Vista. Little girls enjoy inventing panics, which to them are a lovely frightening game.

Willowhaven itself was a smallish, featureless seaside town upon the South East coast of England. It was quite flat, and it prospered because it had sands and was supposed not to have been discovered by trippers. Meadowside Road, which no longer bordered grassland, was at the western edge of the town, at the farthest point yet reached from the smell of fish. Villas with six-foot front lawns and small privet hedges and wooden gates to shut them off from the road stood there side by side in semi-detached refinement. Nobody in Meadowside Road ever 'let' rooms in Summer.

It was true that friends might come and stay, and of course it *might* happen that they preferred to bring in their own food, or even to have a little settling-up at the end of a visit. This was their own affair, and it was most charitably understood by everybody in the road. Meanwhile residents strictly maintained an amateur status that is all-important to English people —as a last relic of aristocracy—in Sport, the Arts, and the Home. They did nothing for money. They entertained the sick and the run-down. They received poor relations, provided these poor relations were not so poor as to look shabby. But they naturally did not dream of having séances, orgies, or mentally afflicted persons in their homes; because, while refusing to be narrow-minded, they wished to remain respectably inconspicuous. British. Sometimes—it was pardonable—they could not help suspecting the occupants of Bella Vista of being foreigners.

They did not *know* The Old Lady or The Daughter. A few of them nodded and half-smiled at them, if it seemed likely that the nods and half-smiles would be returned; but after the first calls by Mrs Pearce and Miss Tozer, when The Old Lady had been so repressively *grande dame*, nobody else had tried to be sociable. They peeped out from behind curtains, and summoned their visitors to do the same, saying 'Here she comes. Quite a character. We always call her "The Old Lady". Everybody seems to call her that. The other one's The Daughter.' It gave them a tiny thrill to share the peepshow, almost as if they lived on the route of processions, or overlooking the county cricket ground. 'You can tell she's *been* something. Just calls herself plain "Mrs". And they pay their bills . . . in time. But you hear the most extraordinary sounds; screams, and like cats, and . . . It's not drink. We've asked the grocer. My husband thinks The Old Lady's probably a bit of a tartar. Well, it's that or . . .' Some things need not be said; a touch to the brow indicates everything.

What was so strange was that it was usually the mornings which were a little queer. This completely puzzled the neighbours.

But it did not at all puzzle Letitia's sister Muriel, who knew, if she did not understand, all that went on in Bella Vista. She always awakened believing that the wall between her room and her mother's would fall upon her because it had been imperiously rapped from the other side. If the sound were repeated, she scrambled out of bed and dragged on her dressing-gown, with a cry of 'I'm coming'; after which she slowed all her movements in order not to be breathless upon arrival, and, with the dressing-gown trailing, swept like a costumed stage queen to the door.

If the sound was *not* repeated, she turned upon her back, thrust her arms out of bed, began gravely to flip the tips of her fingers together, and said aloud:

'Not a wink of sleep have I had this night. My toothache's kept me awake. That and the dreams. There was one in which an ogre in embroidered slippers began to eat raw fish; it was very loathsome. I'm too imaginative. It gives me blood pressure; and that works up through my veins to my head and makes me see splendid visions with disappointing endings. Of course, I need a change. Anybody would, living day after day . . . But I'm so conscientious; devoted to Mother; and really the only one she's got—well, a thing like that cuts both ways, doesn't it. But I've nobody to help me, except Mrs Pepperkin one day a week; and Mrs Pepperkin, between ourselves . . . Too fond of the teapot: it makes her tongue wag . . . I wonder how my gout is this morning!' Muriel moved each foot carefully up and down a few times, testing it. 'Agony,' she remarked. 'I shall really have to do something about it. I shall really have to see a doctor. There's that nice one in the Ferndale Road. He looks sympathetic. But *she'd* never pay his *bill.* I should have to write to Letitia. I always hate asking Letitia, though she's got plenty. Not that I ever do ask her . . .'

Ratter-batter-clatter! 'You'd think she'd got a machine-gun in there; but it's only her auctioneer's mallet.'

'All *right.* All *right.* I'm coming!'

Two minutes later, with a travesty of her mother's dignity, she appeared in the next room. She was very short; her too-long dressing-gown, now largely threadbare, was of grey ripple cloth; her grey hair, which had been cut short by an inexpert hand, stuck out at all angles; her face was ruddy and puffy with sleep. But her mother could not see this, for heavy curtains were drawn across the windows and the room was illuminated only by the narrow lines of morning sunshine which crept like miniature searchlights above and beside these curtains.

'Is that you . . . ugh . . . Muriel?' Not cats or negro spirituals this morning. She was in her hollow mood, fabulously old but most noble, enduring with bravery all the pain and neglect which were her lot in life. Muriel thought: It's the most *sickening* mood of all! So *ungrateful*!

'Did you knock, Mother?'

A sardonic smile bared the Old Lady's gums. Her false teeth were not in yet. She recognised Muriel's sarcasm as a sign that her daughter, having awakened irritable, was ready to yield good sport.

'I was lonely,' she groaned. 'Do sit on the bed, please, dear. We'll have a nice little talk.'

'This room's horribly stuffy.'

'I'm sorry to say my neuralgia's troubling me, dear.'

Muriel plumped herself upon the bed without bothering to express a sympathy which she did not feel. Mother had *no* neuralgia. She pretended. She was really a humbug!

'I wonder you can stand having no window open,' she continued, crossly. 'It's like living in a trunkful of old clothes. Must be very bad for you.'

A faint moan, like the almost inaudible whine of an expectant dog, came from the bed.

'I've been thinking all night of nothing but pain. Pain and misery. Pain and sorrow. I dreamt of Farringdon.'

Muriel shivered. When her mother dreamed—or pretended to have dreamt—of Farringdon, the day was always horrible. This one would be horrible. Although Farringdon had been hated as a boy, and quite furiously cast off when he ran away, and then, twenty years ago, execrated for almost disgracing them, his absence, and the disregard he had since shown, worked in The Old Lady's mind and heart, and made her sentimental about him. Farringdon! Muriel hated his name.

She had begun to feel terrified lest, in a state of—well, one of her states —Mother should suddenly change her will, and . . . Such a situation! You couldn't go to Law with a brother; and yet he'd behaved awfully, and done nothing whatever to help *anybody*, whereas *she* . . . And if that happened what in the world would become of her? 'My life would have been wasted. It's been ruined, I know; but to have it *wasted*, as well, would be so . . . I shouldn't get the Old Age Pension. I should have to go as a charwoman . . .'

'I'll get you some salts,' she retorted.

'I should like to see him again, piteously pleaded The Old Lady. 'Just once, before I go.'

As if she were at all likely to 'go'! Muriel was greatly exasperated. She cried:

'Don't talk about "going". You'll live many years yet. I hope. And as for Farringdon, you know very well, he'd only come if he was broke, and *after something*.' To Muriel, the thought that anybody was *after something* was frightful. If she saw a boy pause by the gate, or a man take a seat near her on the sea front, or if a woman asked her the time, she always thought they must be *after something*. 'I hope, if he did come, you wouldn't be silly——'

Of course they both knew what being 'silly' meant.

'I wonder if I could refuse the dear boy anything,' sighed her mother, very comfortable in her warm bed. She was pleased to think that she had awakened with this blithe thought of a topic which never failed to produce good results. She would soon have Muriel crying, and then the girl would go off sob, sob, sobbing, and looking a sight; and she'd be a sniffing and most amusing pot-banger and fireiron-rattler all the morning. Mornings ordinarily were so dull; one *had* to liven them in various ways. In the afternoon they'd go for a pleasant stroll by the sea, Muriel sturdily distant but—owing to the tears—looking as if she drank, herself very frail, very dignified . . . 'It's so long since I saw him. Dear boy, I hope he isn't ill, or in trouble. I can't help thinking there must be some *vibration* between us, to make me dream of him. Perhaps he was near me?'

'*I* didn't hear him. And *I* was awake all night,' said Muriel, with promising savagery.

'I meant, in spirit,' said The Old Lady, with quiet dignity. 'But that's a thing I'm afraid you'd hardly understand. You and Letitia were always hard-hearted.'

'I suppose all I do for you doesn't count!' cried Muriel, in a loud voice. 'It's nothing at all!'

'Now, you mustn't be unkind,' protested The Old Lady, feebly. 'You won't have me to look after you much longer; and I do wonder how you'll manage without me——'

'Oh!' Muriel was unbearably exasperated. 'Looking after me!' She could hardly prevent her tongue from uttering the angry accusations which filled her mind. 'Mother! When you *know* I'm suffering night and day. Slaving for you, Ill. Overworked. It's too bad! It is indeed!' She choked. Tears began to run from her eyes. 'You're ungra-a-ateful!'

'You still write to Letitia, don't you?' asked her mother, in the same innocent tone. 'I've no wish to see *her*. Too much the father's child. I'm glad she's provided for, of course. I don't think it's quite nice of you to write to her——'

'I don't write to her!' shouted Muriel.

'No, dear,' patiently agreed The Old Lady. 'I only thought you did. With that horrible legal husband. I sometimes feel very sorry for Julian, who's a real *Reynolds*. Is he getting on all right in America?'

Muriel made no reply. Her heart seemed to be standing still. She knew from this that The Old Lady had discovered the hiding-place under the floor of her bedroom, where she kept her treasures, her early Journal, many and many a secret. She knew that Letitia's letters—always addressed to the Poste Restante—had been read; that Julian's notes, which she had kept since the first of them came a dozen years ago, had not escaped, and that a last card of his, sent to the house and too carelessly hidden upon its arrival, had given her mother the clue for painful search; that her whole life had no longer the smallest privacy——.

Mounting realisation of helplessness in the web of so formidable a spider destroyed every fantasy and broke her self-control. Rocking backwards and forwards upon the bed, with her hands over her red and swollen face, Muriel abandoned herself to loud, wretched sobbing. 'Oh-oh-oh! Oh-oh-oh!' She wished she were dead.

The Old Lady continued to lie snugly chuckling to herself in exquisite silence. Happy excitement ran like fire in her veins. She began to twist her fingers about under the bedclothes, snapping them with loud cracks resembling the cracks of burning twigs; and at last, carried ever higher and higher by delight, she could no longer restrain vocal expression of her triumph.

'Prr-murrow-miau! Wow wow! Prr-murrow-miau!' she piercingly warbled. 'Miau! Wow wow wow!' And, in a man's deep voice, 'Open up dem pearly gates! Open up dem pearly gates!' Her arms were brought out of bed and raised high in the air, with the fingers snapping. She whooped with laughter. She kicked her feet in the bed. She miaowed and sang and miaowed to her heart's content. Until at last weariness came suddenly upon her and she lay still again, breathing thickly, still smiling, but once more ready for sleep.

ii

A little more than sixty miles away, in Chelsea, where he lived in a Victorian house close to the Thames, Gabriel Wilton hung an insulting ticket bearing the words KEEP OUT: THIS MEANS *YOU* to the knob of his heavy study door. As an extra precaution he locked this door and bolted the inner baize-covered door which excluded sound. He had been forced into such practices many years earlier, because when they were first married Constance often interrupted his work.

Constance had felt amorously lonely, and she could not realise that what to her was a delicious impulsive visit, much too short to waste Gabriel's time, was to Gabriel literary murder. It could ruin a whole day on which the tongues of imagined people ran into epigram as drops of quicksilver roll together in a saucer.

He had also decreed that even if cook flung herself upon her sword the hotness of a punctual meal mattered less to him than what Stevenson called the heat of composition. To a man as cynical as Gabriel the claim that his work was a mystery could only be a joke; but it had impressed the impressible Constance, who would have been a religieuse if she had been able to understand what religion was all about. Consequently Gabriel had secured peace. And now, when he could hardly work at all because of the pain which racked him and brought violent sweats to his head and eyes and robbed him of sense, he continued to value solitude, and he continued to eat when he wished to eat, and not when some damned kitchen tyrant thought he ought to do so. Cook, indeed, took pride in his eccentricity; she was paid high wages, and received complimentary dress circle tickets for Gabriel's plays and the plays in which Constance acted. She also went behind the scenes. Her knowledge of theatrical scandal was unsurpassed. She would not have allowed herself to be lured elsewhere under twice her present wages.

Gabriel walked up and down the study, planning to help Letitia.

As the dramatist husband of an actress he had always been free to dine alone or in company with able men of every sort at one or other of his four clubs, and at these clubs he knew familiarly, in their hours of relaxation, many writers, actors, barristers, politicians, and business men or Civil Servants. The writers he detested, from a sense of their jealous rivalry; the actors he despised, sometimes because they did not want his plays, sometimes because he thought their vanity fatuous; but amongst the rest, even the Civil Servants, he found an acutely stimulating supply of news, anecdote, and information. He gave, every two or three months, a dinnerparty in a club private room, to which he invited five or seven or eleven of them; and although he was never unreservedly liked invitations to the parties were not refused.

Evidently Letitia had been influenced by, not idolatrous admiration, but knowledge of his habits. Constance. Constance was a gossip and a boaster. Letitia might have believed what she said. She thought he could pull strings. And that he would be ready to do so for her. He was not deceived into imagining more than that. He was never, for long, deceived. No man was so constantly on his guard. As he restlessly walked—at times almost trotting—about his room Gabriel wondered that he should be so eager to help her. It argued unusual naïveté . . .

What shrewd innocence she had! To think that a lover—assuming himself to be her lover—would, without profit, seek to bring honour and advantage to a husband! On the stage the converse was a commonplace— *le mari complaisant*. But then, apparently, the stage represented Alice's looking-glass world; a dream distortion, not a mirroring of Nature. It was no guide to Life.

Sometimes Gabriel was quite deceived by the stage. He had worked for it since youth. He realised that one mustn't mistake stage values for real values; but as a professional writer he observed the theatre's conventions, and, as a successful man, he dwelt so much apart that his view of life was as artificial as Congreve's. Men and women had only one interest for each other; they pursued, or they sought to escape from pursuit. He himself was an escaper. He thought women coarse, acquisitive, unscrupulous, and, concerning the senses, disagreeably serious. His first concern, in flirting with them, was thus to show that he was without seriousness. This bewildered them; it threw their tactics out of gear; it made them, he knew, accuse him of what, in feminine eyes, is a seemingly unpardonable natural defect. But Letitia was different. He had never observed in her any of the coarseness of his would-be mistresses. She was peculiarly chaste. In approaching him she used her sex as nearly unconsciously as a sensitive and extraordinarily attractive woman could do.

He could imagine himself Letitia's lover with none of the guards and precautions it had been necessary to take with other women. He wouldn't want to baffle or torment her, to deny, to evade, to bring her from pride to fawning humility. Neither would he ever run away from any commitment to her. He could trust her. Extraordinary! This *must* be love.

Something was to be done. But you didn't go to the Lord Chancellor, or the L.C.J., to recommend an outstanding barrister for a Judgeship. You wormed your way among the lesser lights who effect such appointments. Or did you? Intrigues weren't always as dirty as those who screamed in the outer circles of politics alleged. Those inside *had* the jobs. They needn't intrigue as much as those outside. The screamers, who *wanted* the jobs, were biased. But many considerations, besides merit, influence appointments. One notorious nepotist justified himself on the ground that he was pledged to appoint only those whom he personally *knew* to be fit. The men of one University, one school, one set, one religion, looked round among their coevals; they thought the rest of mankind a gang of outsiders. The ambitious, it was true, squeezed a great man's lackeys if they wanted this or that. And, great men, without doubt, could be snobs.

Pro and con. Monty was not ambitious: a fatal defect. You could push a man who was already moving under his own momentum; but if you had to dig him out of a ditch his machinery was suspect. Monty hadn't worked for a Judgeship, or even for popular reputation. He was nothing but a lawyer. Monty, however, was a gentleman, immaculately just, extremely able, in every way worthy of judicial honours in a free State. Even Gabriel didn't despise him. The mere mention of Monty's name ought to impress those who valued Justice. It might equally impress the jobbers, who needed good names as window-dressing. He would test this, as a beginning.

He mustn't be over-long; for this damned stone was killing him. They didn't want to operate. The devils! Always protecting themselves and each other! They frightened you by hinting that your heart wouldn't stand an operation. Damn them! What did they know of his heart? He kept it private. Even Letitia knew nothing of it.

Did she know nothing? Oh, come! Constance, once you were past the play of that fluttering assimilative intelligence, was as single-track and slug-witted as a highbrow; and Constance saw something. Constance was already poisoned by jealousy. Letitia—the good—wouldn't miss it. Wouldn't miss it, and wouldn't 'see' it. The tortuosity of the female mind! The blankness of the experienced female eye! The singleness of the female instinct! Letitia saw and knew everything, just as a common tart did;

she merely did not let vanity or avarice intoxicate her. That showed class.

He adored her. 'When I should be half-dead of joy, James Lee!' He'd quoted that to her. But of course, if one was habitually insincere, one could at any time venture a sincerity without risk. A favourable position, rich in disguise!

Backwards and forwards loped Gabriel, his eyebrows working, his shoulders much hunched, his hands clasped in front of him like those of a prudish stone Venus. This was a play indeed! His masterpiece! He saw himself dying in the last act of it; lying upon his limelit bed amid sobs from Constance, drawn silence from Letitia, mute gratitude from Monty; while angels, singing in chorus like the morning stars, waited ready-winged to bear his spirit to Paradise.

iii

Ruth answered the front door bell. That long, lean man with the beard and the funny eyes was there again. His manner towards her was not that of a gentleman; it was too familiar, too presuming. She didn't like him.

'Good morning, sir,' said she.

'Well, did you tell Mrs Boldero that Mr Farringdon had called?' demanded the man, easily.

'Yes, sir; I did. Mrs Boldero said to tell you that she would be at home all the afternoon. She had to go out this morning. You didn't leave an address or a telephone number.'

Ruth could not see his mouth; but she knew he was jeering, and trying to make her uncomfortable. She was glad to remember her brother Dick, who, by much teasing when she was a kid, had cured her of blushing. He'd done her good. Mrs Boldero had helped too, by telling her things, and showing that she trusted her.

'No, I didn't leave a telephone number,' said the man, with familiar impertinence. 'Perhaps you can guess why.' He seemed disappointed when Ruth made no effort to guess. Less derision and more hostility showed in his manner. 'I'm not on the telephone. Mr Boldero at home?'

'No, sir.'

'He's in London?'

'Yes, sir.'

'Mhm.' The stranger was in no hurry to go. 'I see.' The truth was, F. R. had no other pressing business, and would not have minded chatting awhile with Ruth. Ruth realised that. Ruth knew what she looked like; and she knew that some men found her pleasantly exasperating. Some had thought her education incomplete. But those who had supposed this had found her sidestep, and even her slap, reassuringly sophisticated. 'I see,' said the stranger, again. 'Well, maybe I'll come back. I won't promise. I *never* promise, even when tempted by La Gioconda.'

He turned slowly away, having given her a meaning glance.

Ruth held the door open, as she had been taught to do, until he reached the foot of the steps. Her eyes were cast down; she still wore the little fixed simper which suggested that her brain never moved. And yet she contrived, without slyness, to see that F. R. wore economical rubber heels and a stock-size grey flannel shirt from which his long, stringy wrists projected, and to feel quite sure that, promise or no promise, he would come back for his own calculated purposes. She also, in closing the door, saw something—somebody—else arriving at the house. And at sight of this somebody else additional colour warmed her cheeks and her simper took on the mysterious reality of a smile.

The stranger, who had been about to stride away with obviously long legs, checked his pace. He took the sharpest possible look, a much too familiar, eating sort of look, at the somebody else. And Ruth saw Mr Julian, who had been coming to the house, stop as if he had been spoken to. His very handsome face lost what Ruth had been shocked to feel was the expression of one damned. He looked up at the stranger with something very like his ordinary hesitating, languid smile of politeness. The stranger—good gracious! thought Ruth; just as if he was a policeman!—put his hand upon Mr Julian's shoulder, and kept it there while he talked and straddled his long legs and persuasively jerked his head about. Long legs and a long tongue! But Mr Julian wasn't at all alarmed—of course, he wouldn't be, at anything; not even a nasty German spy holding a gun—and spoke to the man, not as if he was a friend, but as if the man had told him something he was glad or sorry to know. The man continued to press Mr Julian's shoulder. He seemed to be urging him to do something—to come with him down the street, perhaps. Then he withdrew his hand, and stood loose-limbed, at last putting both hands, clasped, to his own waist. Ruth could see the waggle of his beard. He talked twenty to the dozen. It wouldn't impress Mr Julian. Gab-gab-gab!

For a few moments Mr. Julian listened in an undecided way. Ruth thought he looked as if he might be wanting to get away from the stranger, as she had done, but as if he couldn't think up a proper excuse. That was Mr Julian all over—undecided. It was the reason he drawled, to give himself time to think up a wisecrack or something. A weak darling, Dick called him. She was not surprised therefore, when the two of them began to walk slowly down the street together, away from the house. As quick as a conjurer, Ruth shut the front door and darted into the dining-room, from the window of which she could see them until they reached the corner of Mallow Street, and turned along it into the unknown world of which she had no command.

That was funny, wasn't it! demanded Ruth, of herself. Mr Julian in America, and now, all of a sudden, here—nothing having been *said*. Didn't they know? That man, who, Mrs Boldero had told her, might be a brother; though Ruth had never so much as heard of a brother. And the two of them meeting and talking—probably Mr Julian hearing his mother was out—and then going off together. *That* was funny, if you like! Ruth began to whistle 'Onward, Christian Soldiers'—not a very good whistle, as far as the 'tune was concerned, but very high and clear, like a wren's song. She liked Mr. Julian almost the best of them. Not as *nice* as Mr Mark; but he rather excited her, as Franchot Tone did in the pictures. Why had he come back?

Mrs Boldero would be upset at missing him. She was sort of fond of Mr Julian—anxious about him. She might not care for his being caught by this Mr Farringdon. Ruth wished it hadn't happened. She didn't trust Mr Farringdon: he thought other things while he was talking to you. That was a nasty trick. The whistle faltered. Then it died away altogether.

iv

Constance had gone to the first rehearsal of 'The Chicks are Cold.' She went by bus to the Imperial Theatre in Shaftesbury Avenue, and saw all the early shoppers and strollers in Piccadilly and up Bond Street and Regent Street; and she mumbled one or two phrases of the play under her breath. She was depressed. If she had not been exhilarated at the thought of having so long a part, she would have been very depressed indeed. It didn't take much to lower her spirits, she knew.

She had a great dislike, which she thought she concealed, for Valentine Rough, with whom she was to spar throughout the play. She did not much fancy one of the girls, either; Rose Cortall, who was as pert as the chit she had been cast to play. They'd *both* been cast intelligently. (Did that go for her, too?) The others were unknown youngsters. On the whole Constance did not relish newcomers. They had superficial good manners; but she found them hard. They stared, feeling contempt for everybody older than themselves, and a sense of injury because they weren't already starred. She would have felt safer if Gabriel had been with her. She needed either a guardian angel or a sympathetic audience. These youngsters had no sympathy; they wanted to hog it all for themselves.

Fortunately Constance liked Cress Marvin, the producer. He understood her. He did not show off before the young or humiliate his leading ladies; and if he should want something changed he would take her to lunch and make admirable suggestions with equally admirable courtesy. She had been through the part with Gabriel, who was a clever devil with other men's words as well as his own, and she was not afraid that she would make a fool of herself; but the first rehearsal was always agitating.

That wasn't the reason she was distressed. Not the *real* reason. To some extent it was reaction, because she'd discovered what was the matter with Gabriel, and she'd cried a little over him. He'd been rather impatient; told her she'd be 'all right', which she knew, if anything happened to him; told her to take her tears somewhere else—all very Gabriel, but at the same time softened by the dread of death and a sort of sentiment. And she'd felt splendid; ready for anything, even sorrowing widowhood. Quite a good, heart-warming rôle. And then Letitia had made him laugh. Beautifully. As if his heart were in it. Divine merriment! What had she said? Damn, damn, damn her!

No answer of course, from Gabriel, afterwards, to her subtle questions. Sighing, she realised that they had not been too subtle. Never more than obvious to *him*. Letitia for the rest of the evening like a cat that's finished the cream jug. No sign of worry. But she'd *been* worried. There was *something* up. Why had she been late the other afternoon? Gabriel? No, no; she couldn't possibly have acted her surprised concern at the news of his illness. *Couldn't* she? She had extraordinary depths; why shouldn't they be diabolical? Constance's suspicions flew up like a genie rising from an uncorked bottle. That was something she'd always distrusted about Letitia—her self-control. Would you ever be able to tell what she'd been up to, or *was* up to? You never would!

'Gosh, I'm depressed!' exclaimed Constance. 'I wish I was dead!'

It needed the dark, mean little entry to the Imperial's stage door to rouse her. It needed the door-keeper's ugly brown face and sourly anti-feminist greeting (he had a flighty wife who wouldn't leave him) to tickle her whimsy. It needed the grim dimness of the staircase, and the Imperial stage, and all the lovely associations of the theatre, and that little circle of chairs, to stir the sense that she, too, like Correggio, or whoever it was, was an artist. It needed Cress Marvin's flattering hail, a moment later, to lift her heart. It needed the sidelong looks of the group of hardly-glimpsed youngsters (sidelong because they regarded her, however unwillingly, as a real live actress, beside whom they, although modern and therefore magnificent, were really only beginners) to make her gay. And suddenly it was as an almost bounding, Ellen Terry-ish friend of all the world that she greeted and—in spirit only—embraced the author of the play, Ronald Lafayette, who stood beside Cress.

Lafayette was nervous, poor lamb! Small, thin, dark, timid; all his boldness in his lines. Like Gabriel as a young man; but better-looking and with less real spite. That was Constance's experience of playwrights: they wrote, to compensate. Like Addison, or somebody, they could scribble cheques for a thousand pounds, but they hadn't a penny on the tips of their tongues. Gabriel had sniggered over the deflation which was coming to Lafayette—'The dramatist, after a first rehearsal of what he thought was a masterpiece,' he had laughed, pretending dazedly to cringe and dodge brickbats—and Gabriel would never pity him. Constance pitied him. Poor lamb; to hear his words mangled! And he was so frightened! He made her feel a grand successful giantess, mother of all men, and a star with her name in six-foot lights and contracts showering. When she richly exclaimed 'Glorious play!' he shrank and smiled tremblingly. Very, very nice! About thirty, she supposed. Poor shoulders; very smartly dressed, not arty, but something of a drawing-room ornament. Yes, silent there, but capable of barbed detraction, as they all were. And now, in the theatre, as shy and self-distrustful as a child at her first school. Constance's heart expanded and engulfed him. Why, he was positively a darling! He could be jollied!

'I don't grumble because I'm made a laughing-stock all through,' she exuberantly told him. 'I don't demand to be let score off these puppies even once——'

'You wouldn't get anything if you *did*, darling!' cried Cress. 'Besides, you already get the sympathy given to underdogs!'

'Yes, but what a litter I feed!' retorted Constance.

'*He's* the boss,' said Lafayette, smiling at Cress. How strange; he closed his eyes in smiling, like an affectionate cat. And of course opened them again very quickly. A beautiful quiet voice. 'I'm powerless.'

'His work's done,' said Cress. 'Ours is beginning. Or should be, now you've come.'

'I wasn't late, was I?' demanded Constance.

'Absolutely on the tick.' Cress looked at his watch. 'One thing I love about you.'

Cress was delicious. You couldn't ruffle him. Constance always said 'As cool as Cress.' He was a good head taller than Lafayette, and an older-eyed man, in type similar to the best kind of gigolo or *maître d'hôtel*, but obviously neither a gigolo nor a *maître d'hôtel*. Not the smallest suggestion of dago about him. And yet—Constance knew that she was getting out of her depth.

'Now, ladies and gentlemen,' continued Cress, raising his voice. 'I've got the author of this very fine play here—Mr Lafayette—and he'll run through the play with us this morning. That's our great privilege. You all know each other, I think——'

'*I* don't,' cried Constance, with her famous squeak, which produced much laughter from the advancing groups.

Somehow they all became friends in that moment, she thought. All, perhaps, except the aloof Valentine, who was far too conceited to be anybody's enemy but his own, and who never made friends because he was so dourly patronising to his betters. Unhappy wretch! He *was* clever, though; he could give edge to any platitude. Oh, fine! Oh, fine! The greatest profession in the world! Constance was so interested, and so pleased with herself for all her thoughts and discoveries, that she felt kind to everybody.

Only somewhere at the bottom of her heart had she the old, old unease which prevented her from being a happy woman. This unease was spelled 'Gabriel'; and it never left her. Never. This morning it was active and alarming, because Letitia, apart from that momentary assumption of Ruth's very self, appearing most grave, had made Gabriel laugh so blithely the night before. Laugh, and *look*. Look as he had never looked at herself.

Damn Letitia! Damn her! She's got everything, and I've only got—this fat part and this jolly crowd of kids and the prospect of a run and (oh, God!) Gabriel, whom I've never really had at all; whistling woman that I am . . . Who would I rather be? Envy's the bitterest evil of all!

v

And Letitia, having missed Julian through a further fruitless visit to the flat near Baker Street station, and having forgotten all about Monty's Judgeship, which to her was not worth bothering about, was at this moment no object for envy. She felt for the first time that her life was over. Now that her children were grown up, she saw no place for herself in the domestic circle. She would grow old; busy to the end with superfluous tasks. Were not Monty's parents the living warnings of outgrown usefulness?

Sitting alone in a taxi, she thought of the children, of her mother, Muriel, and Farringdon, of Monty, of Constance and Gabriel; and her lips trembled. 'All of them sustained by their own egotism. All except Monty?' Loving memory of Monty filled her mind for a moment. It produced such an effect upon her that she said: 'We only feel useless because, just now, our values are denied. That doesn't make us really useless. The values will revive. They can't be dead. No, no; I won't have it! . . . Good gracious, I'm at home!'

She paid the taximan, and ran up the steps. An old lady who lived opposite, and who sat at the upstairs front window all day long, thought 'There's that young creature. She doesn't know what it is to be old. As far as she's concerned, the sun never sets!' And Ruth, seeing her once again, thought 'Thank goodness she's home again. She'll decide everything now.' As they drank together before lunch, F. R. and Julian both thought of her, and F. R. smiling behind his beard, said 'I remember your mother turning on *our* mother, and telling her what she thought of her. I was there, you understand; but I wasn't in the room. They were alone. She never hesitated for a word. She left the Old Lady shrivelled. Hysterical. Squashed. Never been known before. I expect she's changed since then; but I always remember that. She went off—ran away, it was called, in those days—without a penny or a friend. She never asked for anything, and never got anything, from anybody else. The most extraordinary self-confidence. Thought only of herself. You couldn't help admiring her.'

Julian drank again. He nodded, hearing for the first time of his mother's deliverance from evil; but he said nothing.

Five

VISITORS FOR THE PARTY

i

MR AND MRS BOLDERO senior—Mr. Boldero did not object to the 'senior'; but Mrs Boldero, who had never willingly given up a possession, thought it quite unnecessary—lived in a delightful Surrey village. They were proud of their only son, Montague, and of their grandchildren. They were proud of their garden and of the old furniture in their Elizabethan home. They were proud of being English, of being respected, and of being so remarkably sturdy in their eighties; and they were devoted to one another. Each of them hoped to be the first to die; Mr Boldero more earnestly and with great secret shame at his own cowardice; Mrs Boldero because, in spite of all her prides, she thought she would be the less missed.

Mr Boldero strolled in his acre of beautiful garden, napped in a comfortable armchair over large books, most of them biographies of his one-time contemporaries, smoked a high-class tobacco in fastidiously chosen pipes, chatted familiarly with everybody in the village, was jovial with his gardener-chauffeur, and looked back over eighty-four years of good life. He had worked conscientiously as an India Merchant for nearly fifty of them, and upon retirement at sixty-five had sold his share in the business for a handsome sum. His only unhappy period had lasted four-and-a-half years, during the War of 1914–18, and his chief anxiety in that period had been over Monty's safety. If Monty had been killed, Mr Boldero would long since have been dead.

His wife, who was two years younger, worked a little in the garden, snipping off dead flowers and withered leaves, dusted in the house, served tea once a week to a select few, held herself aloof from village dances, whist drives, and laboured sociability, and kept in touch with modern art by sampling the newest books and music, did not smoke or drink, sat up straight in a wooden chair, was autocratic with the gardener and the two women servants, prided herself upon spurring her husband away from slackness, was jealous of Letitia, and humbled her own ego by confessing in quiet nightly prayers all the imperfections she had noticed in it during the day. They were few. Hasty retort was her chief confessible sin; hasty retort and obduracy of opinion. Especially did she mention a lack of kindness towards Letitia. But this lack of kindness drew so little attention from the Being to whom she prayed that she had come to regard it as amusingly venial.

The two old people were lucky in their staff and their home; for their gardener-chauffeur, who mended everything and contrived such comforts as draught-excluders and door stops, was Ruth's brother, Dick, a good-natured and mischievous fellow in the early thirties; their cook had been with them for twenty-seven years and knew how to make almost everything except the local beef digestible; and the Bolderos were known to be so pleasant as employers that when their maids left, to marry and worsen themselves, excellent substitutes hurried to seek the vacant post. In the kitchen 'they' were sometimes smiled at; but they were never condemned with heat as 'she' and 'he'!

As to the Bolderos' home, it had been 'converted' from several Eliza-bethan cottages, in some portion of which it seemed that all the older inhabitants of Marpham had been born; and it had looks. It was also weather-tight, centrally-heated, company-supplied, and fully half-a-mile from the bus route. No cars drenched it with greasy dust; the lane in which it stood was so narrow that even energetic hikers, vehement in assertion of their right to trespass, did not trouble to explore it. But villagers sometimes paused during Sunday evening walks to stare over the hedge at Mrs Boldero's roses, delphiniums, antirrhinums, sweet williams, and stocks. Mrs Boldero, her chair in the living-room, observed the homage with pleasure.

This year the old people had seen most of their flowers and fruits pass. Late apples were all that remained to be picked and garnered. Chrysanthe-mums were well in bloom; wreaths of mist hung of a morning about the thorn hedges. It was time for their Autumn tour, first to London, and then to the home of an old school-friend of Mrs Boldero's who lived in South Devon. They would return home for the Winter, to long evenings by the wood-fire of their living-room, to books and patience, the gramophone, barometer-tapping, and discussion of *The Times*, *Punch*, *Country Life*, *Amateur Gardening*, and *The Spectator*. They still prized the Spring above all other seasons of the year; but they knew well the compensations of Winter, such as exquisite tree skeletons, rime, visible and audible robins, crumpets, and enduring nights.

And nobody ever suggested that it was the duty of octogenarians to put the world to rights. Contrariwise. Mr Boldero, although sometimes grunting—he was given to grunting—at some particularly mendacious claim, reported in *The Times* as having been made at home or abroad by every variety of partisan, had lost the political fire of his youth. He thought you might disturb Nature, but could not improve upon it. Mrs Boldero, it must be admitted, did not agree with him. She had no doubt that, given a free hand, she could improve the social order—chiefly by the method of shooting all those who disagreed with herself.

They were looking forward very much to their week with Monty. Mrs Boldero knew that Letitia would yield him entirely, and could not decide whether she ought to dislike her daughter-in-law for being so sure of him or to admire her for being so gracefully generous to his mother. It would have given her such pleasure to re-capture the boy in face of jealous opposition that Letitia's calm, which was clearly not due to indifference, wounded, she thought, one's *amour-propre*.

As for Mr Boldero, he knew that he would not be quite happy until he was home again; but he was exceedingly fond and proud of Letitia, as his wife knew, and thought Christine the prettiest, most intelligent, and best-mannered girl of her generation in England. He preferred her style to that of any of the drawling young ladies of Marpham, who seemed always to be trying to show what good schools they had been at, which he considered an unpardonable vulgarity.

There was much in modern young women which he considered vulgar; 'not that I don't see a lot to admire, too, if it's only their exhibited physical development,' he said between ruminant puffs of his pipe. 'Of which there's plenty,' he said, 'I admit; and very sturdy.' 'But,' he said, 'it reminds me that they're only flesh and blood, like ourselves.' 'Which, taken in conjunction with the loss of faith, respect, and wonder in other directions,' he said, 'is a pity.' 'And, in fact,' he said, 'one of the few unmistakable signs of modern degeneracy.' He spoke thus when alone. He did not tell his wife what he thought of her sex as a whole. He merely allowed her the satisfaction of knowing that she, Letitia, and Christine lay outside all generalisations.

And so at last the morning came upon which Mr and Mrs Boldero were to take their long drive to London. They would go all the way by road, as they always did, because although it meant a day's neglect of the garden on the part of active and apple-cheeked Dick Sharples (who could never, in spite of his blue coat and peaked cap, be mistaken for a whole-time chauffeur) it saved them all the trials of changing, and scrambling into railway carriages where there were young babies or fidgety little boys or toad-like cigar-smokers, and hiring off-hand porters, and struggling with the defiant windows of taxicabs. Moreover, both Mr and Mrs Boldero took pleasure in observing, in the driving mirror, the reflection of Dick's recurrent broad grin as he thought up pranks to play upon young Ruth when they reached·Kensington and the old uns had been safely dumped.

ii

The day was fair; and the car, although it was not new, was well sprung and in good order. It soon reached the road over the Hog's Back, and Dick did not need to be told that Mr and Mrs Boldero would wish to pore silently upon the great stretch of beauty above which they passed. He therefore placidly waved-on upwards of a hundred more impetuous drivers, so bent upon keeping urgent appointments with money or power or death that they had no leisure for the amenities; and, having reached Guildford and, as a wise driver, avoided its crowded, hilly High Street, was soon travelling smoothly and buoyantly along the ample road to Kingston.

Mr and Mrs Boldero leaned back in their seats and closed their eyes. They were no longer interested in the scene, save at intervals, and, as they had full confidence in Dick's skill, neither needed to drive the car, steer it from danger, stamp in panic on the brakes, or feel indignant with all the little cars which, with ludicrous vanity, tottered and rattled past them—'doing fifty, old man.' Only when London itself was reached would they again, by instinct, open their eyes and look forward, holding the arm-rests and staring like children.

Ah! Here were the red omnibuses!

A few minutes later they were upon Hammersmith Bridge, across it, turning in half-a-dozen side streets to escape the Broadway, and then positively at Monty's door.

'Well done, Dick!' said Mr Boldero. 'You . . . surpass yourself.'

Dick smiled. He helped them both to step from the car, knowing that Mr Boldero, for fun, would lean heavily upon his arm in descending, and that because she had no fun in her constitution he would hardly at all feel Mrs Boldero's weight. His elbow became strangely awkward at the instant of Ruth's arrival; but luckily neither of the old people saw how sharply it darted into his sister's ribs, and Ruth herself, being better trained than he, did not scream. Her buttoned smile had grown slightly more timid under Mrs Boldero senior's glance. Her cheeks were a deeper pink. She fluttered a glance back to the front door, made sure that Letitia was greeting the visitors, and relaxed.

'Clumsy!' Ruth breathed in Dick's ear. 'I'll pay you for that.'

'Oh, did I 'urt you?' asked Dick, suavely; 'I'm all of a tremble. What's for dinner?'

'Eat it, and see,' answered Ruth. "Gimme that end, and buck up.'

Together, they disengaged the old people's portmanteaux from the carrier-straps, and brought them into the house.

'Good morning, Dick,' said Letitia. 'Are you well? And Ellen and Pansy May?'

'Good morning, Madame. All well, thank you, Madame.' Dick's grin was broad with a breadth which Ruth never allowed herself in public. But his eyes had the same glow as Ruth's eyes.

'Pansy May's teeth still giving trouble?'

'Only when she remembers, Madame.'

'And thinks you're forgetting? We're all the same. I must go now. I'll see you later.'

'Very good, Madame.'

Not until, as Letitia withdrew, they put down the portmanteaux, did Dick give his sister a hearty kiss and spank of greeting, which Ruth, who sometimes looked too prim to be true, answered with a kiss and a push. Her smile relaxed, as if it had slipped a button. She might have been a country hoyden.

iii

Now Mr and Mrs Boldero were alone with their daughter-in-law, and Letitia could see how they looked.

Mr Boldero was a shortish, trimly white-bearded man, rather like John Burns, with brown cheeks and big black eyebrows, beneath which blue eyes —sometimes rather fixed, with age—retained a glitter of freshness. He moved slowly, but not feebly; rather as if he were given to communing much with himself, as he was. His wife had never been in the habit of listening to others. Mrs Boldero was taller, plumper, very straight, black-silked with a gold locket brooch, and her white hair was drawn severely back from her brows. This style of hairdressing revealed her bony skull, and heightened the effect of age in her rather sunken raisin-coloured eyes; but most people would not have taken her for eighty, owing to her upright carriage and the precision of her movements.

It was her habit to say: 'Don't ask how we are. We're always well.' Indeed, Letitia, who would never think such a thing, knew instinctively that these two old people, if one of them ever felt ill, would both at once surprisedly be sick unto death.

They had walked boldly into the drawing-room, savouring its miraculous lightness. Mrs Boldero had long ago seized upon the room's secret. She thought Letitia had been clever to see it first; but she gave her daughter-in-law credit for nothing more than cleverness. She was convinced that this house owed its serenity to Monty. Monty was everywhere in it, the calm and beautiful Monty. Monty, her one child, always a model; his taste, his skill, his learning, his nobility of character, were known to her, she assumed, as to nobody else. He could not move or speak or remain still without stirring her approval. It was her constant complacent thought that Letitia had never appreciated, and had not the capacity to appreciate, her luck in being married to him.

She surveyed Letitia this morning, as at all other meetings, with a different measure of criticism from the one she applied to Monty. Letitia was not, by blood, a Boldero or a Littleton—Mrs Boldero had been a Littleton—she was just another woman. She was never seen as a daughter at one remove; always as the appendage of a beloved son. Good enough to look at; certainly thoughtful of one's comfort; still a bit the actress; evidently a satisfied woman—that was Monty. When in larger company, the old lady observed Letitia's ease with more surprise: yes, yes, quite effective—the new word was poise—yes, unexceptionable. She was there all the time, always, startlingly fluid in comprehension. Oh, not a bad companion for the boy. He might have done worse. Of course, he'd formed Letitia; influenced her in every way, taking the pretty worthless creature and giving her a part to play. She'd just been quick, as actresses were. And besides adapting herself, she had grown . . .

At the beginning, Mrs Boldero remembered to have been seriously alarmed. She forgot that, having with uncontrolled hostility threatened every disaster, she had done her worst to stop the marriage and then to humiliate Letitia into a state of vendetta. She had worked in vain, had sulked, had been conquered. Time had softened all her animus, and substituted reluctant, disparaging respect and affection. She would not, now, in any emergency, instantly believe the worst of her daughter-in-law, and might even slightly defend her.

'And now, lunch,' Letitia said, seeing Ruth within the doorway. 'I'm sorry Monty's not able to be here; but he'll be in for tea. So will Christine. So'—this with a glance at Mr Boldero—'you'll be able to see her while she's still a child.'

'Nonsense!' spoke up Mrs Boldero. 'She'll be a child for another ten years.'

'Only two more days,' laughed Letitia. 'She told me. I don't know if she plans yet to leave home.'

'Ridiculous!' cried Mrs Boldero. 'You wouldn't allow it! Monty wouldn't!'

'You must use *your* influence.'

'I shall certainly tell her what I think of such foolishness.'

'She does very well as she is,' Mr Boldero protested in defence of his favourite. 'She's a great darling. When I contrast her with the superfine hussies——'

'Oh, she's *much* more superfine than when you last saw her——'

The old people did not understand Letitia's levity over her daughter. Mrs Boldero suspected her of jealousy. Yes, that would be natural. The baser metal showing as she grew older and went back, as people did, to what she had been as a child. Mr Boldero, marching sturdily downstairs, said:

'Oh, we'll see for ourselves. Make up our own minds.'

'*Quite* sentimental about her,' commented Mrs Boldero, sweeping ahead of him and taking her place at the table. She was eyeing Ruth, to make sure that she had coarsened as a result of life in London. 'Is that a new picture, Letitia?'

'Yes, by a friend of Christine's.'

'I can't see what it's meant to represent.'

'Nobody can. The artist's done his best to explain; but I'm still vague.'

'Some charlatan, I suppose,' suggested Mrs Boldero.

'Not if he's a friend of Christine's,' objected Mr Boldero, who even by twisting his neck could not see the picture. 'She wouldn't . . ah . . .'

'He's a very nice boy,' said Letitia. 'By no means a charlatan. But inspired; so that he hardly knows what he's doing himself.'

'Ridiculous!' Mrs. Boldero looked uneasy. 'A queer sort of friend for Christine to make. I know that one doesn't want to be——'

'I'm sure you'll like him,' promised Letitia, who had known that, in mentioning Christine's familiar friendship with such an eccentric, she would spring a mine upon the old people. 'You may even like his painting, when you see it properly. I do.'

'Did he *give* it to you?' demanded Mrs Boldero.

'No, I bought it.'

There was no spoken comment. Perhaps, even secretly, there was none; for the painting itself, being modern, was of interest only to artist and owner. It was left behind.

The old people, helping themselves from the dishes which Ruth silently brought, thought of what their own cook would have given them, and felt adventurous, a little apprehensive. They watched Ruth fill their glasses with wine of a pale gold, and sighed, and then, becoming aware of their sighs, which had been caused by old happy memories, they smiled at Letitia. After all, it was extremely pleasant to be here, and they were safe and happy; and Letitia was kind and beautiful; never either bored or obtrusively indulgent in manner; but—this was Mr Boldero—really just what a daughter of their own might have been, if they had been lucky enough to have a daughter . . .

It was the greatest compliment he could pay, the revelation of his never-confessed dream. Mrs Boldero would not, *could* not have paid it. Compliments from her were few; and if she had had another child she would have desired a second son to be proud of. But she did at least think what a good job Monty had made of his wife, and how tranquil and ever-welcome they felt in this house, and what a nice lunch they were having; which in the circumstances, coming from Mrs Boldero, was almost equal to a mother's long withheld kiss and a blessing for the hostess. Peace was upon the room.

iv

'Mark *hopes* to be back for your party, Chris,' Monty said that night, across the glowing dinner-table.

Letitia felt her heart jump in her breast, and swell unbearably.

'Hopes!' cried Christine, full of indignation. 'Well, I should think so! What brothers I've got! I didn't even know he was away.'

Nor I. Nor I, thought his mother, in agony. She lost all pleasure in Christine's lovely youth. The others continued placidly to eat. She could see the movement in their cheeks, which in that moment became intolerable. They were like fish in an aquarium. They understood nothing. Masticating at slow speed, casually waiting for more idle news of Mark, none of them could share her suffering or imagine its cause.

Monty, as tranquil as everybody except his wife, continued:

'Yes, I had a note this afternoon. He's sorry he can't be here tonight. Sends his love.' This was to Mrs Boldero, who nodded briskly. 'He's been up in Durham for the last week or so, on a case. He seems satisfied.'

Satisfied! At that distance, *now*! It was appalling! Alone? Then what? He was away, and satisfied, when everything demanded that he should be here, and alert to preserve his own and Stephanie's integrity. This was not fiddling, but droning. The professional lawyer, all black hat and green tape and crackling papers, with a bare cupboard for home, and an eager, dissatisfied young wife running away from him in boredom and chagrin. Appalling! Appalling! Her fists were pressed hard upon her knees under the table. She could hardly prevent the cry from leaving her lips. If Stephanie were with Julian! 'He seems satisfied.' She saw the others in a mist, as if she were fainting . . .

The faintness passed. Monty looked exactly as he always did in his mother's company, a handsome, slightly abashed boy; while his mother, although she was possessive, betrayed such love for him by her glance and the unconscious movement of her lips as she echoed the words he spoke that her possessiveness could not offend. It was so thin, such a shadow of what it had once been, that Letitia pitied her and wished she could give more of Monty's heart to satisfy an old woman's insatiable need.

Across the table from his wife old Henry Boldero, as brown as a sea captain, frisked with Christine, seeing her as if she were still the child in the cradle to whom he had given his heart twenty-one years ago. Whereas Mrs Boldero had a son and grandchildren, he had a son and a grand-daughter. The boys were well enough—fine fellows, and gentlemen;—but Christine was the only girl in the family. He adored her; he teased her in an old man's fond, trifling way, always smiling as if he would like to eat her. Christine knew her power. She kept her dark head high upon her slender neck, archly teasing in return, a lovely child who thought herself a woman. And so Letitia, at this evening's dinner-table, was the only person not engaged heart-to-heart in familiar talk. She was alone, haunted by the living, passionate ghosts of three who were absent.

She forced herself, trying to recover calmness, to ask one thing about Mark.

'Do you expect him back tomorrow?'

'Tomorrow night,' said Monty.

Tomorrow night—to that empty flat. She saw it as she had seen it last; bare save for the empty cup and the torn letters. She heard with dreadful foreboding Mark's voice using the very words she had heard from Julian. 'She's gone. I don't understand this . . .' *I don't understand this*. Oh, God! who in the world *ever* understood the involuntary deceit of love, or the mad follies of lovers? . . . The slight, fantastic wink with which Monty accompanied his reply was intended to establish a loving confidence with herself; but in face of it she was the more alone. A wink meant that he knew nothing of what threatened Mark. Had she done wrong to leave him ignorant? Had she done—Futile creature! She had done nothing but what was wrong. This was why, in bitterness and misery, she pictured both her boys broken-hearted; disaster in the very hour of Christine's triumphant birthday happiness.

'How's his wife?' demanded Mrs Boldero, perhaps with some feminine sense of the anguish which was so close to her.

Letitia became suddenly alert. She must not sacrifice Stephanie.

'Well; but probably feeling very tired of her own company,' she answered.

'Hm. I'd like to see that for myself.'

'You should have asked her here tonight,' cried Monty. 'No doubt you did?'

'I wasn't lucky,' said Letitia.

'I suppose she'll be here for Christine's party?' demanded Mrs Boldero.

'I shall be disappointed if she isn't; and so will she,' answered Letitia, in a cheerful voice.

'And so shall I!' declared Christine. 'As the person most concerned.'

Letitia knew from the brief stare accompanying this outcry that Christine had recognised three evasions and suspected more; but fortunately Mrs Boldero was less alert to replies about Stephanie than she would have been to replies about her grandsons. To her, Stephanie was nothing but the girl who had married Mark, which is to say that she disliked her, thought her untidy-minded, and called her 'Mark's wife' very much as she had once called Letitia 'that girl', or even 'that woman'. She looked at Letitia, ready to detect any sign that Stephanie might be in the early stages of child-bearing; but, seeing nothing to interest her, and finding Monty unperturbed, she returned to her son.

Letitia would have resumed anxious and exasperated thought of Mark if she had not been sure that Christine's bright observation, directed now to herself, would notice any withdrawal and begin to assess its causes. She smilingly sought Christine's eye, as the best form of defence.

It was at this moment that Ruth, whispering, called her to the telephone.

v

'Mother!'

Lighting played about Letitia in the dark telephone box. This was Stephanie herself. She could have screamed with relief.

'Where are you?' she cried.

'Are you alone?' demanded the voice. It was grimly unagitated.

'Door shut. Nobody near the telephone.'

'But in the house?'

'Father, Christine, two grandparents. That's all. Do *you* want to come? Do!'

There was a breathless silence. Then, very doubtfully:

'I don't know.'

Oh, yes, she knew! One didn't say one didn't know, unless one knew.

'Where *are* you? The flat? Lonely?'

'I want to be with *you*. Not the others.'

'That's easy. Ruth shall let you in quietly; whip you upstairs in an instant. Nobody any the wiser.'

The voice said, breathlessly again, almost as if with nervous laughter: 'The conspirators!' After a pause: 'Mother!'

'Yes.'

'I'm not good, you know.'

'How bad *are* you?'

Again that suggestion of nervous laughter. Triumph? Fear? But Letitia knew with certainty that Stephanie was alone, not speaking with Julian at her side.

'I don't know.'

'Not too bad, I should suppose. Let me see you, anyway How thankful I am to hear your voice!'

'I wonder if that's true?'

'Did you know Mark will be back tomorrow night?' There was dead silence. 'Hullo, Stephanie. Did you hear me?' She listened. She faintly heard hurried breathing. At last:

'I heard you.' No other reply. After a further silence. 'Mother, I can't bear to go back to the flat.'

'No.'

'That's why I rang up.'

'Yes. Was it the only reason?'

A long, long pause. Then:

'Not quite.'

'Good. Are you far away? How long will it take you to get here?'

'Whatever I've done?'

'Whatever you've done.'

'About one minute.'

'I'll let you in myself. Come quickly.'

It was Letitia who rang off.

For a moment, being still confused, she dallied. Stephanie had called her 'mother': that wasn't meaningless. Hitherto, when she had used the word, the other children had been there and it had seemed an inadvertence. Tonight it had been necessary to her, a means of claiming, of entreating Letitia's love. Didn't that mean, perhaps, rather a good deal? To Mark's mother? Or was it—Letitia's heart sank—to Julian's mother?

'Oh, one's not in compartments. Stephanie knows that. I mustn't waste time. Now!'

She went quickly away from the corner by Monty's study in which the telephone box stood, intending to go straight to the front door. But at a familiar silken rustle she turned; saw Ruth fresh from the dining-room, standing back in the shadow to let her pass; and at once felt her mind clear.

'Ruth! Have they finished?'

'Yes, Madame. Mrs Boldero said she would like coffee at the table.'

'Ask Miss Christine to pour it. Tell her—very quietly—that I've been called away. Not to remark on it. I'm not going out.'

'Yes, Madame.'

'And, Ruth. Switch on the fire in Mr Mark's room. And the bedside light. And bring something to eat—I think Isabel's got a cold chicken—and a glass of wine. The dry sherry. Mrs Mark's coming. She's very tired. I'll take her straight upstairs.'

'Very good, Madame.' No surprise; instant obedience, as if this were the most natural thing in the world. Almost without noise, Ruth disappeared. Letitia heard the chink of a spoon in a saucer, saw her return, saw the line of brighter light from the room, and stood back. The light came again; and Ruth was running upstairs. With her heart beating very fast, Letitia drew open the front door and went out on to the step to watch for Stephanie. Thank God! Whatever was now to happen, at least there was an end to fear of Stephanie's mistrust.

It was a cool, windless Autumn night, the moon young and clear in an exquisitely still sky. Every outline was flawless; the effect of moonlight was so to blanch the slates and beautify the placid chimneys that the scene brought quietness to a beholder's mind. Letitia bowed her head. There could be no end to pain; but she was not any longer strained by conscious futility. She had a part to play with those she loved . . .

And as she stood, hidden in the porch, the door pulled-to behind her, she saw—she did not hear the smallest sound; but she saw in silhouette against the silvered pavement—that tall figure running upon tiptoe towards the house. It was mysterious and beautiful. Thus must wraiths appear to those who are terrified by them; speeding wisps of shadow.

A moment later Stephanie, with a gasp, a sudden clutch and plunge of despairing thankfulness, was held closely in her arms. Her own heart did not beat more quickly than this other. Warm hands from beneath an enveloping cloak were across her shoulders; a wind-chilled cheek was pressed to hers. She heard a vehement whisper:

'Mother! How lovely! Always!'

'Come in quickly!'

There was resistance as Letitia sought to bring them both into the house; a lower whisper:

'If we could stay here in the dark!'

'In the cold!' whispered Letitia, laughing, her lashes wet. She heard:

'What! You're cold? I'm burning!'

'You're shivering.'

'No, trembling. With relief. Indoors they'll see me. *You'll* see me.'

'Nobody will see you. I'll keep my head turned away——'

'Ridiculous!'

'Ruth's bringing you something to eat. I'll take it from her at the bedroom door. We'll make you snug.'

'Your cure for everything——'

'Come quickly.' Still with one arm about the girl, Letitia persuaded her to enter; and together they went past the voice-ridden dining-room and up the stairs in the mild light of this elderly house. It had been old Mr Boldero's voice, so sharply interrupted by a contradiction from his wife, followed by

Christine's irrepressible laughter, that they both quivered with nervous merriment and were forced to stop. 'Bolderism in epitome,' whispered Letitia; and 'Better *that* than . . .' whispered Stephanie, in return. 'Oh, you don't *know*!' Letitia thought: Than what? What don't I know? Oh, she's far gone—— It was quite half a minute before the journey could be resumed; and Stephanie's body had grown heavier meanwhile.

At last Mark's room upon the second floor was reached, and they found that Ruth had already whipped off the bed-cover and made the room warm and glowing; fit corner for a weary traveller. One could see nothing clearly; but the bedside lamp made a circle of brilliance, and all about the walls were shadows of a rich orderly gathering of what had belonged to Mark's life before marriage. In this merciful dimness Stephanie's exhaustion was not outraged. But as she helped her off with the hooded cloak Letitia felt her fingers touch thick dust, and when she came to shoes they also were covered with dust. Stephanie had travelled far. She was worn out. She allowed herself to be put into a chair and into slippers; and, sitting in the warmth, she clung to Letitia's hand, turning her head and resting it, first against Letitia's arm, and then against her breast. A little girl might have done the same, seeking refuge from fear. A single deep gulp showed how hard she was struggling against the ignominy of a breakdown into noisy sobbing.

In this suspense, neither heard Ruth come into the room with a tray; but when the door was shut again some faint sound or draught caused Stephanie to jump forward in her chair.

'Who's that!' she exclaimed, in a hushed voice of alarm. 'Somebody's there!'

'Nothing. Ruth. A moment——' Letitia disengaged herself, overtook Ruth upon the stairs, whispered some instructions, and was back again while the weary Stephanie was still relaxed in a profound yawn. 'Now we'l sponge your face, get you into bed, feed you a little, and sing you to sleep, she announced.

'Don't leave me!' entreated Stephanie. 'I can't let you go!'

'I won't leave you. That's why I ran after Ruth.'

'She'll gossip.'

'Not a word.'

'How you trust her! I shouldn't. *Couldn't!* But I was afraid it wa Christine.'

'Why were you afraid?'

'She's hard.'

'No. She's severe. With herself too, you know.'

'You mean I indulge myself. I know that. You couldn't say harshe things of me than I do.'

'I *don't* say them, or often think them. We're our own cruellest judges

'I wonder. No, I'm not. That's what separates me from you an Christine. I *do* say the harsh things; but I'm like the repentant drunkar who gets drunk again——'

'Never repent. It's self-indulgence. Cut your losses and "march brea forward"——'

'Is that what you do? But then you haven't anything to repent. Or have you?'

'I'm never sure. I think I'm brazen. Here's Ruth. Thank you, Ruth. Yes, everything, thank you.' The door was once more closed, and she was back at Stephanie's side. 'I can hear Christine playing the piano to Mr Boldero——'

'She doesn't play as well as I do.'

'Mr Boldero wouldn't know that. He likes to feel it's Christine playing.' Stephanie murmured a little petulantly:

'You don't contradict me. I pummel the air. Christine's your real daughter. I don't mean only physically. She's *like* you. Oh, God! I resent and resent and . . .' It was as though she spoke these last words through clenched teeth. She admired and resented self-command in others. Probably in Mark. Presently she said: 'Ruth's like a mouse. Do you really trust her? I trust nobody.'

'Not me? Then I won't ask it.'

'Yes, you. I meant like Ruth.'

'Ruth's a particularly skilful and discreet mouse. She's also brought all you'll need for the night, including a new toothbrush in its cardboard box.'

'I should have expected that. Boldero Service. God! Nothing surprises me here.'

'How funny! To me, the place is a complete surprise packet.'

'But then you're naïve.'

Letitia, followed by this jeer, ran water into the fixed bowl until it was hot; after which, with some contrivance, she bathed Stephanie's face and hands, and even her aching feet, and helped her to undress. The nightdress which Ruth had brought was cast over the lovely shoulders; hair was quickly brushed; and within ten minutes Stephanie was propped up in bed with the tray on her knees.

'Sumptuous!' she exclaimed. She was already better. Indeed, she ate ravenously, and raised the glass to her lips with a steady hand. 'This room's all comfort.'

'Yes, it's been a happy room.'

Something in the coolness of Letitia's tone must have struck Stephanie too; for she looked attentively at the shadowed walls, first to one and then to another. It was impossible to detect any change in her face; but her voice was carefully steady.

'I see what you mean,' she said. 'It's Mark's. What genius you must have felt in bringing me here.'

'Is there another room you'd have preferred?' asked Letitia. 'This isn't a castle, you know. Eat up.'

Not looking at Letitia, but with an odd, diffident half-smile, Stephanie said:

'I *do* trust you. And love you. That's funny. I don't trust my own mother a scrap—I *couldn't* humiliate myself to her. She'd never let me forget it. I don't love her either. Who could? But you're so indifferent to everything that you don't have to be dishonest. No, I know that's not true. The wine's gone to my tongue.'

It was not only the wine.   A tremendous yawn seized her.   As Letitia took the tray, she leaned back, slid down in the bed, and almost before her pillows could be rearranged was fast asleep, her hair loose upon the pillow, her face as simple as a child's.

vi

Feeling guilty, triumphant, but not yet unperplexed; loving Stephanie but dreading the inconsequence of that busy mind, which found all other minds obstinate and incomprehensible; Letitia ran down the stairs.   She had turned the bedside lamp so that it would leave the sleeper's face in shadow; but she imagined Stephanie waking in the night and needing to know where she was and why she was so completely alone.   She felt sure that sensitive awakening to the room's associations with Mark would work in the sick thoughts like a new ichor; and she wished she might attend the consequences.   That was impossible.   She had already been away for too long from her other guests.

But as she ran she could hear Christine still playing his favourites quietly for her grandfather's ear, and when she slipped into the room she felt that she had not been seriously missed.   Away from the piano, listening to it only when she cared to do so, Mrs Boldero feasted as much upon Monty's silence as upon his sparse, always attractive talk.   She sat very upright, obviously alert and content.   Old Mr Boldero lay back, smoking, in an armchair, his feet raised, under doctor's advice, to another chair.   He was happy.   He heard Christine's competent strumming of everything, from Chopin to Scriabin, as if he listened to celestial songs.

It was not of old Mr Boldero that Letitia felt nervous: he was the sort of man to whom one could have said 'I've got a stray daughter-in-law on my hands' without prompting endless inquisitiveness.   It was of his wife and of Christine, the former because her questioning would be peremptory and her judgement rigid; the latter because she had too clear a head to be kept away from the most inconvenient facts in the world.   But Mrs Boldero ordinarily sleepless in attention, seemed to have arrived that day prepared to find everything in place; she now hardly turned her eyes to acknowledge Letitia's arrival, and gave her no sign of recognition.   And Christine, after one droll look which twisted her pretty lips, continued to the end of a Chopin mazurka before closing the piano, giving the old man a friendly touch on the shoulder, and crossing the room to her mother's side.

At the same moment Ruth, who was pleasantly and innocently like one of suburbia's Eastern monkeys, which are supposed to see all and say nothing, brought Letitia some fresh coffee.   Her eyes were shy; the mechanical smile upon her lips was doll-like.

'You must be *quite* glutted, Grandpa.   It's indecent to overeat music' said Christine, as he groaned in protest.   She was as firm in manner as professional nurse.   And, to Letitia, for whom she kindly poured the coffee she added, so low that her voice could not have been heard at a yard distance: 'You're very mysterious tonight, Mother. Are you playing secrets?'

Letitia, drinking, said: 'I'm a very old woman.'

'Did you say "old" or "odd"?'

'I'd so much rather you didn't draw attention to me.'

'But those comings and goings, darling! Attention's been drawn to them. Long ago,' said Christine. There was no need for her to say who had drawn the attention.

'Is it forgotten?'

'Is anything forgotten?'

'I'll tell you a true story—one day.'

Baffled, but with a searching glance, Christine seated herself by Letitia. 'I hope it will be true. There are several stories I *want* to hear, you know. One of them's about somebody who was mentioned at dinner. And another's about why you were so pale about Mark . . . And for one thing I don't believe in mothers having secrets from their only daughters. Especially when the daughters are twenty-one. You did know that, didn't you. About my being twenty-one——'

'It's an obsolete convention, dearest.'

'Red herring, Mama. And I want to *know* about——'

'Please, Chris.'

It was enough. A nod preceded Christine's answering smile. She had pin-pointed the cause of her mother's disturbed evening. Henceforward her own intelligence would be applied, without mercy, to every clue in the relations of Mark and Stephanie.

Mr Boldero puffed at his pipe; Mrs Boldero looked at Monty; Monty in a gentle voice told her a legal anecdote—for in that most absorbing of 'shops' there is a series of anecdotes unending in their interest to laymen;—upstairs Stephanie turned, smiling, in her sleep as if she already drew strength from her surroundings; and Christine felt secret pride because her mother had appealed to her gentlemanly discretion.

Only Letitia, who knew so much that the others did not know, felt her triumph ebbing, her guilt growing more insignificant, and her fundamental perplexity continuing far into the future. She sipped coffee, sending the antennæ of understanding and conjecture simultaneously in a dozen directions.

Six

AT BELLA VISTA

i

r HAD NOT been a very good morning in Bella Vista. For one thing, the himney had smoked a great deal, sending clouds of bitter smoke out into he room, and making The Old Lady cough and scream like a parrot. The smoke had left millions of smuts everywhere, and before Muriel could bring a duster her mother had printed several insulting remarks with her fore-finger upon the polished top of the drawing-room table. Muriel soon dusted them off; but the insults rankled. She would have protested against them if she had not known that this was just what The Old Lady wanted her to do. And so, thinking to herself 'You have to be artful with artful people,' she only banged the books and ornaments down rather sharply after dusting them.

Of course they were quite as dusty again a moment later, with the next puff; and more words were written upon the table.

In the kitchen too, although the fire did not smoke, there were a few mishaps. The black cat from next door, a very clever cat which could shake a window down with his front paws until there was room for his body to pass, had come in and eaten a beautiful kipper which Muriel had set aside for her own breakfast. Muriel was never sure about black cats. You were supposed to welcome them; but the luck they brought seemed to her to be usually bad. And this one, tripping you up, and stealing kippers, might really be a grimalkin, who came upon some witch's horried business. Or he might be an imp from Somebody even more undesirable. The D . . .

Well, what with the smoke and the cat and the kipper—it was a funny thing, bacon never *did* agree with her for breakfast, although it was al' right at other times of the day; but bacon it would have to be because even she, who had the appetite of a mouse, couldn't starve—and a chip of the teapot spout, and another slug who had worked his way artfully up the waste pipe to the sink, Muriel felt that this was Black Thursday. Then she found it was Friday, which meant that she would have to scuttle out in the wind to get some fish before it was all sold; and it was Black Friday, with the black cat as her black enemy. Very likely it was the D's birthday He could have them, she imagined, wherever and as often as he chose.

Bang-bang-bang! came The Old Lady's hammer from the front room where she sat amid the smoke and old relics—some of them really her own, but others just odd antiques picked up at shops and adopted as famil heirlooms—and made up lies about imaginary ancestors, and equall imaginary theatrical triumphs with Irving and the Bancrofts and Kendal Bang-bang-bang!

'All right. All right. I'm coming,' grumbled Muriel. 'It's only a minut since I was there; and a few more puffs won't make much difference. you'd have the window open it wouldn't be so bad, as I've told you; but might as well talk to the Grand Pyramid himself——'

'Bang-bang-bang.' The knocks became a tremendous cannonad which at last impressed even Muriel. But before she could run from the kitchen to the front room she was thrown into the greatest possible tumu by the loud thrring-thrring-thrring of the electric bell, which had its batte and noise-making apparatus high up on the kitchen wall. She was horrified by the noise, which came after such a stormy, disaster-filled mornin and close upon the rappings of Mother's Mallet, that she would have lik to sit down for a moment on one of the kitchen chairs to recover her brea and her courage. But the banging and ringing began again, frightenir the blood from her cheeks and weakening her knees; and she tottered out into the passage with a spurt of desperate energy.

'Hi-hi-hi!' bawled The Old Lady, from the front room. It did not occur to her to get up and answer the door herself. It never did. And thrring-thrring! went the bell. And bang-bang-bang! went the hammer. This was pandemonium. Maddening! 'I'm coming! I'm coming!' screamed Muriel. 'I'm not a tee-to-tum.' She could see a shadow, two shadows, upon the glass panes of the front door, and at once thought it must be the police; but as she could not remember anything she had done which was punishable by the law, she cast aside that fear and plumped for a ferocious bully—a gunman from Chicago—who would force his way into the house and insist upon being fed on the fat of the land until—until she did not know what. Invention always stopped before a cure suggested itself. The whole thing was a dream of powerlessness. She hurried to the front door.

Yes, there were two of them. Obviously gangsters. One was a hugely tall thin man with long arms and a beard like the beards of W. G. Grace or the old Duke of Devonshire. She felt sure this man was a great scoundrel. He made his companion seem quite small, and as his hand was pressed to the bell at the moment of opening it remained in the air, as if aimed in a frightful way at her low throat.

'Be off!' cried Muriel, with tremendous courage. 'Or I'll set the mastiff on to you. It's an outrage, ringing like that!' The pounding of that horrible mallet, and Mother's stentorian 'Hi-hi-hi!' continued to echo through the house.

'Hullo, Muriel!' genially exclaimed the gangster. His beard parted near the top, and she saw in the disclosed cavity a red tongue and some fang-like teeth. 'You're still deaf, I find. And you're fatter than ever!'

'Deaf'? She'd never been deaf. And 'fat' was insulting. She wasn't fat. And 'Muriel': he pretended to know her. Worse, his voice was deplorably familiar. Worse, that beard, which was like a box-tree, when it suffocatingly buried your face, resembled something once seen in an old snap-shot . . .

'Farringdon!' cried Muriel. Her mouth fell open. This was the last person whom she had wished to see in the house. Every portent of that black morning was instantly justified. 'Hi-hi-hi!' bawled the Old Lady from behind her closed door. 'Who is it?' Bang-bang-bang! 'Who is it?' The racket and excitement were enough to drive anybody mad. But at last the bell no longer turned her bones to water. At least no revolver had been pointed at her heart. Mutely, too exhausted to do more, she stood back to allow Farringdon to swing past her; and his companion, a graceful young man who wore no hat, and whose dark pallor and narrow head looked strangely familiar, followed him, smiling, into the hall.

They were like a giraffe and a puma, she thought, in this narrow space! They quite filled it, crowding her to the wall. She herself was as helpless as a rabbit—a very nice rabbit.

'Well, Auntie,' said the young man. 'Don't you remember me?'

'You're—*Julian*!' Muriel was so relieved to know that she had one friend in the world, to protect her from Farringdon, that she shrieked Julian's

name and stood upon tiptoe to hug him with her short arms. Her blunt
nose struck against his cheek; her chin was grazed by the collar of his rough
tweed coat. 'Go in! Go in!' she gasped, to Farringdon. 'And stop that
dreadful hammering!'

'Hi-hi-hi! Hi-hi——' With the appearance of his tall figure in the
doorway The Old Lady abandoned her outcry, and immediately sat with the
dignity of a duchess. She was in a black stuff frock with a gypsy-like scarf
of many colours, and her face had changed in a trice from exasperated rage
to the image of ancient pride. That was easy: her expressions, all artificial,
resembled dissolving views. And at the same moment a monstrous cloud
of smoke came down the chimney and out into the room, choking everybody
and half-obliterating the last words busily printed upon the table by that
poised forefinger—'MY DAUGHTER IS A DILLATTORY SLUT'.

'They talk of broomsticks!' thought Farringdon. 'The ignorant buffoons!
Mine flies by hearse!' He drawled: 'Mother, darling!'

'Farringdon! My precious buo-ooy!' cried The Old Lady, rising
immensely to her feet. 'My dream's come true!'

She was clasped in those long arms, and kissed—she did not kiss in
return—upon a cheek which made him think of oilcloth. Her own clasp,
Farringdon thought, was as strong as his own. She must be eighty-odd.
Marvellous woman! How insincere was the dramatic greeting? She had
always pitched her note high. Well, he'd show that he, too, had some
command of high notes. Given the smallest genuineness, mere relief from
previous boredom, it held unlimited promise. He smiled, his brain
consciously busy.

ii

'We-e-ell, now!' groaned The Old Lady, withdrawing herself at last from
Farringdon's tentacles. 'How are you? My boy! My Absalom!'
She surveyed him with fond pride, still holding his right hand. Her lips
quivered. Not tears, but the pride of Volumnia glowed in her coaly eyes

Farringdon seated himself upon the edge of the dusty table, bending
towards her, and not for an instant suggesting that his hand should be
freed.

'This is a wonderful welcome,' he enthusiastically declared. 'What
I'd longed for. It's extraordinary how you picture to yourself . . . And
then daren't hope . . . You say you dreamed of me? We met in our
dreams——'

'I said so! Muriel, didn't I say so! Where's Muriel? Oh, that girl'
a——' The Old Lady reached for her mallet, which was tied by a long string
to the arm of her chair. A dark patch of battered plaster in the wall was
explained for Farringdon by her action. 'You shall hear from her whether
I——'

'No, no, Mother! Let's hear it from yourself,' coaxed Farringdon
That's what I want to do. Tell me how you are, and how you manage——

'Ah, that's impossible!' groaned his mother, casting her eyes aloft. My sufferings . . .'

'Terrible!' agreed Farringdon. 'Though you *look* wonderful.'

'No comfort. No understanding. I sit here . . .' She shrugged, indicating the emptiness of her boredom.

'Very bravely, no doubt. As you'd do everything.'

'I do my best,' admitted The Old Lady, with hooded eyes. He imagined the savage fury with which she would punish Muriel. He felt almost sorry for Muriel. 'Sometimes a little impatient, I'm afraid. When one's old and ill, and sad, thinking of loved ones . . .' Was she going to speak of his father? If so, he would know that the whole thing was a performance. Twenty-shillings to a tanner! She interrupted herself, however. 'But *you*; let me hear about *you*, my darling boy. My troubles can wait.' With a sad composure she added: 'They *do* wait.'

'At least,' suggested Farringdon; 'tell me how you dreamed of me. How was it? *Where* was it?'

'It was on a ship. A great ship!' cried his mother.

He made an encouraging noise, a rising groan of assent.

'True enough. That's the way I came.'

'Alone?' It was an apparently artless question. He firmly replied: 'Alone.'

'I felt it. I knew it. At night, on a dark, foaming sea. Coming from the end of the earth. You were somehow *above* the deck, and the wind was tremendous. I screamed'—she magnificently declaimed: ' "Farringdon! Where are you? When shall I see you?" You said'—she imitated a hollow, distant voice. ' "Mother! It won't be long now." At first I was terrified. The wind screamed. I thought it meant . . . But wait! I then heard you say: "I'm coming to bring you great news, Mother . . . Great news!" '.

The dream—perhaps it was, rather, a vision?—was apparently ended; for she sank back, as if exhausted, in her chair.

'I wonder what that could have been,' mused Farringdon. 'Not of some good fortune of my own, d'you think?'

'I took it so, my boy.' The Old Lady looked expectantly at him. 'Of *ours*.'

'Not only true, but an omen,' declared Farringdon, who had found his cue in that moment of doubt. 'Your dream was no common dream, Mother. A lot's thought of dreams in these days, you know. We call Time another dimension, and find our way in it with their help. I always said you were clairvoyant.'

'It's true,' agreed The Old Lady. 'I'm forced to sit here, lonely enough; but my thoughts go out adventurously, as far as the spheres. They bring me back wonderful messages; but owing to Muriel's stupidity I'm forced to keep them to myself, and they pass back into the ether. Perhaps other people get the benefit of them—I don't know.'

There was a wildness in her manner as she grappled with rage at wasted inspirations which warned Farringdon that she could easily become over-excited. He did not want her over-excited.

'You shall tell them to *me*,' he told her, calmingly. 'They won't be

D

wasted. Mine go that way, too. It might well be that yours and mine, joined, would pattern together in good shapes. You've read Plato's *Banquet* of course; about men and women as two halves. Give it a wider application. You and I were born to put our heads together, Mother——'

His eyes were solemn. Under his big beard, where they could not be seen, his lips were pressed close to prevent a huge guffaw at the spectacle of himself playing an excitable old fish-woman with fairy tales. But was his mother as self-deceived by her dreams as her earnest manner suggested? There might have been no dreams at all. Was she playing *him*, the old devil? Careful! Careful!

'Yes. Yes.' The Old Lady gave quick, gulping nods of approval. 'To put our heads together. That's true. We'll do it.' The pressure of her hand increased. It grew intense, urgent, and he thought she was going to whisper some tremendous secret of material advantage to himself. He had time to think: 'These emotional old women soon suspect kid from others. One must let them kid themselves . . .' But the pressure was suddenly relaxed. Instead of confiding in him, she whispered: 'Sh! Here's Muriel!' and aloud, in a revealing tone of contemptuous severity, she demanded: 'Well, Muriel, where on earth—— And who's *this*?'

Here was no sign of exhaustion. Dreams were forgotten. Farringdon himself, he felt aware, was forgotten. Dammit, the whole affair had probably been just a show, to tickle her sensations, to fool him, to make him open his hand! She had aged much; but she had not changed. He must be doubly, trebly, on his guard! Darkly turning towards the door, he slid back along the table, trying to reach a point from which all was to be seen.

Julian had come coolly into the room, with Muriel demurely holding his arm as if she came to announce their engagement. The scowl was gone from Muriel's face, together with every sign of the alarm she had felt earlier. Instead, she beamed redly, confronting her mother as though, for once, she scorned her. Farringdon was amused. The little mother cat! He cruelly observed his sister's bad figure, and the flushed jowl which was of a piece with it. A poor lump of flesh, suffering from indigestion and lost pride in herself. As for Julian, he was good enough looking in a pretty way to go to any old girl's head! He hadn't any guts; but he looked good. What was his effect on The Old Lady?

She was giving her performance as a female Earl of Dorrincourt. That was just about the class and period of her impersonation. It had yellow edges. Oh, most instructive to see her in action, when the action was directed to somebody else. Her arms lay along the arms of the chair; her head was drawn back so that it was pressed against the chair; she stared out from under heavy waxen lids; her wide mouth was tightly closed, and its corners were lowered in a quizzical smile. It was a cruel face; a malignant face.

But Julian seemed indifferent to this. He too, was smiling a little, and behind the smile his lean white face masked all feeling.

'How d'you do, Grandmother,' said he.

She continued to stare, but with a slight change—very amusing to Farringdon. Those lids were lowered still farther, and yet she was obviously

smiling out from under them, as if scrutiny had given place to approval.
One arm left its resting-place—it was the arm nearest Julian. Her hand
grasped Julian's wrist.

'You're Julian,' she said, gruffly. 'You write to Muriel. Your brother
don't. I like you.'

Farringdon saw Muriel flush to the colour of beetroot. Why? Clearly
she felt infatuation for the boy. It made her glow like a red lantern; nothing
could make her beautiful. But surely she couldn't value the old devil's
praise of him. Did she resent it? Why all this pother? He must remember
that Julian was a sure key to her confidence. The boy was going to be
extraordinarily useful here. He'd seen that at once. Yes, but why the
beetroot flush? There was something there, besides a plethoric condition.

'I haven't often written to her,' smiled Julian, looking aside at his aunt.

'I know how often,' retorted The Old Lady.

'Mother's been searching the box where I keep my letters,' cried Muriel,
in a rather loud voice. 'I suppose, while I was out. That's why she knows
you've written to me, Julian.'

'Muriel knows all my doings, you see, Julian,' sighed his grandmother.
'Even when she's out. I get no chance to keep a secret. Not, of course, that
I wish to have any secrets. I can see that you're full of them.'

It was a reference to Julian's air of composure, which she felt to be a
challenge. She would have been overjoyed to see him redden or move
constrainedly. But Julian met the charge by polite silence. He looked,
they all felt, startlingly like Letitia, and this deeply impressed both The Old
Lady and Muriel. It worked excitingly in their minds, rousing old emotions
and creating new combinations of fury.

'I hope he'll keep them!' exclaimed Muriel. 'It's what I could never do.'

'That's not for want of trying, Muriel,' said her mother.

Farringdon, amid his enjoyment of these sallies, felt a sudden qualm.
He had been forgotten. The excitement of a few minutes earlier was as if it
had never been. Perhaps it had never been? He grew grave.

'We none of us,' said he, 'expect to have secrets from *you*, Mother.'

The old eyes turned slowly to him.

'I'm interested in my family,' replied The Old Lady. 'I dream about
them night and day. Sometimes I don't understand them. But sometimes
I understand them—better than they suppose.'

'Better than they understand themselves, I'm sure,' answered Farringdon
flattering her, yet allowing his teeth to be seen, framed in his beard.

'No.' She appeared to consider the matter. With immense graciousness,
but with her glance measuringly upon Julian, as if Farringdon had quite
dropped to second place in her mind. 'But well enough. Your mother made
the mistake of quarrelling with me, Julian. She behaved wrongly, and I
told her so. Her stubborn heart fed on the flattery of others. I warned her
of what it would mean. She became furious. Shouted insults, and ran
screaming away. Outrageous. Since then I've not seen her. She may have
said bad things of me.'

'Not one, I assure you,' said Julian, still smiling.

'Hm.' The Old Lady put a hand over her mouth. She looked as if she were laughing. Muriel expected her to burst into a whoop of tempestuous ridicule of something which she could not fail to regard as a lie; instead, for Julian's benefit, she said with an air of lamentable melancholy: 'She knew that one day you and I would meet. The crafty quean!'

Farringdon secretly grinned. This old coughdrop! But Muriel cried out in protest:

'Mother! How can you! To Julian!'

With an extraordinary change of manner, The Old Lady turned upon her, fierce and unwinking as a condor.

'Don't interfere! I'm speaking with Julian. Don't you see his face? He has an understanding of life.'

'But he doesn't understand *you*. I won't have him deceived like this.'

'Deceived!'

'He hasn't seen what you wrote on the table about me.'

'Wrote? I?' Everybody could tell that in sliding along the table Farringdon had partly rubbed out the last insulting comment. Only the word 'SLUT' remained.

Julian, whose face had been drawn ever finer in his effort to remain aloof in an atmosphere of insolence and insincerity, could bear no more. He gave a short, uncontrollable laugh.

'I beg your pardon,' he said, instantly recovering composure. 'I hadn't seen what was written on the table.'

Muriel was aghast at his tone of ridicule: she once again turned a beet-root red. Her eyes filled with tears. She could not understand what maddening pain he carried in his heart, or how angry he had been made by abuse of Letitia, or, because she had lived for so long alone with her mother, how unbearably crazy the household seemed to him. She saw only the desertion of a beloved boy, whom she had just defended.

The Old Lady tightly closed her lips. She looked in turn at Julian, at Muriel, at Farringdon. As if wearily, she leaned back in her chair, an aged, exhausted woman.

'This morning's been too much for me,' she faintly said. 'I must rest now. Come back presently. And you'—to Muriel—'should remember that *luncheon is at one oclock.*' Her voice rose shrilly. Her two hands beat roughly upon the arms of her chair. '*One oclock! Not a moment later!*'

iii

As they walked from Bella Vista, Farringdon triumphantly said:

'A most interesting morning, Julian. It's twenty years since I saw those two; and it's curious to see original savagery bursting through acquired characteristics. Original savagery. I choose my words. When I was a boy there used to be advertisements of a Self-Educator—we were proud to begin at the bottom in those days, and rise to higher things—and on the theme "the Child; what will he become?" they showed superimposed portraits of good and bad men at different ages. The result was a whiskered blur, of course. Well, my mother and Muriel used to represent the results of superimposition; but now they're naked. Mentally naked . . .'

He was strolling idly along, allowing his bony arms to swing at his sides, and looking shrewdly at the bathing huts, drawn up under the esplanade, and at the grey sea, and the long strip of sands beyond the narrow belt of shingle. The sky above their heads was dropsical with low grey cloud.

'Easy to see,' he continued, 'that this place is dead in the Autumn and Winter. It's probably, like so many English seaside towns, never more than half-alive. Dead people moulder all round us. Appalling. But the profits to be made here in the Summer must be enormous. With a little capital, a little dexterity, and the brains to *plan*, a fortune's not impossible.'

His improvised enthusiasm aroused no comparable enthusiasm.

'I have no capital, no dexterity, and no ability to plan,' replied Julian, who had seen the grey water and the shingle and sands only as an exasperating boredom.

'Hm,' observed Farringdon, thinking: The negative young fool! Typical enough! Shirk adventure, and scorn the adventurous! He continued: 'No. But of course capital *can* be gathered. If I'm not altogether mistaken —and I'm rarely mistaken, let me tell you—it could be found in the very house we've just left. Either directly or indirectly.'

'Nothing would induce me to live in a place like this,' said Julian, fastidiously shivering.

'Perhaps not. But then your nerves are on edge, dear boy. You're like so many of your generation; you don't know what you want, but you want it to come easy.'

'If that were true, I should think it profound,' said Julian.

'It can't be true, because it's unacceptable,' calmly said Farringdon. '*Are* your nerves on edge?'

'At this moment, yes,' agreed Julian.

'I'm so far right, then. And you certainly shouldn't disdain the help of your female relations.'

'I'd rather starve than take it.'

'That's where we see differently. For myself, I should be less proud.' Farringdon still gazed about him. He was considering some stories he had heard of successful men. 'I once knew a beach-photographer who divided his working life between such a place as this, in Summer, and Nice in Winter. He made three or four thousand pounds a year, and added to it by gambling. That would suit me very well. I tell you, I've no intention of letting myself rust in retirement.'

'So you said to Grandmother,' suggested Julian.

'No. Excuse me. To Muriel.'

'In fact, to Grandmother,' said Julian, smiling.

Farringdon was amused. He was also not amused. He decided to be amused.

'Quite true,' he calmly admitted. 'Your grandmother tells me that she intercepts inspirations flying through the elements. Sterne says something of the same sort; but in fun. She's always serious; a sure mark of insanity.

All the same, as it's my habit to humour everybody, I thought she might care to receive a ricochet off Muriel.'

'I like Muriel,' murmured Julian.

'A gargoyle, my boy. A gargoyle who might be subtly used; but still a gargoyle. Maddened, I should think, by living alone with a witch. In her place, I should use weedkiller; apparently she hopes to last out. Touch and go whether she'll die sane. What she's after is The Old Lady's money, which she won't get if she's often as indiscreet as she was today.' This indeed had been the infallible conclusion of his watch upon the two ladies. 'Muriel's stupid. She boils. She blurts. She caves in. And she's dealing with a Sadist. So she'll probably find the money's gone to Charity.'

Julian made no answer. He looked with desperation at the grey sea and sky, which hemmed him so clearly that he had some of the sensations of claustrophobia. In his impatience he began to walk very quickly indeed; but he could not out-distance the lean figure at his side. They reached the end of the meagre esplanade, and saw before them tufty, pathless waste ground amid which was spreadeagled the ruin of a derelict stone cottage.

'No thoroughfare,' grinned Farringdon. 'This is what they mean by the end of civilisation. The fag end, *bien entendu*.'

Julian looked at his wristwatch, without seeing what the hands said. He had given no heed at all to his companion's comment upon Muriel. He had not heard it. Immediately after leaving the house he had thought of her with pity; but he had then ceased to think of her. Inescapable misery had closed his mind to everything from without. He cursed the vacillations of an unstable girl, who loved and tempted and betrayed. And out of this misery, stirring within it and rising like a bubble to its surface, came one sudden humane memory. Unconscious of apparent irrelevance, he vehemently cried:

'What's today?'

Farringdon looked quizzically down at him, frowning in a droll way, with a nick between the bushy eyebrows. He saw faint colour in the boy's leaden cheeks. This wasn't the obvious son of Letitia, or the boy who sought to hide anxiety under an air of coolness. It was a different, an emotional creature, who had been shocked at some unpardonable forgetfulness. Amused, not offended, he answered:

'As far as I remember, it's Friday.'

'I must go back to London at once,' replied Julian, with new energy.

'We'll go back after we've eaten Muriel's lunch.'

'No. For me, impossible.' Julian did not trouble to explain himself. 'You must make an apology. It's an urgent occasion.'

'This leaves me rather in the lurch, you know,' objected Farringdon, now annoyed.

'I'm sorry. I must catch the first train.'

Farringdon was immeasurably surprised. This was decision. Or was it hysteria? A family weakness. And damned awkward. He realised that if he were to keep any hold on the boy he must accept. Then he saw that he might be a gainer.

'All right,' he said, with pretended heartiness. 'No questions. You decide, and I explain—to the others. We'll meet again. I need you here, you know. Tomorrow, at the Oriental?'

Julian was walking away.

'I'm not sure,' he answered, as if his thoughts were far away. 'Perhaps. I'll try.'

'Look here, we'll go to the station——'

Both were striding back along the esplanade, meeting a salted wind of which until that moment they had been unaware. Now indeed Farringdon had some difficulty in keeping pace with his determined nephew. But he continued to wear his pleasantest expression; for he was not ready to quarrel with a valuable tool.

iv

As he had supposed, the news of Julian's departure was a shock to the ladies at Bella Vista. It caused Muriel, who ruddily opened the front door, to lose her colour and look piteous. It caused the Old Lady, whose dress had been changed from one of stuff to one of silk, to send fiery daggers at Farringdon and thereafter to repeat under her breath the name of Letitia as if it were the basest of oaths. If he had been differently constituted, Farringdon's blood must have run cold at these portents; but he took a chair with calm and tapped his fingers lightly upon his knees.

'You may have noticed,' he said, to the agitated women, 'that Julian's a queer boy. Not'—with a side glance at Muriel—'a bad boy. On the contrary. But I happen to know something about him. He's troubled. He's in love.' There was a catch of Muriel's breath. 'He loves a beautiful girl who's unfortunately without money. And this'—and he looked directly at The Old Lady—'upsets Letitia. He and Letitia have had a quarrel. Well, the boy's confided in me. He trusts me. I said to him "My dear boy, you must be circumspect. Don't offend your mother. She's got her own way of looking at things——" '

'Hm,' said The Old Lady. 'How she's changed!'

'I said "A boy owes everything to his mother".'

'Hm,' said The Old Lady. 'Not a daughter, it seems.'

' "Except obedience",' proceeded Farringdon, as if he had not heard the muttered comments. ' "Love, kindness, and the rest. And what you've got to do," I said, "is to . . . keep a stout heart." But he's not stout-hearted. He's a delicate-minded boy. He's all for rushing off to America——'

'He's just back from there!' cried Muriel.

Farringdon had not known it. He said:

'I'd thought he was still there, till I ran into him in the street. "Why," I said, "I thought you were in America." It all came out. In twenty words. Holding my arm; shaking it'—He lifted his long arm, and looked at it with wonderment, seeing three inches of bare wrist projecting beyond the grey flannel cuff of his shirt. 'He trusts me, d'you see; one man to another. Well, I'm his old uncle——'

'I thought you'd just come from abroad yourself,' said The Old Lady.

'This moment,' said Farringdon. 'But blood tells. We knew each other at a glance——'

The Old Lady beat her hands upon the arms of her chair.

'Muriel!' she cried, in a furious voice. 'The fish! The fish! Bring it in at once. We'll wait no——'

'I'd got an extra piece for him,' whispered Muriel. 'A lovely piece!'

'I'm his proxy,' returned Farringdon, passing an avid tongue across his lips.

With Muriel gone from the room, accompanied by a bustle of stoutness, he and his mother were grimacingly alone. Their mouths watered for the fish. But they were not thinking of the fish.

'What's the truth?' demanded The Old Lady.

Farringdon innocently regarded her. He could see reflected in the glass of a picture above her head the dismal greyness of the day and some outlines of the houses opposite. And below the reflection was The Old Lady's face, which was that of the Tragic Muse. No, he thought; not the Tragic Muse, but Dürer's Melancholia.

'He's gone back to see the girl,' he answered. 'I was to explain to you that he had to visit his bank before it closed. He wants her to elope. She's got too much sense. He's got no money, and no job.'

'*She'd* see to it that he was dependent on her,' muttered The Old Lady. 'Have you seen her?'

'I've seen nobody,' said Farringdon. He slipped back in his chair, and his bony knees rose in front of him. 'Except you. And you know why I hurried here.'

The Old Lady stared at him. Her look was at first very hard; but it softened as she stared. She had observed his length, which gratified her because his father had been short. She had noticed his ready tongue, which reminded her of her own. She was bored. She remembered what he had told her about his dreams. She remembered what she had told him about her own dreams. What he said of Julian might be true.

'Are you proposing to bring him here again?' she asked, pretending to yawn. Her glance roamed the room, so that he should not interpret her fever of anxiety to have the boy at her side.

Farringdon waited while he counted twenty. He said, as if he had just received a message from Fate:

'How would it be if I got him down here for a few days? I see there's one hotel still open—the Grand. It wouldn't be a bad idea, d'you think?'

The Old Lady gave no sign that she had heard what he said. He knew that this was the most favourable of omens. The truth was that she was trembling a little. Farringdon clasped his hands above a raised knee. So quietly that the sound was almost inaudible, he whistled the first notes of a little tune. This showed that he, too, was rather excited.

Seven

THE PARTY

i

EVENING HAD ARRIVED. The house in Kensington was not at all calm. Lights shone in all the rooms, and upon every stair. There was a hidden fever in the kitchen; in several of the bedrooms dressing proceeded with an intense preoccupation rarely seen here before this day. Stephanie, alone in Mark's room, sniffed, swore, and trembled. Old Mr and Mrs Boldero nearly had a quarrel, so seized had they been by the fury of the household. Even Ruth ran up and down the stairs, wishing there was a lift, as if she had twenty thousand things to do in a minute. Ruth's cheeks were rosier than usual. Her lips were parted, showing small, pretty teeth. Her skirts flew behind her like the dress of a ballerina. She was enjoying the excitement as much as she would have done if the birthday had been her own.

It was useless for Christine to pretend any longer that she alone was calm. She was not calm. She had felt exalted all day long, from the peep of day, when a mound of parcels beside her bed rose impressively out of the shadow like the Rock of Gibraltar at dawn, startling her into wakefulness. Only her Grandmother's stiff back, at a late arrival for breakfast, had saved her from disgraceful exuberance. Grandpa, it couldn't be helped, had then been arch and rather inclined to pule and preach; but Mother and Father had been admirable. Admirable. She had lunched out; gaily, family-free, with three friends. Fine. And now that she was dressed and made up for the evening, with her hair well brushed, she examined herself in the mirror with subdued pride. Eyes a bit wild; otherwise worthy of moderate commendation. The party could begin.

She whirled into the parental bedroom, to find her mother tying Father's dress-tie. Oddly enough, Father at that moment was kissing Mother, a fact which, besides delaying the operation, embarrassed his daughter. After all, they were old; and everybody knew that sexual love, the prerogative of youth, became indecent at thirty-five. However, kissing was a habit. At their age it was a survival. People went on, egocentrically functioning, until their hearts wore out. And while she felt that Mother and Father couldn't *really* not understand that only youth mattered, she didn't go as far as Cedric Martin, whose line it was that everybody over forty should be sent to the lethal chamber. Sometimes Cedric, though as clever as the devil, was a fearful ass. When you saw Father——

Letitia gave Monty's tie a final pat.

'*There*, little man!' said she. 'Christine's friends will respect you very much.'

'That will console me,' replied Monty, in a mild voice. 'I'd rather it had been Christine herself.'

Christine could not help giggling at this antediluvian facetiousness, and wishing to embrace them both, as she might fittingly have done five years

D*

earlier. She felt her eyes grow moist. Somehow one did, in spite of all theory, feel extraordinary affection for one's father and mother. Affection for them, and pride in them. All wrong, of course. In the properly constituted State one wouldn't even know one's parents.

'You both look quite creditable,' she handsomely allowed.

'If we may say so,' responded Letitia, with one all-seeing glance at the radiant child, her costume, and her adornment, 'we both think *you* look . . . creditable.'

Christine shrugged.

'Quite meaningless,' she said. 'But you both look almost *young*.'

'By Jove! It's like an accolade!' exclaimed Monty, with such *empressement* that they all laughed unconstrainedly.

'Sillies!' cried Christine, forgetting that she was twenty-one, forgetting that one didn't do such things; and warmly kissing first Letitia and then Monty.

Monty kept his arm about her. He remembered her as the little girl who had ridden triumphantly upon his shoulder, as his chivalrous opponent at draughts and ludo, as his proud companion at Lords when Mark had overwhelmed them by making fifty for Tonbridge against Clifton, and in one or two tender passages with himself when mischance or disappointment had rendered her otherwise heartbroken. He was old enough not to be ashamed of sentiment. And so, pretending that he was going to tweak her nose with the thumb and forefinger of his free hand, he reassuringly sang in a fine barytone:

'Tomorrow we'll be sober!' And he kissed her again.

Christine recalled, at the moment, none of Monty's cherished episodes. She was young enough to live wholly in the present and future. But if ashamed of sentiment she was not ashamed of her father; and although she disengaged herself from what, after all, had been a restrained and tolerable embrace, it was without brusqueness. Father had cool, dry hands. Like lightning, she thought: 'Cedric hasn't! For all his brains and certainties and contempts, Cedric had detestable hands. In fact, as to Cedric, no. No! Absolutely NO!'

Without premeditation, and because of an instinctively felt contrast, she made up her mind about something which of late had caused her much uncertainty. Furthermore, nothing, she knew, would change the decision. She was Christine Boldero.

ii

One of the birthday presents had been a delicious jade necklace, which Christine was wearing with her evening frock.

'Hullo,' remarked Monty. 'That's a lovely thing.'

Letitia, who had seen the necklace for the first time two minutes earlier, also praised it. She did not ask the name of the donor. It was not her habit to ask questions.

'By Jove, what a tremendous, mysterious people the Chinese must be . . .' Monty, lowering his head, spoke as if to himself; and Christine, who did not wish to encourage discussion of the necklace, took this way of escape.

'And yet we do nothing to help China against the villainous Jap,' said she, accusingly. 'The old gang again, of course.'

'Rather a simplification, isn't it?' asked Monty, reasonably. 'You so often rest content with finding and damning a scapegoat.'

'Unless we simplify,' declared Christine, with spirit, 'and damn, we're red-taped and "this-isn't-the-timed" to death.'

'I'm all with you,' agreed Monty, with a crackle of shirtcuffs; 'about China; except that I think the *practical* difficulties insuperable.'

'No difficulties are insuperable,' said Christine.

He digested this heroic assumption. Then he ventured:

'Don't forget that we're no longer the strongest people on earth, able to threaten and command——'

'What about the League of Nations? We and the French boss that, don't we?'

'It's we who would have to do the fighting. It's not so easy. Take distance as a first difficulty——'

Letitia left them not quite ignorantly but not quite authoritatively discussing the Chinese affair.

She, who judged by emotion, and who could not pretend, as some of Christine's friends did, that an emotional opinion was an expression of the most irrefragable principle, thought the affair disgusting, and its condonation disgraceful. She knew nothing of international politics; her values were only humane. She knew that war meant certain death to millions of the young. And although willing to sacrifice her own life she shared Monty's fear of what would be styled another 'old men's war.' This was the insoluble dilemma of her generation: the enforcement of peace by opinion alone. And so, while Monty and Christine spoke academically, she ran downstairs—as fast as Ruth could have done—not only to survey the dinner-table but to escape an entirely fruitless argument.

There were to be twenty people at dinner, of whom, apart from Gabriel and Constance (Christine's god-parents) and the family, all were Christine's friends. These friends were fellow-students or young writers, artists, and dilettanti, much given to bold denunciation, full of good humour, and extremely pessimistic about the future. Tonight Letitia expected them to talk pessimistically and to tuck pessimism away. She hoped they would enjoy their dinner, and their neighbours at dinner.

She herself would have Henry Boldero upon her right—a pleasant duty —and Gabriel upon her left—pleasure hardly alloyed. Monty would have Christine upon his right and his mother, for once, upon his left: that was right and proper. Constance would be next to Henry Boldero; not so good, but unavoidable. Stephanie would be next to Gabriel, and he would scowl at the arrangement. So also, probably, and more understandably, would Constance. Difficult people! But Gabriel would have liked none of the other guests better than Stephanie; and any pretty girl made Constance darkle! The rest had been arranged by Christine; and Letitia was interested to notice that none of the friends—not even, apparently, the giver of the necklace— had qualified for the place upon her right. It had been reserved for Mark.

Who *was* the giver of the necklace? Christine's silence had not passed unnoticed. Nor had her determination to reward him by proof of its high favour. Happy young man. Temporarily happy! His future would be chequered. Letitia smiled and forgot.

She would have been made to forget almost anything by the magnificence of her own dining-table. It was lit with shaded wax candles; and Ruth, who had a genius for table-decoration, had soared this evening to the grandest simplicity. Brother Dick had in the morning brought from Marpham all the autumn-hued leaves and berries she had previously demanded; and the effect was stupendous. Lines of warm colour spread and were interlaced upon the polished table and the white doilies; the black, cream, or scarlet berries lay clustered in patterns to catch every soft light; the whole was not so much brilliant as superbly, enchantingly lustrous.

Ruth herself, standing back from the table in an artist's rapture of contemplation, looked hesitantly at her mistress, who after the first shock was able to say, most sincerely:

'Beautiful, Ruth. Everybody will love it.'

'Mr Wilton will tease me, Madame.'

Gabriel! *Did* he tease Ruth? How wicked, and how likeable of him! To see what a darling she was.

'What will he say?'

'I expect he'll say "Harvest Festival", Madame.'

'Abominable! He certainly won't mean it.'

No, Madame. I shall know that.'

Letitia saw Ruth's lovely larger smile. It was full of confidence.

'He'll be breathless with admiration. Take notice of his breathlessness, Ruth. And I really don't know how you've managed it, with so much else to do. It's perfect.'

'Thank you, Madame.'

'Thank *you*, Ruth. Miss Christine will be tremendously happy. Is everything all right otherwise?'

'Isobel's rather worried about the ice cream, Madame. She'd like you to see it.'

'What! How alarming! I must go at once!'

It was a vast kitchen, which dated from a time when such large parties as this were a commonplace; but its fittings were modern, so that Isabel, the cook, having both space and gadgets at her command, was as nearly content as a cook can be.

She was not content this evening. As Letitia went down the stairs she heard a scolding voice raised, and heard the last words of a rebuke.

'Don't let me 'ave to tell you again! Wonder you ain't got pockets in your frocks, to keep your 'ands cosy.'

Maud, the sturdy housemaid, and two extra girls who had come in to help the others through this evening were looking red and artificially busy, moving as eagerly as sheep before a dog, and getting in each other's way. Ruth's brother Dick at the same moment disappeared through the doorway to the maids' sitting-room, his shoulders hunched in mock terror. Adorable scents filled the kitchen.

Isabel, who was as tall as a policeman, and who remained mysteriously thin, despite her relishing joy in the foods she prepared, glowered into the electric oven, while with a wooden spoon held in her left hand she continued to stir a saucepan which bubbled above it. A moment later she slammed the oven door and turned viciously upon her slaves, ready to scold them again. At sight of Letitia, however, she gave a sigh and gesture of relief. Her chin shot up.

'Ice cream, Madame!' she exclaimed. 'Glass pudd'n, rather! It's let me dahn! Maud! Just stir this, will you!'

She and Letitia walked gloomily to the refrigerator.

A single taste of the ice cream was enough for Letitia. She might indeed have been chewing glass.

'No,' said she. 'It's a frost, isn't it.'

'And *I'm* a frost!' wailed Isabel. 'Oh, I could beat myself. Tonight of *all* nights.'

'It might happen to anyone.'

'If I'd a took more care over it. But no! Too confident. And left it to these lazy gels——'

The lazy girls were all ears, although they were so busy. The strangers hoped that Old Skinny Izzy was going to ketch it in *her* turn, same as they'd bin doing.

'Cut out the ices. There's no time to get this right for dinner. But we shall be having the iced drinks later; so it won't matter. Don't worry, Isabel. I'm sure everything else is lovely, isn't it.'

Isabel, rubbing her hands in her apron, shook a lugubrious head. She could have knocked that head three times on the kitchen floor in homage to Letitia.

'Everything else is *fair*,' she grudgingly admitted. 'I wouldn't mind *who* ate it.'

'There'll be none left,' laughed Letitia, 'for anybody but ourselves.'

'Oh, there's plenty,' grumbled Isabel. She led the way to her stores of prepared food, some of which were ready upon a great bench which ran down one side of the kitchen; and as Letitia, running her eye over all, and satisfying herself that it was exactly as it should be, expressed enthusiasm, a faint grimace, the nearest thing she could produce to a smile, moved stiffly across Isabel's lips. She immediately frowned murderously at three cheerful faces which she could see beyond her mistress's shoulder, and there was a scuffle of moving feet . . .

Returning to the polite world above stairs, Letitia felt that despondency had settled upon her cheerfulness like a fly. It instantly enlarged itself to frightful pessimism. How, in the face of such trifling, maddening vexations as the ruined ice cream, which were more irksome than hardship, should a spoiled and fêted beauty like Stephanie, who would sooner eat expensively in a restaurant and dance the evening away, make a *home* for Mark? She was as ignorant of cooking as of Chinese.

Obviously, faced with the need for tremendous, distasteful effort,

Stephanie had the impulse to bolt, to say 'It's no good. I can't go on,' and, because she wasn't used to fighting alone, to take a lover. Julian, or another. But if she bolted from Mark her lover would be only another false start; a *pis aller*. Bad to worse. She would regret it all her life. What was to be done?

And how was Stephanie at this minute? She must go up to Mark's room, and see. Mark was not there. There had been no Mark until this afternoon, when he'd called for a few minutes and hurried away again. He had not been alone with Stephanie. Apparently the only secrets they had were those which they kept from each other. Oh, miserable! Humdrum wedlock might bore; but it lasted. This curious domestic anarchy destroyed marriages, and made marriage itself an anachronism . . .

She could *shake* them all . . .

Christine came skipping from victorious political discussion with Monty. She jumped the last four stairs.

'Hullo, Mother. Broody?'

'There won't be any ices, darling.'

'Oh, curse! Really, Isabel's the outside edge. Did you row her? I don't believe you did.'

'I thought you might feel inclined to do it after dinner.'

'I? Because it's my—oh, I see. The dinner's otherwise good, is it?'

They went into the dining-room together. Aladdin's Cave! Even Christine could not control a gasp of excitement. Her severe eyes critically searched every corner of the table for a fault. Her firm young lips were pressed together in a resolute effort to restrain enthusiasm. Her brow was clear as an Italian sky.

'Satisfied?' asked Letitia, surveying Ruth's masterpiece with pride.

'Not bad,' was the airy answer. 'For Ruth.'

The curmudgeon! Letitia, laughing, felt defensive loyalty to her own more enthusiastic contemporaries.

iii

There was great babble in the drawing-room. A dozen young people were talking at once. A few of them pitched their voices imperiously. Grandmother Boldero, however, was not to be drowned; and even Grandfather Boldero, stirred by so much youthful energy, was shouting away to Monty, his beard wagging, as if he harangued a mob. The noise was deafening; the scene lively and unconstrained. Unable to focus it from the ground, Letitia felt that she would have liked, instead of being hostess, to watch, concealed, from some peephole in the ceiling.

'I'm like Keats,' she thought; 'who said he was everybody and nobody at a party. Not himself at all!'

She heard one young man rudely interrupt an ingenuous girl with a high-pitched 'Shawly you don't deny that *Science*——' He reverently called it 'Sarnce,' and his tone caused Letitia to observe that while some of the girls, who wore their hair very short, looked like boys, several of the young

men squeaked girlishly when they argued. Was this ascent to the treble a
fashion? Or hadn't their voices broken? Or were their vocal chords just
weak?

Where were the children? Christine was talking hardly and brightly
to an ugly stranger with a hanging nose and an underhung jaw. It was not
he. Letitia did not know whom she meant by 'he': probably the giver of the
necklace; even more probably, some one or other of these boys who would
make the child's pulses quicken. It seemed unlikely. Christine was a darling;
but also a tough nut. Stephanie was with three or four others in a distant
corner of the room—obviously exalted by the admiration she was causing;
for she was brilliantly flushed. A different Stephanie from the one who
had been seen half-an-hour ago in Mark's room. Then listless, self-
distrustful; now all gaiety. And Mark? Where *was* Mark?

Far away from his wife, amusingly grave under the assault of an earnest,
dictatorial young man who looked as if, like Pooh Bah, he had been born
sneering. It was Cedric Martin, lamentably lofty and fluent; a theorist
with a thick skin, who grabbed what he wanted, and who would ultimately
be thwarted by those more subtle than himself. She respected Mark more
than her other children. He had his father's candour and good looks.
Could any girl who loved him be blind to these qualities? It seemed so.
Tonight, seeing him from a new and more anxious standpoint, Letitia
thought his mouth for once too sensitive to be reassuring. Was he, after
all, as much his father's child as she had supposed? Wasn't he, in an
alarming degree, hers, also? Was sensitiveness to ruin his marriage and his
career?

Before she could clarify these agitated doubts, her attention was distracted
from Mark. The talk blurred, as it were; and when she looked to see what
had caused the blur she found that Constance and Gabriel, who had just
arrived, were making an effective entrance.

They stood in the doorway, an extraordinary pair; white-faced, golden-
haired Constance in the brilliant peacock-blue frock of an old-style Bank
Holiday donah at Hampstead, Gabriel in a silken soft-fronted shirt and a
tailcoat with blue-shot-silk lapels as broad as those of a smoking jacket.
Gabriel, with his head down and his gleaming eyes summing up a wholly
ironic impression of what he saw, smiled darkly; Constance waited for her
frock to bring the fire of controversy among all present.

As Letitia moved forward, Constance took two rapid steps which gave
her dress the effect of an electric flame. In passing, she caught Christine's
hand, jerked it vigorously as she kissed her, and stood for a moment so that
Christine's delicate green garment should falter, fade, and perhaps recover
from the contrast. She then kissed Letitia very continentally upon both
cheeks.

The party was arrested. The clatter of tongues paused. Mrs Boldero
stared. Gabriel, standing against a background of the closed door, and
smiling more darkly still, had the charm of solace for eyes previously dazzled
and bedevilled. He, too, ceremoniously, kissed Christine as if the occasion
were very important; and patted her upon the shoulder like an old grandfather in a Victorian comedy. But he did not remain at her side, though

she touched one of the lapels of his odd bandmaster's coat in familiar curiosity. Children tired him. His goal was Letitia.

Nobody, seeing the newcomers for the first time, almost caricatures of what was to be expected from the Stage, could have imagined how truly simple in character they both were. Nobody, least of all herself, could have accounted for the extraordinary shock of poignant affection—made up of laughter, pity, reverence, and pain—which Letitia felt, at first for her old friend, and then for Gabriel. Especially, it proved, for Gabriel.

She had hardly had time to realise and wonder at this emotion, and to answer Constance's exclamatory 'Aren't I a kingfisher!' when a shock even greater seemed to drain all the blood from her heart. This time there was no pause in the renewed babble. Nobody except herself saw that incoming figure, until Christine with an astonished cry forsook her guests and darted towards the door. Even then, only those with whom she had been talking noticed that an unexpected visitor had arrived, in whom Christine's joy was so great that she had flung herself into his arms.

Letitia slowly turned her eyes to Mark, to Stephanie, and back to Julian. She thought Stephanie paled; but, if this were so, colour and temper flowed swiftly back into the child's cheeks and made her proudly defiant. Her eyes were averted. However thickly her heart might be beating, any visible discomposure was past. Mark smiled incredulously but with delight. Therefore he knew nothing. Julian, unflustered, unsmiling, looked at nobody but his dearly loved sister, who held fast to his arm as she faced the room once more. He was haggard; white with enmity towards mankind. The babble continued.

'How dramatic! Round the world in eighty days!' breathed Constance in Letitia's ear. 'But you, of course, aren't surprised!'

So absorbed had Letitia been in the situation and her sympathy for the children that she had forgotten her friend's nearness. She hardly heard what Constance said, and certainly did not grasp its meaning. But somebody else, equally alert to the spectacle, and less interested in the children than in herself, had also been closely attentive. As she went towards Julian, Gabriel detained her, meaningly pressing her elbow with his long fingers. Perhaps he did it in order to rescue her from self-betrayal?

'I observe all that *you* observe, dear Letitia,' he said, in a low voice. 'Forgive me. I think all that *you* think. I hope all that *you* hope.'

Still confused, she saw that iron-seamed cheek and pointed nose, and those bitterly smiling lips, so close to her that they were magnified to the point of being unrecognisable; but she saw at the same time with wondering realisation the warmth and beauty of Gabriel's piercing eyes. The eyes were like hooded lamps. Their message of understanding startled her. They burned from her mind memory of all his verbal cruelties to Constance, his strange concealments, his fantastic absurdities of dress and manner. What did he know? Why did he feel thus for her? It was with profound and agitated curiosity that she allowed her elbow to remain an instant longer within the firm clasp of his fingers. Then she hastened to Julian.

iv

Letitia sat in her place at the long, candle-lit dinner-table, looking down it at the shining plates and the moving hands and silver, which, except for the faces of those who were close beside her, were all that she could see. Above the feast lay darkness. A stir of noise filled the room; but it was mass noise, an animated drone from which the individual voice was wholly blotted. She knew that the maids, like shadows, came and went from that far, invisible sideboard and the concealed service hatch. But her thoughts were in darkness as great as that of the ceiling. She was like somebody in a dream, who walks into a terrible unknown, without power to call for help or avert the end of her journey.

Half-an-hour ago, or a month, or a year, Julian had returned her greeting with composed affectionateness, as if no explanation of his presence could possibly be needed. He might never have crossed an ocean, never, in torment, have accused her of tyranny, or run, distracted, from that deserted flat. This composure was not what disturbed her. One did not expect confidences amid hubbub, or desire them. But why was he here at all? He had not once, as far as she could tell, glanced at Stephanie. He had not spoken to Mark, who had arrived that afternoon from the North. He had wanted only to see Christine, whom he had monopolised with malignant severity. Now, by Christine's impulsive rearrangement of the order of sitting, he had taken Mark's place at the table. He was hidden in the darkness which lay beyond all but the nearest candle-rays. It was what he must have desired. Stealth, swiftness, secrecy, hidden power and accomplishment, the iron hand within the velvet glove—those had been his fantasies since boyhood . . .

'Strange, young Julian turning up like this,' shouted old Henry Boldero, into Letitia's right ear. 'Not sure that I . . . Great fondness of course.'

'Yes, *great* fondness.' But it was not for Christine that he had crossed the Atlantic. She dared not look at Stephanie. It was intolerable to sit like this, in the dark, understanding nothing. 'Yes, there's always been this bond between them—an extraordinary loyalty.'

It was true. It sounded, in her head, as an insincerity; but it was true.

'Quite excusable,' murmured Gabriel, smiling a deadly smile at the old man. 'When one looks at Christine.'

'Hardly a word to the rest of us,' grumbled Henry. But he grinned at Gabriel's tribute to his adored Christine; and his grin spread affectionately to Letitia. 'However, I'm just as silly about her, I know . . .'

Letitia laughed, raising her hands towards her ears to indicate deafness. 'I doubt if we should have heard a word, in any case . . .'

That was finished. She brought herself with difficulty to taste the soup, which was faultless. But she had not been amused, and she forgot nothing; for Mark, sitting next to his grandmother, was as completely hidden as Julian. Were he and Julian talking? *Could* they talk? Mark was so unfortunately hidden from his wife that he might not, from her point of view, have been there at all.

'It reminds me . . .'

Now Henry Boldero, having eased his mind of Julian's offence, chose to be lively about something, best forgotten, which had happened many years ago, when bosoms and bustles were worn and skirts trailed heavily in the dust. Henry's memory trailed with a similar weight. And Constance, to whom he had politely addressed his remarks, chose in return to be sombre and unresponsive. The truth was that the old man had been dazzled by Constance's dress into hazy recollection of the old fashions and his own youthful curiosity about over-shaped women, and that Constance, more up-to-date in the knowledge of evil, had seen Gabriel catch Letitia's elbow and hold it while he whispered into her ear. Constance was forgetful of everything except that whisper. She looked and looked again for signs to prove that her husband and her friend were guilty lovers.

Gabriel, ignored by Stephanie, wearied by Henry Boldero's sudden fit of reminiscence, and sardonically conscious of Constance's gravity and its probable cause, observed the transit of his hot soup from palate to gullet and so down within him to grizzly darkness. He took a detached interest in this progress. When a boy, he had seen, like the juvenile Art Kipps, a diagram of the human body. He had been at first deeply shocked and then deeply depressed by it. Since that time he had imagined with alarm the effects of foreign bodies upon this complicated system of tubes, noting every little pain in his body as a possible consequence of leak, breakage, blister, or obstruction. In vain he had been reminded of the toughness and the renewals of human tissues; he could not accept what he was told, but was diverted by his own fears, which he encouraged. His present illness heightened both the fears and the amusement. Besides being a valetudinarian, he was an ironist. And as his irony was applied to himself, as well as to others, he had become a conscious coward.

'When the tumult and the shouting die,' muttered Gabriel, thinking of his cowardice, 'say the day after tomorrow, I shall come and see you, Letitia, about my schemes and plots for Monty.'

Letitia turned to him with relief.

'*Are* you scheming and plotting, Gabriel?' she asked, with her indulgent smile. 'I hope not. But you really enjoy schemes and plots——'

'As a midwife enjoys a little stranger,' interrupted Gabriel. 'Well, I do. They take my mind off other things.'

'Serious things? I ought to have asked how you are.'

'Oh, you *did* ask. Most polite.'

'But particularly.'

His expression did not appear to change from that of catlike listening; but he lowered his voice until it could scarcely be heard. She was forced to put her ear closer to his lips.

'I'm like the British Empire. I astound myself by my own survival.'

'In that case you'll live for ever,' she whispered back. 'The same pliable constitution.' She was unprepared for his next declaration.

'Constitution or not, I'm no better. This is true. I say nothing to Constance. Nothing to anybody but you. But I can't sleep. I'm often in—discomfort. Sometimes in agony. I ask myself what good my life is.'

She was horrified. She grew graver than Constance herself.

'Is the treatment giving you no relief?'

'None. Letitia, I don't want you to believe me, of course. Forget that I told you this. Don't hold it against me. And yet I'm trying to frighten you into sympathy. I need your sympathy.'

'Gabriel! You do indeed frighten me!'

He did not look at her. He looked down at his right hand, which lay upon the table, white against its shining surface.

'Does it trouble you? To think of me mouldering? You'd be sorry?' he whispered.

'I never *have* thought it. How *could* I? You're our living friend, Gabriel. We *love* you.'

'Yes, of course. A live dog. Was that "we" discreet or royal, I wonder?' He glanced across the table at the heavy-hearted Constance, and murmured: 'Look, now, at Constance. Can you imagine anybody telling her the truth? I never do. Except for her chastening.'

Letitia followed the direction of his glance; and she saw Constance, who was watching them, give a shrug and a slight roll of the eyes, as if she were intolerably bored.

'You frighten her,' she told Gabriel 'Too much. Endlessly. It makes you seem unkind.'

'You think me unkind?'

'I said you *seemed* so. I know you to be otherwise.'

'Oh, but it's true. I *am* unkind. It's my only defence.'

'Against what?'

'Suppose we say, tears.'

'From Constance? Or from us all?'

'From myself. You can't imagine me crying. I don't cry, in that sense. But tears come easily to the eyes of an elderly sick man. Self-pity, you know.'

'In sickness, that's justifiable. I've never thought stoicism the highest virtue, Gabriel.'

He smiled without irony, saying:

'Except for yourself. And then not a virtue at all, but as natural to you as sleep. Do you tell me that *you* cry easily? Or at all? I can't believe it.'

Letitia smiled in her turn, at his smile and at the regard behind his rallying tone. She shook her head.

'I couldn't disgrace three self-possessed children,' she replied. Nevertheless, at the mention of them, which released all her fears, her heart beat faster; her eyes moved from the baffling line of Stephanie's cheek, which was all she could see, into the darkness which held her boys.

'Who give you constant pain?'

'No. Perhaps, sometimes, painful anxiety.'

'I understand. Thank God I've had no children. But you've this reward. They'll rest on your love all their lives.'

Letitia was so much moved that she could not easily speak as if she still smiled at her children.

'I hope you and Constance could do that,' she said.

Gabriel looked at Constance, at this moment a personified megrim, who suffered from the goading of her own wanton—almost wanton—inventions; and at Letitia, who suffered only for the follies and distresses of others. It was not a cruel comparison; it was not one that he would have expressed to either woman. He sighed. He quietly answered:

'You're adorable. You quieten my soul.'

No more was said. The sound of busy talk, mingled with laughter and the tinkle of glass or silver, came about them like the dawn-song of birds. Everybody in the room seemed to be happy, eating and drinking, ready to toast Christine and ready to dance until morning, as if each look and speech and action were flung into an unremembering void, free of all consequences to themselves or their company.

v

An hour later, the doors between the big drawing-room and a small room behind it were thrown open. During dinner all superfluous furniture had been moved from the drawing-room and the rugs lifted; and all was ready for the dance. A little orchestra pottered in the small room, arranging chairs and tuning instruments. The orchestra consisted of four villainous-looking men. It was being inspected by Gabriel, who took morbid interest in the phenomena of entertainment.

Gabriel returned to Letitia's side. He said:

'The violinist is good. He wipes the resin from his fiddle. It's an infallible test. Are you dancing with me?'

'Later,' promised Letitia. 'Meanwhile——'

She left him. It was important that she should see all the youngsters united. They were upon the stairs, coming up from dinner or down from the cloakrooms; and new arrivals, who had arrived for the dance, were entering the house each moment. On the landing, Christine, brimming with calm, was talking to Cedric Martin, a young man whose assurance never failed, whether he spoke of Bach, Mathematics, Politics, Plastic, the Lawrences, Functional Art, or Pond Life; while shy Justin Greer, who stammered even when he tried to explain the meaning of one of his own pictures, havered beside them. Evidently Cedric had interrupted the other two, and proposed to oust Justin. Equally evidently, Christine proposed, in spite of Cedric's determination, to keep Justin securely within her own orbit.

Letitia's sympathy was with Justin: she detested the cocksure Cedric. Amused, therefore, at these manœuvres, and, although unaware of all their implications, pleased at the certainty of Christine's victory, she continued upon her way downstairs, and was thus a witness of what occurred below.

The entrance-hall was brilliantly lighted, and Dick, as butler for the occasion, was taking charge of all comers. But there was a lull for the moment, which left the doorway empty except for Dick, and the hall visible in every detail. Letitia, halfway down the stairs, was checked by a crowd of young people who were just below her. Stephanie, laughing, came from the dining-room between two obviously ardent admirers, glossy-haired, rather sleek and well fed and—Letitia assumed—fluent rather than witty talkers. Stephanie was still flushed and excited; looking happier than she had done for weeks past, and very beautiful. These were the circumstances in which, stimulated and amused, she was at her best. In that bright light the radiant face, lifted high in conscious beauty, glowed with life.

But just then a dark figure came from the other direction—perhaps from Monty's study. It was Julian, wearing his overcoat, carrying his hat. He was leaving the house.

'Julian! Julian!' Letitia's voice was drowned. Nobody heard her. In vain did she beg the merry crowd to make way for her. They were too tightly bunched to be thrust aside, and by the time they realised that somebody was trying desperately to come down the stairs it was too late.

Julian advanced. He saw Stephanie. Stephanie's laughter ceased. She took an eager step towards him, forgetful entirely of her triumphant escort. But Julian, not turning his head away, but appearing blind to her presence, passed and was gone. Letitia saw Dick grin affectionately at him and spring to the door. There was a breath of cold air. Then the door swung-to behind Julian: the latch clicked; there was silence. The encounter had been refused.

vi

With a vehement effort, Letitia drew free of the young guests who now recognised her and shouted friendly, boisterous greetings to which she must return laughing replies; and an instant later, outwardly serene but inwardly in stupor, she was beside Stephanie, who stood bewildered, as if her heart had stopped beating. She caught the girl's arm, smiled quickly and self-excusingly at the two young men, who, understanding nothing, found themselves waved to the stairs; and somehow—she did not know how it was done—managed to draw Stephanie away to the study, where they were alone.

It was time. Stephanie, silent, breathless, until that moment, began uncontrolledly to sob, with the heavy, noisy, hopeless sobs of a child's heart-broken disappointment.

Letitia locked the door and at once switched off the light, leaving only a table-lamp near the fire, which had a parchment shade, to give subdued illumination to the room. Her arm was still around Stephanie. There was nothing in her mind but compassion. Caressing words were whispered, unphrased and without conscious purpose, into the girl's ear. Indeed, Letitia was not herself calm enough to do more than obey each impulse as it came to her. She heard the sobbing with intolerable confused anguish, repulsion, and sympathy.

As the moments passed, she began to notice the clock's soft ticking. It was a reminder of other life, other lives. It seized her attention, dominated her thoughts. She imagined Julian's rapid steps carrying him away from her for ever. Ever, ever, ever, said the clock. Its pendulum swung endlessly. Monty, Mark, Christine, herself, were all moving in a dreadful shadow-dance, to-and-fro, to-and-fro. Strength was leaving her each minute; Stephanie drawing it away, drop by drop. Tick-tack, tick-tack, said the clock; way-a, way-a, way . . .

A long-drawn quivering sigh, that was almost a groan, checked every other sound in the room. Stephanie had moved; her arms clutched Letitia; they were breast to breast, so that every movement of that stormy body was known to her, and another head was pressed convulsively to her own. A long time elapsed, during which she felt the sobs diminish, until they were almost gone. The warmth of Stephanie's blood stifled her. She felt that she could breathe only with difficulty. Unconsciously she must have moved; for in a frantic whisper Stephanie cried:

'Don't go!'

'No, no; I won't.'

'You were drawing away. Yes. You were. Everybody draws away.'

'Nobody draws away. You imagine everything.'

'Yet *you* saw him.' There was a long pause. A shudder. The arms clutched again. 'He despises me.'

It was out; the humiliation was confessed. Letitia said:

'Then it's over. I'm thankful.'

'What?' Stephanie's inquiry was wondering, vacant, like a drawn breath before a sob. Then the incredulousness which must underlie such vacancy made its meaning clear to Letitia. She was startled. Could some tenacious purpose really still be working, under the sobs of shame and the confession of misery? Was Julian not yet free? Was Mark, even now, to receive shameful humiliation? She cried urgently:

'With a man, contempt is final. You're done with him.' Silence. 'Don't you *want* to be?'

There was no hesitation.

'Yes. Oh, *yes*. But, *Mother* . . .'

'Darling.'

'What you said . . . It isn't true. It *couldn't* be true.'

'No. Nothing's true. Nothing I say. I *want* it to be over. I want you to be Mark's wife, as you were.'

A shudder again ran through Stephanie's body. In a terrible whisper she cried:

'Mother, I *can't*——'

Despair caught at Letitia's heart; wisdom would not receive it.

'Never?' she whispered, in return. 'I don't speak——'

'I can't go back——'

'No. You can't go back. Nor can he.'

'He? Mark? It's all past. *Past*. Am I wicked? I'm not wicked. I simply——' The arms were withdrawn. Her body was partly withdrawn; but she still remained in Letitia's embrace, resting burning hands upon Letitia's bare shoulders. 'You're his mother. You must think me . . . Atrocious, of course.'

'No, no!' protested Letitia. 'This isn't what we're speaking of. I'm Julian's mother, too. Not *less*. Julian has far too much of *me* in him——'

The words, and the vehement tone in which she spoke, caught Stephanie's attention.

'Of you? Isn't it strange!'

Letitia said quickly:

'Why "strange"? Are *you* so simple? Aren't you a dozen people? But, at bottom, you? That *you* needed Mark; that *you* still needs him. He needs *you*, just as much.'

'No,' said Stephanie. A dozen spiteful thoughts of Mark were summed in this word.

'Just as much,' insisted Letitia, not blind to the spitefulness. 'I know Mark. I know his father.'

Stephanie raised her eyes. She was estranged. She disliked Letitia. But the dislike and estrangement lasted for seconds only, as she read the message sent to her secret heart. There was a long silence.

At last:

'I can't *do* it!' cried Stephanie, in a fierce voice.

'You can. You will.'

'No! I can't go *back* there!' She wrenched herself free, and stood alone. 'I can't! I won't!'

Letitia's shoulders, still burning from her grip, felt the cool air strike them. They ached as if they were bruised. Her unsteady pulses betrayed the loss of that energy which had been drawn from her by Stephanie. She almost pushed the girl away in hatred, seeing her as a vampire. But her comprehension and will were greater than her horror. With deliberate effort, she said:

'That's understood, of course. You stay here.'

'With Christine? How *can* I? She'd see everything. With her hard, poky censoriousness. Oh, no. Besides, if I stay——'

'Mark obviously doesn't.'

Stephanie was astounded. She was speechless, knowing that while *she* had felt free to judge Letitia by the cruellest insights, an insight no less piercing, but blessed and strengthened by charity, had enabled Letitia to anticipate every possible reaction. She caught Letitia's arm.

'Mother!'

'Isn't it clear? Can't you see I'm trying to make it easy for you?'

'To go back? To begin that fight over again?'

'Of course. The fight's with yourself.'

'Oh, you're Victorian! You're old! Samuel——'

'I know it. But what, positively, are you? A shirker. If you shirk now, you'll shirk again. Always on less favourable ground.'

'Shirker! Why "less favourable"? I'm far better than that. How you hate me!' The voice, having begun in pride, sank to almost unctuous self-pity.

But when Letitia made no reply, and the banal charge of hatred produced no angry disclaimer, Stephanie's head dropped in thought.

'I ought not to have said that,' she carefully added.

'Say what you must,' entreated Letitia. 'I shan't blame you. But *think*. Whatever you decide, I'll help you to do.'

'Even against Mark?'

Letitia could not restrain an ironic smile at this arrogance.

'Even against Mark,' she added. At one moment she saw Stephanie's flight as the God-given release for Mark from a life of drained energy and thankless effort. He would recover, would marry again, a harder, less greedy, exhausting woman. All would be, except in occasional memory, as if Stephanie had never lived. But Stephanie, who had so much more in her than greed and pride and folly, might never find her mate. 'Never against yourself.'

'Myself,' murmured Stephanie, under her breath. She was not blind. She read the irony and the warning. Colour flew to her cheeks, and ebbed very slowly from them.

There was a continuing pause, during which their wills seemed locked in close conflict. Stephanie's breath was at last drawn for reply—perhaps for angry final refusal—when the handle of the door was turned.

Letitia alone saw its movement, which at first was carelessly rapid, as if the newcomer had not imagined that the door might be locked, and afterwards, as Stephanie's glance followed hers, very slow, with an effect of stealth. Without speaking, Letitia pointed to the chair by the fireside, indicating that Stephanie should sit in it. A light tapping followed.

'Who is it?' called Letitia. Simultaneously a voice cried:

'Are you there, Mother?'

It was Mark.

vii

Stephanie leaned back in the chair; so quietly that nobody who entered could have imagined her agitation. Letitia, looking back from the door, was surprised and reassured by such complete physical self-control. And as Mark came into the room he gave a boyish whistle of surprise at finding these two closeted together. Afar they could hear the plunking and tootling of the band as an unreality.

He was at first silhouetted against the brighter light of the hall beyond, and this made him seem much bigger than he was. In reality he was under six feet, and although broad-shouldered was hardly less slim than Julian. He shut the door after him, and stood against it. All sound from above was excluded from the room.

'Just the pair I wanted!' declared Mark, in glee. 'But why the locked door? I applaud the locked door. It's so English. So private. But at a party? I say, I don't know if we all ought to be away at the same time; but I've got something to tell you.'

'You're right,' cried Letitia. 'I *ought* to go.'

There were two cries of protest, both urgent.

'They're all happy,' asserted Mark. 'We're forgotten. In any case it's Christine's party, and the little wretch manages everything as if nobody else mattered. I can't find Julian; and I couldn't find *you*. Only the elder statesmen and the small fry. It's not very light in here.' He looked inquiringly at Letitia. Then: 'You all right, Stephanie?'

'Yes,' drawled Stephanie, as if she yawned in boredom at his concern for her. 'Thank you.'

Letitia saw him interpret the tone and passingly frown. She said: 'We just prefer the twilight.'

'What, secrets?' asked Mark, with no suggestion that he believed his own word. He was so natural, so much the Mark he had always been, that Letitia smiled in maternal pleasure.

'Not, in your sense, secrets,' she answered. 'As Uncle Gabriel would say.'

'Yes, well, Uncle Gabriel. Hey? Those cushioned lapels! But he's been giving me his attention. I'm always grateful when somebody does that.'

'You're excited,' said Stephanie, from the safety of her shaded chair.

It was true, thought Letitia, that he was unusually garrulous. Otherwise he was normal. Normal and reassuring. He was fully two inches taller than Julian; broader and less dark. His brow was wide, his nose straight, and, whereas Julian's face was thin and clean-shaven, Mark's had agreeable plumpness and colour, and he wore a neat moustache. Mark had good humour, where Julian, who could cry with laughter, had a fitful malice. Julian pretended, and took offence; Mark was reasonable, and free from all affectation. Letitia, loving them both, understood why Stephanie believed herself, at the end of a year, to know Mark too thoroughly; but if Mark started fewer conjectures than Julian he had more character and would last better. It was true that Julian's irritability, in Stephanie's eyes, might justify Stephanie's.

'Would you like us to give you *our* attention?' she asked.

He advanced towards the fire, and stood with his back to it, she supposed in unconscious imitation of his father. Was he, too, one of those who must stand in order to explain?

'If I'm not interrupting?' replied Mark. He looked from one to the other of them; obviously he had moved to the hearthrug to get a closer view of Stephanie. 'I've got an uncomfortable sense——'

'Cut the cackle,' cried Stephanie, who knew that he could now see her much too clearly.

'I've been asked to stand as Liberal candidate for Benchbury. If my family agrees, I shall accept.'

'Why "if"?' demanded Stephanie. 'They'd be enchanted.'

'I mean you, chiefly,' answered Mark.

'Oh, count me out,' she retorted. She was biting her lip. Letitia, who had come nearer, saw that if Stephanie goaded herself thus with harsh words to Mark she would begin to sob again, talk wildly, and rush into a fatal quarrel.

'But Mother, too,' said Mark. He observed Stephanie closely. He did not lift his eyes to Letitia.

'I certainly agree,' cried Letitia. 'How intelligent of Benchbury to ask you! But is it a Liberal place? Why were you asked? Hasn't Labour a superannuated Union secretary to pass in?'

'It's *not* a Liberal place. The Labour man's as dull as a Communist manifesto. I've been asked because the Benchbury Liberals are in a hole. The man they relied on is very ill; and the Tories are strong.'

'Is there *any* chance of your getting in?' persisted Letitia.

'Precious little, I should think,' said Stephanie. 'Liberalism being what it is.'

'I'm relying on Stephanie to pull it off,' answered Mark, smiling with all his father's charm and the added—and in Letitia's eyes highly cheering —confidence of youth. He took another long look at his wife's lowered head. Stephanie was determined not to give him the smallest encouragement; to have done so when her heart was hard to him, when her longing for the excitement of ardent love had been flouted by his brother, would have been a lie which she was not prepared to act. She detested both Mark and Julian. Letitia read all this, and was nervous of saying an explosive word.

'Accept,' she said. 'It will be experience. Very exhilarating.'

'I'll do it,' replied Mark. He rubbed his hands together, as Monty did; but they did not rustle. As Monty would have done, he sent a droll glance in his wife's direction; but without reward. 'I feel—encouraged.'

He had no opportunity to say more; for the door opened once again, to admit a burst of raucous rhythmic sound, and to reveal the inquiring head of Gabriel. This head's curious peering loll was so grotesque that Letitia felt a tremor of loving amusement run through her. She smiled. Mark smiled. Gabriel smiled. And then Gabriel stepped very circumspectly into the room, as if he evaded a low fence of barbed wire.

'I'm looking,' said 'he, 'for peace. I find a Cabinet Meeting.'

'Uncle Gabriel's already put me in the Cabinet,' laughed Mark. 'He says brains, even nowadays, make their way into inaccessible places.'

'Nature abhors a vacuum. The truth is, Letitia, I claim my dance. The noise upstairs is infernal. Youth at its most inept. I dislike youth in bulk. You know what Fuseli, the painter said? He said "Damn Nature! She always puts me out". I'm like that with the young. Unless you come, dearest Letitia, I shall have to put myself out. It's past my invalid bedtime and endurance.'

Gabriel had hardly finished his elaborate self-excuse when Constance, who, thinking that he had arranged a secret meeting with Letitia, had shadowed him, also came into the room. Her face was grey under the make-up. Letitia, seeing such haggard distress, was stricken with an unaccountable sense of guilt.

'Ah, *there* you are !' cried Constance, in a voice of false joy. 'I saw. I thought. I wondered. And I came! How right I was!'

There was something naked, ghastly, in her pretence of lightness which —although Gabriel alone understood it—affected everybody in the room. Stephanie rose quickly to her feet. What she said was unheard by any of her companions; but the glance she gave to Letitia was one of horror, filled with impatience, pain, and despair. She hurried from the room. The four who remained stood looking at one another as if, first Constance's coming, and then Stephanie's going, had thrown them into sudden consternation.

Part Three

TEMPTATIONS

Eight

THE SCHEMER

i

F. R., SITTING ALONE in the brasserie of the Oriental, near Piccadilly Circus, ordered a second gin and Italian. The lights were bright; there was a brisk coming and going of men and women; there were warmth and drink, both very good things for a solitary man. He felt himself keenly observant of the play of life, and, in order the better to relish the scene, half-closed his eyes, leaning back against the red plush, assessing types, reading clothes and gestures, watching the waiters who so deftly conjured with their metal trays, and contrasting what he saw with what he had seen in places two and three and six thousand miles from London.

Waiters were the same in all lands. They were Latin, Teutonic, or Negro; the Latins for savings to be spent in age and in their own country, the Negroes for present wages, the Teutons for politics or the learning of languages. English waiters were shabby, dirty-shirted, obviously ill-paid hirelings. Broken hacks. They were coarse-handed slovens; they had bunions. They were bored; they lost their tips to the bookmakers; they were obviously burdened by large families, as unwanted and slatternly as themselves. No pride in service. These men, on the contrary, moved quickly, felt no shame, and were given to their calling. Why the national differences? It was a subject too complicated to be discussed in this mood of flexible attention. . . .

He would never, in England, employ waiters; always waitresses. Waitresses cost less; they took pains to please; they could be frightened into precision. He understood women. But, by Jove! the foreigner understood the catering business. He was devoted to it. Not ignorantly disdainful, as the English were.

Half-past six. No Julian. A darkness crossed Farringdon's eyes and sank like a cloud upon his hopes. This was awkward. It wounded his vanity. He had thought to command the boy, and to use him. To attract and to fascinate as a man of experience; exploiting and educating the tender, half-sophisticated mind. To use, as bait for the women at Willowhaven. Both of them had quickened to Julian, who had youth and novelty and a boyish beauty. To himself, oddly enough, they hadn't really responded at all. The causes of this lay far back in time, among old . . . misunderstandings. The euphemism amused F. R.

How much money could be touched in that tousled little villa? It was probably stowed under the beds in wrappings of old cloth and tattered silk.

As if thieves wouldn't look there first of all! They couldn't spend much. Mother had the snug comfort; Muriel the ragged, darned, rotten flannel petticoats of an aged Cinderella. She was nothing, herself, but a fervid bundle of them. Fat, deaf, and a muddler. She'd sold her life to the old devil. Mortgaged it, rather, for the sake of a pensioned old age. Most likely, whatever happened, she'd get nothing in the end. She was the sort that got nothing. Poor Muriel! What an air of shabby avarice there was about the whole place! It sickened him! Now if *he* handled the money it should *work* for him. . . .

F. R. was lost in the scene before his eyes. He planned. Ten minutes later, he awoke.

That boy wasn't coming! Damn him!

There were two young blondes over in the corner, both of them suburban would-be-smart, in cheap furs and careful finery, who had a stupid, white, puffy-faced middle-aged man in tow. The bore had probably got a wife of his own kidney, left at home with her feet on the fender and a sloppy novel from the library in her hands. She, thankful to be rid of him as long as she was still respectably supported; he, impotent enough, dully proud of entertaining these third-rate wenches; but fundamentally uneasy in case somebody who knew him should tell his wife. You could see him wriggling. He was buying himself drink after drink because he was uneasy. He wanted to get into a state of half-fuddled assurance. He'd never do it. Men who'd made a little money in business were furtively doing the same thing wherever moral opinion shackled licence. All were uneasy.

Who was easy? F. R. looked at his own drink, and finished it. Nobody knew him. If he had left a wife at home it was by cool calculation. Once the door closed behind him she ceased to exist. He was afraid of nobody. Whereas, if that fellow yonder made a slip with one of those girls, and put himself at her mercy, the wife would be a threat, removable only by murder. Farringdon's affairs would never come to grief. He had only to pack a bag, step aboard ship, and disappear . . .

Citizen of the World! He caught the waiter's eye, and knew that in a minute he would be noiselessly served with a third drink. In a place like this he was a king! By God! He'd swear those blondes—both were eyeing him—wished they were sitting here, listening to the stories he could tell. He'd swear they'd imagined the joy of having *his* money spent on them. They imagined more than that, poor sex-starved dolls! No limit to it. They were probably the bore's typists. Their key words would be 'ladylike' and 'dainty'; their thoughts foul enough. . . . He revelled in contempt.

Meanwhile he was alone. Young Julian wasn't here. He wasn't coming. The truth was Letitia had him under her thumb, the extraordinary woman. She had everybody there; Monty not least.

Except himself. Oh, *he* wasn't afraid of Letitia. It was just that, in dealing with her, he'd always felt . . . Something intangible. As if he wasn't getting away with it. In that business twenty years ago: he'd stuck to the story of a frame-up. She hadn't believed it. She hadn't said so. She'd come handsomely to the rescue. But she hadn't for a moment believed it. She'd looked—amazing!—as if she was sorry for him. Damned insulting.

Sometimes he was sorry for himself; naturally. He would endure pity from nobody else in the world.

Well, if Julian wasn't coming, he must dine alone. Alone. Sombre word; like a knell. A word for heroes. How all those others—including the blondes and their escorting bore—would hate it! 'You're alone, aren't you?' Why, they'd pick up *anybody* for the sake of answering 'No'. They knew they were never anything else. Not true of himself. He had always a plan for company. He had one now; its ramifications as engrossing as the moves of a Capablanca.

Then he saw Julian. His heart leapt. The boy had entered quickly, had seen him in the instant of arrival, and was picking his way between the scattered tables. At once, Farringdon threw off all melancholy, and grinned. It was not only with relief, or at the fulfilment of a design. It was with delight, also, and pride in his nephew's good looks; seen with affection. This boy was of his own blood.

ii

Julian had the sense of being engaged upon an adventure. He disliked his uncle; but Farringdon, for all his air of seedy intrigue, stirred curiosity. His bearded length and fang-like teeth, which showed in the middle of that forestial acreage of whisker, suggested tenacious strength. No doubt the man was bogus, or Mother would have talked of him with fun. She'd have had amusing anecdotes. He'd have been in and out of the house, now or in the past, a slightly ridiculous personality, full of yarns and elaborate discretions. His letters would have yielded merriment and foreign stamps . . .

Never mind; he was somebody who had never heard of Stephanie. He treated one, flatteringly, as a man. It was interesting to watch his mind hooking and unhooking like a piece of an old-fashioned wire puzzle. One could put the puzzle together. As to Aunt Muriel, for example: what was he up to? Wouldn't it be interesting to find out?

'Good evening. I'm sorry to be late.' No need to explain that one hadn't been able to break away from the chance of seeing her in the distance, or that one had been quite determined until ten minutes ago not to come.

'What will you drink?' demanded F. R., easily. In seeing and resenting Julian's lack of cordiality he felt like a lover who woos a cold beauty. 'Waiter!' The boy was spoiled. Something on his mind. Brusque, pointedly indifferent; probably knew that an elder man wouldn't wait for him without good and complimentary reason. Ignore it! 'Short of pure contemplation, this kind of scene's the best for an observant eye.'

'Is it?' asked Julian, glancing coolly at the flattered blondes.

'A mind at ease can see nothing that doesn't answer,' retorted Farringdon. 'You know your Jane Austen, I suppose,'

'No,' said Julian. 'Do you?'

'Intimately. You're surprised,' commented Farringdon. "Good boy. It's a capacity I've outlived.'

Julian laughed outright.

'I'd as soon watch mouldy cheese as this crowd,' he declared. 'I'm no protistologist.'

'Your mother's kept you fastidious,' said Farringdon, whistling under his breath. He intended a taunt. But he could not trace the effect of his taunt upon that secretive temperament. 'An excellent but limiting trait.'

'You know my mother better than I do,' said Julian.

'I've known her longer, at any rate. We used to say she belonged to the genteel side of the family. Not the artistic.'

'Grandmother being the artistic?' Julian was at last interested. He had a habit of dropping his eyelids very slowly when his attention was engaged. It was unconscious, and suggested languor, without weakness.

'Not Muriel, I need hardly say.' Farringdon was happy again. He drank, seeing the blondes in a pleasant glow of light, keeping an eye half on Julian's face and half on his hands, which were restless, and inwardly relishing perceptions of Muriel as a comic, abortive personality. This was the kind of talk he enjoyed.

'She's genuine,' said Julian, frowning thoughtfully.

'Muriel? She keeps bats. Now The Old Lady—what did you make of The Old Lady?'

Julian shrugged. He was no longer thinking of that household. He had been seized by a white heat of adoring detestation of Stephanie. He saw her, warm and tempted, before him. He felt her body within his arms, crushing, crushing, as she screamed in agony; and he thrust her away so savagely that she fell shrieking into the cavernous blackness of oblivion. The bitch! He abhorred her! Hate! Hate! . . .

He stared; perspiration darted; his jaw dropped. And then madness passed, and he was cold again, listening to his uncle's mockery and guessing —so that he might disappoint expectation—at the reply which should be expected of him. Avoidance of the obvious was essential to his intellectual vanity; he must always say 'puce' or 'onyx' when they supposed he could not escape 'red'.

'She appeared simple,' he studiously replied.

Farringdon was not deceived.

'There must be rare bouts at times,' he said. 'You saw what she'd written in the dust? Oh, I wouldn't be surprised if murder was done there one day.' His teeth showed. 'Yes, murder.' His shoulders twitched as he laughed. 'That would be amusing. But very awkward for *us*.'

'Us?' Julian was disdainful of the association.

'Yes, my boy; us. Have you never considered the repercussions of murder? Notorious crime ruins a family. Young Johnny's career; young Doris's fiancé. Almost any family submits to blackmail to save its younger generation. It'll starve itself to pension a black sheep. Anything to keep him out of the newspapers.' He smiled broadly. 'I *know* this.'

Julian started. His first thought was: 'Ah! Is that what happened to *you*? Did Mother? How God-awful!' The second: 'Christine! Yes, I'd . . . No! Ridiculous!' The third, which he expressed, was:

'An advantage if it shook us all up.'

'You're *for* it, then?' asked F. R., with elaborate gravity and watchful eyes.

'I'm against stuffiness.'

'Who steals my purse steals trash . . .' My God! thought Farringdon; I'm rivalling that old bore, Polonius! This is the wrong tack! How did I get here? Exploration and education of this boy's heart; but also my clairvoyance, maybe. His tone changed; he grew false with confidential *bonhomie*. 'The truth is, I'm tired of roving. I'm getting respectable. I want to settle quietly——'

'By the sea?' asked Julian.

Farringdon smiled. But he had almost winced. Merciless boy!

'Let's go in to dinner,' he said. 'Away from the cheese-mites. I'll give you some insight into . . . one of my plans. It doesn't involve murder.'

iii

F. R. fixed the *maître d'hôtel* with a steely eye. He saw that the *maître d'hôtel*, a grandee, was showing them to an unimportant table in the middle of the restaurant. It was an affront, product of a summary glance and a crude estimate of F. R.'s spending power.

'Oh, no,' he said, firmly, and pointed to a table by the farther wall.

The *maître d'hôtel* shrugged, contorted his face into a very black scowl, and shook his head.

'Dat is engached,' said he.

'I know,' retorted Farringdon. 'For me.' He caused himself to tower high in the air, like a cat walking stiff-legged past a possible enemy. 'Or I go, my friend.'

Without verbal reply, the *maître d'hôtel* preceded them to the table, whisked away the 'engaged' ticket, and handed his two guests to another grandee of lower rank. This other grandee, who brought a notebook from under his coat-tails, was more affable. He made suggestions; with little drops of the head he accepted decisions; the dinner was ordered to meet F. R.'s wishes. F. R., stretching his legs under and his arms across the table, looked slowly about him. This busy, moving scene! He felt he had done well. Even Julian, for whose elegance he was sure waiters would more impulsively hasten, could not fail to be impressed by his control of men and menu. Would he be also rendered malleable by the dinner? This remained to be seen.

In any case, thought Farringdon, that's immaterial. All I want to do is to get him down to Willowhaven again. To *prove*. There's money: what's he living on? He said:

'Am I right in thinking you've a coolness on your hands at home?'

Julian, whose head had been down, lifted it suddenly. He had been taken by surprise.

'On the contrary,' said he, almost sharply. 'Complete warmth.'

Nothing short of Counsel's contemptuous 'As your Ludship pleases', could have surpassed F. R.'s bland air of unbelieving patience.

'You're just back from America?' he inquired.

Julian saw the meaning of an earlier hint. His uncle evidently pictured him as a remittance man! How amusing! But how extraordinarily impertinent!

'I come and go.'

'Yes? I'm interested.' F. R. ostentatiously leant a little nearer. 'It costs money, doesn't it?' When the answer was no more than a smile, he added: 'I should like to come and go, myself.'

'Don't you?' asked Julian.

'I'm not as independent as you seem to be.' Farringdon pretended to be watching the waiter who served them with hors d'œuvres.

'I have no money at all,' said Julian, frankly.

Well, that was one ascertained fact. Farringdon nodded in mockery.

'Fortunately your father can support you indefinitely,' he remarked. 'He's prosperous. Your mother's got nothing. Mine saw to that thirty-odd years ago.'

'I *said* she was simple.'

'You have the right word for everything. She hates Letitia, as you saw.'

'Was that hate? It surprised me.'

'Letitia's told you nothing? She's always been very discreet.' F. R. gave his nephew a conspicuously ironic glance. 'Her past's a sealed book to you, I suppose.'

'Oh, yes,' said Julian. 'She's never mentioned *you*.'

Oho! Oho! This was decidedly a counter-attack! One must take great care. *Great* care.

'So that, in a sense, you're taking *me* on trust?'

'Very much so.' Julian smiled again. 'Is that wrong?' F. R. drew a quick breath. The boy was extraordinarily handsome. Why did these children all ape Byron? Yes; but he was artful. He threatened by means of impudent candour. As his mother had done. Of course that was one reason for his present attractiveness. When he smiled he was the image of Letitia at the same age.

'No, right; *cela va sans dire*. This was why I asked how The Old Lady struck you. At bottom, she'd do you a mischief. You saw, of course. Whereas *I* mean nothing but good. That clear? We're both charmed by you. You don't need telling. So is Muriel. You could get something from Muriel.'

'I wonder what,' said Julian, slowly, as if he were musing.

'If your father became less prosperous. If he died. The Old Lady won't live for ever.'

'Do *you* hope to "get something"?'

F. R. leaned back, beaming. He said:

'Like you, I suffer from filial affection. I always have done. I never cared tremendously for my father. As I told you, he was genteel. But Mother's a character. Inexhaustible. I've been trying to understand her for fifty years. Is that how you feel about *your* mother?'

'I'm still trying to understand *myself*,' replied Julian.

'Come down with me to Willowhaven.'

'I? Again? Why?'

'To see your grandmother. Your aunt.' F. R. saw the quickly shaken head. 'To help me.' He could not decipher that incredibly melancholy calm. As well try to read the Sphinx. There was probably nothing behind it but obstinacy; but he must try everything. 'I'd foot the hotel bill.'

What! thought Julian. Leave *her*! He could hardly control his shudder. Although he hated her, although he despised her, there was the eternal chance that she'd relent, capitulate as she *must* do. She knew how to reach him in an hour. He'd waited in his lodging, ground by bitter agitation, hour after hour, walking back and forth from the window to the door and to the window again, waiting, waiting, with his heart feeling like a swollen balloon which would at any instant burst. . . . She *must* come. She *must* send. The alternative was suicide. He felt the cruellest contempt. If she came now, he would refuse her. He would insult her. . . . He couldn't endure defeat. She was not strong; she was wayward, weak, like water in her evasiveness. She'd already almost yielded herself—*almost*; letting 'I dare not' wait upon 'I would'. What a coward!

His head was shaken.

'No,' he said with grim pallor, not at all thinking of his uncle, or of the ladies at Bella Vista. 'I stay here.'

Indignation so heated F. R.'s mind that he missed the meaning of Julian's excessive sternness. Something else, also, besides indignation, caused him to grow suddenly deaf, as if the world had stopped for a moment in hideous warning. It was the thought: This is defeat. It presages ultimate disaster. shall be beaten!

'Well, I'm sorry,' he said, as if he were laughing in secret at the whim f a child. 'That's a blow! However, we'll say no more about it. They'll e disappointed.'

More, much more, they would know that he could not perform what he romised. Damn! Unknown to himself, F. R.'s demeanour lost assurance.

Meanwhile Julian, back in the restaurant after his electric flight through notion, weighed his uncle's prospects of money from Bella Vista. Had he got plenty of money, then? There would be no help from Muriel. She disliked him. The Old Lady? That was different. Less certain. But, for a different reason, perhaps niggardliness, just as unlikely. Why did the man ant *him* to go? Didn't it suggest the desperate scheming of a needy character? Beware?

'I'll go down one day by myself,' he smilingly promised.

'That will be fine!' cried F. R., with great gaiety. 'I'll tell them so.'

iv

He remained uneasily furious for the rest of the meal, as inattentive to lian as Julian was to him, but never as indifferent. While Julian, knowing at he had failed, could not let himself realise the loss of Stephanie, F. R. uld not, knowing that he had failed, let himself yield his hope of Julian. returned fitfully in the midst of all his wilder plots. But the wilder plots

became each moment more ferocious. Unquestionably he must go alone to
Willowhaven. He must frighten Muriel into being an ally, or a helpful
enemy, or a fluttered non-hindering observer of his appropriation of her
inheritance. That would be decided later. . . .

They parted at last, with cool thanks from Julian and a hurried turning
into the crowd; with a warm handgrip from F. R. and exactly the right
measure of avuncular preoccupation with adult affairs. The warm hand-
grip had always been one of F. R.'s deliberate gestures. It belonged, in his
view, to the bunch of English illusions which one must flatter; wear tweeds,
drink beer, smoke a pipe, look a man honestly in the eyes, and never offer
a flabby hand. By such habits, in this country, you were judged. It was
extraordinary that any great people could be so simple. He, too, turned
into the crowd, walking through it, up an almost deserted Regent Street,
over which arc lights, like judges at the Last Trump, shed a ghastly stare,
to Portland Place, and so home to the flat near Regent's Park. He saw
nothing of what he passed. It was by instinct alone that he carried his head
high and swung his long arms; for in the last two hours his courage had
shrunk to nothing.

Normal litheness and pretended unconcern were achieved as he let himself
in at No. 39. Thelma mustn't guess that he was dissatisfied. He would
have to meet her distrust, and show that it left him unmoved. He assumed
his part. And of course he succeeded to perfection; for Thelma had nothing,
nowadays, of any value to withhold, and he could ignore her without acting
at all. She would be sewing in the kitchen. She was always sewing in the
kitchen. As it happened, she was sewing in the kitchen. It was a room so
drab, with its dead walls and black grate and brown dresser, that she seemed
tediously to belong to it, like a standard fitting. And she raised her eyes
from ugly brown stuff and brown cotton to give him the usual blank eyes of
hostile inquiry. All was as he had foreseen.

'Poor light you have,' remarked F. R., jauntily circling the kitchen.
He flung off at the last moment his broad-brimmed hat and great woollen
muffler, which slid from the dresser and lay jumbled upon the floor. And
as he sat by the fire in an old high-backed wooden chair he at once dug deep
in his outer pockets for pipe and tobacco pouch.

'I have no better,' answered Thelma, continuing to watch.

By God! She drove him out, with her aggrieved dullness. She was like
some old white cow. Not, of course, sacred. But pleasure in tormenting her
made him smile in revived good spirits. Good! Good! He had still some
power left. Yes, he felt brighter.

'True. You need fear no rival,' said F. R.

'You want some supper?' she asked.

'I've dined.'

'You are so gay, I felt sure of it,' answered Thelma. 'It would have
been courteous to invite me, too. But I must naturally not expect it.'

'Another time,' said F. R., suavely. 'We'll celebrate.'

'You were with friends?' she persisted.

'One friend.'

'He paid?'

'Hardly that. He'll prove useful to me.'

'When will that be?'

'Time's your tyrant, Thelma. Like your husband, he won't be driven.'

Thelma picked up her ugly sewing. It was her tastelessness that made all she did a drudgery. She never had anything pretty. Her one thought was to make what would last, that they might never be without food and covering. She was terrified of want. She said:

'He has a long white beard and a scythe.'

F. R. crossed his legs, and puffed his pipe.

'Charming! Cryptic! You're always the poet, Thelma.'

She was silenced. Her head fell. She no longer watched. With wounded sullenness she continued to sew.

Presently, without speaking, F. R. went into the front room which he regarded as his own, and, going to the cupboard, drew from it some parcels hidden there earlier in the day. They contained four new shirts, which were very necessary, some new soft silken collars, a couple of dandyish ties, a pair of good shoes, a pair of beautifully soft slippers, three pairs of socks, suspenders, two suits of pyjamas, and a silk dressing-gown. He hummed with satisfaction. He had never owned anything finer. With a stealthy smoothing of the brown paper he laid these possessions in a pile and brought from behind the window curtain a splendid new small pigskin dressing-case, in which, still quietly humming, he began to place the clothes. These things gave him strength. They were also, tangibly, good investment. They had been bought, before his meeting with Julian, as essential to a stay in the same hotel as a young man who, if he had no money himself, enjoyed a wardrobe provided by his opulent father. One must dress one's part. And F. R. had for too long allowed Thelma to mend and cobble his clothes, until he felt that he carried darns upon his person like ungraceful scars received in a brawl.

Willowhaven. Julian. The house in Meadowside Road. He had become obsessed by them.

'The essence of planning,' said F. R., aloud, 'is corroborative detail. Omit nothing in corroboration. *I* omit nothing.' He hummed again; his song being 'Lead, Kindly Light.'

A faint flicker of air interrupted his preoccupation with his clothes and his next adventure. He looked up to see that Thelma was standing in the doorway observing him. Her broad white face was without expression. She might have been sleep-walking. But she was not asleep. She had been for some moments attentive to all that he did.

'Tomorrow,' said F. R., as if he were not surprised at her presence—indeed, as if he resumed a conversation which had hardly been interrupted, 'leave you. But not for long. *That* would be unkind. For three or four busy days. Then I shall come back again; it may be with good news.'

'You are going to make your fortune?' asked Thelma, drily.

'I hope so.'

'You have a costly trousseau there.'

'To impress . . . friends.'

'Is one of them a woman?'

'Oh, my difficulty is always *not* to impress women. Didn't you know that? As flies to amber. The trousseau was to impress a man.'

'I spend my life mending, so that you shall make a good impression.'

'Not a *good* impression. A shabby genteel impression. Admirable in *some* companies; useless in this one.'

'You are going to see Letitia?'

F. R. smiled broadly at such futile guesswork. Appalling to be married to a woman of sluggish wits! He shook his head. He wagged a finger. His wagging finger, although he did not know it, made a dreadful shadow upon the wall behind him. It fascinated Thelma, who ceased for an instant to look at her husband with anger. She started when F. R. replied:

'I hope never to see Letitia. If I saw Letitia now, it would mean that I was in serious trouble.'

'I see,' said Thelma. 'One goes to her in serious trouble, then.'

Across the white face passed a smile which F. R. did not trouble to interpret. He continued to pack his clothes into the dressing-case.

'Don't misunderstand me,' he courteously replied. 'Understanding I *never* expect.'

'Wouldn't you like me to *mark* your trousseau?' asked Thelma.

'Decidedly not,' said F. R. He was struck by a thought. Embroidery scissors! He must remove the makers' names from all these things. It was not urgent; but it was something to be done as soon as he was alone and a free agent. 'I shan't be trusting them to a laundry.'

'To your wife, perhaps?' asked Thelma. 'Like the pigskin case?'

'Only to my wife,' answered F. R., with happy gallantry. But her last words horrified him. He thought: Hell! What a fool to get a pigskin case! Absolutely unmistakable! Worse still, let her see it! Damn! Fool! Fool! He felt a constriction of the throat, as if he were suffocating. He could hardly keep still.

v

That night F. R. slept badly. He could not shake off the conviction that he had made a fatal slip. Perhaps, after all, it would be better not to attempt this bold scheme. He could go straight ahead with the other, applying to Letitia for a thousand pounds, and taking a sound commercial chance. That would be the safe course. He was nearly fifty. Wouldn't be better? But no; he had always been an opportunist. Besides, why the panic? He wasn't going berserk. He was committed to nothing at all. Merely going to Willowhaven again, to sound his mother. No more. The shadows which had gathered behind, the dark unspecified devils of his imagination, were secret; they could immediately be discarded. If they were discarded, this would become but one more of his day-dreams, of which there had been a million or more, breeding rapidly and now forgotten.

His nerve had been shaken by the knowledge that Thelma menaced liberty. She was stupid; but with the obdurate memory of a child. She knew, pryingly, altogether too much for safety. Either he must remain tied to her or he must escape for good. Bella Vista held the key. And the plunder.

Morning came at last, very late, a grey peep of watery autumnal light, in which darkness lingered. A chill breeze flickered from the north-east, strong enough to recall wintry Channel crossings, or awakenings upon long distance journeys after other restless nights, when one saw through the bleared windows of creaking railway trains the silhouettes of cities previously unknown. There had been many cities, many such journeys, in his life. All of them were as grey as this morning. But he could not doubt his cleverness had been too self-confident. The case, the case; *there* had been his error. It had been bought to suggest careless affluence. It had become an indestructible label.

By full daylight, F. R. had shaken off his fear. He saw that he had been over-elaborate, even melodramatic. His mother's chief fault! Something shoddy about her. His own keener sense of reality, which was due to experience of hardship, was a protection. . . . He hummed as he took his bath and as he dressed in some of his new clothes. After all, the case—of which he was very proud—could bring no danger, because all he was going to do was as open as the air of England. Those other tentative designs were no more than the Devil's whisperings. They beset him at night.

He set off in good heart. Once he was in the train, and the dreary backyards of railway-side London were giving place to red roofs and squares of lawn and larger spaces of tree-fringed green, he left every care behind. The stubbornly silent men and women in his compartment, who showed no reaction whatever to his quizzical applications of good nature, were focused as curious homunculæ. The thought of being boxed with them for a couple of hours, at first so choking, rose to the pitch of a fantastic joke. Thelma did not exist. Julian was a ludicrous prig. He himself was d'Artagnan riding a pigskin horse through the town of Meung on his way to M. de Tréville, the King, Richelieu, and Fortune. . . . The countryside streamed past; the sun pierced the clouds; jauntiness jerked his shoulders and stimulated his heart.

When Willowhaven was reached, and the draughty marine wind caught his breath as he walked sharply down the street leading to the sea, he threw back his head. Days of boyhood, in which he sailed with other boys and smelled salt upon the breeze, and stood in the prow, naked, to feel it biting his skin, recurred to him so strongly that he could not at once bear to enter a building. What a love of adventure he'd always had! Heroic, sensational! He had it still. He was eternally young. He would never die!

Shunning the original centre of the town, which led to the barren dunes, he turned westward, still carrying the conspicuous pigskin case, meaning to go not quite as far as Meadowside Road but to 'reconnoitre', coming back later along the Front to his centrally placed hotel. With a triumphant glance he took in the sepia rollers which rose and flattened below him in their white, madly running lace of foam. He ridiculed the doddering old men who crept beside them, warming untempered bones and flesh in the autumn sunshine. He exchanged laughing glances with a girl who was being dragged along by two leashed Aberdeens. Ah! She needed the

muscular strength of *his* arms! Not a charmer. If she had been, he was
still the man for a rapid affair; and here was opportunity ready-made.
Then something caught his eye as he strode. It seemed like an answer to
prayer. It made him shake, almost cough, with merriment.

At the corner of Meadowside Road stood a large, ugly red house, big
enough and vulgar enough to assault everybody who approached. A very
fortress of respectability, with iron balconies and marble steps, a pseudo sun
parlour, two absurdly discomfited stone lions, and a wide green front door
speckled with polished brass. It might have been—perhaps it was—the
dream-home of a retired publican or a self-made jerry-builder. But, if that
were true, the jerry-builder publican had met his Waterloo. In future he
would not be as rich as he had been. For outside this bastion, as dear as
solvency to the heart of every dweller in Meadowside Road, were two
tremendous pantechnicons. About them stood the swollen furnishings,
brass pots, upturned chairs, and more ignominious possessions of the
departing household. Several men in short baize aprons moved in and out
of the doorway, bringing more and more treasures, while two others stacked
lavish bedsteads and wardrobes within the leading van.

He went nearer, as engrossed as a boy, sniffing well-remembered odours
of straw and removal-matting, and looking from the furniture to the house
and back again, noting the local name on the pantechnicons, calculating the
number of rooms in the house. Then an estate-agent's board, not yet erected,
but lying inside the gateway all ready to go up as soon as the place was empty,
attracted his attention. He screwed his head upon one side, and read:

FOR SALE OR TO LET ON LONG LEASE
THIS COMMODIOUS MANSION
One drawing-room, 30 ft.×20 ft. One dining . . .
Four principal bedrooms . . .

Catching the eye of a red-faced moving-man who seemed to be as much
interested in F. R. as F. R. was interested in the board, F. R. said:

'Big place, this.' The red-faced man grunted, valuing him with a shrewd
blue-eyed half-smile. 'I see it's to be let. It might suit *me*. Why are they
going? Money scarce?'

'They 'aven't said,' answered the man, drily enough. 'I must ask.'
F. R. did not care much for his slightly ribald expression. After standing
long enough, therefore, to show indifference to ribaldry, he skirted the
pantechnicons and looked up at the house from the farther side. Too much
staff needed to keep it spick and span. Rates high, for town-improvements.
What offers? Too many people impoverished three years ago in the spread
from American financial crashes. It would stand empty. Deteriorate.
Big houses were done for, and this one was a white elephant. But extraordinarily opportune for use in his scheme. Either way. Either actually
or as a lever. Under her melodrama, mother craved display; under the
craving lay a conventional woman . . .

F. R laughed again. A weapon against a miser lay ready to his hand.
He nodded his head, again skirted the pantechnicons, and went to his hotel.

vi

As he had supposed, the atmosphere at Bella Vista became, in the afternoon, frowsy with all absence of ventilation. He had arrived to find Muriel and The Old Lady dozing by the fire; and now, at teatime, they gave him the impression of living in sleeping-bags. He felt uncommonly sleepy, himself, after striding in the wind until he was tired. More than once he had been unable to hide a colossal yawn.

'Yes,' said he, smothering a smaller one. 'I saw the boy last night. He dined with me, in fact. Desolated at not being able to come down to-day. He'll join me.'

'Ah!' said The Old Lady, working the joints of her left hand, for the pleasure of hearing them crack. Why, thought F. R., the hand's dirty! Good God! I never thought of that! 'I wonder if he *will* join you.'

'That's true,' agreed F. R. 'They disregard their elders. Last night he was very late. No apology. Complete sangfroid. But a delightful boy.'

'Silent,' ruminated The Old Lady. 'Beautiful but silent.'

'He thinks the more!' cried Muriel, loyally. 'He's not a chatterbox.'

'That's the last thing I should call him,' declared F. R., disagreeably, with distaste observing Muriel's dumpy figure in—what was it?—some sort of home-made dressing-gown? a hold-all?—yes, that was it, a daylight sleeping-bag! *En-tout-cas!* That's to say, for all purposes. She had much too red a face. She flushed easily; but the constant redness was due to bad digestion. Tk-tk! Good-hearted, she would be called. My God! thought F. R.

'I've dreamt of him,' announced The Old Lady, with dignity. 'In my dream I saw him clinging to a pillar——'

'No doubt, myself,' suggested F. R.

'Crying out "Oh, save me! Save me!" It was most affecting. I laid my hand on his arm. He was quieted. I never saw a sweeter smile. This dream's occurred more than once. I assumed he needed saving from his mother. In that case the effect of my touch would be very symbolic. It would mean . . .' With fixed eyes, The Old Lady helped herself to another sandwich of potted meat. F. R. realised that she had already eaten five of these, and that he had no chance of catching her up. As far as he could tell—for she was largely hidden from him by a very considerable tea-cosy—Muriel ate nothing; but drank many cups of sweet tea.

'It would mean he'd made a mistake,' said Muriel, rather rudely.

'Not a *mistake*,' corrected F. R., smiling in his beard. 'The truth is that a young man's troubles aren't on the surface. It's been said that every boy's in love with his mother. Now, as the only *son*——'

'Who's been away more than half his life——' cried the flushed Muriel.

Ah, yes; she'd taken fright. That was perfectly obvious. But should he soothe or terrify her? F. R. determined to terrify now, and, if advisable, to soothe later

'As the only *son*,' he repeated, 'I know the hold a mother has on her boy's heart. It's not unlikely that Mother, who's clairvoyant, really did help

Julian. I think she did. My impression is that he's been kept down by Letitia. I put it to him last night, point blank. "Have you?" Of course he denied it——'

'Of course he did!' cried Muriel. 'He adores his mother!'

'Yes? Yes?' demanded The Old Lady, drumming both her dirty paws on the arm of her chair. 'You were saying, Farringdon?'

'The very *promptness* of the denial——' began Farringdon.

'Of course!' agreed The Old Lady. She relapsed into muttering thought. 'Have you dreamt of *me* again?' asked F. R., pathetically, after a long pause.

'Hm. I do nothing else.'

'So she *says*!' murmured Muriel, behind the tea-cosy. 'Whether it's *true*——'

'I'm glad of that,' said F. R. 'Do I seem to come nearer?'

'Vividly!' exclaimed his mother. 'Such happy, exciting dreams! Close at hand; helping me. I sleep more comfortably after them.'

'Isn't that fine!' said F. R. 'I've been wondering . . .' He could feel Muriel glaring at him over the cosy. He settled himself more easily. 'You're glad I'm here for a few days? I shall be in and out, you know. Pot luck, if I may.'

'Of course,' agreed his mother. 'Muriel! You hear this?'

'I wish you could dine with me one night at the Hotel. Or lunch, perhaps.'

'Lunch would be better. I mustn't over-excite myself.'

'Lunch, then. Tomorrow? I thought of staying till the weekend.'

'Why?' asked Muriel.

He beamed at her.

'Love. Filial and fraternal love. Surely you're not surprised?' Then, as if upon impulse—but they knew it was not upon impulse—he asked: 'How would you like me for a neighbour?'

He felt a tremor run through them both Across The Old Lady's face shot a spasm of triumphant joy. It disappeared, and she leaned majestically back, tapping the tips of her fingers together. But Muriel's cheeks were a deeper red. She sat straight up, alert with suspicion.

'Do you mean for ever?' she demanded.

'Well,' drawled F. R., enjoying himself. 'I've a great inclination to settle down. Preferably by the sea. This air suits me. And as I came here today I noticed that that big house on the corner . . .'

Oh, they were impressed! He could hear the intaking of deep, incredulous breaths. They had discussed him. Mother had been his good friend Muriel his detractor. He was sure of these things.

'By yourself?' asked Muriel, with the most scornful suspicion imaginable

'Did you think you'd like to come and look after me?' he said, in a soft voice. 'The loving sister, tending her *two* dearest relatives?'

'It would be a wonderful position.' The Old Lady was dreaming of luxury. This rich son of hers! Her fancy was captivated by the picture of herself entering that thirty-foot drawing-room. How her voice would echo in it!

'*I* don't want to look after you!' snapped Muriel. 'I was wondering what sort of people you'd bring there. A lot of sharpers and rogues, I expect.'

'That's your love,' teased F. R. Reflectively, he added, as if for her ear alone: 'No man's a hero to his sister, perhaps.'

'Not a man with *your* history.'

"Mine? I wonder what you mean?' he inquired.

Muriel's eyes filled with tears. She was growing over-excited. In a few moments she would begin noisily to sob, quite unable to control herself any longer. Knowing this, The Old Lady sent a stealthy, enjoying, approving glance to F. R., encouraging him to provoke Muriel. Her eyes glittered. She tapped her fingers continuously together, as little girls whirl a skipping rope through salt and mustard and vinegar until they reach the whizzing fury of *pepper*. If he made Muriel rush, boo-hooing, from the room, she would not be able to resist shouting and miaowing with glee. It was a grand sensation. He was a wonderful boy. The past was forgiven. How her heart had ached for him! He could give her new, enchanting delights of domestic strife.

'I was delighted with the house,' said F. R., closing his eyes, and speaking as if he saw a vision. 'It's preposterously ugly. Think of it filled with cheery people, crowding into the dining-room to a great meal. Paper streamers. Champagne. Coloured lights. The sight of Willowhaven. I should be tempted to call it the Grand Babylon——'

'Our quiet town!' gasped Muriel.

'Why not?'

The drumming of The Old Lady's fingers had ceased. She had become suddenly exhausted. F. R., not looking at her, but certain of the effect he had provoked, knew that she had grown pale with enthralled excitement. There would be a reaction. She would grow frightened. Tomorrow she would entreat him to abandon his scheme. But now she was in joy. He would say no more. Showing his big teeth in a baffling grin, he made a boyish lunge and caught his raised, skinny knee in clasped hands.

'Wheeee!' screamed The Old Lady. 'Miau-wow! Miau-wow! Wheeee! My son's come home!' She rocked with laughter. 'My Absalom!'

Muriel jumped to her feet. Her face was blotched. She was quite distraught.

'An impulse,' said F. R. 'Nothing's done. Don't be alarmed. Naturally your approval's a *sine qua non*.' Hugging his knees, he spread calm upon them by his determined tranquillity. He was very pleased indeed. His mother would come. Meanwhile, as he had intended, he had Muriel hysterically at his mercy.

vii

When Farringdon had left the house, wearied of their company, and ready to dine quietly by himself at the Hotel, The Old Lady and Muriel were in different rooms. The Old Lady sat by the fire, as usual, without book or sewing to distract her mind, which was alternately grey and vivid and almost blank. Muriel, having refrained from going to the front door with Farringdon, had first watched his departure and then gone into the dark kitchen to escape what she knew would be coming.

As she sat down upon a wooden chair she noticed that the kitchen fire had gone out. She would have to re-light it in order to cook the evening meal. This seemed to her to be the cruellest misfortune of the afternoon; and the big tears rolled unstaunched down her cheeks, and down the front of the shapeless dress she wore. To have to re-light the fire when her whole body seemed to be clenched in an effort to resist the Devil was too bad! 'Too bad!' she kept saying to herself, in a childish moan. 'Too bad!'

She was afraid. Farringdon was a very bad man. He meant them harm. Herself, chiefly. She'd seen him look about the room, and at the ceiling. He was after what was hidden. He might kill her. But what was there that she could do? Anybody to whom she told her fear would laugh at her. The policeman who strolled around the streets; the prying neighbours; the grocer—all would laugh. She already saw them laughing as she went by. They ridiculed her. If only Julian had come. Now that Mother knew where she had hidden her letters, she dared not write anything that called for a reply. It was the same with Letitia. But she saw it all. All that was coming. She would be killed. She would be turned out of doors, to beg her bread. 'Move on, move on, there. Move on.' That was what they said to poor shabby old women who had no homes or money or food. Should she run away that night? She had nowhere to go. The fire was out; it would defy her, smouldering and dying, as it often did. What *should* she do! 'Too bad! Too bad!' she grumbled, as the tears fell. 'I'm frightened! They've no right to frighten me so!'

Rat-tat-tat-tat-tat! sounded the auctioneer's mallet on the sitting-room wall. Rat-tat-tat! Rat-tat-tat! The Old Lady's strong wrist never tired. It was the wrist of one who would mercilessly live for ever. 'But *my* wrist's *weak*! I can hardly lift it. See?' She held aloft her hand, which showed stumpy fingers spreading almost directly from a thick wrist. 'I couldn't do anything with that! Sometimes I think I haven't got an ounce of strength left in my body. I don't bleed, you know, if I cut myself. I keep going by will. If once I lost my will, I should fall down. They'd send me away. I don't know *what* would happen to me. The workhouse, I suppose. Or worse; the Morgue, whatever that is.'

Rat-tat-tat! Rat-tat-tat! She could hear her mother calling. 'I haven't the strength to go. I'm very ill, with my veins and back. I really need to be in bed. Yet I'm pursued and tortured from day to night. And at night, if I sleep, I dream. Only I never sleep. She says *she* dreams. It's my belief she doesn't tell the truth. Oh, how wicked she is!'

At last the knocking and shouting grew so insistent that she dragged herself along the passage into the front room, knowing that her mother would at once see that she had been crying. She could not even take the trouble to wipe the tears from her cheeks, so that when she entered the stuffy, over-heated room they dried at once and began to tickle.

'I wondered if you'd been taken ill,' said The Old Lady in a severe tone although immediately she had spoken she smiled with both present and retrospective pleasure at sight of the tears.

'I *am* ill,' replied Muriel. 'Anybody else would be in bed.'

'If you're ill, you'd better be sent away,' said The Old Lady. 'For I can't have anybody who's ill. I'm too old. But where you could go I don't know. I can't think anybody would want to have you. You wouldn't like the workhouse. It smells of carbolic and dirty clothes. You wouldn't like *that*. But you haven't the money to pay, and I don't think Letitia would help you at all. So you'd better feel better soon. If we're going out to lunch tomorrow with dear Farringdon I must have a bath tonight and you must find me some clean clothes to wear. Is the kitchen boiler nice and hot?'

Despair crushed Muriel. Her mother must have known by means of a devil's whisper that the kitchen fire was out. Probably the same devil had first put out the fire with his dry, sooty black hands. He worked incessantly to tease her. The tears began to roll again from her eyes. She turned away, saying very bitterly over her shoulder:

'You shall have your bath. You shall have your clean things. It doesn't matter to you if I'm dying—as I am.'

She heard her mother laugh, with a pleased, low, rasping chuckle.

'What a temper you have, dear Muriel! A terrible jealous temper.'

'I haven't.'

'Oh, yes. It's growing worse. Now Farringdon was always sweet-tempered. He's loved me dearly from a child.'

'He showed that, by running away, I suppose——'

'That was his father. A cruel man. He was always hard on my baby. He said he was wild. You see how thoughtful he is now. Oh, what a change! His coming's made me happy, dear. It's completed my life. I may not be with you much longer——'

'You might try living with him in the house at the corner——'

'That splendid house! Too big for us, I fear. But wasn't it kind of him!'

Muriel, sickened by her mother's false tone, choked back the accusations which rushed angrily to her mind and tongue. She tried in turn to be archly insincere.

'Wasn't it!' she exclaimed. 'It wouldn't *cost* us a great deal, I'm sure. Only every penny we've got!'

'Miau-wow!' carolled The Old Lady. 'You're very like a cat, Muriel, with your rough tongue. You're spiteful!'

'I should look under your bed every night,' said Muriel. 'He's after something.'

'Only love and tenderness, dear. You can tell, by the way he looks at me.'

'We'll see if you say that in a month's time. I must light the kitchen fire. It takes me all my strength to do the work of this house; so I've no time to waste on fine words and loving glances. He's too much like a bearded pard for me——'

'A what, my dear?' asked The Old Lady, in a frail voice.

'A wolf! A wolf!' cried Muriel. 'Don't you know what *that* is?'

She fairly ran from the room, slamming the door after her. When she had gone the old lady stooped, opened the door of the fireside coal box, put in a bare hand, and threw a great lump of coal upon the fire. She then clapped both hands together, and sat back in her chair. Her silent, secret laughter shook her body. She thought cynically, but with fond sentimentality and whirls of passionate affection, of Farringdon; cynically, but without sentiment or affection, of Muriel. Muriel was cantankerous, quite silly at times; Farringdon pleased her. He pleased her very much. He was her only son. She loved him. And as she thought thus of her children she passed quite suddenly into dream-filled sleep.

viii

Farringdon, having dined critically and ill in the smart, deserted, half-lit hotel dining-room, went up to his smart, claret-coloured, mechanically-furnished bedroom, and switched on the electric fire. Now that the curtains were drawn, and the firelight set everything in a glow, the room, if small, was agreeable. He might be comfortable enough here. The bed had been prepared for the night. In the middle of it a small mound showed that an earthenware hot-water bottle had already been placed within. Good. But the bottle should not have been put into the bed for another hour.

He opened the pigskin case, which had been left locked; and took out, first of all, the half-dozen cheap editions which he had bought for the solace of lonely hours. These books he set aside on a small table near the fire. The armchair was much too small for his comfort. The whole room was much too small for his comfort.

'No matter!' said Farringdon, aloud. He had business on hand.

Now for the labels in his pyjamas. From his pocket he produced a pair of folding scissors, and with their sharp points he nipped the makers' names from everything he had bought. Minute needle-holes were left in the material; but after rubbing these with his finger he thought they ceased to be obvious, and gathered every label and every tiny fragment of cotton into one of the hotel envelopes. Just so did the Sherlock Holmes—one remembered—gather together his clues! But, alas for Mr. Sherlock Holmes, there was a coal fire in the smoking-room downstairs, in which everything would burn.

Meanwhile, looking back upon his day, he was content. He heard the sea thudding along the beach like incessant heavy gunfire. He pictured his mother and sister in the villa to the west of the town. He remembered the flat near Regent's Park, where Thelma, no doubt, was sewing in the kitchen. It did not seem to him that anybody in his immediate world could compare with himself in adroitness. And he felt sure that he knew to a hairbreadth the arrangement of his mother's house.

'Yes,' yawned F. R. 'I've done well. It's been a good day.'

He picked up one of his books, had a final drink at the bar, burned the labels which had been in his clothes, and settled in the smoking-room—slightly annoyed by two sighing, coughing elderly and most superior commercial travellers who seemed to be making up their orders at neighbouring desks—for a quiet read. Presently his long legs moved, the knees came high, higher than his head, his head slipped sideways, and he forgot everything. Expression gone from his sleeping face, he looked from a distance exactly like a trustworthy man. To an eye brought nearer still, he would have seemed forever the boy who, forty years ago, gaily breasted the sea winds and with his friends of that time played the superb, dangerous games of shipwreck, smuggling, and piracy.

Nine

THE MOTHER

IF LETITIA HAD been asked to describe herself she would have been aghast. What a question! 'Why, I'm nothing but a walking muddle. At fifty-three one's cautious about *most* things, even possible enemies; but oneself! Quite floored!' Nor, in saying this, would she have been insincere. Her interest was in others. She had always been incapable of self-analysis. And she was seriously indifferent to her own importance. In fact, a completely pre-modern type.

Waking, therefore, at her regular hour after the tumult of Christine's party, she began the day, not by thinking of her waistline or her wrinkles or any peevish discontents, but with bland generalised pleasure in the obvious happiness of all the guests. The party had been a success. Christine, who certainly would lie late this morning, had shown as much before yawning her way triumphantly to bed a few hours ago. Without wasting words, she had pressed her cheek to Letitia's and patted her mother twice upon the shoulder. Then with a smiling nod, she had departed, without thought leaving the ruins of the evening to be cleared by others.

'Most gratifying!' Letitia had said to Monty, with consuming laughter. He had added the adaptation of an historic phrase:

'A double pat, that said everything, and will probably set you dreaming.'

To herself, Letitia had thought:

'Excited. Happy. Heartwhole. I wonder who gave her the necklace. Darling!'

This morning she still wondered who had given the necklace. She hoped it was not Cedric Martin. Cedric's eyes were too close together. He had immense self-assurance, and would go as far as he was allowed to do in both conduct and career. A hatchet-sharp but fundamentally vile mind. Would Christine know all this? Certainly! Besides, he was mean. No, it wasn't Cedric. Was it Justin Greer? Justin, the shy, speechless boy of uncertain talent? Not unlikely. How amusing if his timidity had roused the mother in her adamantine Christine! Amusing and touching! Wonderful, Christine!

But, as daylight grew, Letitia had less pleasant thoughts. Those three wretched children needed her help. Yet none of them, except perhaps Mark, would accept her judgment. Terrible!

What *was* that judgment? Julian to go back to America; Stephanie to go back to Mark; Mark to abandon pride and career, and stay uxoriously at home? If she delivered it, all three romantics would detest her. Well, then, Stephanie and Julian to bolt together; Mark to divorce Stephanie and re-marry—some steady girl? Much nastiness, and an eternally broken family. In six months, when the consequences were apparent, all three realists would blame her for vicious immorality.

Was she vicious? What were *they*? They couldn't think straight about their own actions.

She knew this, that Stephanie had slept alone. Mark, failing to find his wife, had returned, rather agitatedly self-possessed, to herself.

'Stephanie?'

'Mark, dear; don't stay. Lunch with me somewhere. A restaurant. Yes. Oh, wherever—yes, the Café d'Azur; splendid. I can't explain anything tonight, you see——' She had made a gesture referring him to the crowd.

He'd said: 'Something serious?' She had known that he felt suffocated with alarm.

'I don't think so, if—— But meet me. Try not to worry about anything——'

'What a phrase! From *you*!'

'I know . . . I'm idiotic . . . Save it until we've talked.'

'Where is she?'

'I hope, in your room.'

'Here?' He had taken a moment to grasp that. Then: 'Any good my seeing her? Of course, I knew she was ecstatically bored——'

'No good at all. Far from bored, darling! Wait till tomorrow.'

Even then, less precipitate than Julian, he had remained for a time, dancing once with Christine, mixing with the others. perhaps hoping in spite of everything that Stephanie would reappear in changed or at least directly challengeable mood. His pride was less petulant than Julian's where Julian could sulk and torture and affront, Mark had Monty's self control. He did not, as Letitia completely understood, feel less deeply On the contrary.

So she had Mark before her. Was it to be a meeting of half truths Of kites on his side, and effronteries or abominable discretions on hers Candours? Protests? Exasperations? What was she to say? Not so much *what* she said, as *how* she said it. As usual. People would take any criticism of themselves, if it were given lightly, affectionately, without contempt. The needed to know that they were loved. But there must be neither accusation nor blame. Self-esteem would not stand them. How, without treacher or impertinence, did one invade the very heart of married life?

It was frightful! Letitia felt she could not bear to stay in bed, or b inactive, for an instant longer. She was tempted to rouse Monty, pack bag, and fly with him to Lhasa, like a comically guilty pair in a play b Gabriel. Why? To escape from the stuffiness of rebellious young wive and lovers. Yes, stuffiness! They stifled her! She threw aside the bedclothes and jumped out of bed.

Monty slept. A moment passed. She bent over him, listening to almost inaudible breathing. Seen thus, relaxed, his face was that of a man nobly free from evil. A man dead. She shivered, imagining him lost to her for ever, herself uncompanioned for the rest of her life. She could not disturb him.

ii

Letitia was habitually punctual. It was expected of her. But punctual as she was for her lunch with Mark, she found him waiting.

On the previous night he had been clear-headed enough to name their quietest restaurant, where one might eat without pseudo-Gipsy music, the cacophony of cultured Englishwoman's voices, and exclamatory raids from quasi-friends. The Café d'Azur was in a turning between Regent Street and Bond Street. It was well warmed, costly, and not quite luxurious enough to tickle the ultra-smart. Apart from the costliness, thought Letitia, Mark had chosen well. Even the costliness, for this occasion, did not altogether displease her. At least he didn't lunch his mother penuriously!

Her first impression was: He's slept! That's good! But immediately afterwards she knew that she had been too facile. His hands were steady, and he was quite normally well-brushed; but his face had the shadowed pallor of troubled thought. There was burning darkness at the back of his eyes.

'Well, Mother.' He took her arm, and led her the length of the grey carpeted room. They sat side by side, both facing the entrance, but a good deal hidden by a big vase of scentless flowers and the gold and blue shaded table lamp which shone only upon the intricately patterned blue and yellow cloth. When they had ordered, he began at once: 'You told me not to alarm myself——'

'The stupid thing one could beat oneself for saying——'

'Take my alarm away. Or confirm it.'

'You certainly don't wish me to confirm it.'

'Must you?' He was very still.

'No!' She was perhaps over-emphatic. 'No! I can't do anything, except say what I think *you* might do.'

'There's something I can do, then?' He thanked the waiter for bringing their aperitifs; but neither he nor Letitia touched a glass. 'Surely *that's* hopeful?'

'I think so. I didn't want you to try and see her last night, because——'

'It's another man?'

'Because she was very much upset. I think it's primarily discontent.'

He leaned back in their seat, thinking. Then he said:

'Discontent. I realise that. But when I've tried to cure it, I've failed. Perhaps I've tried wrongly.'

'Mark! She *is*—to you—worth all the trouble in the world, isn't she?'

'The last ounce.' His tone left no doubt in Letitia's mind. Well, it was something. It was a great deal. Where else did they go?

'I'm thankful. Of course you're right.'

'I've often wanted to wring her neck.'

'Naturally. Most understandable. But you'd never hear the last of it.'

He was smiling; but he slightly shook his head.

'Oh, it hasn't been quite what you suppose,' said he.

'I suppose nothing but good of you both,' answered Letitia, calmly. 'I know you're not absolutely crass. Perhaps you're too modest. Elastic. I think she loves you dearly, with great pride; but at times sympathy and patience are intolerable to a young wife. She'd prefer injustice. One can fight injustice.'

'She could fight my election,' suggested Mark. Letitia, for all her lambent maternal regard, caught a glimpse of his imaginative limits. He was unaware of them. Those of others are always more apparent than our own.

'Well,' she demurred. 'With no benefit to herself.'

'Not directly, I agree; but surely——'

'Mark, Queen Victoria's dead. In some ways I'm sorry; but bear it in mind. Stephanie's very young; not tremendously experienced. She's had this overwhelming love for you. Now she's—not lost it, but found it insufficient. An awful misery. She's reached the point of throwing in her hand. Cutting her losses. In fact, running away.'

'From me?'

'From what she feels can't be borne another hour.'

'Oh!' He had been taken aback by these new aspects of something which he had long pondered; and as Letitia saw that he might grow indignant she softened her blow by making it less direct.

'From *every* surrounding.'

Mark at once felt better.

'Do you mean the flat? I see. It's small.'

'Worse than small, Mark. It's like solitary confinement.'

'Stephanie chose it herself,' he said. 'Is it the flat, and boredom, only?'

Perhaps because she was unconsciously ruffled by his male indifference to a wife's screaming hatred of imprisonment, or distracted by some old, uncharted memory, Letitia replied with too little care.

'Probably a good deal more than that. Being alone. Being worked up. Perhaps the bad advice of friends. You know how they——'

'Friends!' He reddened and grew arrogant. This was a shock to Letitia She realised, for the first time, how bitterly he despised Stephanie's friends hangers-on of the arts, who drank and trooped and sniggered at all the decorums. Not appreciating Stephanie's need of excitement and applause and her pathetic, puzzled loyalty to old associates, he would measure her by this contempt. That would be fatal. It would double the barrier between two ardent prides. 'Does she discuss our affairs with *that* crew?'

The meaning was plain! If Stephanie betrays my privacy to such vulga sensationalists, she can go. I'll have no more of her!

Letitia read all this, blamed herself for indiscretion, and like a docto who cures hysteria with a slap, interrupted his anger by a warning cry:

'No, no, no! Of course not! Mark! You know perfectly well that Stephanie doesn't discuss; she suffers.. Her feelings grow unbearable. They're unbearable now. To me, she appears merely desperate.'

Mark again recovered; but, as his next speech showed, Stephanie was still linked in his mind with those others. He said:

'She's a sensationalist. They're all sensationalists. *All* unreal. Pretentious humbugs. Would it do any good, d'you think, if I turned melodramatic, and beat my breast?'

'Indeed, no! You confound her with a tail she can't escape. It's not clowning she needs, but time to think, to *settle*. If all her feelings for the next six months could be crowded into a day, and the accumulated hysteria exploded with a pop, she'd be thankfully in your arms tomorrow.'

He laughed a little, annoyance mingling with his amusement.

'What a wonderful dream! We can't just stop living for six months. It's like Tom Sawyer wanting to "die temporalily." Things go *on*.'

'But they needn't go on getting worse,' said Letitia.

Mark remained silent for several moments. She could see almost without looking at him, that he was learning quickly, and thinking of much beside what they had said.

'Is Julian involved in this?' he suddenly asked.

Letitia could hardly check a movement of consternation.

'Oh, I don't think you need fear *any* other man,' she said, quickly. 'Except, perhaps, as a means of escape.'

'But Julian in the offing?' suggested Mark. 'Like me; *un*like me. Perhaps a better second choice? They're popular. Familiar, decent, inscrutably exciting: what?'

She was horrified by his analysis. When spoken, it seemed all edge, without substance. Yet it was a part of what she herself had once, ages ago in the life of sensation, thought possible. Had this uncovered long-standing jealousy of Julian?

'*No* other man,' she nevertheless insisted. She had already been made wise by some of those unseen mental adjustments which she had wanted Stephanie to crowd into a few hours.

As if he had not heard, Mark reflected aloud:

'I wondered why he was here. Why *is* he here? Is America exhausted? When he avoided me last night I thought—"Hullo! Why the hangdog hostility!" He's not as a rule hostile. Never so crude. Never so hangdog.'

'He's hostile to us all. He knows it's wrong.'

'Because of Stephanie?' asked Mark. 'It's the same sort of hostility as hers.'

'Yes.' Letitia had been warned by her shock that she must keep near the truth. He had penetration. His pride was alert. 'I think it is. No, I'm sure it is.'

Mark had drawn a quick breath. He was staring before him.

'Not pleasant,' he exclaimed. 'I've been going on, quite——. Thinking she was with me. Of course she wasn't. I've even thought she might be going to have a child, and didn't know what to do about it.'

'It might be so,' said Letitia. 'That might help. But she hasn't said anything to suggest it.'

'She mightn't know,' observed Mark, coolly. 'She's as ignorant as a booby.'

Letitia felt an inward shiver at his tone.

'If you speak *to* her with that detachment,' she said, 'she may well be doubtful.'

He turned with his old affectionate smile.

'What *am* I to do?' he asked.

Letitia, who had been in doubt until that instant, spoke as if she had long since decided what advice to give.

'What would you think of this? Go straight to the house after lunch. Be nice to the old people, who'll be very tired after the party. Wait for Stephanie. When she comes, be as natural as you can——'

'I was, last night——'

'You were, last night. She couldn't be; there was a reason. To-day she'll need most particularly to feel you love her. I know this. Ask her point-blank if she feels like an election-campaigner——'

'One minute. Where will you be?'

'——In the Liberal interest. (I'm going to see Aunt Constance.) Be a little Liberal. If she says "yes", suggest dinner a hundred miles away, and take her off at once. *Never* ask her to go back to the flat. Refuse to go, yourself. Say you want a house with plenty of room for the children. That will make her jump. If she says "no", be unsurprised, acquiescent. Tell her you're ready to give up the campaign.'

'But I'm not, Mother!'

'Isn't that one of her troubles?'

He looked puzzled. 'Is it?'

'You'll find out. You're forcing the pace, remember. If she wants to quarrel, quarrel. Be as angry as you feel. Reproach her. Say you've relied on her—as you have. Risk the irrevocable. It won't, in a quarrel, be *quite* irrevocable; it could only be that if the emotion were one-sided.'

'It's never been one-sided,' he interrupted, very urgently.

'At any rate, prove it. Don't be patient. Give her something to fight. And leave her. Walk out on her, so that she knows the next move's with her. Give her time to settle. She can stay with us as long as she likes. That will be till Christine's interest drives her away.'

He whistled.

'You're drastic. In any case, Christine's a hard little beast.'

'No. Only composed. And inquiring. I'm only just beginning to see that she's sagacious. But to Stephanie she seems like a policewoman. She makes Stephanie feel splashy. Stephanie hates feeling splashy. She wants the reassurance of ardent love.'

'I thought she had it.'

'I think she has, and that she knows it. The fact that she's staying at all means that she needs *us*.'

'Or Julian?'

'My dear boy, if she'd wanted Julian, she'd have run away with him already.'

She saw Mark jump. He understood what his danger had been. What risks one ran by being patient but logical! He said:

'You think she wants me. But she's had me. Do you imagine I've neglected her?'

'No.'

'That I've become a Victorian husband? That I've been pedantic? Humiliated her? Been a coward? In fact that I'm somehow to blame for the whole business?'

Letitia could not help laughing.

'All those things had occurred to me. I don't say they're true, of course.'

'Well!' exclaimed Mark, as if something unpleasant had fallen from the sky. He drank his aperitif, looking down. He rubbed his chin. He turned his head so as to see, very accusingly, his mother's face. Some colour had returned to his cheeks, which had grown ashen at the reference to Julian. He said: 'All this time you're on *her* side!'

Letitia, with a shaken head, made no other answer. She knew he was wounded, but she met his glance very candidly; and no son, not even Julian, who had his own processes of judgment, could have doubted her love for him or her confidence in his determination to do right. It was so smiling, and so loving an expression, indeed, that Mark for an instant wished his wife had his mother's temper, and not her own. He did not wish this for more than an instant, however; for his mind broke violently from Letitia to picture Stephanie with rapture in her floundering immaturity.

Letitia, now rather exhausted, in turn drank her aperitif. It was time. She had done her best. She had given him hope, fear, some glimpse of possible shortcoming, and the impulse to fight for his wife's love. But she had been left, in turn, needing the comfort of love.

iii

Gabriel Wilton, at half-past two, was nearly ready for lunch.

He was striding about the study with his hands behind his back, bending far forward, and looking like Felix the Cat. The rich crimson rugs on the floor were so thick as to silence every step he took in his superb slippers. Upon the walls around him were the coloured and gilded covers of four thousand books. Upon his desk was a sheet of blank paper. It represented his work since nine o'clock that morning, when he had barricaded the study in order to note in peace the early entrances and speeches of characters in a comedy about a hypocrite.

This comedy had been commissioned over dinner the previous night, before witnesses, by Roderick Gore. Gore, grumbling about his inability to get anything but tepid domestic plays from modern dramatists, had said: 'You, Gabriel: why do *you* never write me a play?' Gabriel had replied: 'I? I should never presume to write a play for that profile.' Roderick had said: 'There's something *behind* that profile, my boy! Come now; write me a *real* play!' . . .

Gabriel had stung him by saying he'd never dare to produce a new play on a seventeenth-century theme. Gore, thus challenged, had called upon the company to note his promise to do so. He had written it down, and the rest had added their solemn convivial signatures. Gore, thus adroitly cornered, would get what was coming to him. When he read the play, he would be in a panic. He would protest. He would try to wriggle out of his promise. A row would follow. Gabriel enjoyed rows, with other men; not with women. He especially enjoyed humiliating actor-managers, whom he considered entirely preposterous.

By a master-stroke, he had landed Roderick with a part of which every shade could be drawn from Roderick himself. He knew Roderick. He had known two of Roderick's ex-mistresses, both of them malicious to the core. His 'sense' of Roderick was perfect. And yet Roderick should have his final curtain—showing the hypocrite's triumph over the Englishman's shibboleths, honour, decency, and order. Well, wasn't that all divinely involved in the dramatist's art? 'Hee-hee-hee!' laughed Gabriel, fluttering his fingers behind him. What was so good was that, behind his adored profile, Roderick was self-protective enough to see how unmistakably, if he rejected the play, a character-actor could impersonate him!

That, of course, would be a delicious end to the episode! 'Hee-hee-hee!' Let him turn it down, at his peril! He'd be the laugh of inner, civilised London; and all the smart semi-wits outside that circle would strain thereafter to see a joke which their masters had relished. They would pretend, being fastidiously stupid, to revel in it. For fear of being thought less stupid than they were. . . .

Much of Gabriel's morning had been spent in an armchair by the fire, not reading or sleeping, or planning his comedy about Roderick, but reflecting and dreaming. And the subjects of his reverie had been two women—his wife, and Letitia. He believed that even men who ranted in public about society and usury and the oppressed common people were in private wholly concerned with the women they loved and the inconvenient women whom they wished in Jericho. And it was interesting to Gabriel to consider that a man had as many standards of value—and virtue—as he had shirts, or socks. But then Gabriel was always enchanted by peculiarities, especially his own peculiarities, and never hesitated to carry memory and imagination to their limits. He was called a cynic; he considered himself a realist. For this reason his thoughts of Constance, which seemed to him both natural and curious, would have seemed only cruel to another person.

Now, having decided that he needed lunch, Gabriel unclasped his hands and prepared to leave his sanctuary from domestic persecution. He knew that he would at once come face to face with Constance. He did not wish to come face to face with Constance. It would be a great strain to his nerves, especially as he would have to check his tongue whenever he spoke to her. But one of the penalties of marriage was that one came face to face with one's wife several times a day. Another was that one had to check one's tongue even in sleep, when it was most dangerous.

He should never have married. Single, he would have been a rich man and a free man. His left hand could have known what his right did. His desk and privacy would have been his own, his flirtations of no consequence, his domestic staff adoring, and his house untenanted by an ever-active reproach. In other words, Constance, in her ubiquitousness, was a bit thick!

His pain, he was persuaded, grew a little worse each day, stabbing at his self-control. Sometimes it was acute. It made him sweat. In private, he screamed. He was afraid. But these devils would not operate. Instead, they took X-ray photographs, and had mysterious consultations, and used soothing words, laughing indulgently when he accused them of deceiving him, battening on him, knowing nothing whatever about their job . . .

'Well, I'm in pain,' thought Gabriel. 'Among these ghastly convolutions inside me there's gravel or stone that ought to come away and doesn't. If they'd cut it out, and sew me up again, another would form. But I should have three or six months free from pain. But then, once I'm cut, I sink under the anæsthetic. My heart stops. I get half-a-column in *The Times* and half-an-inch in the picture papers. "Curtain for Dramatist" or "Wrote Plays: Dead". Once I were dead, I should think no more of Letitia. Oh, God! I don't *want* to be able to think no more of Letitia!'

It was a pity he should have spoken that name aloud, as if he quietly sneezed just at the moment of his encounter with Constance. For Constance was coming, with slightly forced vivacity, down the stairs to the dining-room; and although her smile did not vanish at the sound of her friend's name it grew a little stiff.

'Well, Constance,' began Gabriel, piloting her with mock respect into the dining-room; 'how was the rehearsal? P. B.? Your boy friend there? How's Cress? Cross? And my beloved Valentine, damn his eyes! Is *he* well? How I hope he's as sick as a dog!' As he spoke his own eyes were darting like a pair of toads' tongues at the dishes upon the table, and at the wooden-faced parlourmaid, Howard, who was so different in every respect from Ruth; in particular so dull, so untinged and quicksilvered by contact with Letitia. Ugly woman! You felt she was always chewing! What was for lunch? Something he could eat? Whatever it was, he would suffer for it. He saw his infernal jug of barley water. He muttered: " "And *aye* we'll taste the barley bree!" Well, that's a lie, to begin with; it's insipid to excess!'

Constance replied with stagey brightness to his inquiries.

'Oh, we're getting on; murdering the lines nicely. No, of course Ronald wasn't there. *Much* too busy! He's had a new play accepted by Roderick; so he's off to see *him* this morning.'

Gabriel, conscious of a responsive twinge, read the malice in her tone. She knew nothing of his last night's triumph. She meant that Roderick Gore, the man with the profile, was hard to please. In Gabriel's case, too hard. The fool! To match *her* malice with *his*! So she was running that boy as his more successful younger rival! Ridiculous! He said calmly:

'Hm. I suppose Roderick's re-writing his own part.'

'No, darling; casting for early production.'

'Not too sanguine about it, then, because he begged *me* to write him a play last night. Urgently. He insisted on commissioning it.'

'Really? Oho!' Her face had grown radiant with surprise and pleasure. She was still proud of him, the sentimental fool! 'Well, *that's* pretty good, isn't it?'

'Is it?' He said nothing of the comic scene at dinner. She'd miss the finesse in her joy at his continuing success. Besides, she'd blab. Roderick, hearing all about it from his spies, would cry off privately tomorrow. 'Not too good for Ronald's hopes of a run. I've been working hard on it all the morning.'

What a farce it was to talk like this! When he'd spent the time thinking of Letitia, and detesting Constance! It would be crueller to speak the truth. More effective.

'It'll be a distraction for you, darling!' cried Constance, masked in liquid powder. 'I wish you didn't dislike poor Ronald so much. Seen kindly, he'd amuse you.'

'He *does* amuse me. But not enough. He's like a poor *carte de visite* of myself at his age. No surprises. Nothing. Now, Valentine's dislikeable; and I dislike him. I *like* disliking him. He *doesn't* amuse me.'

'But you're not jealous of *him*, Gabriel,' cried Constance.

'As a man, yes,' handsomely owned Gabriel. 'He's younger than I am. Stronger. Ruder. He's got fine padded shoulders. He can glower.'

'Not as *you* can!' declared Constance, with derisive flattery.

'My frown's due to preoccupation,' said Gabriel. 'His to headache. He tries to understand all the words he can't spell. By the way, what *is* this?' He held up on his fork a piece of the meat provided for his lunch.

Constance was immediately flurried. She was always defensive about her housekeeping, to which she gave anxious incompetence. Of course— as Gabriel had implied—Letitia managed better. Of course, Letitia was better in every way than herself. Wiser, slyer, more competent! A new delight. It would be funny to see now what she said to a few of Gabriel's old amours! Hateful creature! Oh, what unjust bitterness to a beloved friend! Constance hated herself for the bitterness. It was shaming to her. Yes, but what *was* the truth? She was mad with jealousy!

'Isn't it nice, dear? It's chicken. Or should be.'

'It's delicious,' said Gabriel, having played his trick.

'Oho!' laughed Constance, in relief. 'You terrified me. I thought you were determined to be characteristic!'

'Wasn't I?' asked Gabriel, grimacing over his barley water.

'At any rate I'm glad to have got something you like. Are you going out after lunch?'

'I ought to rest,' answered Gabriel, wearily. 'Why?'

'I thought I'd go and see . . . Letitia.' How did he look? Evil! The cad! The adorable cad! 'I'm consumed with curiosity about those children. I want to know why Julian's back.'

'Isn't it obvious?'

'What, Christine's birthday? They've always been devoted——'

'My good idiot!' snarled Gabriel, turned almost sick by severe pain. 'Didn't you *look* at Letitia?'

Constance, recollecting Howard's presence, smiled without replying. Gabriel's pain subsided. Both continued to eat in silence, consciously holding their tongues, with expressions of long-suffering.

At that moment they heard the front door-bell ring; and Howard, deserting her place near the sideboard, went to answer the door. Husband and wife exchanged glances of inquiry and confessed ignorance.

'What did you mean?' asked Constance, under her breath. She abandoned long-suffering as useless. It gratified him too much. 'Be quick!'

'No time. No time,' protested Gabriel, waving his fingers.

He was right; for as he spoke Howard opened the door again, and Letitia appeared. Gabriel jumped up, flung down his napkin, gave her both his hands. Under his dark skin there was a dull flush of colour. Constance, more relieved than he, if less overjoyed, was close behind. Their welcome was the welcome of old affection, as Howard had known it would be. Howard herself, usually so dour, stood in the background, seeing with content that she had acted rightly in giving them this dramatic surprise. She watched her master and mistress draw Letitia to the table, and heard them beg her to join them. When she refused, they resumed their meal without ceremony.

'Though I should have liked you to taste the chicken, because Gabriel, apparently, can *eat* it!' exclaimed Constance, spicing with unconscious pathos her jeer at the epicure. 'You may find it incredible.'

'You always cry stinking fish, darling!' cried Gabriel, beaming, however, at Letitia across the table. 'Letitia wouldn't expect me to praise ill-cooked meat and islands of greenstuff.'

'She doesn't know such things exist!' cried Constance, recklessly. Then, bending nearer, she whispered: 'Howard's gone. Out of the room, I mean. What a relief! Letitia, I was coming to see you. Darling, we're spiteful with curiosity. Both! A moment ago, I ventured one little obvious remark; and Gabriel was down my throat like a scorpion——'

'Ignore her, Letitia! Listen to me! *Look* at me, darling!'

'It appears I missed something, dearest. One can't, of course——'

'Sh!' hissed Gabriel. A tremendous 'Sh!' like the hiss of a first-night audience.

Letitia said:

'I've come into a cockatrice's nest!'

Howard re-entered the room, with humdrum, easily-digested pudding for Gabriel, and a delicious pancake for Constance.

'An agapemone, Letitia,' continued Gabriel. 'Witness the tapioca. But we congratulate you on the party, and want to know about *everything*. In fact our visit was such a stimulant that we'd both resolved to come and see you again this afternoon——'

'*I* was resolved. Gabriel felt he ought to rest——'

'I was coming by myself——'

'Over my dead body, dearest.'

They had both spoken so quickly that Letitia had been unable to interject

any reply whatever; and now that Howard had again withdrawn, she had
no protection against two who were determined to ransack her cupboards
for skeletons. They were both ravenous ghouls! All the same, she observed
that behind Constance's vivacity lay gloom and doubt, and that behind
Gabriel's kindness was glittering excitement as well as a new warmth which
held embarrassing flickers of passion.

'I'm glad you *didn't* come,' she said. 'Because I said at home that I
was lunching with you——'

'You'd be unconscious by now!' declared Constance. 'If you *had* been!'

'Sh!' from Gabriel. 'With *whom* did you lunch?'

'With Mark.'

'Oh, *is* she leaving him?' demanded the impatient Constance. 'Be
quiet, Gabriel: I can't rest until I know. I was always sure it couldn't last,
darling! She so *outrée*, and he so staid . . .'

'I lied to the old people. They're staying until Wednesday. Christine,
fortunately, wasn't up——'

'Yes, but little Forget-me-not!' cried Constance. 'Christine and the
Ancients are no more than nice red herrings.'

'They're absolutely central in our house!' laughed Letitia. She *could*
not discuss family affairs with the glibness expected at this table. 'I devote
myself to them. Well, now, to answer your question, I can't suppose
Stephanie will ever leave Mark. Why should she? Mark's going to stand
for Parliament as a Liberal——'

'Yes, why a Liberal?' asked Gabriel. 'As well marry a corpse!'

'But what about Julian?' demanded Constance. 'Such a mysterious
stranger at the ball! So aloof! So unaware of our existence! Really, one's
curiosity was—do I mean titivated?——'

Letitia glanced at Gabriel, who had fallen back in his chair and was
observing her with the most sanguine delight and understanding. His
chin was upon his chest. His arms were stretched straight out, so that the
long hands rested quietly upon the table. His heavy brows did not conceal
his eyes, but heightened the ardour of their expression. She felt her heart
stir in response to that expression. She, too, leaned back in her chair, sighing
as she turned to the impatient Constance.

'I know nothing of Julian,' she answered. 'As you say, a mysterious
stranger. At least, a cross between a mysterious stranger and an early
Cinderella; for he fled before ten o'clock. Why he came, where he is, what
he's doing, are all a puzzle.'

'Strange,' said Gabriel, forgetting politics. 'He must have wings.'

'Unless he's in love,' added Constance, looking searchingly at Letitia,
whom she no longer trusted.

'Love gives the mind wings,' remarked Gabriel, with a little cruel movement of the shoulders. 'Constance knows,'

'It makes some men spit venom,' retorted Constance.

Letitia thought: I wish they wouldn't use me for their ricochets! I
that boy home? Has he seen her? Is he—extraordinary to think—*at thi*
very instant quarrelling with her? I'm dying of excitement.' She said, t
excuse her confusedness:

'What with birthdays and elections and old people, I need quiet. How are you, Gabriel?'

'He's better,' splashed Constance, with a nod and grimace of warning. 'He's writing a play for Roderick Gore. He's very pleased about that. We both are.'

'The pleasure's of different quality,' suggested Gabriel, in a tone of resignation.

'Mine's pure!' cried Constance, with a peal of laughter. 'How nice it is to see you, Letitia! One can't think ill of you to your face: you always make me happy. Though you're a little oblique, evasive, and obstructionist about your children. You always were. Defensive, I suppose.'

'It's because I'm so ignorant,' said Letitia.

'*I* shouldn't be. I should know too much!'

'How they'd hate you!' murmured Gabriel.

'I expect so.' Constance's brightness was clouded. Because she had been hurt, she dashed off after something else. 'I love Julian best. I always feel he'll either go on the films or commit a crime!'

'I wonder what crime?' asked Letitia, smiling, thankful that Constance had been distracted from hotter pursuit of Stephanie. 'His most probable crime will be inaction.'

'Profound!' ejaculated Gabriel. 'Profound!' He glowed with pleasure. His fingers hid his lips, which had suddenly trembled.

Letitia had not seen Gabriel's mouth before he covered it. She only saw Constance's agonized glance at him, of love, anger, misery. Though, upon what she knew, it was almost inexplicable, it struck her to the heart.

iv

Letitia, forcing herself to dawdle, in case she should be home too soon, stopped to look into a curiosity shop. It was full of ugly things, testifying to the empty ingenuity of those who make new and useless *objets d'art* in every generation; and she had a sudden glimpse of that perverted taste which, from vanity, is amused by outmoded monstrosities. Gabriel was not innocent of such humourless cruelty.

It seemed as though Constance and Gabriel could only endure each other as pincushions. Gabriel was like one of dark red velvet from which the pins, when they were withdrawn, are always rather rusted; Constance had been made of scraps of orange and scarlet satin, and was heavily embroidered in other bright colours. But the pins which Gabriel stuck in this pincushion never rusted. At heart, Constance was good and true. Was Gabriel?

He was ill, and in pain. He no longer loved Constance.

There shot through all Letitia's awareness the clear warning: He loves *me*. No wonder she's unhappy!

She turned away from the window of the curiosity shop, and began to walk homeward, glancing about her at drab women who looked as if they trailed, exhausted by life, from one unkempt home to another, and at the children who had come out of school and were dawdling in small knots, or running along, kicking sparks from the kerb with the metal tips upon their boot-heels, to tea and more noise in the back streets of London. Above their heads grey, smoke-dulled brickwork rose above the shop-fronts; along the road passed red omnibuses and vans of many hues; the air was acrid with the smells of the town.

Letitia was aware of these sounds and smells and the profusion of energy about her, and she was too familiar with them to be depressed anew by their continued presence; but she now walked faster. She was disquieted. This was not because it was a new experience to her to attract men, or because she had believed herself to be too old to be attractive to them. It was because, to her concern, she felt no displeasure at the thought of Gabriel's love. On the contrary, she was conscious of a lightened heart, almost a new vivacity in her limbs, which in spite of anxiety to know this afternoon's truth about Mark made the journey too short for her needs.

She had begun to go more slowly again when there were hurried steps behind her; a voice spoke her name; and she found Gabriel himself at her side.

He was a little breathless, and was forced to stop, half-smiling in deprecation of the signs of age, but greatly tried by recent haste. Compassion seized her. He had been running. It must be bad for him to run, to hurry. He ought not to do it. Poor boy! There was swollen pallor beneath his eyes; an agony in the eyes themselves . . .

'I . . . hoped . . . I might catch you,' was what he said. His fingers were quite naturally about her elbow; her elbow was in no way incommoded. Their shoulders had briefly touched. She saw his long lips parted, revealing the malicious teeth and that tongue upon which words seemed to receive a last caress before they sped forth to destroy.

'You *shouldn't* have run,' she reproached him.

'But, dammit, you . . . walk . . . like the wind. Hey, I'm breathless. I've had a long pursuit. I wanted to talk. No chance at home. And Constance . . . so . . . curious.' He began to laugh. 'There! I'm better! I could tell you a history of my devious paths. No more of that.' But he laughed again, with enjoyment of deceits successfully practised. 'Oh, I'm expert. I *have* to cheat Constance. My only chance of privacy. You understand?'

They walked on. He still lightly clasped her elbow, as if, being tired, he had need of support.

'You know,' continued Gabriel, 'I really *was* coming this afternoon. Constance saying that she was going put me off. One doesn't advantageously hunt in packs. On such an errand. I wanted to ask the questions *she* asked. But differently. She gives one's answers such *publicity*. Rather loud, I think. Is there anything I can do for you? That was my first question. You remember you wanted to ask me something else—this was it, wasn't it? Mark, Julian . . . I haven't forgotten . . . the other things you asked. They're less urgent.'

It was not strange that Letitia's mind should have changed in an hour towards those questions. Constance had confidants by the dozen, most

of them ladies richly stored with the private affairs of others. She used
secrets, without conscious treachery, as conversational gambits. However
lovingly, one was on guard with her. It had been so, in the past, with
Gabriel. But Letitia now believed something which gave him a kinder
place in her thoughts.

'It was about all three—Mark, Julian, Stephanie,' she finally admitted.
'But in a few days everything's in a new pattern. I don't think I need *ask*
you anything. I can *tell* you, if you like, what's happened.'

Gabriel caught at what she had said. Almost with eagerness, he
amplified it.

'That new pattern. Isn't it strange? All, at the moment, so frightening.
And then the fragments, the colours, the relations entirely altered. Fear's
gone; one's whole concern is different. It happens all the time. Personality's
the only constant. Very likely you don't believe in personality; the word's
become a vulgarism. In some moods—how many one has!—I don't, myself.
You say this Julian affair's solved?'

'It's far from being only Julian's affair——'

'My dear Letitia! All our affairs are involved and re-involved. We
can't stir hand or foot——'

'No, I meant that Julian was never the centre of it.'

'At one time you felt he was.'

She was forced to admit that this was true.

'I'd forgotten. Yes, I did. First I thought Julian, then Stephanie, now
Mark——'

Gabriel laughed.

'Yes. Yes. And why has it changed? Just through your own contacts.
You're a chameleon, Letitia, as we said. You know it. You now think
Mark's squared it up with that untidy minx——'

'Gabriel!'

'You must allow me my own judgment——'

'Who could dare not to?'

'Well, and so you're happy again? You've put it all right with your
lovely kindness?'

She was serious.

'No. I haven't. But I'm happier. I *want* the happy ending.'

He smiled broadly at the admission.

'Love's so unruly. We're ashamed of it,' he teased. 'Sometimes we
brazen it out, of course. When brazened, it sounds too much like the
farmyard. Isn't that so?'

'We're divided between now and eternity,' said Letitia.

'You, too? I'm for now. Let eternity hang!' cried Gabriel, who stood
nearest of them all to eternity. 'We've got rid of the old Christian metaphysic
of fear. Now it's each man for himelf. Darwin taught us that. Look what
it's done for the world. Especially, look abroad, where they're more easily
infatuated than we are.'

He touched his cheek against her shoulder. He had grown breathless
again at the beginning of his speech, and what followed had been spoken
with his old ridicule. 'Letitia, darling; I find my tongue runs away with

me. It's your influence. You've listened, I'm sure, to interminable confessions on Autumn days, in the concealing dusk. You know I'm a frightened
man. I needn't disguise it. I may have a week or six months to live. They
won't say. Every moment's joy's precious to me——'

'Gabriel,' murmured Letitia.

'You're sorry. You'll miss me.'

'I can't bear you even to say that.'

'Yet you didn't, until recently, like me? No, it's not a fair question.
No. No.'

She had stopped in the twilight-saddened street. Gabriel looked up,
looked at her, and then around him, and saw that they were at the end of a
familiar road. He exclaimed:

'You see? Everything's against me. I grow eloquent, and we're at your
door. With Mark, perhaps, waiting to blow a trumpet. The moment's past.
Letitia! Not now, but soon, will you lunch with *me*, as you did with Mark?
Alone? I'll bore you less than he did. But isn't my best way to your heart
a demand for help? Then I want your help as much as Mark or Julian can
do, I assure you.'

His face was very close to her own. The lines in it were like those of a
spider's web; but she did not see them. She saw only that he was smiling,
looking at her as if he would interpret thus her smallest reluctance to endure
his touch. But the smile was beautiful, and the searching glance free from
evil. His love was not disguised. When she, too, smiled, and gave him
her hand, he stooped and kissed her wrist. A moment later he had withdrawn
into the dusk, and she was alone, her heart quickened and tears in
her eyes.

Ten

TWO VISITS

i

THELMA HAD FINISHED the dress she had taken such a long time to make.
She had tried it on, arranging the bedroom mirror at every possible angle
to see the creases which, in spite of her pains, always appeared round the
shoulders of her frocks; and she had shaken her head, as usual, at unaccountable saggings and tightnesses elsewhere which no cobbling would remove.

'It is another failure,' she said, in her careful English. In this matter
she was, temperamentally, the artist. But the verdict, nevertheless, was
true. The dress was a failure.

It was as drab in colour as a grain-sack, and made of material chosen
only for its stoutness. It was suppose to fit closely, and it could not do so.
It looked too long; yet when she pinned up the hem she excessively displayed
her sturdy legs, which were of a shape to justify Victorian concealment.
It might be true that the dress would wear for ever; but all those others

which lay between white paper in the dressing-chest would do the same. They might rot; they could never be worn out.

Thelma's white face, being square and thick-skinned, was incapable of expressing the softer emotions. It could, and did, show the gloom into which she had sunk after seven days of lonely, industrious dressmaking. As she took off the dress, and stood, stumpily preoccupied, in her underclothes, she would have served excellently as model for a realistic painter. Her heavy figure, the dark room, the borrowed mahogany furniture, and her melancholy aspect could punningly have been entitled 'Brown Study'. But there was more in Thelma's heart and mind than brown. There was a scarcely perceptible flame, which, licking hungrily at patient courage, kindled it for action.

She knew too well what F. R. thought of her. An inelastic bore, whom he could insult and cheat and summon at will. The knowledge went far back into the past, and stung her with angry shame at former blindness. How unhappy she was! At first she had been fascinated, breathless, gladly a victim to Papa's anxious encouragement of the match. Later, she knew that Papa, aware of coming death, had merely determined to give her a new protector. He had been quite unscrupulous about Farringdon. Farringdon had been equally unscrupulous in his own designs. A battle of foxes! She, the supposed prize, had been no prize but a lovesick creature. She had clutchingly loved Farringdon, weeping heavily at night with jealousy lest some flimsier woman should snare him. And her tears and vows had been all too surely answered. . . .

That was over. She still wept at night; or, after their quarrels, drew him obstinately into her arms, fighting to conquer the preoccupied boredom of his response. At such times she had no dignity. Were there other women? She continued savagely to hate such imaginable women. But her fear of them was only physical; it was often joined with sick indifference. He was contemptible. And so, by day, she worried him to make his promised fortune. She thought he might do so if he would *stick* to something. But she knew he was too idle, too greatly infatuated with his own cleverness, to persist. When she was alone every hope died. This stolid mood of dullness, of conscious failure, gathered as into a reservoir of pain the tears which it would so exquisitely have relieved her to shed.

Having cast aside the new dress, she now thought she caught a gleam o sunshine across the roofs of neighbouring houses. The gleam prompted her to turn away, to wash with slow thoroughness, and to put the dress on again. At least it was new. It was respectable. It would make somebody see that she was a lady, perhaps? There was *something* wrong with it. But *what*? Frowning doubtfully, she did her hair afresh, put on a small brown velvet-trimmed hat resembling a meat pie, and a newly-mended pair of shoes which gave her broad feet room to breathe. There was no full-length mirror in the flat; she saw herself as a rule in the mirror-background of the dry cleaner's shop not far away. Her best handbag; her umbrella; it was not yet so cold that the absence of a coat would be remarked. She was going out.

'I am going *out*,' said Thelma to the absent Farringdon, hardly unclenching her set teeth. 'As I said to you, I should do, I am going to see the pretty sister. You understand? *That Letitia* whose photograph you carry. I shall give her news of her brother. She will *like* that.'

She did not smile. She was very excited, both angry and resentful; in no state to make a new friend. She walked along the sober street looking neither right nor left, but always ahead. Nobody took the smallest notice of her, or was even aware that she had passed.

ii

Thelma always travelled by omnibus. She was frightened to go down below the surface of the earth, for fear she might never return. She said to herself 'I need the sun. Without it I should die.' But the truth was that she feared suffocation. Besides, in an omnibus one hurried untouched through the streets. One saw those straggling crowds of the truly stupid from a slightly superior height. It was good to do such things. In England there were too many people. Though they were polite they were not interested in her. Nobody was interested in her. That, she said, was as she wished; one thus remained dignified, and entirely private. But the sense of mass indifference was oppressive.

She first of all took an omnibus to Oxford Circus. Then, after inquiry, she travelled by another omnibus past Hyde Park and into a region hitherto unexplored of this weariness of brick. The number of buildings was another cause of oppression; and when she reached her goal, the road of tall houses in which Letitia lived, courage had forsaken her. The houses were so grim, so much like the blank-faced police of nightmare, that they seemed already to ask her business, and what she carried in her bag and her gloves and her mind. They were the first to look superciliously at her new dress, pointing out that it was obviously home-made, creased at the shoulders, and too short in front and too long behind. They noticed the rubbed sides of her newly-mended shoes. As if they were too remote to hear her replies, they exchanged cold glances with one another, full of meaning and proud callousness, which heightened the sound of her beating heart and made her over-warm. She tried to walk upon tiptoe; but her knees were so clumsy and her feet so much like lead that she clattered as if she wore clogs.

These bitter sensations caused Thelma to press her lips very tightly together in an expression emphasizing what F. R. called her likeness to a white toad. They made her draw her arms close, so that her shoulders were raised and rather hunched. She began to look like that anomaly, a stout cripple. And it was in this semblance that she forced herself to mount the steps of the Bolderos' house and, swallowing heavily, to ring the bell.

There was a dead silence. She could not keep her feet quite still. She was stubborn, angry, unhappy. And at the sight of Ruth, whose fresh colour and prim little mouth were a reproachful challenge to middle-age for having grown slack, she was at her worst, a foreign-seeming, awkwardly ugly woman with a bad manner. She knew it. Her voice grew harsh, and her tone rude, in sympathy with her appearance.

'I want to see Mrs Boldero,' said Thelma, as resentfully as she might have done if boys belonging to Mrs Boldero had thrown stones at her pug-dog.

Ruth had several thoughts. But she knew that Letitia would be able to deal with any difficulty. She stood back.

'Will you come in, please.'

Thelma was like one who had charged a stout door which yields at once. She was used to narrower privacies. She entered the house, astounded, saying to herself: 'There, you see! The English give way when one is firm with them!' But her assurance was not increased. Once the door was closed she had been trapped. It was as bad as going underground. It was like being a spy in a wartime hostile country. What was to prevent this Letitia from calling her an impostor? From driving her forth? She had no place in such an atmosphere of tranquil luxury. It oppressed her. The very breeding of this girl who led the way was an intimidation.

Now she was in a room, a room with books and armchairs. She gave her name, 'Mrs Farringdon Reynolds.' It produced no awe, no recognition. She was alone, the walls rising high. Soon a tall cool stranger would come, very haughty, fair, with hard blue eyes, and say 'What do you want?' She was to say 'I think we are sisters-in-law.' She said it now, under her breath. 'I think we are sisters-in-law. I wish to know you. Forgive me for defying etiquette. I am well aware that I should have waited for you to call on me; but—excuse me—you didn't do it, so I thought—I think—sisters-in-law should not stand upon much ceremony with each other . . .' How stilted! How impossible! In the night, when her speech had been composed, the words had sounded quite plausible, quite easy and dignified. Now they were absurd! Letitia would look down her nose! What was she to do? Go? Yes, go! If she opened that door——

She was sitting far back in an armchair—far back, because it had been her first timid impulse to sit far forward—and she now drew herself some inches nearer the front of the chair in preparation for flight. One remained sitting. One gave one's hand without emphasis. The door would open; the maid would return. 'Madame is not at home'; or that imperious creature would herself come, as to an anteroom, shake hands, perhaps say she is going out . . . 'Who *are* you? I didn't know my brother was married. How singular!' Meaning, how incredible! Clearly she would refuse to believe it. 'If you ask your *husband* to call upon me, I'll try and arrange a meeting. At present I'm busy . . .'

'Listen to me, Madame. It may be true that Farringdon has not told you he was married—I can believe it. I know him, you see. I realise that he has peculiar ways. Who should know better than I? But surely that does not absolve *you* from some responsibility? Some hospitality? I had hoped that you would at least . . . What, do you wish to see the certificate of our marriage? Surely, between ladies . . .'

Confused and wretched, Thelma crouched in her chair. She had done wrong to come; she had been unwise; she had placed herself in the position of one who invites an affront.

The door opened. The maid reappeared. Now for the affront!

'Will you come upstairs, please?'

Oho! Oho! thought Thelma, scrambling out of the chair. So the lady receives me! That's the way to deal with English ladies. You entreat; they repel. You insist; they politely acquiesce, delaying their snub until they have well examined you. No, they can't deny themselves *that* great pleasure. To be sure! . . . This maid walks upstairs well; her body is flexible, her carriage excellent. It shows training. Her dress is well-made. It fits her shoulders. She knows all this. The walls are full of mellow light. The house is pleasant. Perhaps Letitia is less frigid than one fears. Perhaps, after all, she will be the friend I need. I've forgotten what I was going to say. I'm dumb. What can I say? No words. I haven't any breath. My hat has slipped. I'm hot, awkward, a toad, squat, ugly, ashamed; the last person who should come in any circumstances to such an elegant house . . .

She was in a room which in some extraordinary way held whatever sunshine the London afternoon provided. It made her heart rise. She became instantly much happier. And yet, at her first glance, she did not like Letitia. Letitia was not the frigid lady of her fear; neither was she the overflowingly warm-hearted creature who would take one's hand, or hear one's troubles, with matronly sympathy, exclaiming: 'Ah, yes. Yes, Thelma; I *do* see! How very wrong he is! My husband shall find him a good position; I shall introduce you to all my friends; your life for the future shall be all happiness. I feel so warmly for all you've suffered!' No, she was too calm. Too elegant. Too self-assured, with a smile which one would have to analyse before one could be sure how much ridicule lay behind its superficial kindness. She would never be one's friend . . .

She was not young; she was not old. She was not at all like what one recollected of the photograph which Farringdon carried. That photograph was of a young girl. Her hair was dark; her eyes, too. Her body—not her eyes—made one feel stout and ill-dressed. One's hands seamed with house-work. One's back less straight than it had been. One felt 'Please, I'm the old washerwoman, come to ask if you wish some cleaning to be done . . .' She had an effect. One felt desirous of her interest, her affection. But hopeless of engaging either. She made one feel . . . she made one feel that one should bow; or perhaps smile . . . that one must, this very instant, sit down because one's legs could no longer bear any burden whatsoever.

'How d'you do?' said Letitia, smiling still more kindly.

'How d'you do?' echoed Thelma, with a look in which terror, uncertainty, and supplication were blended. She felt her hard hand warmly clasped by a soft one. She felt herself guided to a chair. She glanced quickly over her shoulder: the maid was already gone; she was alone with Letitia. Her breathlessness had returned. She had reached her goal. But she was afraid; she had no armour against somebody like this.

iii

They had not gone very far in the first five minutes. Thelma had been unable to remember those memorised words, and could think of none to take their place. She had stammered: 'So good of you. I thought . . . as I was in London . . .' And, finding her visitor so much embarrassed, Letitia had said outright:

'I've not seen Farringdon, you know. Did you know that? He called here one day. I was out. He didn't leave a message, or an address.'

'No, you would not know.' Thelma stared blankly at her. 'You . . .' The sentence faded away. She swallowed twice, and could not continue.

'I haven't seen him for twenty years. Have you been here long?'

'No. Not long.'

'Perhaps you've thought me unkind? But then I didn't even know——' As, breaking off, she laughed instead of saying how astonished she had been by Ruth's announcement of an unsuspected sister-in-law, Letitia's heart sank at sight of this poor heavy woman stubbornly watching her, not smiling or showing any readiness to quicken into accord. That Farringdon's wife should be unhappy did not surprise her. That she should be so inelastic was a puzzle. Farringdon had always been impatient, almost mercurial. They must have been married for some years. Had she once been vivacious? Were there children? What could be done about her? If a diversion would help, how soon would Christine be home? Christine, softening now that she was grown up, was going to become an unfailing ally! What a blessing, and what a surprise!

At last:

'You didn't know I existed,' said Thelma, slowly. 'He didn't write to you?'

'No. Never a letter-writer.'

'He has never written to *me*. But that's because we are together. Obviously. You are not the only sister. He is not more . . . communicative, I think, with the other. He is secretive. Perhaps you are like him in that?"

'I don't seem to have many secrets,' said Letitia, frankly. 'Just as well. They're such a weight on the memory.'

Thelma thought: You have a million. Nobody ever yet read your mind. That air of something childish, of levity, *must* be assumed. It *could* not be natural. But you may perhaps be sincere in what you say. For you, they're not secrets but reserves. I understand. I am very subtle. Aloud, feeling more confident, she said:

'I think I should tell you how great a courage it's taken to come here. How much defiance of Farringdon. I have begged him. In my loneliness. But he won't come, it seems. I don't know why. He said he would only come to you in extremity. You understand that? I felt sure you must be without feeling. But perhaps he has behaved badly to you in the past?' There was no answer or encouraging smile. She must continue. 'I know

F

he . . . admires you. He keeps an old photograph of you always . . . near him——' She touched her breast.

'That's odd!' said Letitia, 'I didn't think he had *any* family sentiment.'

'He has none,' answered Thelma. She thought for a short time; and then said 'Naturally, you can't tell me anything about him——'

'He's not *lost*?' asked Letitia.

'Oh, no. Of course, he seeks a fortune. An easy fortune. I don't, in a way, want help about him. Except that I'm . . . curious . . .'

'Can I help you about yourself?' asked Letitia, quickly. 'It seems more possible.'

She saw the white face grow less white. Beneath that coarse skin blood flowed. The black, expressionless eyes were turned to her.

'I mustn't ask you to do such a thing,' said Thelma, stiff with pride.

'Why not? At least, why not let *me* ask? You mustn't, please, having come to see me, feel that that's the end of it. You must let me be your friend.'

'You have your own friends,' said Thelma.

'I have. I'm glad of it. But we're not made in compartments. That would be more simple. Do sit back. Ruth will be bringing tea in a few minutes. Would you like to take off your hat? I'll tell you about Muriel my sister.'

'Yes? He says she is . . . He doesn't respect her.'

'One doesn't. She doesn't respect *herself* enough. But she's really kind and simple——'

'Ah, you love her. You warm when you speak of her. Yes, it's possible however different she may be. Do you also speak as favourably of you mother?' asked Thelma, with a sharp look. 'You understand I have no opinion of my own. It's what I hear.'

'No, she's one of my antipathies. I haven't seen her for a great many years. We had a very disagreeable quarrel when I was a girl; and—I ran away. Besides, I'm hard——'

'It may be true,' said Thelma, watching Letitia, noticing her composure which was a sign of hardness.

'But Muriel isn't. She's too accommodating. She has a very difficult life, with our mother.'

'You help her?' asked Thelma, intending to disconcert.

Letitia was not disconcerted.

'It's almost impossible to help her, except in trifling ways.'

'I see.' Thelma could not imagine what 'trifling ways' might be. To her, money was far from a trifle. Farringdon had called Muriel a lickspittle and worse. He had called Letitia a prig. One didn't always understand his use of words; and he was often prejudiced. In this case, for example. She felt increasing trust in Letitia, and, stirring in her chair so that she might adopt a more confidential position, she continued: 'I've been married to Farringdon for twelve years. He came to South Africa. My papa was doctor there—I had no mother. I mean, my mother died long ago. I was always Papa's child . . . Papa died; and we were in love. I asked Farringdon to write to you, and he said he would. To his family; not you alone. There was no reply, because of course he didn't write. As you say. I didn't know that, then. I was young. It seems strange to you, no doubt, to see me a mature woman. I'm thirty-four. I've come suddenly. I feel, intruded. Perhaps you would like me to tell you something more about myself . . .'

She was at this point startled to find that Ruth, who had silently entered the room again, wheeling a tea-wagon, was at her elbow. She was unused to such interruptions; they troubled her. The girl should knock. One ceased speaking of private matters before a servant. She held her tongue, frowning as Ruth bent to say something to Letitia.

Letitia said:

'Yes, of course he's to come up.' And to Thelma: 'A friend's here. He's coming to join us. You won't mind, I hope. He's very kind—though you mayn't at first think so . . .'

A moment later, before Thelma had been able to do more than stare and nod, Gabriel was in the room. He swept in, the picture of eagerness and vanity, stooping, half-running, smiling with joy and secret amusement, and starting elaborately at the presence of a stranger. Yet he must have been told that Letitia was not alone. That was *acting*. Thelma immediately felt such dislike of him that it made her heart beat fast.

iv

What was the relationship between this man and her hostess? Such impudent ease! Such ugliness! Was Letitia his mistress? Watch!

He had an affected manner. He would obviously say anything; often, thinking it an amusement, the opposite of what he meant; as Farringdon tried to do. This man was more insincere than Farringdon. He was sinisterly quick. He had polish. He reminded her of something she had read or heard of Disraeli; it might be a portrait she had seen. Was he a Jew? She disliked Jews. No, not a Jew. A great dandy; probably one of the English rich, the class she had been taught by Papa to despise as parasites. Papa had been wise. Until his throat became too bad for much speech he had told her many things of importance. Most of them were warnings.

'You see I can't keep away, Letitia,' Gabriel said, as soon as he was inside the door. 'Oh, how d'you do? I've heard of your husband from Letitia. I've been expecting to hear that he'd called again. You're his representative; I'm sure a most efficient one. Are you new to London, or born and bred here? Ah, South Africa. Then I expect you miss the sun; we all do. And the snakes, and the veldt, and the inspanning and out-spanning—which are all English novelists can tell us about the country. I suppose the sun's authentic? It isn't, here. Like our new laid eggs. That's the reason why we all come and see Letitia. She dwells in sunshine. You've noticed that, I'm sure. Dwells in it and bestows it. A wonderful gift. Darling Letitia, I've been slaving all the morning. I'm exhausted. I feel like Balzac; who, when he knew he was dying, begged his doctor for six weeks to finish a book. The doctor—incredibly candid!—shook his head.

"Six days!" entreated Balzac. The doctor shook his head. "Ah, my friend," groaned Balzac; "give me only six *hours*!" What an artist, eh? But the doctor still shook his head. Even Balzac knew that six minutes were no good. Whether the book was *Le Deputé d'Arcis* I don't know. But what a tragedy! It purges me with passion and terror. It must frighten anybody who embarks—as I've done—on his masterpiece.'

'Mr Wilton's a playwright, who's just begun writing a new play,' explained Letitia. 'He talks, as you hear, rather extravagantly.'

Gabriel raised his long hands in protest.

'Really, Letitia! What cynical philistinism! In any case, you should allow Mrs Reynolds to form her own opinion of me.'

'That's what I *shall* do,' grimly retorted Thelma, smoothing her skirt across her knee. 'I am never deceived.'

Gabriel did not venture to look at Letitia. His ridiculing glance ran over the visitor, from her stockiness, the intense disapprobation of her set lips, her tasteless, shapeless dress, her shoes, back to the small black eyes, as expressionless as blackcurrants, marooned amid that white space in which no other features were memorable. Thelma knew that he had made up his mind, and that he was indifferent to her. She grew resentfully hostile. She was a stranger. She would always be a stranger to this dapper gentleman, who disliked strangers.

It was otherwise when he looked at Letitia. As Letitia must certainly know, he found *her* the most fascinating woman in the world. He brimmed anew with tenderness whenever he glanced at her. He sought private communication with her eye. In English Society, Thelma knew, morals were often a matter for clerical censure. Had she stumbled, at her first—perhaps her only—visit, upon an example of English morals?

'Have you really been slaving, Gabriel? Or was that a gambit?'

'Darling! You're cruel!' Gabriel, sitting down, and stooping with his hands upon his knees, set himself to shock Thelma. 'Whenever I wasn't thinking of *you*, I was slaving. I wrote two pages!'

'Two pages'. What a *farceur*! To regard such fiddle-faddle as slavery

'Evidently I was *quite* neglected,' laughed Letitia. 'Was Constance with you, or was she rehearsing?' She said to Thelma: 'Though Mr Wilton never met Farringdon, his wife did so, many years ago.'

His wife! Thelma moved her head slowly, as a cow does. But Gabriel quite well comprehended the reproof which Letitia had administered to him. What a demure darling she was! That lovely mouth—a tantalization Sacrilege that it should be wasted in rebuke, or in conversation with th sour lady. No wonder the lady was sour, poor thing. She was married t an adventurer! Was she here to get money?

'My wife and I never agree,' he explained to Thelma. 'On the other han Letitia and I agree perfectly.'

Thelma stared; Letitia laughed.

'You understand him well enough now, don't you?' she aske Thelma.

'This slander by innuendo!' cried Gabriel. He looked over his shoulde 'Ah, here's Ruth. And, oh dear me, here's Christine!'

Thelma saw that it was true. Ruth had brought the tea; and, with her, a young girl had come into the room. She was what Letitia must have been as a child of the same age. Not tall; very slim and dark; dressed plainly and smartly in dark blue. She was much too assured. Thelma unconsciously shook her head. She felt like a tortoise which has peeped from under its shell in a moment of security, and must now quickly draw in again at the approach of a young, relentless cat.

'You here *again*, Uncle Gabriel!' exclaimed Christine, with inhospitable raillery. 'I'd wanted a quiet talk with mother——'

'We all dream of it,' said Gabriel, sighing and grimacing.

'This is my daughter. I haven't asked you——'

'Oh, how d'you do.' Christine came to shake hands with the new aunt, giving her a brief direct glance—such as she might have given to a book which she immediately put down again. She turned back to Gabriel. 'But yours is only flat selfishness. Mine's for the pursuit of knowledge.'

'Your mother flies eternally from that pursuit,' Gabriel said. 'But you're like the Canadian Mounties. There's a look in your eye.'

'Purpose,' agreed Christine.

'I cross my fingers,' said Gabriel. He held up his crossed fingers. 'Please ask me nothing.'

'About Stephanie?'

'Not even about Stephanie.' He teased Letitia with impudent eyes. 'Or Mark. I'm bound by respect for the confessional——'

'You'd spill it, all right. Obviously you don't know a thing.'

'Christine. The tea,' interrupted Letitia.

'He's a complete impostor. I suspected it when I was a child——' Christine brought Thelma a cup of tea and a plate, and offered her a tiered cake stand. 'Now I'm sure.' She gave her aunt another quick, smiling glance in which Thelma, fumbling for a scone, saw only self-confidence. But what a trim figure! It was too thin, too boyish. Her hair was too short. She was distressingly without ceremoniousness or warmth.

'Oh, dear!' sighed Gabriel, taking his own teacup from Letitia's hand, but refusing her mute offer of anything to eat. 'These ancients of twenty-one! In my day we were young up to forty.'

'You and your friend Barrie!' retorted Christine. 'I'd suspected the child-complex. You're awfully like him. Had *you* met Uncle Gabriel before? The original Peter Pan.' She spoke disconcertingly to Thelma, who, being taken by surprise in the midst of distaste for both tilters, could only shake her head.

'She shakes her head as meaningfully as Lord Burleigh,' exclaimed Gabriel, enchanted. 'But as to Barrie, no, no. He's a melancholiac. That gloomy ingle-nook: a place for self-torment. Besides, I never admire my fellow-dramatists. I admire practically nobody. Your mother, of course——'

'Mother's *all* admiration. Or should be. But her dramatic taste's for "Our Boys".'

'Mark and Julian?'

'You have sons?' Thelma asked Letitia, rather pointedly. And, upon being informed that this was so, she nodded again, raised her shoulders as if in resignation, and was silent.

'She's got a daughter-in-law too,' announced Christine. 'Whom I don't see, by the way, Mother. Has she left us?'

'At least, she's not in the house,' replied Letitia, with pleasant calm.

'No note or message? Will she be back to tea? I thought she was a little distraite last evening. . . .'

'I long to hear about it,' cried Gabriel. 'The excellent Mark, I assume, was *not* here. . . .'

'Electioneering alone,' interjected Christine. 'I think he offered to let her take his place.'

'Indeed. Indeed. . . .'

'Is Farringdon in London now?' asked Letitia, leaving the two chatterboxes to spar more quietly. 'I wonder whether you'd like to bring him to dinner one evening? Or would you——'

Thelma gave her an expressive, silencing look. It was to say: Please! That's impossible! But I can't speak frankly before these foolish, impertinent others. I was interrupted, you remember.

'If I might come again to see *you*.'

'Of course.'

'I shall write.'

'You and I must also meet again, Christine!' said Gabriel, in a low voice. 'For speech together.'

Christine frowned at him.

'I prefer adult minds,' she said. 'Analytical minds.'

'Even they, however, need living material for their contempt.'

'Not contempt. You're regarded tolerantly as a back number.'

'Say, rather, a sealed book. I'm half-way to being a classic, waiting for tardy justice from the National Theatre.'

'Embalmment. Material for pedants in mime, decor, and the arty-crafty. Naturally we active minds don't bother about the classics. We're modern. We look to the future.'

'Idealistic escapism. As you say, you're already old.'

'At any rate, we're not infantilists.'

'Or even ripe.'

Thelma heard and did not hear this exchange. It sounded quick and remained meaningless. It left no room for serious intimate conversation in which one enlarged upon one's troubles and sometimes received the gratifying confidences of a friend. She would never reap such gratification from Letitia, who would deceive, but not complain of, her husband. Letitia had not mentioned him. She had not boasted of her children's health and success. She had not, even tactfully, referred to Thelma's childlessness. She now allowed the talk to be monopolised by this old buffoon and the aggressive chit, who should be humble and who was pert. It was bad. was wrong not to hush them. They were without respect for each other and courtesy to a stranger. They ignored or ridiculed her. She could feel them smiling behind her back.

'You, madame,' said Gabriel, with mocking gravity. 'I feel sure you find the London young very soft within, though hard without? Too quickly cooked?' He had come near. From beneath his deep lids he was taunting her, she felt, with being a frump and an outsider.

'I don't care for them,' she replied, with glum candour. 'They are too much encouraged to be rude.'

'You think I encourage Christine? I'm her godfather. If Letitia and Monty were to die, I should stand *in loco parentis*.'

Thelma stared. Letitia came to her rescue.

'Mr Wilton's such an old friend that he doesn't cultivate our respect. We force it on him, which is a nice revenge. We go to the first nights of his plays, and laugh, and shout "author" at the end of them. Then we're told the author isn't in the house—though we've seen him lurking there all the evening;—and we let him take us out to an expensive supper, to celebrate his success.'

'My plays are always successes, Mrs Reynolds. I have a clause in the contract.'

Thelma would not smile. She stubbornly said:

'I go little to plays. I have not seen yours.'

'You must come and see my masterpiece. But I doubt if you'll find it amusing.'

Letitia, seeing that flippant self-detraction would be taken, as he was willing that it should be taken, as an insult, cried:

'You do yourself much less than justice, Gabriel. Even Christine will think it better than Congreve.'

'I doubt if she's so much as *heard* of Congreve.'

Christine, caught by this sudden attack, indignantly exclaimed: 'I have! I've even read his poems!' Thelma, with a stony face, glanced at the clock upon the mantelpiece.

iv

Thelma left the house, handsomely sped by the self-complacent jesters, and given warm encouragement by Letitia to return. And while Gabriel watched from the window to see her go, wishing that Christine might soon follow, and Letitia stood for a moment alone, re-living the early awkwardnesses of the encounter and wondering what more she could have done to give this poor woman much-needed hope and interest, Thelma was grimly thinking:

'I shan't go *there* again! That's *quite* certain. The stupid fools!'

A slight shudder ran through her, as if a ghost had touched her back. She could have cried in the street; but, because she was too proud to do so, yet disappointment poison her mind.

They were all stupid and heartless. She didn't understand them. They didn't understand her. They openly mocked her. They thought her a clumsy, ignorant nonentity. It wasn't true. They were both blind and cruel. Letitia was a frivolous woman. She had no depth. Only the stupid calm of English breeding. All Englishwomen were the same. They sneered at whatever

was unfamiliar to them. She would never go again. Never. Never.
Never.

Heavy with failure, she travelled back to the flat near Regent's Park.
The loud noise of traffic and the silent progress of immense crowds embodied
for her the simultaneous blatancy and indifference of London, where all
were self-engrossed. Not a single person here loved her.

The moment she opened the door of the flat, instinct told her that it
was not empty. Whether she smelled the reek of F. R.'s tobacco, or whether
there was a sound, or some quality in the atmosphere, she could not have
said; but her nerves were suddenly taut. Without doubt, as Farringdon
always produced this effect upon her, Farringdon had come home again.

She went to the bedroom, and looked at herself in the glass. The face
into which she gazed was cold and stern. It was the face, she thought, of a
woman of courage and equanimity, who had greatly endured. Not a smiling
face; not one with the middle-aged piquancy of that which she had first
seen an hour ago. What care that creature must take to keep young! The
exercises, the cosmetics, the potions, the treatments! To make herself still
charming to her lovers. Her lovers—that buffoon, and others like him!

'My God!' exclaimed Thelma. 'What lovers!'

There came into the face she saw in the mirror such sly, eyebrow-lifted
cynicism, and to her arms and shoulders such a tremendous shrug, that she
was astonished. At once the arms fell to her side; the expression disappeared.
The face had no longer any expression at all.

As she had known she would do, she found Farringdon in the kitchen,
brewing himself some tea, and cutting giant slices of bread and margarine
and plum jam. He had not troubled to lay a cloth; the caddy and milk-jug,
teapot, bread, and butter-dish were all strewn at large upon Thelma's scrubbed
table. Water had been spilt there. It was a shocking, abhorrent, gipsy-like
mess, which in other circumstances would have roused her to abuse. He was
being over-generous with the margarine, too, like a greedy boy. That
offended her thrift, as the untidiness offended her sense of order; but today
it also endeared him to her.

'Hello,' was Farringdon's greeting. He looked quizzically at her new
dress, and whistled a little tune under his breath. She saw suspicion enter
his mind. He followed her movements with a speculative glance. She was
pleased to know that he could not imagine where on earth she had been
and, for all his whistling and pretended indifference, was irked by this doub'
and her silence. She had power over him.

'You are back,' was all she said. They did not kiss. They never kissed
except to excite one another.

'I wondered where you were,' remarked F. R., as if he were laughing
'Did you fear you had lost me?'

'I know you're full of engagements.'

'Where should I go?'

He made no reply. He was in excellent spirits, she could tell; for thoug
he would obviously do his best to discover where she had been (which sh
would not tell him), he had an air of active merriment, and looked at th
singing kettle with expectancy. She noticed that he was brown, as if he ha

been much in strong air; the backs of his hands were as brown as his face. When he stepped across to the kettle he was buoyant. So. He had been to the sea. His eyes were clear. A pleasurable emotion stirred within Thelma; expectant echo of old joy in him. It grew vivid, irresistible. Her voice was thick.

'Was your business successful?'

He was filling the teapot, his back towards her.

'I have hopes,' he replied. Then, as he turned, she added another cup and saucer to the spread, and a plate, to show that she, too, would eat and drink. They both sat at the table, and in reaching her chair she brushed against him in good humour. She knew he would misunderstand. And yet understand. This cordial acceptance of his return, and of the untidy, uncovered table, was fully half—although F. R. did not know it—a gesture of defiance to the sophistication of Letitia's home. It was as if, with the fury of one who punches an aching tooth, she said: 'This is the way *I* live. You would think it uncivilized. I prefer it. What *then*?' But it was also a sign of her need of F. R., as to which both were clear. She saw his lids drop in male amusement.

'You make good tea,' she said, stinging with detestation of Gabriel and Christine and amorous proprietorship in her husband.

F. R. yawned.

'My good woman, I do everything well. I'm a first-class cook.'

'You could cook,' she grudgingly admitted. 'If you cared to.'

'Yes, if I cared to,' he indifferently agreed.

They ate ravenously. When F. R. had finished, he drew out his pipe and loaded it, sitting comfortably by the well-roused fire. Thelma, having cleared the dishes away, put them aside to be washed up, and went to change her dress. As she reached the two doors, which were side by side, she looked into the room where Farringdon kept his secrets. Yes, the exquisite pigskin bag lay on a side-table: it had come safely back. What was in it? She listened. There was no sound from the kitchen. He would enjoy his pipe to the end before moving again. She snapped open the catch.

Only his clothes, dirty and otherwise. She drew the dirty ones out, knowing that she would have to wash them. What else? A pair of new gloves, unworn, of fine kid. Strange! What did he want with such things as these? He never wore gloves; yet the size showed that they were for himself, not for a woman. She could think of no explanation. Even as she considered possibilities she noticed that something hard and flat lay in a side pocket of the bag; it proved to be his passport, well worn but with its renewal still valid. Her heart froze. That was alarming. It frightened her. Had he been abroad? Why should he pack a passport? Should she hide it, for safety? He might kill her. Now search became feverish. Her fingers trembled. This little oblong box: it was new, but she had seen such boxes before. Quick! Quick! Yes, it was what she had guessed it to be—a safety razor. A safety razor for a bearded man: extraordinary! What did all these things mean? They could only mean something which threatened her own security.

Seriously alarmed, Thelma bundled the clothes back into the bag and

F*

snapped it fast. Noiselessly she went out of the room and into the bedroom. She could not think. She *would* not think. As she struggled to bring her clumsy dress over her head, and while she was still enveloped in it as if in a sack, she heard her heart beating very loudly, and felt as though she were suffocating.

v

Gabriel was alone in the sunny drawing-room when Letitia returned there. He had left the window, and was standing with his back to the fire. The tea-things were gone. And Letitia, entering with her quick step, caught him grinning in malicious observation of his own pain.

'You shouldn't have been unkind, Gabriel,' she said. 'It wasn't nice of you.'

The quality of Gabriel's smile changed. It was now all sweetness.

'In your world one's to suffer stupidity gladly,' he said. 'There's to be no retaliation.'

'She's an unhappy woman.'

'I'm an unhappy man.'

'Are you? I know you're ill; and I'm sorry. But you've got blessings —genius, a loving wife, loving friends. She has nothing.'

'Not even charity!' he declared. 'Did you miss that? How could I see her misjudge you and not resent it? If *you* wouldn't resent it. I don't like you as a moralist, Letitia.'

'With you, then, every judge is his own executioner?'

Gabriel laughed. He cried eagerly:

'Are we quarrelling? Our first quarrel! Doesn't that suggest something to you?'

Letitia would not rise to his raillery. She said:

'It was my fault. I should have done better. Well, I always feel that.' She sat down again, rather put out, in her former chair. 'I've never been a hostess; and I never shall be.'

'My dear! The best hostess in the world. You give your guests freedom.'

'Not to hurt one another.'

'But really! Didn't you see her sitting there, thinking unutterable things about us all? Thinking Christine a monkey, myself a mountebank, you a *demi-mondaine*? What parochial smugness! What a dull, narrow clod of a woman!'

'No.' Letitia shook her head. 'I saw somebody paralysed by shyness; who was humiliated by the disdain of a clever girl and a brilliant man who, if he wished, could always make rings round his inferior self.'

He had been moving about, irritably, at her protests; his hands fluttering and his feet unsteady. The compliment made him smile; but he continued to speak with impatience.

'How sentimental you are, for all your wisdom! This woman's made her own bed. You can see that. Yet you're so morbidly family-conscious —you do realise it, don't you!—that you take your wretched brother's sins on yourself. Absurd! Why waste time and intelligence and compassion on the worthless?' Changing his look and his speech with intimidating ease, he then said, most persuasively: 'I'm *much* worthier of your kindness. God knows how I need it!'

'Poor Gabriel!' She returned to a kinder consideration of his ills. 'Am I blaming you for being Gabriel?'

'I'm a sick man. No, I *won't* plead that.' He took two or three steps from the fire; but as they led away from Letitia he was soon back again. 'I don't want the pity you lavish on bores. *Parlons d'autres choses.* That's what Madame de Sévigné so often said. Tell me about Stephanie. Much as I dislike that sensual chit, there's something fluent in her veins. She's not a bag of self-pity, like this other.'

His sharp tongue uttered verdicts which Letitia would never forget. Nevertheless, she spoke as if she had not heard them.

'There's nothing to tell. Mark couldn't sweep her off her feet. He hasn't the sweeping temperament.'

'Nor I. It goes with insensitiveness.'

'But he must have been outspoken.'

'As *you* directed. How women despise each other!'

'She told me he was extraordinarily unkind—suspiciously well-informed.'

Gabriel smiled at a glimpse of Mark's forensic eloquence and Stephanie's shrewdness.

'The jury obviously affected. But passing notes to the judge. And *you* said, as to unkindness?'

'I said unkindness could never be all on one side. It was everywhere. In fact I've been a Devil's Advocate to both of them, and very Jesuitical. I'm ashamed. But, as I love them both, basely triumphant.'

'A loss to the Bar, as well as the Stage.'

'By this morning she'd decided that he's her abiding cross; so she telegraphed to say that she was joining him in the North. She said "Liberal Party wins a new recruit. Meet me Central Station three oclock". I put her on the train.'

'Excellent. But trains can be stopped. Did *you* draft the face-saving telegram?'

'I helped to keep it to essentials. But it was she who made up her mind.'

'Naturally.' He laughed in silence, bending down and looking at his pointed shoes. 'Well, you're a wonderful woman. I love you dearly, Letitia. I don't know what you think of *that*.'

Letitia caught the tremor in his voice, saw his rigid hands and the flush in his cheeks; and realised that everything he had said and done that afternoon had been an improvisation. They had reached his single purpose, which was to declare his love for her. His shyness, his humility, was really touching.

'I'm very proud,' she replied, sitting quite still.

'Thank God you don't immediately speak of Constance.' He had turned away, his chin upon his breast.

'I think of her too much to do that,' said Letitia. 'She's my old, loyal friend, Gabriel.'

'Loyal?' His head was lifted. 'Yes, I suppose that's true. Loyal, in her own crazy way, to both of us. She's had a great—a ruinous—effect on me. In one way, she's the stronger personality. I can't stand noise; and she's noisy.'

'It's to hide feeling, Gabriel.'

He laughed.

'As the drummer bangs to drown his sorrows. No, she's noisy because it's a relief to her feelings. Her feelings are superficial. You have feeling; but no feelings.'

'Have I not!' exclaimed Letitia, who had not moved.

'Remember, I understand you very well.'

'Not *too* well, I hope.'

'By report for many years.'

'Constance's report,' murmured Letitia, smiling.

'By direct route. And by inspiration. All together, those three are irresistible. I know you're family-conscious, because for twenty years I've seen you wasting your strength on the children——'

'Never wasting!' she protested. 'There you *can't* understand.'

'I don't mean, interfering with them. Or henning them. Assimilating *their* experience, secretly adjusting your stance to catch them if they should tumble off their tightrope of juvenile pride. Doing that even with Monty, with Constance, with that poor feckless sister at the seaside . . . Positively a juggler! Yes, you're a juggler. You drop nothing . . . What *did* you do for Farringdon?'

Letitia shook her head.

'I'm taking no part in this,' she said.

'I can guess. I say he embezzled, and you, somehow, finding the money without telling Monty, got him out of the country. If you aren't careful, you'll soon have to do the same again.' He watched for any sign that she was distressed by his relentless rebuilding of the past. Then he grew impatient with himself. 'Oh, but this isn't what I *want* to say to you. This mortuary mumbling of old bones! I want to talk about myself. I want to canalize your . . . sympathy . . . You see I daren't use the word "love".'

'I'm listening,' Letitia said; affected, but amused by his naïvely oblique introduction of the forbidden word. 'With sympathy.'

'Without passion.'

'With . . . emotion.' She felt her cheeks grow warm. 'I'm giving you more than you ask. All I *can* give.'

He was deeply moved.

'Bless you, Letitia.' When he could speak again, he said: 'Twenty years ago I should have tried to steal you from Monty. It would have been an adventure. Would you have come?'

'I might, through unwisdom.'

'Ah, you're conventional!'

'Monty's my strength. You would have been my weakness.'

'Have you considered it? Not with me. No. With other men?'

'Have you thought me so staid? It hasn't been convention. It's been Monty.'

'I hate the fellow!' cried Gabriel, with momentary conviction. 'However, I understand. It's a Pickwickian hate. I'm really quite worthless. A coward, you know. That's why I'm spiteful. I expect you've heard more than all about me—from Constance?' He was uneasy; defending himself against her insight, yet desperate to seize this chance of expressing all that he hid from others. 'She doesn't paint a pretty picture.'

'She makes it attractively exasperating.'

'She's stupid. Abysmally stupid.'

'With the nimblest mind and the most beautiful readiness to sacrifice herself.'

'To what? To her self-portrait. Don't imagine I'm indifferent to her.'

'I *shan't* praise her. That would be *really* smug. But she's a positive: I'm altogether negative. It's most discouraging——'

'Oh, but we've got an endless topic!' cried Gabriel. 'Our own imperfection. Let's dwell on it!'

'At six o'clock?' As they both heard the hour chiming, she nodded towards the mantelpiece.

'Damn! Love should be timeless. The theme for a desert island; with the rescue ship not too far away. Well, we've talked. I've told you my heart. Not my heart; that would be the longest story in the world!'

He grew pale as he spoke. She saw that when his lips were pressed so tightly together every sign of illness was emphasised. There was perspiration about his eyes.

'Gabriel! You're in great pain!'

He smiled. Thus, he knew, might a seraph smile; but she could read sincerity behind insincerity, and he did not intend to deceive her. With complete naturalness, he said:

'I was in pain this afternoon, when you thought me cruel. I'm now in pain. Unless they do something quickly, I shall die of pain.'

Letitia was upon her feet.

'Sit down, Gabriel. Stay, while I——'

He saw in her action love, kindness, true sympathy; and he was so overwhelmed by despair at this tenderness and the dreadful silences of death that he could bear no more.

'No, I must go! To shame myself before you, to be ill here, would be intolerable. In any case, I'm better. Forgive me.' For the first time, he put his arms about her, and, kissing her cheek, rested his own discoloured cheek against it. 'Darling, I adore you.' He held her hand. He checked another speech. Then, his eyes no longer dry, he turned away and hastened to the door. Smiling there in farewell, he was gone.

Eleven

IDYLLIC

i

LEFT TO HERSELF, Letitia was wretched indeed. She scorned the tears that ran down her cheeks; they had come too easily, and in no way represented her deep pain. She reproached herself. She had seen an old friend, a lover, put aside his endearing affectations in order to stand unconcealed; and she, incapable of equal sacrifice, had given him, in return, the frigid condolences of a queen. Yet she had not avoided treachery to Constance. *That* was unpardonable. No wonder she stood, with lowered head, feeling perplexed shame.

'He's perhaps dying,' she thought. 'And I give him nothing. I can't *bear* to give nothing . . . I'm really very stupid. I'm so stupid that I don't know what to do . . . I meddle in other lives; I can't manage my own. Nothing but a fraud!'

She seemed to be listening; but she had already heard Gabriel's departing steps, along the pavement below, and could not imagine what she was listening for, unless it was some crack in the voice of conscience. About her, everything was in confusion; as if, being the juggler of Gabriel's image, she had lost all control of the flying particles which spun above her head. What an incompetent juggler! An apprentice! The actions of other people were independent. Why was she forever tied with as many strings as an old lady's parcel, and hampered by ridiculous over-anticipation of what others might expect or need of her?

Because, even now, when she was despairingly ashamed, she had tasks to perform, she roused herself to go and perform them. She walked from the room as impetuously as ever; but without elasticity of mind. The demon of self-condemnation had seized her.

That demon worked so hard, in conjunction with fear of what might have happened to Gabriel, that she was driven at last, just before dinner, to telephone to Gabriel's home. It was Constance who answered the telephone; Constance in a gush of exuberance like that of bottled beer on a Summer's day.

'Splendid of you to phone, darling. I'm alone. I needn't say that. Yes, Gabriel's gone off to plot. You know how he plots. At his club with kindred spirits. They haggle and cackle over all the literary and political reputations, like a lot of *passée* old hens. Such *nasty* jokes hens share, I always think; they laugh as if they were going to be sick. I don't know who Gabriel's cronies are. Anonymous. Pseu. Like "A Harley Street Physician". Oh, Gabriel's all right. He has his bouts; but they're soon over. I get frightened; then I laugh. One can't do anything else, with him. What? Now? Well, it's marvellous of you; who else is *there*? Oh no, I don't think I will. Too ordealy. If *you'd* been alone . . . Cook's going to give me an omelette; I shall have a little drinkie. Sober as a judge. Thank you, all the same. *You're* not lonely, are you? Sound a little "down"

How are the children?—oh, she *has*! What a disappointment! I've been a croaker, haven't I! I've read too many plays with modern girls in them. I've come to the conclusion that dramatists know nothing about us primitives. Hey! Can I come to tea, *alone*? Thursday? Right! Like a shot! Oh, well, I've got to the point of being sick of my part. No, no; not sick of *myself*. Never that! I let other people get sick of me. *Don't* you? . . .'

Monty, waiting for his dinner, objected that Constance had the longest tongue in Christendom. Christine, who also was dining at home, suffered a slight delay with charmingly pointed patience. Letitia, feeling like a naughty child who has just caught a valuable dish as it was falling through her carelessness, took her place at the table with apparent calm. She was happier. She could smile back at Christine, feeling sure that Christine was still reading hearts in such terms of one syllable as ache, break, give and take.

There was more to the heart than that.

ii

It was the same in the morning. She was as restless as a young girl after her first dance, still dazzled by the lights and the programme under her pillow, and the interest of her supper partner. It was preposterous, when troubles over the children were momentarily at an end—though Julian remained silent and unreachable,—that other agitations, both more and less acute, had arisen. It always happened. This was less acute because she was not incapable of plain-dealing with herself or with Gabriel; more acute because for once she was extraordinarily confused in mind and spirit.

How ridiculous it is! was her thought. She was embarrassed. But she wanted most irresistibly to see Gabriel. She wanted to hear him talking, as he had done yesterday, without the mockery which represented the wrappings of his pride. Was she only curious? Flattered? Hypocritically concerned with Constance and Monty? She could not tell. The house, and housekeeping, and all the duties imposed by a lifetime's accumulation of unobtrusive good works, had become abhorrent to her.

'How like Stephanie I am!' she said, at one moment. Then: 'Didn't I tell her so! There was a time when Monty picked up my scattered letter-tearings. How I detested him! I thought I couldn't bear it another hour. The impulse to break away, to fly. I nearly went. If I'd gone? Yet I've persuaded Stephanie back into the cage. Immoral woman! Oh, I'm hateful!'

Such thoughts drove her out of doors in mid-morning, when early fog was yielding to the sun, which hung aloft in the murky sky, looking small, like the yolk of a poached egg. The fog would make her cheeks grimy, and bring specks into the corners of her eyes; but it would also be kind in giving her solitariness, whether she walked by the winter-lighted shops or by the Round Pond or the Serpentine. It was not her enemy.

She did all these things. She glanced at the bright shop windows, which took her into short flights of planning, irrelevant to her dominant concern.

She entered Kensington Gardens, where under the bare trees, no children sailed their boats upon the Round Pond and no dogs defied the regulation against bathing. And in time she reached Hyde Park, making her way along beside the Serpentine; and, by stopping at the water's edge, she brought greedy ducks inquisitively to her side, their horrid little eyes the merest spots of calculation in solemn, comic faces. About them, the water had the greyness of ice. In the breezeless day it was almost unruffled; only the smallest movements, like the promptings of temptation, occurred as it lapped the bank. Across the water came idle sounds from the farther shore, which was shrouded in mist.

Letitia did not loiter; but neither did she hasten. She knew the value of her freedom; and if the sun would grow a very little stronger and give a very little more warmth the day would be ideal for the indulgence of her present mood. She felt newly happy, active, deliciously a truant; for nobody could possibly find her here. Lovely!

At last she had come to the great turmoil of traffic at Hyde Park Corner, where automobiles from the crossing streamed through to the North, and a bunch of red omnibuses, eastward bound, had gathered, as ready for release as a crateful of pigeons, beyond the railings. What should she do? Go home? Her heart sank. She thoughtfully ventured a step into the roadway. It was at such a point in freedom that knights errant were always needed. About sixty per cent of oneself wanted security; the remainder wanted urgent change. That was true of men and women alike. Whichever one had, reaction followed; reaction upon reaction upon reaction!

'The truth is, I'm hungry,' said Letitia, aloud. 'That's my trouble. And the thought of lunching alone in a woman's club's enough to send me to a snack bar!'

She was laughing to herself, unconsciously radiant, when a taxi stopped abruptly at a distance, and amid some horn-hooting and a few shouted candours, a beautifully dressed man, who wore a furlined coat and a broad-brimmed black hat, ran through the traffic from the very edge and limit of the Park, where Piccadilly begins, changed his course as she followed a nursemaid with a perambulator across the Row, and at last, in the nick of time, reached her by the exit gate.

'Hey! Hey!' he was panting, as he caught her arm. 'Letitia! Stop!'

Poor Gabriel was breathless. His cheeks were grey. He was forced to stand for a moment, clinging to her for support. When he could speak, he said:

> ' "My dust . . . would hear her and beat,
>   Had I . . . lain for a . . . century dead."

Not to mention my eyes, . . . like "a pair o' patent . . . double million . . . magnifyin' gas microscopes" . . . They see through fogs, crowds, buildings, vehicles. . . . In fact I'm here! Henri de Lagardére!'

He was triumphant. Letitia was filled with gaiety. The passers smiled and were glad to see two happy, apparently amusing, people who had met by the luckiest chance. More sunshine appeared through the fog.

iii

'I wasn't, you know, *looking* for you!' declared Gabriel. 'I say, let's lunch together. Can we? Superb! No, the latest word's "super". Or is it "wizard"? Detestable fixities of cliché. "Oh, definitely!" Just a moment: a taxi? No, we'll go to the Ritz. Yes, I wasn't looking for you. My genie led me. My genius. I've been to Harley Street. I was hurrying back; and there, lo and bold——'

'What did Harley Street say?' Letitia, with his hand tucked into the crook of her arm, had first to be satisfied of this. But she was delighted by his high spirits. These continued.

'Oh, I'm better. They say the pain's nothing. I said "Nothing to *you*." Discreet, butlerish laughs. What a wag! However, the fiends think I'm yielding to their diabolical treatment. I'm not; but I'm not to die yet. Less interesting than I'd hoped. Now how does it happen that *you're* about, so free and easy? You look glorious, as I needn't say.'

'A bit black in the face?' asked Letitia.

'Not to notice. I think you're glad to see me?'

'An answer to prayer. I'm famishing.'

'Yes, the first was bold; the explanation a corrective. You telephoned Constance last night. Was that conscience or conscientiousness?'

'Concern,' Letitia told him.

'Dear, dear, dear; all these cons! And I'm the old pro. Alas! How d'ye do?' He relinquished Letitia's arm and swept off his hat to a fur-trimmed lady who passed them. 'That's somebody I know. I can't think who, at the moment.'

'Probably a friend of Constance's,' suggested Letitia.

'You feel she'll go straight to the telephone? Oh, no, it's Lady Smudge, or some such name. She doesn't know Constance. I've kept them apart. A man must have *some* friends of his own.'

'You don't seem to know her *very* well.'

'Well enough. Well enough. Not her name. After all, names don't matter. Hers is Sarah. Does my knowledge of that rouse your dislike?'

'At any rate, we *passed* her.'

He pinched her elbow.

'How happy I am!" he said.

They passed into the big building, and were met at once by warmth and brilliant lights. Beneath their feet were thick carpets. Through the glass of great doors they could see black-coated figures, and the array of the restaurant.

iv

'How I should have relished this, thirty years ago,' sighed Gabriel, as he looked at her across the table. 'Luxury, food, and . . . you. I'm sixty-one. Thirty years ago, the jingle of hansoms, motor-buses unborn; electric lights not killing the eyes. And my name for the first time on the hoardings! The ink used to peel, I remember. But it *was* my dream come true. Marvellous! . . . My original dream was to write a play for John Hare, and I never did. At least, I sent him two; and got them back. I don't even know if he read a word of either. I'd like to know.'

'Were they produced?' asked Letitia.

'One was. The first of them. It ran three weeks at the Old Terry's. Frightful! "Sweet Lavender" come again, with heredity in the background. Heredity was in vogue. But I was only twenty-five. One learns more by failures than successes—but not much by either. After it, I decided—I'd got sick of third and fourth-rate problem plays—that I'd rather be a twentieth century imitation Congreve than a twentieth century imitation Ibsen. In the end I've been neither.'

'No, you've been Gabriel,' she told him, affectionately. 'Quite a good thing to be.'

He shook his head. She saw his eyes roll in a characteristic way, and the lids fall over them. His lips drew back from his teeth as he spoke, and he looked maliciously good-natured.

'I haven't. Gabriel's a timid little nonentity. Most men's real selves are that. I've disguised Gabriel as Pantaloon and got away with it.'

'Rather preposterous to say that,' observed Letitia. 'To any woman. Because of course the Pantaloon's such a bundle that all the darlings you've known have wanted to see what's inside it.'

'Is that why they've worried me so? You've no notion how I've been molested! I used to think I liked women bad. I found I didn't. So I thought I must like them good. *Just* as tiresome! Excepting you, darling.'

'Good or bad, they become too attached to you,' suggested Letitia, smiling. 'And won't let go when you grow out of them.'

'They shouldn't be serious. It's not their *métier*. But don't let's talk about *women*. I'm trying too hard to interest you in myself; it's like having a message. Like feeling "responsible". Think what *you* would have been without responsibility!'

'Giddy,' Letitia said.

'Grand! So should I! We've been stultified!'

'You wouldn't like me if I were incurably giddy.'

'Still, you ran away from home as a girl,' he mused. 'That was all right.'

'I've never regretted it.'

'I should have run away more often. Constance has always carried a lasso. It's demoralizing. I've been forced to invent ciphers, and hide things, to occupy her mind.'

'Not to escape her?'

'Oh, I've got a few secrets.' He smiled complacently.

'I shouldn't be too sure of that.'

Her murmur seemed not to reach him. It had been derisive.

'If I hadn't followed my own technique, we should have been living in rooms in Brighton, she touring the smalls, and I picking up odd guineas by hack work. As it is, I've given her a life of her own that she doesn't know how to use. I've made some reputation. And remember this: I

can—with impunity—take you to lunch!' He laughed in glee at the thought
that he had dodged Constance.

That laugh, and the small triumph it disclosed, were revelations to
Letitia. Though she smiled at him still, her heart had slightly dropped.
This formidable man, famous in his craft, was still the ambitious boy of a
poor home, frightened of women and ill-success. Nothing essentially but
that: the rest was an intangible superstructure of panache and prestige.
Wasn't it illuminating that he always, in talk, returned complainingly to the
subject of Constance! True, Constance was the original link between them.
True, Constance complained quite as much of him as he did of her. But
Constance was a woman, bogeyfied by centuries of subordination; no man
of such parts should be such a niggard. Could it really be that Constance
was to blame? 'Should *I* have done better? Am I jealous of Constance?'
Aloud, she said:

'I think Constance is a part of yourself; your eye.'

'You think I protest too much about her? It may be true.' He lowered
his lids as he considered this. 'It's a sign that we're unfree. Not you, of
course; you're always detached. I don't mean that as a present *reproach*.'

'It isn't true, in any case. I'm much too much involved; like something
caught in a spider's web. This morning I've run away. But it's a very short
flight; after lunch I shall go home and get back into the spider's web.'

'I wonder who the spider can be.'

'Perhaps it's civilization.'

They both laughed at her rueful tone.

'Which we ourselves are making all the time. The blessings of civilization! You know, don't you, that we're in the early stages of the new
tyranny? Liberalism's dead; the future's with the bigots. There'll be wars
and persecutions galore in our lifetime—in *your* lifetime—because intolerances
as great as any of the old religious intolerances are rising. They'll sweep
the world.'

'Are *you* tolerant, Gabriel?'

'Me? I *suffer* life. I'm an anachronism. So are you. You represent
the Ten Commandments. Particularly the seventh.'

'I can never remember their right order,' replied Letitia.

'They're your spider's web!' he cried in triumph. 'Oh, dear. How
nice to chatter here; I wish it could go on for ever. Not for what we say—
all's the voice, the look, the emotion. You love me enough to bear with
me. That's very sweet. As for me, I think of you with happiness; not with
torture . . .'

v

They had parted, she to drive home alone in a taxi, he to walk to his
club, in which—such was the force of habit—he would pretend to Constance
that he had lunched. Letitia did not know this. But she was still thinking
of his contradictions when she left the taxi. She remembered him in the days
of early brilliance, when he thought so quickly that he had no time to calculate

the effects upon others of *anything* he said, when he and Constance had sparred as coarsely and brilliantly as Benedick and Beatrice. Weren't they in love? Had they even then chafed and hardened each other? It had been amusing: everybody had laughed, seen the Shakespearian analogy, and prophesied a tranquillising marriage. Perhaps they had been influenced by this analogy and common expectation? It was more likely that Constance, flying into love, had been determined, and that he, in love with himself, had been outmanœuvred by her logic. How quick they had both been!

He was not in love with himself now. Success had filled him with self-distrust, the disease of the middle-aged. Nor was there more than a shadow of old brilliance in his light talk. But he still had extraordinary charm for her; the charm of easy gesture, malice, kindness, and, naturally, in her own case the wish—the conscious power—to please. . . .

Letitia went upstairs to take off her hat and coat, to wash her fog-grimed face, and to brush her disarranged hair. It was past four o'clock, a fact which quickened her heart with naughty satisfaction. She felt that the day, and the meeting with Gabriel, had lifted all oppression from her heart. But they had also, by affording just that rearrangement of particles of thought and feeling which she likened to the action of a kaleidoscope, made clear several doubtful matters of some importance. She knew now, since the morning, that while she loved Gabriel she would never be more than a very little in love with him. She remained, and to the end would now remain, herself. But he did her good. He flattered and amused her, and quickened her kindness. Above all, he made her feel once again young and undaunted. *That*, however anachronistic, wasn't in these days a bad thing to be, was it?

The clock in the drawing-room chimed the half-hour as she entered carrying two or three letters which had arrived by the afternoon post. Ruth had drawn the dull-golden curtains, and the room was lighted only by flame and reflection from the fire, where a log burned. Half-past four: she had been away from home for five-and-a-half hours. Hours of happiness, of release. What a fortunate woman she was!

Twelve

MURIEL

i

NOW THAT SHE was awake, Muriel remembered everything. Not that she had been asleep. Oh, no; she had not slept at all. She never did. How she kept her strength she could *not* understand! Will-power. She passed wonderfully from the stormy sea of sleeplessness to the calm waters of being awake. Everything was very wonderful. Very.

She cautiously stretched and drew up her legs. Yes, the gout was very bad this morning; and her back ached. She really ought to see a doctor.

But he'd frighten her so much. It was better to go on worrying than to *know*. She had dreamed that she was being chased by an octopus which ran as fast as one of those big spiders. The octopus, which was very bright-eyed, had a big beard, and laughed; but although she thought it had a strong likeness to Farringdon it breathed like Mother.

From this vague memory of discomfort, which made awakening quite pleasant, Muriel went suddenly—as if she had turned a page in an anthology of creepy stories—to immediate physical fear. She grew so agitated that her really quite goutless legs gave a convulsive kick. Farringdon! He had been here and here and here, at all hours of the day, sometimes extraordinarily fascinating, but sometimes horrid, like a mesmerist. Mostly horrid. Mother had lent—given—him a key to the front door. She was idiotic! He had never returned it. Oh, that was terrible! . . .

His eyes glared so. He might do *anything*. Muriel had heard him say 'Any corner would do. Then I should be here if anything happened.' And Mother had said 'Muriel could turn out; go into the attic.' He had answered 'Oh, don't disturb her yet.' What was *going* to happen? There could only be one thing. He wanted her room. Why? What was he after? Were they plotting something together?

She was sure he knew where all the money was kept. Nobody had told him. He'd found out, somehow. All sorts of questions to herself, in the kitchen. None to Mother. To Mother he'd been all sweetness. But that was because he was artful. In the kitchen he was a different creature. He sat on the table with his long legs half across the floor, sneering, telling her frightening, thrilling stories about helpless women, and great big green snakes, and being eaten by sharks. Sometimes she'd been so alarmed that she hadn't known what she was saying. What *had* she said? If you were mesmerised you said *what they wanted you to say* . . .

He'd asked if the house belonged to Mother. How they managed to live. What she thought about banks. Mother's investments. Her will. Any changes in it? The lawyer; did he come often? What about the doctor? What time they went to bed. If Mother took sleeping draughts. If anything happened, what would Muriel do? What did Muriel get out of it all? Why did she stay? Such nasty hinting! Oh, horrible!

He'd dropped all talk about the big house on the Front as soon as he found that Mother wasn't going to give him any money. Mother had been excited about it at first. Tempted, Muriel thought, by grandeur. After he'd gone, she'd sat brooding; turning it over in her mind. But then she had laughed. She had said 'Master Farringdon! *Master* Farringdon! Well, I'm not so simple!' Muriel had said 'Nor am I. It's what I always told you, Mother. About Farringdon. Only you p'tend to dream about him.' 'Dream?' she'd said. 'Yes,' I said; 'that's what you *say*.' 'I dream about all sorts of things.' 'You tell him you dream about *him*, floating in the rigging, and bringing you wonderful tidings.' 'That's true; so I do.' 'Well, I never know when you're making it up. There's lots better things you could dream. Why don't you dream about *me*?' Mother had gone into one of her horrible fits of laughter, and miawed like a dozen grimalkins. Had Muriel said something funny?

Sometimes Muriel had watched Farringdon. Crept after him. She'd found him once on the upstairs landing. 'Where are you going, Farringdon?' 'Just to the lavatory.' 'That's the door to Mother's room.' 'Oh, sorry.' As if he hadn't known! The lavatory door had been ajar. Oho! He'd glared *then*, as if he could kill her. She'd felt her legs go cold. She was sure he . . . Sure he . . . hated her. He might, if she stood in his way . . .

She lay shivering, staring up into the darkness of the shadowed ceiling. There must be hundreds of spiders there, all watching. What did they think about? Flies? It was not really light yet; but there was a late moon in the morning sky, and the gleam of it bleached the sky and a kind of paleness came in at her bedroom window with the cold air, and made the air colder, like crystallised moonbeams. She hunched the bedclothes up round her neck; but that did not keep her nose warm. Her nose was so cold that it burned. Sometimes you couldn't tell if things were very hot or very cold. 'I'm cold,' thought Muriel. 'Beginning with my nose, I'm gradually freezing to death. If I knocked my nose! My ears will break off; they're as brittle as ice round a milk-bottle. I once read about a goldfish frozen in a block of ice. When the icicle was melted it swam about. That was very interesting.'

She knew exactly what she was going to do. Shaking with excitement, she crept out of bed, and with the faintest scratching of a match lighted a candle. Holding it well away from her in case she caught fire, she listened, standing crouched in her flannelette nightdress, and straining her ears. When she had struggled into the old grey dressing-gown she put one ear against the wall of her mother's room. That was the way you made sure.

An instant later she nodded and smiled.

'Snoring,' she said. It was a satisfaction to her. They had often wrangled about snoring, each accusing the other and denying that she herself ever snored; and this proved Muriel right. She was safe for a little while, perhaps for an hour, perhaps, on a cold morning like this, for two hours. . . .

But she must wash downstairs, in the scullery. Stop up the cracks beside the blind, in case a man saw her. Men were always looking in at that blind; at all blinds. It was a sort of nastiness men were prone to. She sometimes called out to them: 'I can see you! Go away!' Once she had bravely dashed open the back door, crying 'Boo!' But she had not caught anybody. They were always too quick. Scampering.

Was—you know what—all safe? There was one big bag under the bed, and the small bag was in the bottom of the wardrobe. Both were crammed. She had borrowed Mother's keys to unlock the bags and had put those keys back without being observed. Mother often peeped under the bed at night, to make sure the bags were there, and sometimes Muriel heard her pulling and pushing them about as if she had been counting and gloating; but yesterday she had not seemed to trouble, and Muriel had very artfully substituted other, similar bags, filled with newspapers. The real ones were *here*. She would take them downstairs, and hide them in the larder.

So, putting the candle in the shadow of a chest on the landing, she set out down the stairs, her dressing-gown trailing. It was very difficult to make the journey in silence, as the large dressing-case was bulky, as well as heavy; but she had strong arms, and the stairs were carpeted, and she was able to slide the case from the edge of one stair to the edge of another, until the passage from the front door was reached. Then she brought down the candle and the smaller bag. But this time she was no longer cold. Her nose tingled as if she had thrust it into a fire. Perhaps she'd caught erysipelas! that made her shudder anew. . . .

While the kettle boiled on a gas-ring she continually stepped out into the dark passage, to listen. She was now trembling so much that her teeth chattered, and as she unconsciously whispered 'Oh, dear! Oh, dear!' the words were prolonged by this chattering and the noisy intaking of cold air. She had never done anything like this before: it was dreadfully exciting. Even now, she might be found out, might hear the mallet, might be accused and forced to confess. Mother would never understand. You *had* to take drastic action. 'Drastic'; wasn't that a nice word! But at this distance no noise was audible from The Old Lady's room. Up there in the stifling, curtain-draped room, covered with a mound of blankets and quilts, Mother was snoring.

ii

An hour and a half passed. It was nearly nine o'clock, and everything had been done which had to be done in the house. The blinds were up, a fire was alight in the hastily-swept front room, and Muriel had drunk a cup of tea and eaten a little bread and butter. This suspense was much worse than all that had gone before. She waited for time to pass, and time crawled.

If Mother didn't wake up, she'd go. If Mother woke up, she had her breakfast all ready to cook, and would carry it in, and then go.

The clock must have stopped. No, it was ticking. The front-room clock said just the same. Nine o'clock. At half-past nine she'd go. The bags were both in the larder. She had her overcoat and hat on a chair in the kitchen; her outdoor boots on. But she was shaking so much that if the hammer *did* bang it was sure to put her in a state. Mother would notice, and bully her. . . .

'I can't *not* go now. Now I've screwed myself to it!' There! She'd said it aloud. That sort of fixed it. You couldn't, having said such a thing aloud, go back on it. Most likely he'd come to-day—*what if she met him*! He'd come up to her, getting taller and more frightening each minute, and glaring. 'What have you got in those bags? Hey? Hey? *I'll* carry them. *I'll* carry them . . .! If *he* carried them, they'd be gone for ever. He'd walk off in the darkness with long strides. . . . Muriel put her trembling hands to her mouth, lest she should scream.

She began to walk up and down the kitchen, brushing against the chair and the table, and feeling her legs grow weak. She couldn't go. She couldn't possibly leave Mother alone all day by herself. It would be heartless, inhuman! And coming back—how would she ever be able to walk into the house, defiantly, to darkness and reproach! Oh, no; she couldn't go.

But as she felt this, and said it to herself, her heart grew cold. Such bitter disappointment possessed her, such hopeless realization of defeat, that she sobbed twice, and allowed herself to grizzle. Her chin sank to her breast. In another instant, if she had obeyed the impulse to sit, to unbutton her shabby boots, she would have accepted misery and penury for ever.

The Old Lady's giant mallet destroyed cowardice. Bang-bang-bang-bang! Muriel's heart flew into life, with such thudding that it seemed to rival the mallet itself. But simultaneously all that the mallet stood for made her stiff again. She was reminded of past servitude and present danger. She *must* beat Farringdon! If she didn't, they'd both be robbed of every penny. Dashing at the tray, and shouting angrily that she was coming, she hastened, red-faced, to climb the stairs to her mother's room.

'I've come as soon as I could!' she shouted, rousing herself to false, artful indignation as she swept into the dark room. 'No need to bang the house down! Too *handy* with the old mallet!'

iii

Nobody saw Muriel leave the house with her burdens. The neighbours were in their kitchens at the back. In some instances the front blinds were still undrawn; in a few the parlours had not been used on the previous night, and in Winter were not used at all. She trudged along the deserted road, turned away from the town, and did not change direction until all who might know her by sight had been left behind. Strangers merely saw a short, red-faced woman carrying her luggage to the station. A minute later, so familiar was such a sight, they had forgotten everything about her.

But Muriel had made the detour in case she was pursued. Terror was at her heart. She was panic-stricken at finding the door of the bank she had chosen still closed. She would have run away if there had not been a police-man standing just across the road. He'd seen her. If she now ran, he'd arrest her at once, she was sure. So, with a faltering smile, she stood looking innocently at the bank door. How her heart beat! She must pretend to be simple, deaf, ignorant . . .

The policeman gave her a smiling nod. It was meant to encourage, to remark that she was out early, and to tell her that bank clerks guarded their morning privacy until the very hour struck. When it did so—and, pang, pang, pang, pang, a clock with a chime like that of a japanned tea-tray began in that very instant to announce the time—the door would fly open . . .

She was inside the bank. Her right arm ached as a result of carrying that heavy bag so far. She could hardly speak from nervous excitement; but gaped, and drew breath, and made no sound, looking like a red-headed fish with a black body. At last she gasped 'The Manager!' and saw the smile exchanged by the two fresh-coloured young men behind the counter. She wasn't offended. They had never seen, she supposed, a more curious figure than herself. And yet, when she gave them a stern glance, they must have realised that she was—somebody of importance.

That was her phrase of dignity: somebody of importance.

Then she was in the little cubicle which they called the Manager's office. It was fitted with highly polished light-coloured wood, all very new and handsome, but, Muriel felt, not very *industrious*. And she saw that the Manager was a tall, most respectable, frock-coated man who looked like a Cabinet Minister, a fact which gave her great confidence in him. He was most courteous; his hands were beautifully white. But he cocked his eyes at the ceiling a little strangely; and he had an air of *not* looking at you which showed that he had in fact turned away at that very instant. How funny! He couldn't really *know* anything.

'I want to leave . . . this money here,' gasped Muriel, with the sense of burning her boats. She pointed to the two cases, smiling and unconsciously shrugging her shoulders in her nervous fashion. 'In your strong room. Have you got a strong room? I should like to see it, one time. I hope my . . . money will be quite safe. There's a great deal. It's quite . . . tired my arm; though of course I'm strong. I'm really . . . But we'd better . . . I felt I must take drastic action. Drastic. After what I've seen. Seen *and* heard, you understand. *Anything* might happen to it.'

'Certainly, it would be safer in our charge.'

The Manager looked more polite than ever. He really made his face most remarkable, as if he had drawn a blind down over it—a white sun blind. Muriel could tell that he was much astonished. Not quite impressed, perhaps: astonished; rather as if he was pinching himself to make sure that he was awake. She was so excited, and, not amused, but in some degree hysterical, that she gave a small giggle which made him jump.

'A *great* deal safer,' he effusively agreed. 'We must count it together.'

She lifted the big dressing-case, with—'Allow me'—some assistance, to the desk. He didn't give *much* help, she noticed; he wasn't used to it. More a gesture.

'Good gracious!' cried the Manager, growing pink. Muriel hadn't known that people really started back in surprise. 'Have you *carried* this? Excuse me.'

'Oh, yes. I'm very strong. Well, you *have* to be, to do all I've done . . .'

At last he showed that he admired her. In fact, he stood away in awe as Muriel unlatched the case. There, within, folded, rolled, singly and in packets as they had been received from other banks, were hundreds of bank notes. They were stuffed as tight as could be; all the money Mother had ever collected and changed and hoarded. Many of them were tens, more were fives; a few were fifties.

'But these will take some time to count, Madame. There must be an immense number of them! I don't know . . .'

'I can't wait long!' cried Muriel, in a flurry, which made her tone imperiously loud. 'Surely you can count them in a little while . . .' She was imagining Mother in pursuit; perhaps Farringdon; and then complete failure. 'I'm going to see my sister in London. Mrs Boldero; perhaps you've heard of her. Mr Boldero's a famous lawyer, you know. Somebody of importance.' She thought: I'd better say that, in case he thinks I've . . . He does look away so very strangely. 'I came to you in preference to the other bank, because it's on my way . . . Besides, I've always preferred your bank. It's got a more attractive *name* . . .'

The Manager bowed. She could not be sure whether he had heard of Letitia or not; but unquestionably everybody had heard of Monty. He had often got people off.

'Mr *Montagu* Boldero,' she added, graciously. She saw again that queer doubting expression disappear as she looked earnestly into the Manager's face. He said smoothly:

'Of course it's a most distinguished name. Of course. Were you wanting to open an account, Madame?'

Muriel was taken aback by the suggestion. But she was enchanted also.

'What, you mean have a cheque book? Yes, that's splendid. I never thought of it. Chiefly, I want to leave this money safe . . . in your vaults . . . so that nobody can steal it. Banks don't steal money, do they? I know my . . . er . . . a relation of mine . . . thinks they do; but I never . . . I feel that if they were going to do that they'd hardly be likely to build such very substantial premises . . .'

'Oh, *quite* safe,' the Manager assured her.

'They wouldn't trouble to have everything so handsome——'

The Manager gave a hollow laugh.

'On the contrary,' said he, with distant pride in a revered institution.'

'I only want this kept for me,' cried Muriel. 'It's so *important*.'

'It is, indeed,' responded the Manager. 'Do you know how much there is here? I think we must get one of the tellers to help us. Do you object to that?'

In ten minutes the notes were piled high upon the Manager's desk. The sound of their crispness was in the air as each was unfolded. The Manager and his assistant counted and checked and counter-checked the treasure which had descended upon them. They were quite absorbed, it was clear; and Muriel, watching them with the eyes of an eagle, saw that not one of the notes was slipped surreptitiously into a pocket or under a boot-sole or into a false-bottomed drawer. 'One has to be careful,' she said to herself. 'They're impressed. You can tell that. It's a great deal of money. At ten o'clock in the morning.'

She suddenly shivered as she watched, feeling exultant, and then imagining Mother at Bella Vista, having eaten her breakfast, and washed, banging unmercifully to be helped down to the drawing-room, and receiving no answer. She almost told the Manager of her escapade. The words, the laughter, were on the tip of her tongue. It would have been lovely to tell somebody. But the Manager wasn't, somehow, quite the right sort of person.

'A bit starchy,' thought Muriel. 'Quite trustworthy, I should think, poor dear; though his cuffs are a little frayed. I wonder if he's married. I think they *have* to be. Or haven't to be. Or is that clergymen? Farringdon doesn't wear cuffs. You see his wrists. As if he put his hands deep in other people's pockets.' Aloud, she said: 'If I leave the money here nobody but me—I—can get it out again, can they? . . . I mean, unless I say . . . No, no; I thought not. That's why I came, you see. I want to be *quite* . . .'

She smiled. I must really buy myself a wrist-watch, she thought. She heard the clerk mutter 'Four thousand . . .' He had still many notes to count. So had the Manager. They had the figures written down on slips of paper—so many fives, so many tens, so many fifties . . . It was beautiful to feel about herself, for the first time, the admiring respect which is always accorded, in banks, to the affluent . . .

But she began to be in a great hurry. If Mother came out into the street, and told a policeman, it would be so difficult . . . 'I took it, to prevent somebody else taking it . . . Oh, nobody you'd know. Excuse me if I don't . . . I haven't spent it. It's all in the bank . . .'

They couldn't *do* anything to her, could they? She was very much afraid of policemen and magistrates. One was so helpless. The redness of her cheeks was undermined; she breathed heavily, watching the two men. She was beginning to feel terribly sleepy, with excitement, and this tiny room, and the lovely soothing rustle. If she could quietly drop off to sleep . . . No, no; that would *never* do! Oh hurry up! Hurry up! There would be a description of her all over the town. . . .

Once she was in the train, she'd be safe. In London. Letitia would tell her what to do. Darling Letitia: that was what was so nice; *she* wouldn't want a single one of . . . these . . . these lovely crisp notes! They would soon vanish. . . .

If the men didn't finish soon, she would get hysterical. . . .

'Five thousand,' said the fresh-complexioned clerk, sighing a great sigh, and flinging his leonine hair back. Both he and the Manager had some distance to go. . . .

iv

Cunning caused Muriel to leave the train before it reached Liverpool Street station. She gave up the half of her ticket, straining her ears for a recall, and half-prepared to run if it came. Then she went for a walk in mud-churned streets, where multiple stores abounded and everybody looked like everybody else. Then she caught an omnibus which took her to the alarmingly congested centre of the City.

It was so long since she had been there that she did not know which way to turn; and she did not dare to ask anybody for help, lest one of the decent-looking folk about her should be a pick-pocket or even a White Slaver. She had never understood what White Slavers did; but the name was very gruesome, and she had a vague dread of being sent to work in a salt-mine, where her hands would eventually drop off. Nor could she ask a policeman, in case he whipped from his pocket a description of her and took her into custody on a charge of stealing seven thousand, two hundred, and thirty-two pounds, the property of accused's mother, Mrs Reynolds, of Bella Vista. . . .

Shuddering, Muriel scrambled aboard a big red omnibus which was just about to leave the kerbside. As she reached the platform the conductor rang his bell, put his arm out to steady her, and called out 'Ole tight, Mother!'

Muriel staggered. It was very amusing that he should call her 'Mother!'
'Quite a good old Cockney!' she thought. She also laughed a little because
she had staggered. 'I'm not as used to this as you are,' she said to the
conductor. 'Where yer for, lady?' demanded the conductor. . . .

She had handed him twopence. That was something she remembered.
For twopence you could go anywhere by bus in London; so you always
gave twopence, and hopped off when you felt like it. Afterwards, as the bus
swayed along the winding streets like a pleasure boat, she clutched the
ticket, and stared out of the window ahead, over the driver's shoulders,
trying to see the hidden sky. This must be the Royal Exchange. Was it
Cheapside, or . . . How exciting everything was! It really didn't seem
possible to believe that she'd left Bella Vista only a couple of hours ago.
Lovely! She'd run away!

That was what mattered. Never mind the evening. Never mind
anything!

'I'll go and see Letitia this afternoon.' At that moment, Letitia was
leaving the house in Kensington, escaping just as surely from the habitual
as Muriel had done. 'Or shall I go and ask her out to lunch? What a
surprise! "Well, Letty, here I am. How about lunch at the Ritz?" It
would be frightfully daring! Letitia wouldn't want to lunch with a shabby
old thing like me! She'd rather we went to a teashop, in case anybody
saw me. Would she? I don't think so. Would she? I'm very shabby.
I realise that. I expect if I wore smart corsets and high heels, I should
look . . . I shouldn't like to look *not nice*. Well, I'm getting quite hungry!
Oh, there's . . . What was that street? . . .'

Muriel jumped to her feet.

'Excuse me. I've just remembered——'

She had not long to wait for a stopping-place; but when she stood
in the crowds of midday she was confounded by them. She grew seriously
forlorn. She had been driven by an irresistible impulse to get off the bus.
. . . But she didn't know . . . Where had she put Julian's picture postcard? Had she brought it in her handbag?

She went and stood in a shop doorway, hoping that no muscular thief
was watching her. She had so many things in this handbag, letters, and a
penknife, and old shopping-lists that she hadn't liked to destroy. . . .
Everything began to drop out of the bag as she searched; and she tried to
pick it up, and felt that everybody was smiling at her. . . .

But she found the postcard, and she had been right. Julian lived near
here! Her dear Julian! She would go and find him. "Hullo, Julian!
What about a spot of lunch?" That was what one said. But wouldn't it
be a shock if they only served a spot! Men's language was full of under-
statements.

She looked again at the address on Julian's postcard. What if he was
out? 'Oh, how unfortunate! I'm his aunt . . .' That was a nice thing
about Julian. He wouldn't mind one claiming relationship. He wasn't
ashamed of one for being . . .

What a shabby building! There were names painted on the wall just
within the door; but Julian's wasn't there. Had she made a mistake? Such

a dark entry; and the wall seemed to be streaming with wet. What should she do? Miserably loitering, for her heart sank upon the smallest excuse, Muriel hovered under the lintel of this uncomely building. But just as she felt she must run away from it she heard quick steps in the street, braced herself, and, as somebody unseeingly passed her, caught his arm with a yelp of relief.

'Oh, Julian! Julian!'

It was he. At first, coming from daylight into gloom, he didn't recognise her; and she had a painful instant's sense of rebuff. But then a smile drove away his frown. He kissed her, and let her hug him.

'Hullo, auntie!'

'Hullo, Julian! What about a spot of lunch? I'm up in town for the day.' It sounded splendid, so carefree; not at all as if she had been saying it over to herself. Had he hesitated? Not her darling Julian!

'I'm absolutely filthy, Auntie. I've been shopping. I'm off to America tomorrow.'

'Again?'

'Well, there's nothing to keep me here.' He looked as if he might cry.

'Aren't you . . . Well, at any rate you've got today. Can you spare me a little of it? Or would you . . .' Muriel felt the tears start to her own eyes.

'You're a godsend, Auntie. An absolute godsend!' He gave her elbow a quick little clutch. She saw his white teeth. Handsome boy! Handsome, unhappy boy.'

'Aren't you happy with us?'

'I'm not happy with anybody,' said Julian, with a little spiteful emphasis. 'My own fault.'

'Have you told Letitia?'

'She knows.' Julian was leading the way out of doors again. 'Shall we go to Soho for lunch, or where?'

'I'm paying! I'm rich—today. I've done something so awful! Julian, you won't give me away!' It was rather difficult to talk to him, for he walked so quickly, and she grew so soon breathless. 'Where you like. I don't care. Is . . . d'you mind . . .' She looked down ruefully at her shabby clothes. 'You look so very——'

He helped her into a taxi. He was the sort of young man, she felt, who always went by taxi. Not like his old aunt: a twopenny bus old aunt. What was that song? Hee-hee! Wasn't it lovely to be here, beside Julian, sitting back in a taxi, with her feet dangling! If only it could go on and on. . . . Quite without warning, Muriel felt dreadfully ill, as if an ague had seized her. The escapade lost all its lustre. Her bones seemed to press hard against her skin. If Julian had not been beside her she would have whimpered; but instead of whimpering she held his arm.

'What is it you've done that's awful? Run away?' asked Julian.

It sounded so lovely as he said it that Muriel giggled.

'Isn't it naughty of me!' she cried. 'It's just what I *have* done.'

'For good?' asked Julian. That was frightening!

'Oh, I couldn't! You see, I'm so . . .' That horrid vagueness came upon her, in which she *could* not understand anything clearly. 'I'm such a creature of habit,' she glibly answered. 'I wanted to ask Letitia's advice.'

'Best thing you *could* do.'

'She's so wise, I always feel. And she doesn't——'

'Doesn't *what*?'

'I'm afraid I've forgotten.'

'I didn't know, until lately, that *she'd* run away.'

'Did *he* tell you? That was long ago. She was a child. I wish I'd done the same. It's right, sometimes; when you . . . But I . . . hadn't the courage. I was afraid. I thought I was being clever. I wasn't, really; only a coward . . .' The tears had quite filled Muriel's eyes. They would splash over in a minute. She mustn't disgrace him. . . .

'We're all frightened of seeming dull,' said Julian. 'It's the tyranny of sophistication.'

'Oh, *very* tyrannical,' breathed Muriel, wiping her eyes.

The taxi had stopped. Something was at an end. A moment had gone for ever.

v

After the blissful lunch, when she had laughed a thousand wonderful times, and grown thrillingly young, Julian must have noticed—although she hadn't said anything at all about it—that she was afraid. He took her arm as they came out of the little restaurant; and Muriel held him close to her side, looking up into his face; and smiling whenever he looked down at her. When he did not look down she did not smile. She felt very strange inside, as if her heart were as big and heavy as a football, pressing against her lungs and stifling her.

Without asking what she would like to do next, he took her to a big building which stood a short distance away, where in beautiful darkness extraordinary drawings were flashed upon a screen, and fantastic animals danced and sang and played musical instruments until the whole gallimaufry of Muriel's old, forgotten childish dreams came to life and was made into magic fun. Everything was so wild and so swift that she laughed, caught at meanings, lost them, and became sightless and without thought. Tears streamed down her cheeks. She sat holding Julian's hand in the darkness, as merry as a child, gloriously happy, as if there were only such days as this to come for the rest of her life. But every now and then she shuddered.

She thought:

'I don't think . . . I don't think I *dare* go and see Letitia. She's too direct. She'd see, without saying so, or letting me see what she was seeing, how very wrong I've been. It *was* wrong. It's been lovely, and Julian's a beautiful companion—you couldn't wonder at any girl falling in love with him and being quite flustered; but my—— They're such funny little animals! Not really animals; but sort of *ideas*, all dancing. One seems to leave the earth. What ridiculous faces! They make me feel as if running away, even to the moon, was the most natural thing in the world; which of course

it *isn't*. But oh, dear me! how frightened I am of going home! It's dreadful!
If I could suddenly *die!*'

She could bear to look no longer at the dancing animals. They had
become devils of hate and fear. She held Julian's hand, instead, more
tightly than she had done, and shut her eyes. At last she whispered:

'Could we go? I'm not really . . . very well.'

He jumped up at once. Muriel stumbled, and dropped her bag; and as
she stopped to pick it up her head was bathed in uncomfortable stars, as
if she were going to faint. She must have staggered, for Julian put an arm
round her as they groped through the darkness in pursuit of the usher's
moving spot of light. In the half-lit entrance:

'How d'you feel? Better?'

'Rather dazed.'

'I'll take you straight along to see Mother,' whispered Julian, leading
her through the theatre's vast spaces.

It made Muriel tremble even to think of that.

'No, *you* must go,' she said, breathlessly. 'I *couldn't*. Don't tell her
you saw me.'

They were out of doors, and in the afternoon dusk. It was very astonish-
ing to see the street lights, and to breathe the cool air. There were lights in
the shops, too, although the sky was still pale and clear. Men were running
by with evening papers; curious men in rubber shoes whose feet made no
noise upon the hard pavements. Muriel did not like such men: were they
what were called Bow Street Runners? There was something frightening
about them, as there was about the Autumn wind.

'But you wanted to see her,' Julian reminded his aunt.

It took Muriel a moment to understand what he said, and he repeated
it, shaking her arm in a teasing, encouraging way. At last, she thought of
an answer.

'I've seen you, instead.'

Julian rallied her.

'You haven't told *me* anything.'

'No, I daren't. I never had any courage. I shouldn't dare tell *her*.
You see, I've taken all the money. To a bank. To keep it safe. In case—
sh, sh, sh, sh! And it isn't really mine; that's what's so awful. I don't
know what will happen to me.'

'Well, then, come and see Mother. She'll put you to bed and look after
you. She always does.'

How lovely that would be!

'Does she, *you?*'

Julian was silent. He walked along rather faster, and did not look
down at Muriel.

'She does. I haven't been very decent to her.'

Muriel forgot her own terrors.

'Oh, Julian! And you're going away. Poor Letitia! You *ought* to see
her.'

'Perhaps I will.' Muriel saw him smile. Again as if he were ready to
cry. The poor boy! He must be very unhappy. Now *that* was something

Letitia would always be able to cure; her children's unhappiness. She would understand it. Muriel's one bewildered way of curing, she knew, would be by a bribe, some kisses; and bribes and kisses somehow weren't cures for what lay within.

'You *must*. Promise me. It's been so lovely to-day.'

'Come *with* me.'

'I must go home.' The tears seemed to have welled into her throat. 'Back to . . I can come again to see her.' She thought: 'I shan't. She's like conscience. What *will* happen to me?' She was terribly frightened and unhappy, clinging to him as the one link she had with tranquillity. 'You see I've left *my* Mother all alone. I just walked out of the house this morning——'

'Good for *you*.'

'Now I feel like a murderess for doing it. What's the time?'

'Somewhere about four o'clock. Come and have some tea.'

Easy, darling boy! He must know how charming he was; but to waste such charm on a shabby, red-faced old aunt! It made her want to cry again.

'No, no. There's a train at half-past four. I must catch it.'

'Really?'

'Really. You've been the dearest boy.'

'Have I? I feel *most* inadequate. I do wish you'd come along and see Mother.'

'No. But *you* must go. Promise me. Promise me.'

She was deeply moved, beseeching him to do what she would herself have done, if she had had the courage. Tears spread in the deep wrinkles about her eyes, which swelled until they looked as large as the eyes of an old, patient cow. Letitia was a haven. A haven she had missed in the day's pressing excitements; but a haven for which she now felt sick longing. She had only pretended to dread Letitia's dear sight. What mattered more was Letitia's love. It was what one always thought of as motherly; although Mother had none of it. . . .

How unhappy she was! She was afraid she was going to disgrace herself by bellowing!

vi

Julian saw the grimy train leave the grimy platform, its red tail light ominous in the murk. Auntie had not waved to him from the window. Probably she could not see him. She had even been rather fussy, telling him not to wait, and sitting firmly back in her place with her eyes shut. He had bought her some papers and magazines, which she clutched but did not examine. And then he had felt bound to stay until the train moved; and, as it had taken a very long time to move, he had stood in cold and semi-darkness justified by nothing but this obstinate purpose. But now the train was only a shape; and in a moment there was no sign of it at all. Red lights dotted the darkness.

Something about the Autumn day, and the sense of having bidden fare-well, perhaps for the last time, to a poor old woman for whom, although he loved her, his affection was stained with contempt or distaste, heightened Julian's melancholy. He was not naturally patient with old women, or thoughtful of them; they taxed his nervous energy without giving him any-thing in exchange. But he felt pity for Muriel. He glanced up at the big illuminated clock, noting mechanically that its minute hand had just passed the half-hour, and stood irresolute. Should he do what Auntie had begged him to do? Mother? It was embarrassing to meet anybody who so nakedly knew one's heart, one's discomfiture.

But the thought of returning now to his cold lodging, and of leaving later for his three thousand mile journey across the Atlantic, without having seen Mother, sent him hurrying westward. At once his heart was lightened. He caught himself smiling, almost whistling, in glee; and very quizzically raised his brows in not very ardent self-scorn. Did one *never* grow up?

It was better still when he reached the house, which enfolded him with almost every joyous memory of boyhood. Ruth, always his friend, brightened in welcome; and he found with relief that Letitia was alone. Moreover he was able to go into the room, and kiss his mother, with a silent composure which he felt to be creditable. He knew that she would not be in the least deceived. He knew that, with her, no excuse or explanation was ever necessary. Nor desirable. With Letitia one came and went as if one had never been away; one asked and received; one gave only what one wished freely to give. However, former words of his own, spoken in bitterness, hurt him now. He couldn't apologise for them; he didn't suppose they were remembered; but they gave him such pain that he could almost have knelt to Letitia.

'I'm going tonight; back to New York,' he told her, as casually as he could.

'I'm sorry you're going,' Letitia said, just as calmly. 'I wish you'd been able to stay.'

'Nothing to stay for,' observed Julian. He almost added: 'Thanks to you.' What he *did* say was: 'I'm quite tired of London.'

'I wish we'd had a chance of tiring of *you*,' replied Letitia. 'Chris will be sorry to miss you.'

Julian pressed his lips tightly together. He was never so bored as he seemed; and with Christine, because she was a girl, his feelings had always moved more easily. Mother knew that, of course.

'She had a good party,' he declared. 'Enjoyed it, I should think.'

'As far as I could tell, not a blemish.'

He saw her smiling, but thoughtfully, as if she were testing her memory anew, searching for unseen blemish in Christine's happiness. This gave him a glimpse of her loving care of them all, especially of himself. God! He'd been frightful to her!

'Well, she had everything her own way,' he said, of Christine. 'That's what Chris likes.'

'Don't we all?' asked Letitia, with a broadening smile.

'But she *gets* it.' He walked moodily across the room. 'We don't.'

G

'Sometimes she doesn't, because she bounces so. People are curmudgeonly to a bouncer. Repressive, you know.'

'Like you,' Julian muttered, meaning to tease, but not quite hitting the note.

'I'm afraid so.' She sighed. 'It's so easy, afterwards, to see where one went wrong.'

'Of course I didn't mean that.' Julian had reddened. Damn! He couldn't say anything about it. You couldn't *bring* yourself to it! Well, it wasn't desirable. 'I think young Chris has always had a grand time. I think she knows it, too.'

Letitia laughed at a living sense of Christine.

'She's becoming quite motherly!' she exclaimed. 'She's going to be tremendous. I'm not at all afraid of her now.'

'"Of" or "for"?' He saw that he had been sentimental. 'I wish I wasn't going. I'd like to see the comedy.'

'Stay and help us to play it.'

He shook his head.

'No. I'm on a good thing in New York. I'm learning a lot. I mean to learn more.'

'Splendid.'

'But the comedy's absolutely . . .'

Letitia looked up and his voice gave out.

'I'll keep you abreast of it,' she promised. 'But you may also hear something from Chris. Something meaningful. She's not brimming with confidences to me.'

'Assumes you know everything.'

'I don't.'

'At any rate, you won't be told. It's so much easier to hope that you understand what one doesn't understand oneself.'

'An enormous mass of credit,' laughed Letitia. 'When I die I shall startle everybody by saying "What *have* you all meant in the last twenty years?"'

'We shall say: "What you *thought* we meant".'

'Yes. What *was* it?'

'Three words, but I must go, darling,' said Julian, hurriedly. 'We can't go into all that now. I want to run up to my room. And then go. I'm dining on the train; sleeping on board. We leave Southampton first thing in the morning.'

Letitia held him close to her; but Julian's arms were not less firm, and his cheek was pressed for an instant very hard against her own. He said 'Goodbye, Mummie,' and waved radiantly from the door, leaving her warmhearted and not quite dry-eyed. It was not until he was in the train, *en route* for Southampton, that he realised that he had said nothing about his afternoon with Auntie. How extraordinary! Mother washed everybody else out while you were with her!

The poor old girl, in the cold railway carriage, blubbering . . . And that blasted bitch, with Mark! . . . She could rot! She could whine and whimper to get him back. No! Thank God he was done with her!

They were all women.

vii

Muriel, in the gloomy compartment, with an old top-hatted man opposite who forbiddingly held the evening papers in front of his face, so that she could not have been sure that he had a face at all, sank deeper and deeper into the corner. She was very cold, and very small; and the other occupants of the carriage were nothing but darker areas in a blur of dreadful tears. She clenched her work-seamed hands within the rusty black woollen gloves, and felt the wool catch upon her rougher skin until she could hardly bear the disagreeableness of that sensation. The palms of her hands, although she was so cold, grew moist, She could feel the tip of her nose tickling where the dribbling tears congregated in spite of every surreptitious pat of her sodden handkerchief.

In vain did she try to lift her spirits by remembering the happy meeting with Julian, the lovely lunch, and the ridiculous antics of the dancing animals. All were avoidances. They could not hide reality. She was now returning to that miserable home, to Mother, to the continuing threat of Farringdon. Farringdon became taller in her imagination, an immense and grasping force against which there was no defence. Nobody could protect her. Everything she had done would be useless. Farringdon would *command* her to give up the money. She wouldn't do it. *Mother* would command her. She would refuse and refuse. And then they would make her.

All that merry time at the bank was just a silly dream. Silly! It wasn't only the money. It was everything she had done since before dawn. She had only played truant; playing truant wasn't any good. It was silly. Not even grown-up. Silly and wicked. Punishment was coming nearer and nearer. She was wicked, wicked, wicked!

Wicked, wicked, wicked, agreed the train. Wicked. It jolted all the time, saying wicked, wicked . . . Outside, everything was dark. In Muriel's heart the darkness was greater still.

Thirteen

AT BELLA VISTA

i

AS F. R.'S TRAIN was running into Willowhaven that morning, it was halted at the points about half-a-mile outside the town. He noticed that the speed was slackening; and one or two people in the carriage seemed to think the train had arrived, for they expectantly gathered themselves together. F. R., however, had now made the journey so many times that he remained immovable. He thought: 'You see? I don't budge. We're half a mile out. Such a man as myself *knows* a thing like that; but of course these gaping geese never observe *anything*.' It was not an unpleasant thought. From beneath lowered lids he looked about him at the stupid.

Stop. All heard the train's whistle, which said: 'I'm here. Let me pass!' There was a wait of several minutes, during which the passengers coughed, and two of them peered out of the windows, steaming the panes with their breath. Then, with a rumble, another train passed them, going towards London. It was moving slowly, and F. R. was by the window nearest to it. He saw, but did not recognise, a small plump figure in black sitting alone in a compartment, holding down its head as if it did not *want* to be recognised. He was too full of his own plans to imagine the plans of another person. He was too convinced of his own stealthy wisdom to suppose that anybody else could guess what he was thinking.

With another whistle, which said 'Thanks!' the train began to move again. The gleaming up-line rails slid by. A goods train standing by the second platform explained their delay. The darkness caused by a station roof made everything in the carriage black. When the others had scrambled out, F. R. followed slowly. He carried no bag today. He was not staying. But, to F. R., no holiday was without its deeper purpose. How, within the secrecy of his beard, F. R. smiled to think of his own cunning!

His plans were almost complete. But they were so secret that he hardly allowed himself to peep at them in their entirety. It was as if he were several men, members of an Edgar Wallacian Fellowship, who all took instructions from the Big Shot, and who were kept by him in ignorance of the larger purpose of everything they did. Only the Big Shot himself knew that purpose. He indicated it now by a dry smile.

How artful he'd been! He knew the whole business, through and through; and every inch of the house. Practically none of the money was banked or invested. The will was at the solicitor's. So were the deeds of the house. All right; they couldn't be seen; and it didn't matter. The money was here, as any burglar would immediately guess. Ideal. He'd persuaded The Old Lady that he ought to be in the place, for fear anything happened. For fear. Subtle suggestion! That was a blind. He'd never be there. What he proposed to do was to take the money, not all at once, but with precautions against discovery;—and then, one night, at the right moment, have a party at the local hotel, take the two old dears to the local theatre, race back to Bella Vista to make a few dispositions, rejoin them, and bring them home to overturned furniture, ransacked drawers, and—naturally—rifled suitcases. Perfectly simple. He heard his own voice saying:

'Leave this to me! *You* don't want the police. Blunderers! *I'll* get the money back . . .'

No, they wouldn't want the police. They were the sort of people who were frightened of being bullied. *He* knew. As she came out of her terror Muriel would suspect him. But those notes, some of which he had seen, were too old and miscellaneously collected to be traced; and he *thought* The Old Lady was in his pocket. How sympathetic he had been: 'Well, you must let *me* help you.' Why not? With that money, he could carry out all his schemes; and for The Old Lady's lifetime he'd gladly be her banker.

This wouldn't have been necessary if she hadn't been stingy. Why hadn't she offered him a couple of thousand? He'd been driven to plan when he found she wouldn't part with a stiver. 'Now, is there anything wrong with this scheme?' F. R. demanded of himself as he strode along the promenade. Perhaps he needn't fake the burglary. The notes could mysteriously have disappeared—oh, long ago! How often were they pored over? He'd see. They were uncountable in detail, now, under several hours. . . . What majestic luck!

The wind whistled in his ears, and blew his beard apart, revealing his smiling lips and the big, good-natured teeth. There was blue sky overhead; but the sea was grey and weed-ridden after a storm. The coast was exposed. That damned house was draughty and liable to be full of smoke. . . .

He approached it, and, using his key, entered. At once there was a terrific banging and shouting—Bang! Bang-bang-bang! Bang-bang! The shouting was ferocious but blurred, as if the shouter's mouth were covered, or—which was more likely—empty.

'Hey! hey! hey!' called F. R., very jovially. 'What's all this?'

Bang-bang-bang-bang! was the reply. By Jingo, what a row! That hammer must be a formidable weight. A weapon. Yes, in strong hands decidedly a weapon—a lethal weapon! Didn't the neighbours ever complain of it?

'Mother! Muriel!' He opened the door of the downstairs front room. The room was empty. What had been a good fire was sinking to dull red and grey. Bang-bang-bang! Then the bawling voice: 'Come upstairs at once! Come upstairs at once! *You naughty girl!*' Completely puzzled, F. R. darted up the stairs two at a time.

The noise came from the front bedroom. He launched himself upon the door. A moment later, he saw The Old Lady sitting up in bed in her night rig, and was convulsed with laughter.

ii

The heavy curtains had been drawn back, admitting daylight; but an electric light burned over the bed. Upon a heavily-flowered black silk eiderdown—it was no more than the uppermost surface of a mountain of bedclothes—was perched a tray, all the articles upon which, however, had at some time travelled with speed into one corner where they remained huddled. And The Old Lady, well-supported by pillows, the great mallet lifted high, glared from beyond the eiderdown. A fantastic sight.

Upon her shoulders was what had once been a handsome quilted bedjacket of pale pink silk with a pattern of exquisitely small forget-me-nots. Her false teeth were missing, so that she had hollow cheeks and pursed lips in the middle of a strange sunken place between nose and chin. Her hair, which was in twists of paper, looked like the head of Medusa. And so wild and furious was the light in her eyes that if F. R. had not been cocksure of his power to deal at once with any woman he might have been alarmed by it.

'Why?' 'Eh?' The toothless gums showed in a grin. 'Oh, I don't know. Why not? So she ill-treats me. Now she's gone out and left me.'

'Does she do that?' A thought leapt in his mind: if she goes out like this that gives me immense opportunity. Ha! 'Often?'

A poor old head was feebly shaken. Bright eyes glittered in it. What a contradiction!

'I don't know,' sighed a forlorn voice. 'Lying here, what do I know?' F. R. smiled in his beard. He was impressed by his mother; but he was not deceived by her. He was amused by her performance; her old mind groping about behind all complaints, all histrionics, dealing with secret thoughts to which, at present, he had no clue. What the devil *did* she think?

'Well, what about getting up?' he demanded. 'And frightening Muriel!'

He saw those burning eyes fixed upon him. They held a malignant amusement which gave him a slight shock.

iii

An hour had passed. Muriel had not returned. F. R. and his mother were sitting together beside the roasting fire downstairs, she with all her curl-papers removed, her teeth in, her hair neatly brushed, her black silk dress on, and at least her face sufficiently washed. Her hands were a different matter. She was otherwise outwardly a duchess. But F. R., keeping her in play with unlikely tales of ghosts in the Australian bush, snakes in South Africa, and extraordinary vagaries of work and wealth in the United States, knew that he had softened only the surface of her mood. Below, he was convinced, devilish punishment was hatching for Muriel.

But he was content. More than once he had seen those hooded eyes blink. She had dozed for a second or two. 'Doze, doze, my darling,' he had thought. 'Doze, while I get busy.' But she had always opened her eyes again too quickly. Not too quickly for his guard, of course, which was unsleeping.

'I'll tell you what, Mother,' said he. 'I'll look in the larder. I've cooked meals—quick meals—superb meals—in every part of the world. In barge cabins, and under the stars; in Madrid slums and New York luxury apartments. I've cooked snakes; and sheep a farmer didn't know he'd lost; and chicken; and terrapin; and plain sausage and mashed. I might manage something here——'

'She'll have left nothing,' grumbled The Old Lady. 'You don't know Muriel. She's a fool. Where *is* she?'

F. R. found that his mother was unjust to Muriel. There was much in the larder, including some astonishingly fresh fillets of sole, and some sausages and a small piece of beef from which his experienced eye told him that he could begin to make a delicious grill. A tomato or two (alas, he had no kidney!) and some fried potatoes and whatever this fragmentary green-stuff in the box proved to be; a meal was assured. Good! Hunting more

deeply, with an electric torch, he discovered to his joy a bottle of Pommard·
Phew! phew! phew! How had it come there?

'Good God!' he whispered. 'The Fates are with me!'

He went back to the sitting-room, glowing with promises.

'Give me an hour!' he said. 'We'll eat! And we'll *drink*!'

In London, Letitia had walked through Kensington Gardens and was
standing by the Serpentine, looking across to the opposite bank; and Muriel
was scrambling off the big red omnibus in order to go and find Julian. Here,
The Old Lady brooded, and F. R. wrapped about himself a pinafore of
Muriel's as he gathered the ingredients of this fateful meal. The pinafore
nearly reached his knees; it fitted his circumference without strain. F. R.
smiled, and was busy. He was humming with satisfaction; the tune he
hummed was 'Lead, kindly Light.'

iv

After lunch, when the dishes were removed to the kitchen, where, with
the pots and pans, they made a noble assembly for a washer-up, he lighted
his pipe. Smoke from it drifted across the hearthrug, sometimes quite
into the face of The Old Lady, whose hands stretched over the arms of her
chair, clasping them with a firm caress. The big mallet hung, ready, upon
one of the same chair-arms. He saw that long, fleshy nose, slightly reddened
by the meal, responding to the smoke. It was like a pig's snout. He noticed
how untidy The Old Lady's hair became when with a sudden gesture of
exasperation she pushed it away from her ears. He realised how much she
must enjoy being cruel when he saw the long, rather thick lips pressed against
each other in what seemed to be a voluptuous contact. Did she beat Muriel
still? Or was it done by tongue, deprivation, such malicious acts as that
writing on the dusty table?

This old woman, he remembered, had always raved when she lost her
temper. Raved and screamed and stamped and thrown. He had seen her
strike his little father, and strike to do more than affront. Strike to kill.
She was a savage. In youth she must have had some strange beauty and
possibly voluptuous charm; but he didn't believe her tales of theatrical
success. What success had she ever had? None, except in marrying his
father.

'How did Father die?' asked F. R., suddenly.

The old face, if it changed at all, merely grew more baskingly content.
She had enjoyed her lunch. She had eaten heartily, and under his careful
guidance had drunk two-thirds of the rather over-warmed Pommard. Now
she was drowsy and smiling. He thought she might really answer his
question. However, she did not do so. She said:

'He didn't take enough care of himself, my son.'

'Hm. We're different, you and I. We take care of ourselves. We're
still alive. You've made a good lunch,' suggested F. R. When she nodded,
he continued: 'So you haven't missed Muriel as much as you thought you

G*.

went without sound to the doorway, turning once again to assure himself that her sleep was not simulated.

V

'A fool', thought F. R., 'assuming eagerly that she was really asleep, would fly up those stairs three at a time. I'm not a fool. I go first to the kitchen, make up the fire, and pretend I'm washing up. I run the water; I pile the dishes. It takes five valuable minutes; but it makes for probability. It's finesse. By God, I'm clever!'

He ran the hot-water tap in the sink, and deliberately clattered the dishes as he put them to soak in plenty of soda. Then, drying his hands quietly, although he was in such a ferment that they shook like the hands of a toper, he walked, humming, back to the front room. She still slept. Her head was a little more on one side. With what seemed to him to be incredible boldness he spoke to her.

'You all right, Mother?'

Her snoring was uninterrupted. He had time now. He had all the time he wanted. The greying house was open before him.

Now indeed he allowed himself to run, deft-footed, to the first floor; but he stopped upon the landing to listen. Caw . . . caw . . . caw . . . A flight of rooks, homeward bound upon an evening of threatened rain, would make little more noise. Before going downstairs she had closed her bedroom door. Was it locked? Wait! The gloves! He drew his unworn kid gloves from an inside pocket, and put them on. No, the polished china handle squealed as it turned, and the tacky varnish chattered as he pushed open the door; but the room was as it had been first thing in the morning. Foul! Foul! Dirty water stood in the washstand basin; a used towel had been flung upon the eiderdown. Beyond the heavy, square-posted bed, thrown to the floor, was what his mother wore at night. What an atmosphere! What suffocating associations with heavy sleep and an over-laden body! F. R. priding himself upon fastidiousness, gave a pretended shudder. In reality his mind was set upon his single object.

That object was within his grasp, and he hesitated. He could not bring himself to the final act. But, in the midst of hesitation, a stronger impulse drove him forward, and he sank to his hands and knees. It was dark under the bed; he could hardly see the two cases. They had been pushed, in supposed cunning, far to the middle; but such long arms as his were not to be foiled. Groping, he dragged out the bigger one. God! It grated! There were bare boards with nails in them, under there in the darkness!

Fury seized F. R. He brought the case to his knees, and found that it was locked. But a hundred little keys jingled upon a string in his pocket; and while one, two, three of them, to his impatience, were useless, the fourth turned as a knife in butter. You see? thought F. R., with revived assurance. These cases are all alike; no difficulty with any of them. Snap-snap . . He smiled broadly, in excited satisfaction. Now for the feast of notes!

There was something odd here, however. Newspaper. Newspaper.

Folded newspaper, as tightly packed as the notes should have been. Wads and wads of newspaper. Good God! He turned and tossed them aside; more and more; until he saw the bottom of the case. There was nothing here! He'd been cheated!

F. R. fell back upon his heels, pale and sweating. His quick breath hissed. He could not believe what he saw. Newspapers? It was impossible! What had the old devil meant? She'd said the money was here. He'd known it was here—in these very cases. Had she, clairvoyantly guessing at his plan, as she washed and dressed, changed its hiding-place? No, no; there had been no opportunity. It was a job needing thought and time and skill. It had been done earlier by a plan as astute as his own. When? By whom? Muriel? Was *that* why she wasn't here? Had she taken everything to Letitia? F. R. swore in despair.

He stared about the room, to the tall wardrobe, to the dressing-table; and, in rage, drew forth the smaller case. This time he was prepared. It, too, was filled with neatly-folded newspaper. There was no money.

The substituted newspaper made a mocking litter, spread upon the floor in its neat little bundles. It taunted him with ruin. Completely stupefied, F. R. continued to kneel by the two bags, his head down, his eyes half-closed. He felt sick; not yet able to grasp more than the fact of his disappointment; quite unprepared now, for further search or effort. Finished! How had he lost his way? Why had he been deceived? Miserable, unfortunate. . . .

It was in this moment of blank hopelessness that, with a crash, he felt sudden, violent pain in the head; had an instant's sense of being dazed and blinded; and, half turning and rising upon one knee, received a second terrible blow. He pitched over sideways to the floor, unconscious.

vi

An hour later, some returning thread of awareness made F. R. open his eyes. He saw a finger of light in a dark forest. It flickered, as—although he was unaware of this—it had done previously; but after flickering it became a little stronger than before. He groaned. His head ached. The sickness he had felt earlier was increased, and a dizziness forced him, as he struggled to rise, to sink again to the floor. This time insensibility was short. He stirred anew, and put a gloved hand to the stinging patches amid his thick hair. It came away stained, and he was horrified. That must be blood. He could not bear the sight of blood. Horrible! He put the hand from him. At last, moving with caution, he caught with the other hand at what proved to be a great bed, and pulled himself to his knees.

Where was he? The day was not quite gone, but dusk was filling the room with shadow. There seemed to be a window over there—he didn't remember that. It admitted all the light there was, but as the room faced away from the sunset everything in it remained grey and unrecognisable. It floated like a cloud of smoke. Was he at the flat? Memory began to return. He saw white folded newspapers all about him upon the floor, and possible sounds. But nothing happened. The boiler re-filled itself. There was silence.

Ever-glancing at the passing light, sometimes sure that he heard stealthy movement in the house or a key in the front door lock, F. R. forced himself, as quietly and methodically as his shaking hands allowed, to wash all the dishes, the pots, the pans, and replace them as nearly as he could in their proper order upon dresser and shelves. If he had once dropped and broken a dish, he would have lost his nerve; but he was fortunate. It seemed an endless, a dreadful job in the gathering darkness; and when at last it was done, and he could dry his hands and mop his head, a sudden flare of bright light from the next door kitchen made him pant. He drew back into shadow. But when the light was switched off again he missed it and was all at sea for a few moments in the dusk.

Afterwards, made cooler by success, he took a duster and rubbed all the surfaces upon which he could by any chance have left finger-prints during the day: the door-handles, the pokers, the coal scuttles, the backs of chairs. The hammer he had never touched. The Pommard bottle he put, when it had been wiped free of every sign of use, far behind all that stood upon the larder floor, so that it was no more than another empty bottle. It was now completely dark. He did not dare to use a light, for fear it should be noticed and remembered. He did not dare to go again to that dreadful room of death and disaster. A picture of the still body ran before his eyes wherever he turned, and brought panic upon him again. Catching up his hat and coat, therefore, with sweat running down his trembling legs, and his teeth chattering with fear and relief, he stumbled, cursing, against every obstacle, groped his way to the door, and left the house as if his mother's ghost already clawed at his very coat-tails. 'Farringdon! Farringdon! You're forgetting the money, aren't you!' The devil! The witch!

The horror of the house continued upon him. Dread and failure haunted it. He shuddered again and again, perhaps at the evening chill striking through to his hot body; and, ducking his head, feeling the sweet wind upon his cheek, avoiding every lamp, he swept onwards in the darkness, not to the town, not to the station—such places were dangerous,—but by instinct along the broad motor-road away from Willowhaven, towards London, where, unseen himself, he might discover some sure way of escape. Nobody knew his address. If he could get home, back to the flat, he would be hidden, an unknown, unseen creature, lost among the eight million inveterate strangers of the city. That was his prayer.

Out of doors light was reflected from an opal sky; but F. R. knew that in such a light a man was a shadow. Even when he was passed by an occasional car with sweeping headlights he believed himself safe. A rapidly walking figure, though it might be one of exceptional height, would never be identified. But he must leave the road soon. He must hurry to whatever point would bring him first to the railway; for until he was in London he would not have shaken memory of that dreadful room from his mind. It came again; the stench of it, the disarranged bed, the marbled water in the basin, and that cold figure which had lain for so long unheeded between himself and the window. He ran a few steps, coughing in his disgust. If

one had wings, or could seize a boat and go out into unknown waters.
. . . This had been a terrible day. A terrible, a fatal day.

As F. R. strode through the increasing darkness, he found that the road
continued to lie quite close to the railway line, concealed from it at first
by motor service stations and plastered shacks, and then by a difference of
level and a long line of trees. Between the bare branches red signals lamps
were visible against the sky. Wonderful things! They filled him with
longing. They had always done that, since boyhood, when his longing had
been for movement into the adventurous unknown. Adventure! It had
been his dream. Now, alas, he was sick of adventure. The lamps represented
safety.

Even more powerful in its effect upon his mind was a fully-lighted train
which, coming slowly towards Willowhaven, was stopped by a signal at a
point above the road and not more than two hundred yards from it. The
sight of the stopped train made him shudder. How long had this nightmare
lasted? He drew out his watch, trying to read the time by the train's lights.
It was a little before a quarter to six. A moment later the train went on;
the lights passed; he was in darkness. He did not know that in the corner of
one compartment of the moving train Muriel was reaching home, crestfallen
and reluctant, after a day of escape from which so many consequences had
sprung and were to spring.

The inspector came back into the room, seeing her crouched in the chair. 'This mallet, now,' said he. 'We've been having a look at it, ma'am; and we find it's got some grey hair on it, ma'am, and a little blood. Quite fresh, ma'am, as if it had been used to strike some sort of a *blow* on somebody's *head*. I wonder if you could suggest any explanation of that?' He'd looked sly. More than sly. Triumphant. Muriel saw at last that he was her hateful, diabolical enemy. She screamed. She did not hear what else he said, or what he threatened or demanded. Everything was blurred by the one searing flash of realisation which had come to her at sight of his hidden grin. 'You horrible man!' she cried. 'You horrible man! I know what you mean!' She was upon her feet, shaking violently, screaming again, and then growing pale with dread. 'You're horrible!'

'I must do my duty, ma'am,' said the inspector, quietly.

ii

Letitia was mending. A basketful of work stood beside her chair. But she was also in a kindly, dreamy state which would presently make her impatient. She believed that whenever one felt kindly and dreamy it was a sign of unreality or smugness. But this afternoon she was kindly and dreamy. The best of us slip at times below par. She thankfully accepted Julian's grand gesture of love for her. She was not sure of deserving it, but the love was very sweet. She was even less easy about Gabriel, whose kindness towards herself was likewise exceedingly pleasant. And she had Constance upon her mind. Not quite upon her conscience; but upon her mind, as somebody to whom she had lately, for an instant, turned a blind eye. Hence her dreaminess. In the cant of the day, a defence mechanism was at work; candour fought against an impulse to put the best face upon everything. Candour would win. But the best face was, as it were, batting first.

Gabriel was a very amusing darling. Julian was less amusing, but was more her own sort of darling. Gabriel's scruples were those of the sophisticate; they could be brushed off like dust on a topper. And Constance was her friend. Constance had muffed her marriage through lack of that reserve which, in Letitia, she would call cold-heartedness. But then Letitia, being Letitia, wasn't positive that Constance was wrong about Letitia. Perhaps Letitia *was*—she had thought it herself—abominably disinterested. Less pleasant words could be used of her. Constance's candours——'

Ruth was in the room, with that discreet flutter of silk.

'Mrs Wilton, Madame,' she murmured. 'I said you were alone. She's here.'

And at that instant Constance arrived, with a bounce and a flounce which were intended to prove that, come weal or woe, she was still undefeated. It was obviously a pretence; for under the paint and brilliance she was haggard. She had greatly deteriorated in a month.

'Letitia, my angel!' cried Constance, sweeping forward. 'That basket! So domestic! Are you *expecting* somebody? To impress? A beau, for example?'

'No, you've caught me with my visor up—or down, or whatever it is,' laughed Letitia, embracing her friend. 'I'm so glad you've come. I was thinking about you.'

'With remorse?' The tone was edged. But Letitia replied cheerfully: 'All my thoughts are remorseful. Or merely melancholy.'

'It's the mending, darling. It's so like a penance that one assumes the sin. The sin is thrift, or the doctrine of service; or some other wretched Puritanism. The truth is, everything should be thrown away after one use. Like paper napkins. Thrown into a giant incinerator. Is it an incinerator? Something that rolls everything out again and makes it into raw material? I forget. I'm always haunted by the barking noise people make when they say matter's indestructible. I don't know if it *is*. Ridiculous that we should suffer so much from ignorance. We guess. Watch our thankfulness when we guess right! *You* don't guess: I don't mean that. Except about visors, when you're shaky. I mean that *I* do.'

'About visors?'

'Don't be absurd! Visors must come *up*, to show the nose. No, I meant about everything. Nobody *tells* me anything; so I have to put two and two together. They *always* make at least *forty*; usually a headache.'

Ruth brought in the tea.

'What sums are you doing just now?' asked Letitia, innocently.

'A dozen. You and Gabriel, for instance.' Constance's words became almost inaudible, from breathlessness. She sat transfixed, looking *away* from Letitia, lest she should read on her friend's face some intolerable emotion.

'Constance!' Letitia's dreaminess was dispersed as if by a thunderclap. But at the same time a flash of self-accusation rent her. If she, for instance, had seen Constance in the same relationship with Monty! How stupid one could be!

'It's been on my mind for weeks,' gasped Constance. 'Forgive me for blurting it out, darling. Are you trying to think of something to say? I know every word. I've heard it a dozen times—from other women.'

'All with clear consciences, I suppose,' said Letitia, looking at Constance and seeing with horror how greatly she was suffering.

'At least, with glib tongues,' retorted Constance, who held one trembling hand with the other, in order to check their trembling. 'Such as you could easily surpass.' Her glance flew past Letitia. It was stormy; but if it held the hatred or distrust of her words that was not the impression it made upon her friend.

'My conscience isn't absolutely clear,' said Letitia, quickly. 'But I don't think I've done anything wrong.'

'One may have a very elastic sense of that,' cried Constance. 'About one's own conduct.'

'I?'

Constance hesitated.

'Even you, in this case.'

Thinking aloud, Letitia slowly said:

'You torture *yourself*. *I* haven't hurt you. And I won't hurt you.'

In other words, a dangerous man to oppose. She neither liked nor disliked him; she was conscious of instinctive resistance to him.

'Won't you sit down? Do you mean she's been run down by a car, or something?'

'Er . . . no, Ma'am,' said the inspector, thinking to himself: Hm, takes it coolly. Too much the lady to let anything show, I expect. She won't lie much; that's one thing. Some of them lie like Orientals. 'It was at home. Would you mind if I asked you one or two questions?'

'Not at all.' Letitia was puzzled. 'Perhaps, when I've answered them, you'll tell me a little more? I think I'd better explain that I haven't seen my mother for some time. A good many years.'

'Indeed, Ma'am.' The small blue inspecting eyes gave her a sly peep. So there was no love lost. That was interesting. And important. 'But you see your sister, Miss Reynolds, don't you? Occasionally? When did you *last* see her?'

'Oh . . .' Letitia considered. It was just as Constance had said: one's mind went blank. 'About six months ago, I should think.'

The inspector was evidently pleased. As he had thought! And he'd jumped in before they could fix the alibi. Smart work! He smiled as he nodded.

'Not more recently than that?' he carefully inquired. 'Not yesterday?'

'Certainly not yesterday. I can find out exactly when it was. In April, I think. Why?'

'It's of no importance, Ma'am. I'm just making a few inquiries about Miss Reynolds's movements yesterday.'

'But why?' insisted Letitia.

'Well, *you* didn't see her. But she was supposed to be coming to see you.'

'I'll ask my maid if she unfortunately came while I was out.'

'I've asked the maid,' said the inspector. He was extraordinarily pleased with himself. 'She didn't. Now, Ma'am, has your sister any money of her own?'

'Very little, I should think.' Letitia was alarmed. None of course. Otherwise, why did she so often 'borrow' a few pounds? But what did this red-faced man mean by his questions? No good, she was sure. He looked as if he were purring. She must find Monty, at once, to ask his advice. Meanwhile, as the questions found her so much in the dark, she must answer them as she could. She prayed that she might be doing so without indiscretion. 'I don't know.'

'Not some thousands of pounds?' asked the inspector. 'You'd know *that*, wouldn't you?' His eyes were almost shut. A very little of the respect which he had previously shown slipped from his manner, which had a cynical archness.

'I'm sorry to say that I *don't* know. She's lived with my mother, and looked after her, for many years. My mother's eighty. There may have been some gift, to avoid death duties. I've no reason to think it. I could probably help you more if I knew the object of the questions.'

He looked very artful indeed.

'Ah, that might be,' he said, smiling. 'But then you might know what answers to give. And I should be telling *you* something.'

'Why not, to both?' asked Letitia.

He saw that she was not frightened of him. Well, that was as it should be. He didn't want to frighten anybody, except for their own good, or to make them tell the truth. If he made enemies, he got no help; and if he got no help he couldn't do his duty, which was to prevent crime. This here was different. This was murder.

'I don't know as I can tell you just why not,' said he. 'But The Old Lady, as they call her, died from injuries to the head, and we think we've got the cause of them. Miss Reynolds, that's to say, your sister, tells a rather confused story—a *very* confused story; and we're satisfied that there's what's called a prima facie case against her, and so we've . . . ahm . . . just . . . ahm . . . detained her for a while, till we've made some other inquiries——'

'What!' exclaimed Letitia. 'Detained! You mean you've arrested her? For murder? It's ridiculous.' She felt the blood sweep to her face. She was fiercely indignant at this stupid man's power to frighten and humiliate Muriel. It hadn't been stinted, she was sure. It was latent now; he hadn't to get anything from her but indifferent answers. But it must have been made cruelly threatening to that simple, easily-fluttered nature. 'Surely you see she couldn't kill a mouse! No doubt she tells a confused story. I should do so myself——'

'Now, now, Ma'am,' protested the inspector, quailing before Letitia's anger. 'I'm only doing my duty in asking these questions.'

She said quickly:

'Of course you are, Inspector. But what you've done to my sister may unhinge her mind. I *know* her, you see. Would you mind if I telephoned to my husband about this? Ask any other questions, of course——'

She had recovered outward calm. Indeed, her calm impressed the inspector. Having interviewed many synthetic ladies, he thought it the sure proof of gentility. But also suggestive in its contrast. That other old party, the sister, hadn't been at all calm. Why not? Wasn't the answer clear? 'Unhinged' the inspector's foot! She was as artful as a monkey.

'Well, Ma'am, I was going to ask you what terms the ladies were on; but I don't know as you could tell me that from personal observation. Terms and money . . .' He considered; he referred to some notes. 'I've got the solicitor's name—about a will. I think you've answered the only questions . . .'

She could tell that he was a little sheepish; for his neck and scalp had grown fiery under the orange hair.

'Should I be allowed to see my sister tonight?'

'At any time, Ma'am. You, or her legal adviser. You'll find her quite comfortable. If I may say so, really better off than if she was alone in the house——'

'I shall come, then. Being alone and *free*, of course, is one thing; being under arrest quite another——'

'Detention, Ma'am!'

'Does she appreciate the distinction? I can't wonder she's told a confused story! . . . Putting aside the question of my sister, are you satisfied

that my mother was—intentionally killed by somebody else. It couldn't
have been self-inflicted; or an accident?'

'Ahm . . . I think I may say we're satisfied, Ma'am. The truth is, we've
got the undoubted weapon.'

'Did my sister *tell* you she had seen me?'

Inspector Blackburn shifted his feet, and thought for a moment, with
his head down. At last he said:

'No, Ma'am. No. She didn't. She said she'd seen nobody. But
yesterday morning she took a lot of money in notes—seven thousand
pounds, odd—to a bank in Willowhaven, and left it there—for safety, she
said. She mentioned your name to the manager. Said she was going to
town to see you. She left two suitcases at the bank. We found two others,
exactly like 'em, under the bed in the room where . . . ahm . . . the
deceased was found. They were filled with folded newspaper, which your
sister admits to putting in them; and there was fresh blood on some of the
newspaper . . .'

Letitia jumped to her feet. She could sit still no longer.

'Thank you. It sounds terrible. I shall speak to my husband, and come
straight down to see my sister.'

'Very good, Ma'am. Ahm . . . I *had* thought,' said the inspector,
with immense tact, 'that as you hadn't seen your sister yesterday, or your
mother for so long, it mightn't . . . ah . . . be necessary . . . I mean,
Mr Boldero's name, and that . . .' He coughed meaningly. 'I had
thought——'

It was another blow at Letitia's heart. To be associated with murder.
Monty, Mark, Chris! She was stricken. Were they all to suffer because
of this; to become conspicuous for something which was no concern of
theirs? Had she any right to refuse this escape, on their account? Thank
God she knew at once what they would all say. She shook her head.

'That was very kind of you, Inspector,' she answered, with a steady
glance. 'Thank you. I shouldn't be much of a sister——' She could no
longer speak.

The inspector, slightly amused at an emotion outside his range, stood
again to attention.

iv

Letitia found that Constance had gone. She had eaten several more
of the scones and had drunk the tea. A note, written upon Letitia's own
paper, was propped against the clock.

'Though goggling, darling, I go. Tact! Repletion!! Confidence!!!
I still hate you, but not murderously. We'll resume your expiation another
day. Hope no bad news.

Will give your tender love to G. Ugh! Your C.'

Letitia hardly understood the words she read. Constance and Gabriel
were both far away from this emergency. She could hear, like a whisper,
the sound of their distant laughter at a bizarre happening. It would be
succeeded by sympathetic kindness; but the laughter would come first.

She herself could not laugh. Now that the inspector had gone, she could free herself a little from amazement and experience the sensations of Muriel, who was faced with death. She must be in an agony of fear. The beasts! The *beasts!* Of course they didn't *mean* to drive a poor woman mad by hectoring her with unanswerable questions. They didn't *mean* to kill her with threats when she had just, perhaps, made a ghastly discovery and was beside herself with shock. But they were determined that while she was still unprotected she should fatally incriminate herself. It gave them an immediate kill. But they shouldn't have their kill. She put her trust, her never-disappointed trust, in Monty's skill and wisdom. In this, as always, he would act well.

Monty was called to the telephone. After two minutes of explanation, he said:

'You're going now? We shall be able to get back late tonight. Call here for me. I'll see young Child, of Littler's; and get him to come down with us. He'll get hold of that very good doctor, Stedman, who's been in several cases with me. Useful chap. Don't be afraid. We'll see the poor old girl through.'

That was all. There had been no exclamations, no rueful silence, no caution; but an immediate understanding and application of the mind.

'This is *my* family,' thought Letitia, with anguish. 'Mother, Farringdon, Muriel: all mine; not Monty's. But he doesn't blink.' Pride in him brought tears to her eyes; she had been much tried this afternoon, and the reaction was violent. What would Monty's parents say of her now? His mother! She could guess. She had brought into their discreet respectability a colour indistinguishable from mud. Narrow-minded neighbours, calling and staring and gossiping, would rub in the ignominy. How they—being conventional, as well as good—would loathe it! How they would loathe *her*!

She hurried from the house, leaving Ruth with a message to telephone to Constance. Gabriel would receive that message, too. Constance would be sure to speak of it with unconquerable malice, *à la* Rochefoucauld, doing thereby so little justice to the native goodness of her heart. . . .

Imagine Muriel's terror! Alone, 'very comfortable,' watched, distracted! Through living so long with a crazy bully, without change or society, Muriel was not brisk enough in the wits nor confident enough of her own character to deal with anybody like the inspector. Spying the worst, impervious to any sensitiveness which would interfere with the ambition he called his duty, he'd keep on asking questions which frightened her beyond self-control. She would answer wildly, getting deeper and deeper, and always more satisfactorily, involved in contradictions. She would be convicted a thousand times out of her own mouth. Poor creature! Poor creature! Imagining her present state of mind, Letitia grew desperate.

Mr Child was waiting with Monty at Monty's chambers. He was a young partner in Littler's, the firm of solicitors from whom, during Mr Littler's control of the business, Monty had received many of the firm's most important briefs. Now Mr Littler was ill, and Monty's association with Littler's was in jeopardy. But no sign of this appeared in the manners of the two men, and an unsuspecting eye would see nothing but friendliness in the young man's plump, smiling, clean-shaven face, his light grey eyes, or his air of candour. If she had been less versed in the evasions of the fashionably bred, Letitia would have been content. Even now she liked him, and accepted without question Monty's reliance on his capacity. In ten years, at fifty, he would be tremendously experienced, and would appreciate experience in others; at forty he felt excessive pride in his own judgment, and smilingly recorded the signs of faltering in his seniors.

They had a first-class carriage to themselves. Monty held Letitia's hand, and pressed it when, as her feelings grew unmanageable, she became strugglingly silent. As soon as the bad moment passed he leaned forward again, attentive to all that passed. Mr Child listened very seriously to everything she could remember of the inspector's visit, and, nodding, made some notes upon a memorandum tablet.

'As one would expect,' he smilingly commented. 'Mrs Boldero's the ideal witness. She recollects everything, and has it in perspective. What sort of chap's the inspector, Mrs Boldero?'

'Very red—red-haired, red-faced—and tenacious. I should think very ambitious. Limited and merciless. He frightened me, because I don't think he's as stupid as he seems.'

'All the same, limited,' said Child, hopefully.

'But tenacious,' Monty reminded him. 'And apparently convinced.'

'Don't you think that's a point to us?'

'We want a clear acquittal,' said Monty. 'That is, if they charge her. Not a score.'

Child accepted the warning with a smiling duck of the head.

'Subject to your decision, I suggest we find out first of all, hour by hour, what Miss Reynolds really did yesterday. They don't know. She seems to have foxed the inspector a bit there; perhaps trying to conceal something. She'll probably tell *you* more than she'll tell anybody else, Mrs Boldero. We must know if she *did* come to London. Or, if she didn't, where she was. There's the question of the money: I'll see the bank manager. When did she take it to him, and when did she say she was coming to you? It's not clear how well she knows the bank manager. Well, now, the weapon?'

'He gave no hint.'

'But blood. A blow, therefore. You're quite sure there's no question of her ever raising a hand? No, well, you know her. Is she frail? No. That's bad. We must try and find somebody who saw her on the train, or in London. I'll work through the local man——'

'Not too much through the local man, I hope, Child,' murmured Monty 'This is murder. I'd rather trust *you*.'

Child, ducking again with his amiable grin, looked comically at Letitia

'He's an anti-provincial!' he said. 'Great regard for the gemmen from London! There's a very good local man—Smart, by name. My idea would be to use him; not to appear too much, in case the red-faced inspector gets the wind up and brings London down.'

'If London riddled the police case, and freed Muriel, that would be best of all,' said Monty.

'The policeman's evidently got *something*.'

'The body, for example. And the weapon. At a first glance those are *two* considerable things. Our resistance is based on my wife's certainty about her sister, which, knowing my wife, I find unanswerable. *You* may allow yourself greater scepticism. Child, these *times* are most important. You've seen that. The police case, I take it, is that Muriel killed her mother, scuffled the notes together, and took them to the bank. Talked largely about my wife to establish an alibi, and then, waiting for some time, pretended to discover the crime. But what was the state of the body when it was found? Stedman won't be able to ascertain by examination. Will the police doctor be clear as to the facts?'

'He'd better be,' smiled Child.

'And would Muriel have been so simple as not to destroy the weapon?'

'Mother would have been much more likely to kill herself and *plant* a murder on Muriel,' cried Letitia.

'It's done in fiction,' murmured Child.

'Fiction's only a coloured copy of life,' said Monty. 'You get the drab in the Sunday Press.'

'I meant that Muriel's incapable of it,' explained Letitia. 'She's the sort of person who couldn't strike in cold blood, and in excitement collapses.'

Child nodded.

'*I* know. Flops like a jelly. Well, Stedman's coming down tomorrow as soon as it's light. He'll check all the police medical details. He's a terrifically astute fellow, Mrs Boldero. Pity he won't see the body *in situ*. But I bet he's smarter than anybody the local police are likely to get. They won't know that. They won't know *him*. The thing will be to let them keep the whole affair local. Assizes aren't far away; they sound as if they're over-confident. . . .' He smiled angelically.

Letitia blanched at his insistence upon the technique of manœuvre. She turned anxiously to Monty, with a slightly shaken head.

'Oh, we'll manage something,' said Monty.

He took Letitia's hand, and tucked it under his arm. She was soothed and restored to hope. The train rumbled and swayed on in the darkness, now through a tunnel, now past a cluster of lights, but always nearer and nearer to ordeal.

v

At Willowhaven, while Child went to book a room for himself at the best hotel, the name and site of which he must have known by instinct, as it was not the garish place on the promenade, Monty and Letitia made their way to the police station.

She had never been in such a place before, and its echoing bareness heightened her dismay. But the inspector was there, and in Monty's dignified presence was at once a host and one temperamentally subordinate to the highest. He was like Matron when the surgeon visits his patient. He led Letitia up some stone stairs. She braced herself for Muriel.

She had imagined forlorn collapse, perhaps even hysteria. But Muriel was not as she had imagined. Muriel sat, a stumpy figure in black, by the fire in a small, airless room with plain brown walls. She looked almost exactly as she usually did, if a little pale, and held in her hands some futile knitting. Upon a table beside her were a few battered books, of which the uppermost was *The Scottish Chiefs*, and a jug of water without a glass. There was also a pack of Patience cards. She looked up, blinking; and at sight of Letitia shrank back in her chair as if a ghost had entered. Her knitting fell softly to the floor.

'Oh!' exclaimed Muriel, in a combination of mortal disquiets. 'Oh, you *shouldn't*!'

'Muriel, dear.' Letitia kissed her, and felt both hands caught and held with fierce intensity. They hadn't been so close to one another since childhood, when Muriel, repenting of spite, cried and begged her to make it up. But the intensity relaxed. Muriel sought no embrace; but rather drew away, and stiffened, as one might do who doesn't *wish* to make it up. Letitia, as she drew her chair close, saw and was wounded by her sister's constraint. She saw the reddish face growing redder, and the chin rising. It looked as though Muriel disclaimed all relationship with her. And then Nature won; tears filled the curious furtively-peeping eyes. They were not the eyes of a criminal, but those of an elderly woman doomed by seclusion to suppress all secret thoughts of a world magnified by fear to the gigantically grotesque.

'Oh, I *hoped* they wouldn't *find* you!' cried Muriel in a whisper. 'Letty, I didn't want you to be *troubled* with me. *Stained* and *marked*. You're so . . . It doesn't matter about *me*; I'm *nothing*. But *you* . . . This is all so *horrible*!'

'We're here to help you,' said Letitia, quickly. 'What did you expect, old girl? And *you* must help *us*.'

Muriel gasped:

'Oh, I couldn't. I shouldn't know how to do it.' Then earnestly, with a hand upon Letitia's arm, she continued: 'You mustn't have anything to do with me. Nothing. I'm . . . like a leper. I didn't tell that horrible man. He finds things out. Horrible things. He finds them out *all wrong*; and I can't . . .'

'But we *can*. Monty and I can——'

'Monty! Oh, dear, this is terrible. Just what I tried to . . . what *does* he think of me; disgracing you——' She began to cry. The big tears rolled down the ruddied cheeks. Her nose looked swollen with weeping. She sobbed several times, weakly, while Letitia closely held her hand and received in return small jerks of emphasis. When she was able to speak again, Muriel's voice had changed. It had become childish, mournfully helpless. 'I'm so frightened, Letty. Being alone. I don't know what to do. I know I've been wicked; but——'

'Wicked!' exclaimed Letitia, in agony, feeling her heart stabbed and lacerated with pain. 'Of *course* you aren't wicked—except in saying so!'

'Aren't I?' The poor red face was discoloured. The ugly lips were drawn in and down to the accompaniment of a snuffling breath. Muriel was trying to control her tears. She began again: 'But it's *you*, dear. I didn't want *you* brought into it. With Monty and the children. . . . Those . . . It's such a disgrace—all their lives!'

'It won't be if you help us,' whispered Letitia. 'Help us!'

'I can't *think*,' exclaimed Muriel, raising both despairing hands to her head. 'Can't concentrate. I don't know *what* that man thinks I've done. . . . He keeps on asking me things. . . . He asks if I'm strong. Well, of course I *am*. I've lifted Mother, and done . . . But you see . . .' She broke off with a startled glance. 'There's so much I mustn't tell you, dear——'

'Fiddlesticks! Why "mustn't"? Of course you must tell me *everything*,' entreated Letitia.

She was in despair at the swiftly shaken head.

'Oh, no. I couldn't. I've been wicked; and they've found out all about it.'

'But they say you *killed* Mother.'

'I *know*. Isn't it absurd!' There was no sign that she realised her appalling danger. She might have said the same if she had been accused of picking up somebody else's change. Did she suppose innocence was enough? Did she not care whether she lived or died? Letitia, seeing her eyes moving restlessly as if she looked for something near her upon the floor, and then seeing this restless gaze grow fixed and vacant, was caught by consternation.

'But, Muriel, dear, we must prove that you didn't, and couldn't have.'

'Yes,' murmured Muriel, upon a falling, reflective note which suggested that she had not understood.

'What *did* you do that was so wicked?'

Muriel had taken refuge in a dreamy silence which sometimes had checked even Inspector Blackburn, who thought it aimed at justifying an insanity plea. She stared blankly at Letitia. But Letitia, holding her hand, and smiling because she knew how often in the far past Muriel had feigned stupidity in order to escape an explanation, would not be denied. In the end the effect of her loving amusement was too great for Muriel resist. She looked away, peeped back into her sister's eyes, half-smiled, as offended, grew serious, and began, at first haltingly and always with evagations, but in time as if it were a relief to open her heart, to explain about the money and her trip to London. It was not all quite ingenuous; did not all quite convince Letitia; but it was an advance. At last Muriel brought herself back to Willowhaven, to the dark railway station, and the journey through the town to Meadowside Road.

'I felt so ashamed. I *couldn't* go straight indoors. I went for a little walk. Then I went home. The blinds weren't drawn. I went in, and put the light. I could see she'd *been* in the front room, because the fire was all alight. But it was nearly out. I thought it odd that she didn't knock shout. So I went into the kitchen for a minute, and made a little clatter. You see, she *could* look after herself, Letty, if she *wanted* to. She didn't want to. It was only my being there all the time. . . . I thought she'd come up to bed, to frighten me. Well, I *was* frightened. My teeth chattered. could hardly get up the stairs. It seemed so *ominous*. Then, when I into the room—I didn't put on the light there at first. I'd got it on outside the room, on the landing, in case she was asleep. But I saw the bed wasn't made. The room all dirty. Tk-tk! I didn't know *what* to think. . . .'

Sighing, Muriel fell into a muse, shuddered, peeped at Letitia, and relapsed into blankness. Letitia, too, shuddered; imagining Muriel alone in ignorance of what she was to discover.

'And then you found her.'

Muriel started, recalled from a mental journey to some great distance. She said, almost impersonally:

'I put on the light. It was a great shock.'

'What did you do?'

Muriel blinked.

'Oh? I don't know. I can't remember. All I remember is this horrible man, and the policemen tramping. I asked them to draw the curtains for me. Everybody staring in. It was . . . They say I ran next door, to ask if they'd got a telephone. But I don't remember. I think the shock, and all the questions . . . You can't distinguish between what you've dreamed.' She smiled apologetically, tearfully. She gave Letitia's hand a tight little squeeze. Her mouth went down at the corners. 'I feel I've been punished enough for my wickedness, Letty darling; and I want to go home. Why shouldn't I? They could always find me there. I feel they *ought* to let me go. . . . But I don't want you punished, too, dear. Or anybody. *Anybody.*' The tears brimmed over. Hopeless sobs shook her body. 'Oh Letty, I'm *so* unhappy!'

Unhappy! They were *both* unhappy, and greatly afraid. Letitia's fear was such that she sat still with difficulty. If she could have allowed herself to do so, she would have hurried away, crying. But she neither cried nor ran away. She said:

'Of course you're unhappy, darling. It makes me unhappy only to hear what you've suffered. It's a dreadful story. What they've made up is still more dreadful. But you *must* trust us to get you home again—presently. We'll do it. We'll look after you. But *you'll* have to tell me everything you remember. All of it. Didn't you see *anybody* in London?'

The brimming eyes were turned away.

'Nobody, Letty.'

'But that makes it so much harder——'

'Nobody,' repeated Muriel. 'I saw *nobody.* *Nobody.*'

Letitia was in despair.

vi

She and Monty travelled back to London together. They had had supper with Child, who was staying, and they had caught the last train. It was a slow and trundly train, very cold; and Letitia was increasingly miserable; affected by what was almost a sense of doom. What hope, this moment, was there?

Wherever she turned, she saw menace. She had been horrified by the chance glimpses of Muriel's life with their mother, and moved to distress and fear by the story she had heard; but above all she was crushed by her inability to see a way of escape for the innocent. She saw that Child, with his smile and his ducked head, which made him appear, against reality, sleek and too-well nourished, was definitely committed to manœuvre. He believed that only so could the circumstantial evidence be shaken; and he could not accept her first point of faith, which was that Muriel could not commit a crime. On the contrary, he thought Muriel an artful old cuss. She had bagged a small fortune, and was as shady as could be. All was told in his smiles. They cowed Letitia; they made her suppose that any jury would think as he did. Her one comfort was that Monty, who knew all that Child knew, and who was, in addition, a wiser and more experienced man, continued staunch.

At first, when they were alone, Letitia and Monty did not speak. They travelled for some distance busy with thoughts of the evening. But at last Letitia could not restrain an indignant comment on Child.

'I'm sure he doesn't come near to understanding Muriel's nature,' she cried. 'He's too clever, He doesn't see her simplicity; only her cunning. I admit the cunning.'

'It's the cunning of inexperience,' agreed Monty. 'Child sees the motive he'd have himself. It's the commonest mistake of sophistication, which is unimaginative. Muriel's motives are all improvised. They can hardly be said to be motives at all; only tangents of impulse. But why *did* she hurry the money to the bank yesterday morning?'

'She *says*, because she was taking a day off duty, and there had been strange callers.'

'It's an awkward coincidence. It wasn't her money. Is she shielding somebody?'

'If we knew *that*——' began Letitia. 'She'll have to be made to say. But I don't know *how* she's to be made.'

'You can do it.'

'I hope I can. But she's against herself. Even the money. I'm sure he didn't mean to *steal* it. But she may have meant to safeguard her own enjoyment of it.'

Monty smiled, and was preoccupied.

'I'm afraid they've got a case,' he said.

'Oh, Monty!'

'Only a case. Not a conviction.'

'Bad enough. Quite bad enough to ruin her life. There's something more, too. When I think that she and the policeman have both tried to keep *us* out of it, I wonder whether I haven't madly committed the Bolderos too deep. Blood's thicker than water; but one needn't throw good blood after bad.'

'Nonsense!' cried Monty, turning with his old teasing love. 'You mustn't be afraid. We're going to get an acquittal. Even if it's my last case.'

Letitia sat back, breathless. She felt the warmth drawn from her cheeks, and felt it rush back again. He was going to defend Muriel himself.

She made no reply at all. She could not have spoken. But the proud love she had felt for him for thirty years was renewed and heightened beyond measure by the assurance of his abiding love for herself.

H

Fifteen

F. R.

i

SITTING IN HIS armchair in front of the gas fire, F. R. waited for Thelm
to bring him the evening papers. There had been nothing in the mornin
papers that day or the previous day; and he was at a loss. Of course h
could not go out. He had been to the window a hundred times in the tw
days, craning his neck in an effort to see the big boots of some uncon
vincingly casual figure projecting from a selected doorway. Somebod
who would signal to others by means of a peculiar method of striking matches
. . . He had seen nobody.

Suspense tormented him. Finding it impossible to remain in his chai
he began to walk backwards and forwards across the room, approachin
the window first from one side and then from the other. Nobody. Throug
the window opposite he caught a glimpse of movement, but it was only th
mother bringing a broad-leaved green plant back to the window-ledg
She had been giving that damned plant its water for the day. What a sill
happy face! Small pleasures. Small pleasures. F. R. supposed tha
there was a husband somewhere. An insignificant four-pound-a-wee
fellow who arrived home long after dark. 'Well, Mother! 'Ad a good day
. . . At any rate, the woman could not be spying upon *him*, for she nev
lifted her eyes, and disappeared again into the darkness of her room.

There was a click from the front door along the passage. Thelma ha
returned. In a moment she would bring him the papers. He could hard
restrain himself from going to meet her, from snatching them out of her ug
hands. But Thelma was dangerous. She had already noticed sweat upo
his face. She had spoken suspiciously of it, and of his uneasy expressio
Damn the woman! She had the temperament of a spy. She watched hi
as a cat watches a mousehole. Only long experience in baffling her had ke
him ahead of her guesses. Even so, he felt that fear of him had becon
subtly less powerful than ever-encroaching contempt. What inferenc
was she adding together behind that Dutch Madonna flatness? Dan
her! Why didn't she come! She was hanging it out; keeping him o
tenterhooks for those papers!

She was coming at last. He threw himself into the chair and picked u
his book. When she entered, he yawned, and scratched a cheek with th
forefinger of his free hand. His quizzical frown was intended to sugge
that she had disturbed him; but he put the book down upon a small tab
at his elbow rather too quickly for his own sense of considered timing.

Thelma gave him a solemn stare, behind which lay penetration. S'
handed over the papers, which he took indifferently—noting, however, th
they had been opened and clumsily re-folded; and before going again s'
picked the book from the table and examined its title. It was a blue-bou
cheap edition of Bagehot's *The English Constitution* which of course he h
chosen at random.

'Hm,' said Thelma, replacing Bagehot and looking down at F. R.
'This is rather a change for you, isn't it?'

F. R. cocked up an inquiring eye.

'Change?' he asked.

'I thought you only read murder stories,' retorted Thelma.

F. R. could not control the plunge he gave. He was furious. He felt
he would choke if he held his breath another instant. He replied with
forced coolness:

'I should be considered a widely-read man. Unlike you, of course.'

'Ah, yes. But I have no time. I work. All the same, this must be a
nice relief.'

She was gone, leaving him in ferment. By God! Had she seen something in the papers? Was *she* searching with curiosity as great as his own?
Had she guessed something? She was all through his things the moment he
slept. Yes, but 'murder': that was the word she had used. It was the word
that printed itself across the darkness as he lay sweating in bed. He sat,
ignoring the papers, carried back to the panics of two nights ago. 'I can't
stand this! I can't stand this!' he was muttering. Almost whimpering.
'What in God's name does she *mean*?'

With trembling hands he straightened out the first of the newspapers,
his glance flying over the headlines in search of the thing he dreaded. Nothing
here. It was extraordinary. It was more alarming than ever; because they
often kept silence in the hope that a man would betray himself. There was
nothing. He had possessed himself of all the front-page headings in the
three papers, and not one of them concerned himself.

Flinging the papers down, F. R. thought: The eye turns blind. I've
missed it somewhere! Then he thought: What if Muriel went off and hasn't
come back! The house unvisited. No discovery made!

It did not relieve him to think this. It made him feel worse. With
each day that passed the appearance of murder might increase. How many
people had seen him visiting the house? And as he wondered this he brought
both his hands to his beard, pressing them into its crisp softness. His impulse
went to the razor lying in the pigskin case. A man with a beard; a pigskin
case. At the hotel, 'Mr Reynolds'. God! What a clumsy fool! He might
as well have painted himself red, to attract every eye!

ii

Not that day, but the next, F. R. found the paragraph for which he
had been looking. It was very small, and owing to the fact that nobody
had as yet observed the news value of such a story it was set obscurely in
a corner of every newspaper.

SEASIDE TRAGEDY

The body of an elderly woman with severe head injuries has been
found in a house in Willowhaven, the S.E. coast health resort. The
woman's daughter has been detained.

That was all. It made F. R.'s muscles stiffen. The whole kaleidoscope of his thoughts turned, into a new pattern. First, he felt wild with relief at finding that he was not being tracked. But his blood ran cold. A murder charge! Well, was it justified? He was the only person who knew the truth. The risky truth. Unless Muriel knew. Where had they found Muriel? Oh, God! This meant endless trouble! Groaning, he began his caged walk from wall to wall.

He sat down again, quite unmanned. In some corner of his brain words formed which told him to go at once to Willowhaven, to the police there. Yes, he must go. He must explain. 'I was on my knees.' 'What were you doing on your knees? Praying?' He'd think up something: 'My sister was out, gadding; I thought I'd better do a handyman's job.' Grinning scepticism: 'Emptying the pot?' 'Well, look at my head.' He had already had difficulty with Thelma about the damage and bloody bruises on his head. He had told a circumstantial story of catching his heel and falling against a moving lorry in the darkness. She hadn't believed him; but she had bathed the wound. A mixture of unbelief and tenderness. Like other women, she preferred her man helpless. It gave her a false sense of power.

If he was going, he ought to go while the evidential damage could be seen.

'Ye-es,' they'd say; 'but why not come straight to us?'

That wasn't unsuperable. His tongue was easy. 'I'm the sort of fellow who can get away with murder.' But God! That was just his present danger! Could he? No, too late. Too much explanation needed. To quick-witted or imaginative people—they might not be identical; but either could respond —a simple statement of lost nerve would be enough. Not to the police. If he admitted that he was looking for money? No.

He gnawed his finger-nails, sitting twisted in his chair. What an ironic situation! Of course they wouldn't be able to convict. That was unthinkable. That poor worthless old sponge and sycophant . . . Crawling on her belly for more than a quarter of a century for the sake of rewards to come. A quarter of a century's 'grace': For what we are about to receive . . . Twenty-five years of lickspittling; and then—so near and yet so far—accused of murder of the golden goose! Fantastic!

He ought to go. A White Man would go.

He was afraid to go. People would *think* he was afraid. Absurd. But why interfere? They couldn't convict old Muriel. She couldn't knock even a nail in. They'd soon see that.

'Thank God I've never been a Pukka Sahib,' sneered F. R., laughing in his nose and pressing his hands to his mouth and chin. He ought to go. But this was a murder charge.

Suddenly he sat erect, almost screaming. The first thing Muriel would do, to clear herself, would be to incriminate *him*! 'My brother! Ask my brother!' Oh, indeed, indeed, he'd left it too late! They might even now——'

Was the place being watched after all? He went again to the window. His face was as white as chalk. His throat felt as if it were quite closed.

iii

It was Thelma who saw the next stage. She had been out for the final
edition of the evening papers, of which F. R. now felt insatiable need;
and while he searched the first of them she went straight, with her own
feminine directness, in another to what he had not yet found. She read it
very intently, glanced at the haggard Farringdon, saw his hawk-like
absorption in the quest, and handed her paper to him, a finger upon the news.

'This is it,' she said drily. 'This is what you're looking for.'

'What?' F. R. tried to quell her with a frown; but the pointed finger,
so much firmer than his own raised hand, was too insistent.

SEASIDE TRAGEDY

MURDER CHARGE

MOTHER OF FAMOUS K.C.'S WIFE

Today, at Willowhaven, Muriel Reynolds (57) was formally charged
with the murder of her mother, eighty-year-old widow of the late Sebastian
Reynolds. Defence was reserved. Mrs Reynolds was the mother-in-law
of Mr Montague Boldero, the famous K.C. A week ago Mrs Reynolds
was found in her home with severe injuries to the head, which it is
alleged were inflicted by accused. Accused had lived with her mother
for many years in the pretty little villa which both occupied in the
popular seaside resort. The case is arousing much interest in the district,
which is well known to many Summer visitors from London and is
renowned for the number of its resident octogenarians and nonagenarians.

Portraits of Monty and Letitia decorated the paragraph, which was
thus made to fill several inches of space.

Farringdon put down the paper and stared. Thelma, also, under her
triumph, was disquieted by the sense of danger, and saw that he was in a
state of paralysis. There was no colour at all in his cheeks; he sat as one
completely exhausted. At last she said:

'What are you going to do?'

With a ghastly effort, he tried to show indifference; but she shook her
head at him, to show that she was no longer to be intimidated. She knew
him too well.

'I didn't do it,' he ejaculated.

'Your accident?' asked Thelma. 'Did *she* do that?'

'What? Of course not.'

'Why are you afraid, then?'

'*I'm* not afraid.' He sat up; but no colour returned to his face. 'But I
shall have to go down there. I ought to go and explain.'   •

'Can you explain?' She seemed to smile. But that was because her lips
had nervously twitched. It was not a real smile. She realised what risks
he ran. They were extreme. Her thought was 'What should I do without

him?' When his response was a sound which she imagined to be a groan, she menacingly brought her will closer to his, showing thereby that hers was the stronger. 'I don't know what you did; but this is what you were expecting. The seaside; that was where you went. To see your Mother. Did you kill her? You knew she was dead.' Waiting a moment, until she felt herself infected by his terror, and then carried to sudden panic, she whispered: 'Let's get away—quickly.'

He forgot secrecy. He said, thinking aloud:

'Safer here. They watch the ports.'

'Why should *you* be afraid? Were you there?'

'I was there. Nobody knows I was there.'

'Then get away quickly.'

'No.'

Thelma rose impatiently, really because her nerves were overstrained. She pushed back her chair, pushed the table, pushed her handbag which lay on the table, so that it fell with a soft clink to the floor.

'We should go now, before——'

'Don't be a fool! I've told you why not. In this labyrinth one's safer than anywhere——'

'I can't stay here. It makes me scream—inside. Unless we go, I shall go by myself.' She stood watching him, half contemptuous but half frightened lest she, too, should become involved. 'They hang people for murder——'

F. R. hissingly drew his breath.

'It's *not* murder, I tell you!'

'The paper says it is.'

'The paper knows nothing!' he shouted. But he caught up his own paper, and sought in it another account of what had happened. It was there, again with a portrait of Monty as a link between the known and the 'insignificant'. 'These damned papers! No conscience! No decency!' He choked, casting aside the sheet and standing up. But his legs would hardly bear him. His real thought was: 'She's right. We could slip out now, while they're not looking. Not later. Holland. A Dutch tramp without wireless . . .'

'Why should *you* get mixed up in it?'

Why, indeed? Wasn't it his most ardent longing to *escape* being mixed up in it?

'Be quiet!' he shouted.

'What has she ever done for you?' Thelma was undeterred. 'You did nothing, you say. Well, then, it's nothing to do with you. These *sisters*! What are they! Cold English ladies, who think only of themselves!' She thought hysterically of her visit to Letitia, of Gabriel's impudent contempt, and her humiliation. Memory gave spitefulness to her bitter tongue. 'They've always despised you, seen you as a mountebank. It's because they saw through you, as I do——'

Though he raised his arm threateningly, he thought her right.

'Saw through me! You couldn't even *understand* me!'

'No? It hasn't taken twelve years. I knew everything in three months. Well, I shall leave you.'

It was impossible to silence her. He did his best to do so by an unavailing sneer.

'By all means, go. It's a dream of mine! I shall do better alone.'

'Perhaps the police will do that.' He shivered. 'They will like to see your fine case, and the funny razor, and your passport——'

'Will you be quiet!' God! She was intolerable!

'But your gloves seem to be lost. I *do* hope you didn't leave them behind you. It would be so inconvenient to have to explain them. Don't you think so? Oh, what a fool you are! Pretending to yourself! I've known everything, all the time!'

He would have swept her away with a blow; but the table stood as a barrier between them. She understood his mind too cruelly; her meanness would rob adventure of every lustre; she reduced him to her own level of ignominy. But she knew too much; and the malignance she had shown towards his sisters, while it irked him, pierced to old wounds and reopened them. It was Muriel who—first, long ago, poisoning her mother towards him —had brought about this whole affair: he saw how she had opposed him from the beginning, and, shamming simplicity, had tricked him. The treacherous fat beast! Didn't she deserve the punishment of her present distress? As for Letitia, she had once unforgivably helped him—of course in order to hush up an exposure that would be inconvenient to herself and new respectability: wasn't it ironic that she should be the first, now, to be spot-lighted? She and Monty, the prig! Both prigs. Though at a glance he had been shocked by the spread of this thing beyond its true orbit, he was now amused. Serve them all right! . . .

Why hadn't Muriel betrayed him to the police? Wasn't it in the same spirit of hypocritical hushing-up? Could it be true that she had not betrayed him? For long enough to let him get out of the country? It wouldn't last, if she realised her own deadly danger. At any moment! . . . White again as chalk, he said:

'The razor's no good, my dear, unless we stay in London. Consider the passport! By the way, I threw the gloves out of the train on the way home. You'd better go by yourself. In any case, they'll stop you and ask questions.'

'I shall refer them to you,' Thelma answered, very calmly. 'Here.' She was trying to remember whether she had given Letitia her address. It had been a mistake to go to that grand, hateful house, where they were so pleased with themselves. Let them take the consequences! No, she felt sure she had not given it; so she and Farringdon were safe. But she was desperate to get away from England, where all women were belittling strangers, and where everything had gone wrong. How was it to be done? Whichever way she turned, she found a blank wall. Except in the exhilarating knowledge that Farringdon was, and knew that he was, at her mercy. Even that had its flaw. She mustn't by some too severe taunt lead him into the sacrifice of his liberty. Nor must she lose her hold upon him. She could not do without him.

'I'll go to Willowhaven first thing in the morning.'

So she had a night! Did not his very postponement until tomorrow suggest a weakness?

'If you go, I shall not wait for your release. If you *are* released. Everywhere, all over the world, the police need victims. It's their justification. Here it is veneered. They won't let you go. How could you explain?'

Farringdon said, in a false voice:

'I'll tell them the truth.'

'It's something you could never do. However, go. We shall say good-bye. They use stout ropes to hang a man.'

F. R.'s head fell to one side as he felt his throat grow dry. He put one hand, under the beard, to his hairless neck. He was being terrorized into cowardice.

The struggle continued hour after hour.

iv

A week later, they were at sea. It was a bitterly cold night, and the wind was blowing a half-gale. Stars were very bright in the black sky; but they often disappeared as the quivering ship rolled under the assault of heavy seas. F. R., holding firmly to whatever support he could snatch, managed to shelter under the lee of some hardly distinguishable shape forward of the mainmast. He was alone. He heard the wind go whooping past the small ship, and imagined himself the spirit of Vanderdecken, lost to all contact with the earth and the craven ways of men.

All that horror was behind him. He thought of men dashing about the streets of London like dogs upon the scent of fortune, of women painting themselves to hide the ravages of bored exhaustion, of men and women staring greedily into the windows of the house in Willowhaven; and although he could not help shuddering as he shut his mind to any picture of those he had left struggling with ordeal he had such relief and poignant misery as he had never before experienced.

Thelma was below, sick and repellent. Poor bilious soul, how he detested her! Her own hatred was pretty clear; but she couldn't do without him. *There* lay his power. At present, owing to difficult circumstances, she'd got a little out of hand. But once they were through this discomfort, she'd feel the bit again. There'd be some satisfaction in tightening it. His arms grew rigid as he imagined tightening it.

People spoke of one's inability to resist going back to the scene of an unpleasant happening. Quite wrong. He hadn't the smallest inclination. Not a morbid type, of course. . . . By God, if he could once get into some place in Africa where a man *was* a man, and his recent experiences were not too closely inquired into, he'd show them! He'd make it clear to Thelma that she'd have to rough it. Do her good! Get her out of this curious . . . As if she knew *everything*. Pure delusion! What women did was to grope round in their little box of tricks, threading needles. If they threaded one, they were jubilant. They'd threaded all!

Well, he despised women. All his troubles, except one, had been due to women; and even in that one his late papa-in-law had worked through and for Thelma. Palmed her off!

I should have been a rich man, but for that,' thought F. R.

How the wind howled! Rather alarming on a ship as small as this. But not seriously alarming. Ships were built to take enormous strains. Thelma had arranged it all. He'd had nothing to do with it. Simply sat at home, devouring the papers and sweating hot and cold at all the stuff about Monty and Letitia, while she worked like a fiend. Passports, luckily, in order; and luckily South African. Nobody had known that. All really rather smart. . . .

He was getting frozen. Once you couldn't hold, you'd be done for. He'd better hang on to a few more fixed parts and make his way down the companion. It would be foul down below. Fouler still in the water on a night like this—though it wouldn't last long. He clung rather more vigorously, in some alarm, as the ship wallowed and he found himself, with slipping feet, looking straight down an almost perpendicular deck at the boiling sea; and was thankful when a moment later, with another tremor, the ship righted itself and drove forward into the darkness. Water swept the deck, washing about his knees, and spattering in a dense shower upon his head and shoulders. His beard was wringing wet. However unpleasant it might be below, he would feel safer than he did now, in the cold buffeting wind and sluicing waters of the stormy night.

Careful! Mustn't skid or stumble! Too valuable a life! Inch by inch he drew nearer to the boxed warmth of the ship's interior. When he reached it, and was overpowered by it, the contrast between storm and suffocating stench was so great that the brave words of his soliloquy turned to misery. He continued to hold to every stable projection; but no longer with former intentness. His eyes were closed. Near the top of his sodden beard a cavity showed which was caused by an uncontrollable parting of wearily flaccid lips. He could hardly, from reluctance, go forward to what lay ahead.

Sixteen

CURTAIN

i

BACK IN THAT crowded London of which F. R. and Thelma had so gladly shaken themselves free the loss of undistinguished migrants was unnoticed. The Press had discovered the Bella Vista case, and while Inspector Blackburn continued to go about his duties with outward serenity he was already troubled by doubts of his own discretion. He had begun by snubbing reporters—always a fatal thing to do. But as soon as he had, partly in self-defence and partly by a slip of the tongue, mentioned the name of a distinguished K.C., he had seen himself deserted. It was in London that the real meat lay. Back to London swept all the young men in grey flannel bags and tweed jackets who had once threatened to bring London to Willowhaven.

H*

They besieged Kensington. They lay in wait for Letitia; they incessantly used the telephone; they were ` ound upon doorsteps and back doorsteps. They teased Ruth; they were suppliant and intrusive whenever the cook left the house; they desperately re-wrote a few snatched words as a quarter-column interview. And since time was short (for Assizes in the Willowhaven district were close at hand) they imparted to the case an extraordinary family importance. It was livelihood to them; they dared not leave a single stone unturned for its possible revelations. They buzzed and were insatiable, and so even if the Bolderos had not in any case been giving Muriel's affairs the thought and energy of every hour, circumstances would not have allowed them the smallest respite.

But what did the pressmen glean? In sum, nothing. The mother of a barrister's wife had died violently; the person charged with killing her was a daughter and sister. There was little else to be said; only a domestic privacy to be outraged. Within a week news editors were dropping contemptuously into wastepaper baskets such copy as was supplied to them, and were calling off their baffled dogs. Letitia could once more walk out of her front door without meeting smiles of entreaty and raised hats of eager but interested obsequiousness.

She spent several of these early days at Willowhaven, with Muriel. But beyond noting in Muriel a steadily growing lassitude, which implied that the poor creature's reserves of strength were slipping, she learned nothing in her visits. Far too much of the time was lost in what she thought was her own trifling business and Muriel's apathy. She even spoke in vain of childish memories: they produced no reaction. And only faith sustained her belief in Muriel's innocence. She more than once saw Child and Stedman, and she talked much with Monty. Moreover she brought to bear on one single aspect of the case every intuition of which she was capable. It began with an unexpected reflection of Stedman's.

Letitia liked Stedman, the doctor. He was a solid-looking youngish man who had played full-back for his hospital Rugby team, and who had the shoulders and rock-like head which one supposes necessary for the stopping of forward rushes near goal. But inside rock ran fluent thought. When Stedman made his discovery, Child brought him round to see Letitia.

'You've had no luck, I suppose?' Child asked. But he looked blandly excited.

'None,' said Letitia, disliking the blandness as much as ever, bu favourably affected by the excitement. 'She still says she saw nobody.

'And you still disbelieve that?'

'Still.'

'Well, now, listen to Stedman.'

Stedman, speaking laconically, but standing straight up with his arms loose, and looking into the distance as if he watched a scrum there and was ready to anticipate the flight of the ball and the movement of hostile three-quarters, said:

'Struck me. The hair on the hammer. Silver grey.'

Letitia was puzzled.

'Wasn't Mother's silver grey?'

'White. Know anybody with silver grey hair? Miss Reynolds' is grey, of course; might be hers; but she wasn't injured. I've asked. Besides, hers is longer. This is three inches long. Same length as your mother's. We've assumed it *was* hers. Police did; I accepted. But hers was white. I've looked at it again—very carefully. I think this may be a man's!'

A man's! Suddenly Letitia received a signal from unsuperficial thought. Farringdon! He'd called upon her. Wasn't he the only *man* whom Muriel would be likely to shield?

'Something coming through!' smilingly guessed Child.

'My brother.'

'Ah. Where is he? Let's find him!'

'He may be anywhere in the world. Probably in London. . . .' Letitia was lost in wonder. 'But in that case, why hasn't he . . .'

The doctor exchanged glances with Child.

'I say——' Child was quite pink. 'D'you think there was a slogging match? "Have at you!" Eh?'

'I'd like to see the room,' said Stedman, briefly. 'Bet that fool's missed something.'

'We'll get him. Get him to take us round.'

'Shall I see my sister, and mention—my brother?' asked Letitia.

They were all reanimated by this discovery.

ii

'Do you remember when Farringdon hid in the chimney, and frightened us,' Letitia asked, laying out the Patience cards. She paused, with a card between her thumb and forefinger.

A look of distaste darkened Muriel's face.

'A hateful boy,' she grumbled. 'He always tormented me.'

'You let him see how much you *were* tormented.'

The sly old eyes glanced quickly at Letitia.

'I never wanted to be an actrèss,' said Muriel. 'I don't mean you, dear. Yours was self-control. But Mother's was acting. So was Farringdon's. He was a sort of playboy.'

'I wonder if he's changed much.'

'You *know* he's grown wicked. You saved him, didn't you?'

'But that was twenty years ago.' Letitia finished laying out the cards.

Muriel's eyes closed. She had not looked at the cards. In a stifled voice, she said:

'He's worse, now.'

At last! Letitia, with a great effort, delayed her reply. Very quietly, clasping her hands, which were now free, she continued:

'He called one day—about a month ago—at our house; but I wasn't there. His wife came to see me.'

'His wife!' Muriel was deeply flushed. 'Oh, no. It couldn't have been his wife.'

'Yes. They'd been married twelve years, she said. She was a South African. At least, they'd met in South Africa.'

'Fancy! Married! I didn't dream . . . Poor woman!' muttered Muriel.

'I think she *was* a poor woman. I mean, unhappy.'

'Of course she was unhappy.' Muriel was quite breathless. 'He pretended he was single. Told *Mother* he was single. I *heard* him.' She fell into a reverie. The red face worked. It seemed to become swollen. Then, with violence, she exclaimed: 'Letitia, you've no *idea* how wicked he was! He was trying to get everything into his own hands. He came to see Mother. Think of it! Yes, came to the house. As cool and calm! I said—I was never one to . . . I thought they were Chicago gangsters——' She stopped abruptly, her eyes filled with tears.

Letitia knew that she must not say anything, not move, not warn Muriel by any quick glance that this was all new and important in her own defence. She saw Muriel boiling and fuming, growing redder and redder, and jerking her arms and stamping the little feet which hardly reached the floor when she sat properly in the chair. When anger reached such fury it was clearly dangerous, and Letitia was forced to venture a diversion. Stupid as it might be of her, she felt she could not refrain from asking:

'Do you mean Farringdon brought somebody with him? Not his wife?'

'Wife? Oh, no; I told you I didn't know he was married. Oh . . .' Muriel let her anger pass from her, and with it passed all her strength. She grew smaller, just as her mother could grow smaller. 'I've forgotten. I don't remember. Everything goes.'

'When it's too exciting to bear?' suggested Letitia, although her heart was beating quickly.

'Yes, he was exciting. He told me exciting things—on purpose. I didn't believe them, fortunately.'

'Of course you didn't.'

'I'm not stupid, you know.'

'On the contrary.'

Muriel smiled; she was pleased at such praise. She said:

'I *am* fond of you, Letitia. I know we're very different; but I feel I *trust* you. . . . I wish we'd seen more of each other. Been together a lot. That was Mother's fault.'

'Well, we must see more of each other in future.'

Muriel trembled. She said:

'*If*——'

'Never doubt it, darling. I never do.'

'I don't when you're here. You've got such . . . But when you aren't here——' With a heavy sigh, she let her head fall against the back of the chair. Her lips quivered. 'Hour after hour, listening to *nothing*. Like something in a cage. It's so dreadful; so frightening. . . .' She closed her eyes, and grew pale.

For a time Letitia made no attempt to interrupt the sorrowful silence But she forced herself to do so.

'You know I come as often as I can.'

'I know. Darling Letty!'

'And after everything's done you'll come and stay with me.'

'Yes.'

'Get right away from here. Forget all this.' There was a sigh. But Letitia felt that her errand was still undone. Ugly and painful though it was to both of them, she *must* try to gain a further inch, and a further inch, not for curiosity's sake, but for the truth. How clumsy she was! 'Farringdon came twice to see me, I think. I didn't see him. How long ago did he come to see you? How did he look? Old? Young? Grey-haired?'

Muriel vaguely shook her head.

'I can't tell you. I only remember his wrists sticking out of his sleeves. He wore soft flannel shirts. His arms were too long for them. Oh, and great bristling eyebrows——'

'You didn't see *him* in London, by any chance?'

Muriel stared, and went on shaking her head for a long time. Almost with animation, she cried:

'Farringdon? What a horrid thought! When I had such a *happy* day!'

'Did you? I'm very glad.'

Muriel peeped once. Letitia could feel that glance of suspicion, and the withdrawal which followed. She saw the lips close. She knew she would get no more. When, presently, she left, Muriel clung to her with more pathetic affectionateness than she had hitherto shown. Her last words were:

'Don't *tell* anybody, will you! What I said about F.'

Letitia smiled, but gave no promise. Their farewell showed her that with one secret gone Muriel would have better rest that night.

iii

Back at the hotel Letitia found that Child was impatiently awaiting her. He was most excited; but he made her repeat as much as was discreet of her conversation with Muriel before he gave her his own news. When she had finished, he cried boyishly:

'That's our man, then. Even if he's only a red herring! Oh, we're getting on. Very much so. You and I must go back to town. We must see your husband at once. By the way: bit of luck—Sconce is leading for *them*. Complete duffer. . . . Of course, looking for your brother in London——'

'*If* he's in London. I feel that, if he were there, he can't have failed to see something about the case. Surely, if he'd seen anything, he'd have come at once to see me?'

'Frightened, perhaps. Cold shivers down his back.'

'But his sister! I think he *must* be ignorant of it. Do you think there's any chance of finding him?'

Child grimaced.

'Not in time.'

Dashed by this recognisable truth, Letitia had her second inspiration of the day.

'Supposing he's gone. We could get him by wireless, couldn't we? His wife's a South African. They might be on their way back there. Does that help?'

Child stared at her. He smiled brilliantly.

'Wireless. Great! I'll make inquiries about sailings. Don't count on it too much, will you. Now I must tell you *my* news. We've found blood on the bedpost. And—Stedman says—definitely a white hair on it. He's busy reconstructing. The inspector's got an incipient headache; but he still looks on Stedman as an amateur, thank God!'

Letitia felt sick; but Child, to whom reality was a formula and detail its corroboration, went jubilantly away. He was working for an acquittal by manœuvre; Letitia's notion of acquittal by faith seemed to him not only sentimental but lacking in virtuosity.

Letitia, painfully aware of this, lost confidence in the day's discoveries. What did it matter if they changed the culprit? Muriel would still be labelled as an accessory. They might even say she'd delivered the fatal blow in Farringdon's presence. Child was too easily pleased, as she had been by her own ingenuity.

'I *must* do more!' Urgent desire made her go back through every word of her exciting talk with Muriel. Some of the words grew fiery in her memory. She repeated, exactly in Muriel's tone: ' "When I had such a *happy* day!" ' And she put herself in Muriel's place. One didn't say that of a *lonely* day. Muriel had spent it with somebody she loved.

Now Muriel knew nobody. Since her arrest not one person had made any inquiry after her or offered her any help. She said with mournful, self-pitying pride that she had no friends; and Letitia believed her. If Farringdon be ruled out, there must be somebody else; somebody quite obvious, in whom Muriel had such loving happiness that, for fear of blackening it in the eyes of others, she quixotically refused to speak his name. There was no need for further search. That somebody could only be Julian.

Letitia felt so great a relief at certainty that she began, proudly and secretly, to cry.

iv

'Mrs Wilton said would you please ring her up, Madame,' said Ruth.

Weary from excitement and the journey, and from an hour's subsequent talk with Child and Monty, Letitia did not at first understand what Ruth had just whispered, but Christine came running down the stairs and took possession of everything. She was in her most managing mood.

'All right, Ruth. *I'll* see to it.'

Letitia thought: 'Whether I *want* Chris to speak to Constance is another matter! What mightn't Constance—if she's angry—betray!' Then she thought: 'However, this is no time for prudery. . . . Oh, how tired I am of secrets and ingenuities! I'd like to burst out with everything that's hidden in my chest!' She repeated her afterthought to Christine, who was delighted with it.

'Oh, *do* burst out, Mummy!' she entreated. 'Your bursting out is what I've always dreamed of. To bring you down to my level!'

'If the secrets were mine!' groaned Letitia, missing this strange testimony to her own superior calm from one whose calm was like enamel. 'Unfortunately it takes two foolish people to make one idiotic secret. One's gagged and bound twenty times over by mistaken loyalties.'

'This bad old-people's world!' cried Christine. 'Petticoating truth! How much wiser *my* generation is! It's so frank and courageous—as, the newspapers say.'

'*Your* generation!' scoffed Letitia. 'You so much enjoy talking about forbidden things that you're quite hypocritical. You're neither franker nor more courageous. You just omit the graces of living.'

'Now, Mother! You're making a noise like an old goose!'

'Quite true. I'm demoralized. I need some tea. Ruth will bring it, mercifully without talking. Meanwhile, ring up Auntie Constance while I'm dabbing my face.'

'Before you've dabbed a dozen dabs!' cried Christine. 'I'll be gagging you with another secret. By the way, in view of the goose-like noises, perhaps it's as well you're gagged.'

Her return was less spectacular. She came slowly, frowning, into the bedroom.

'Yes, dear?'

'Cantankerous woman demands *you*. The complete egoist! She says she can't talk to a child about such dreadful things. When I told her I knew all the facts of life she began to sob histrionically.'

'Tk, tk. I hope you haven't upset her, poor thing!'

Letitia hastened to the telephone. 'Constance. I'm this moment back from——'

She was not allowed to finish. A deep, tragic voice drowned hers.

'Letitia! *Awful* news! They're going to operate. Tomorrow morning. He's *gone* to the nursing home, terribly brave, like a Christian martyr. Darling, I'm in despair. I don't know what to *do*. I know you're busy; but *could* you . . .'

Filled with trouble as her mind already was, Letitia could still respond with a plunge and sinking of the heart to this fresh shock. Gabriel! He was so little able to bear the strain of such an operation, temperamentally and physically, that he might not fight it unless support came to him from without. No wonder poor Constance was distraught. She, too, all nerves and display, wanted the right sort of stamina. Of course she must be helped. Gabriel must be helped. But was there to be no end to this cycle of disastrous events?

'I'll come to you at once,' Letitia said. 'Be brave, darling!' And after replacing the receiver she went back to the drawing-room, obediently drank the tea which had been poured for her, and listened half-attentively to Christine's further sharp comments upon her seniors.

'I can't help blaming you, Mother. You encourage everybody. But I do think Auntie Constance should bear her own sufferings. She never has done it. She's always put them on your shoulders. That's what she's doing now. It's absolutely unimaginative to speak of you now as "busy". "Busy", indeed; when you're half out of your wits. But it's just like her.'

Letitia, thinking agitatedly of Gabriel, and her last meeting with him, and all that had passed between them, said:

'The sufferings in this case aren't hers only, dear. You *must* allow more for *my* affections.'

Christine was outwardly a little taken aback.

'Yours? Oh, I see. I'm sorry, Mother. Do you think I haven't any?'

'I think you're full of them. I wish you weren't. No, I don't. I'm glad you are. But they always involve suffering.'

In a muffled voice Christine said: 'I thought you thought I was hard.'

'If I ever did, I don't now. Far from it. Chris, I'm thankful for you. I don't know what I should do without you and Father.' Letitia rose quickly and kissed her daughter. 'Be patient with me.'

Christine wore a most peculiar expression. One might have thought she was going to cry. But that, of course, was quite impossible. She said, in her coolest tone:

'I hope you're not sentimental about Uncle Gabriel. He's not really any good, you know.'

Letitia was upon her way. She dwelt less upon Christine's summary judgement than upon her uncontrollable expression.

v

They had put Gabriel to bed, and he was in less pain. He lay under the clothes, and owing to his thinness he hardly raised them from the level of the bed itself, so that it looked as if he had no body at all. When Constance frantically remarked this, he murmured 'All Soul', and shook with laughter; but it was true and affecting to both women that his fine eyes and good brow were all that could be seen of him as they invaded the room.

'Oh,' said Gabriel. 'You've *both* come.' He seemed amused by this fact.

Constance, tense and flurried, cast a despairing glance at Letitia, who sat down at a little distance from the bed; and Gabriel peered at each of them in turn.

'How are you? How d'you feel? You look as if you'd got no body at all. Have they given you anything?' began Constance. 'Has Compston been yet? The nurse is too pretty.'

'Ye-es!' Gabriel was again amused. 'I'd noticed that. But she's stern.'

'Did you give her any reason to be?'

'Oh, they're always stern, at first,' smiled Gabriel. 'It passes off.'

'Are you in pain? I couldn't bear to come alone. I persuaded Letitia to come, though she's tired out. *Look* how tired. She's been very kind. We thought—at least *I* thought—she'd cheer you up. . . .'

'Splendid. Bless you, Letty! They've given me something to ease the pain. Compston's coming later. I've had most of the staff in. They don't often have a dramatist here. Nothing under a countess. One of them's already asked if I take my plays from life. I told her I did. But not from nursing homes. She said I must have been over a bit of grass.'

Constance laughed loudly. She jumped up and brought the sheet away from his mouth.

'He's terrible, isn't he, Letitia!'

'He's teasing you,' said Letitia.

Gabriel, looking over the top of the sheet, thought: 'The two women I've loved. Constance for a fevered month, long ago; Letty with all my being—for the same time, and for ever. Mark her calm. It soothes me. I could die happy, holding her hand; and even *that* will be denied me.' To Constance he said: 'Sit down quietly, quietly for God's sake, where I can see you both. This is an audience, don't forget.'

'We're the audience!' cried Constance, sitting down again. 'Always a necessity to you, darling!'

'We all need one,' retorted Gabriel. 'How's Chris, Letitia?'

'That little malapert!' cried Constance. 'She told me she knew all the facts of life!'

'She meant to help me,' explained Letitia, smiling. 'She's just discovering a few of the facts of human nature. Beginning with herself.'

'Dear kid! You understand her well.' Gabriel spoke breathlessly, with a slight effort. He had felt again, at that moment, the shadow of his former agony, and was anxious to brace himself against an exhibition of weakness. 'Her tone's too bright, in the musical sense.'

'Like mine!' cried Constance. She added, in a low voice, to Letitia: 'Worried about the show. We're supposed to open next Tuesday.'

'Oh, you'll open. Whatever happens,' gasped Gabriel.

'Not with *this*——'

'Darling, you *must*. It's the convention. The brave wife; but an artist first.'

Constance rolled her eyes.

'I should collapse!'

'Wonderful advertisement,' murmured Gabriel. 'What would *you* do, Letty?'

'Oh, she'd carry on, whatever happened,' interrupted Constance. 'Look at her now, with Muriel next door to eternity.'

'Like me.' Gabriel's comment was inaudible. He smiled.

'I'm very hopeful,' Letitia said, seeing the smile, and thinking it was one of sympathy. 'We've just realised that she was with Julian. I've cabled him this evening.'

'What!' Gabriel momentarily forgot his pain. 'Oh, then your troubles are over. I suppose it was you who realised. I'm so glad, Letty. So glad. That's a load off my mind. Oh, yes. . . . You realise why I haven't bothered you——'

'Everybody else has!' declared Constance. 'The damned ghouls! Haven't they, Letitia?'

'They've been astonishingly kind. Neither inquisitive nor cold-shouldering. Monty's mother, *splendid*. She even offered to come and stay with us. She must hate it, of course.'

'Oh, but I'm delighted,' gasped Gabriel. He felt the agony returning. It began to seize him, to tear him from within, so that words were no longer possible, so that he was half-strangled in the effort to restrain screams from betraying his pain and his fear. With a last gesture of strength, he put his finger to the bedside bell and waved them desperately away. 'I'm sorry, girls . . .' Then, as there was a lessening of that ghastly strain, he grimaced in what he meant to be a smile. 'I'll . . . see you . . . tomorrow, darlings. I love you . . . both . . . very much.'

Sobbing, Constance bent and kissed him. She waited, watching with burning eyes while Letitia, reading his entreaty, also kissed him and yielded her hand to his vehement clasp. And as the nurse entered Constance took Letitia's arm and passed crying from the room.

vi

Gabriel was early awake the following day. He found himself alone, and did not remember where he was. They had given him a sleeping draught which left him drowsy and stupid but not bereft of characteristic sense. He thought: 'That ceiling's a bit high. It doesn't seem to be there, in fact. Rather odd. "Impalpable". But this damned bed's here, all right. Damastes. I'm trussed like an old fowl. I expect I've been snoring. . . . Well, how d'you like your last day, my boy? . . .'

He was really afraid to think that it might be his last day.

'I wish I'd finished that play. I wonder what Letty would have thought of it. I don't think she'd have approved. Funnily enough, I see that point. One lowers oneself by guying a guy. By malice. She's a darling; but she makes one wonder if one's best lines are as good as one thought. If they're justifiable. They aren't, of course. If I'd married her—not that she'd have had me. No, that's clear. I should have been a different man. Whether a better writer's arguable. How strong *is* her personality? One tends to exaggerate the virtues of the quiet . . .

'I ought to have written tragedy. *That's* my métier; not cynicism. I was never a cynic. But a modern tragic writer would be an anomaly. We've never got over eighteenth-century rationalism, when they made Tragedy something fatly Roman. My God! Nothing survives pomposity. But then realism killed it by generalising it. Not the great, but the downtrodden, who're a bore. Besides, ambitious men jibbed at a five night run; and left it to the poetasters. The poetasters aimed at the stars and were quite good if they hit the garden fence. What a game!'

He had moralised thus when his nurse entered, crisp and brisk and impersonally kind. It irked him that she should be impersonal. The rest he took for granted; but he was, after all, Gabriel Wilton, and his reputation for diabolical cynicism was not generally disregarded by women.

'Good morning, nurse. Do you prepare the lamb for sacrifice?'

Her cool fingers were upon his pulse. To her he was a patient. She had no humour, as yet.

'I've come to get you ready. Mr Compston will be here at eight.'

Gabriel's humiliations had begun with her impersonality. They became indignities. He was in time given an injection. Later he was helped into the operating theatre, and stripped of his dressing-gown, while Compston, his surgeon, and the anæsthetist, unrecognisable in white, and Compston already masked, dominated the scene. Another drowsy jest trembled upon his lips. He felt insensibility descending upon him; and as consciousness faded he heard low voices already speaking of him as if they thought he could not hear. He was terrified lest he should feel the knife and see his own blood.

'I'm not gone yet! I'm not gone yet!' he stuttered.

'All right, old chap. All ri . . .' No more.

He felt himself crying. He was very unhappy, but no longer in pain. There was a smarting sensation in his body, as though something pressed hard upon him and drove a stubborn weapon into his vitals; but it was not a pain. Dull colours wove themselves in dreary intimidation before his eyes. He imagined he could feel his heart fluttering.

Others were beside him. He thought he heard quick movements. They were putting something over his face. What the devil did they think . . . Was there a flurry? They were hurrying over something. Had he come through too soon? He heard a whisper; but was too weak to understand. Indeed, at this moment he was preoccupied with an amused thought, which was gone before he had grasped it. 'Cunning Nature,' he heard himself saying. 'When Death's due, she lowers our resistance. We give in.' The thought that he was giving in was not unpleasant. He'd had a busy life, restless, with some happiness and a little success, and many boredoms. He didn't grudge it. On the whole this sensation of passive weakness, of surrender to Peace, was rather amusing than alarming. Yes, amusing rather than alarming. He wondered if he would ever wake up again; and in wondering he sighed deeply and was still.

Seventeen

COURT OF LAW

i

OUT OF DOORS a wintry drizzle had robbed the Assize pageantry of its ordinary splendour, and had thinned the crowds of onlookers. The drizzle had darkened the Court itself, giving it a smeary dullness offensive to the eye; but upon Letitia's spirit there was an oppression such as she had not felt since her first day at school. She felt sick with apprehension. Her friends, glancing at her, were reassured by an apparently steady flame of courage; but that was because they saw only one aspect of her, whereas she knew the labyrinths of uncertainty through which her spirit daily passed.

She heard again and again the squeak of an unoiled door at the side of the Court, and saw with concern how crowded was the small space reserved for the public. She saw the uniformed policemen who came and went; harmless big men who to herself would be all helpfulness and to local wrong-doers, or even to suspects, grim giants of threat. To Muriel exactly that. Successive stirs indicated the arrivals of counsel or witnesses; there were louder stirs when the proceedings began; Muriel was brought into the dock.

Muriel was so small that a murmur of astonishment ran like a breeze through the Court. But the Judge himself was hardly taller, a little thin man with florid eyebrows whose deceptive portrait Letitia had often seen and associated with height. She knew that Monty admired him; and in such matters Monty was her guide. She was satisfied. Neither she nor Monty, nor, it appeared, Mr Child, admired Sconce, the prosecuting counsel. Sconce was a snuff-taker with blackened nostrils. He jutted out his blue chin in a way to impress shaken prisoners; but he had a narrow understanding and an ugly, rasping voice.

'Are you guilty or not guilty?' said the Clerk.

'Not guilty,' answered Muriel, with a guilty air.

Oh, Muriel! Muriel! Letitia could have beaten her hands in rage upon her knees. To prejudice oneself by such furtiveness! And then she could have wept at the sight of this poor humbled woman, made small by the Court and her groping sense of inexplicable danger.

That rasping voice sawed the air. It was dry, experienced, dreadful to hear. It was the kind of voice which made the hearer imagine a tickling in his throat, and so it produced a harvest of coughing among those present. It went on and on, reciting all that was so falsely known and misinterpreted, directing itself to flattery of the jury, to the blackening of one who had never in her life, Letitia knew, been other than good, in spite of all her nervous and defensive fear of the future.

'If I could speak out the truth!' thought Letitia, in angry despair. 'All this elaborate torture would be ended. I'm not allowed to speak. Nobody is allowed to speak, to interrupt specious arguments, to put the truth as it's known to them. They must only answer questions; questions far off the mark!' Now she hated the rigid frame of the Law, that giant sieve, through which the subtleties of truth passed like water.

What did the jury think? They had come primed with all they had read in the newspapers. They looked in solemn vacancy at Muriel, at the Judge at the people sitting in Court; but they did not look at the egregious Sconce when he scraped out a perfunctory warning against prejudice. One of them, a long-cheeked man with a spoonbill's nose, stifled that cruel yawn which affects naturally somnolent individuals in Law Courts; another, a woman, made sharp movements with her hands which showed how much she missed her knitting needles. The rest looked like waxworks.

'I shall submit to you,' said the grating voice, 'that nobody but the accused had the motive or the inclination or the opportunity to commit this crime. The doctor who saw the body within two or three hours of death will tell you . . .'

All was familiar. Letitia could have recited beforehand what Sconce would say, and what the inspector would say, and what the doctor would say. She knew that her mother had died from suffocation as she lay unconscious after a heavy blow. She knew that Muriel had taken money to the bank in the morning, and that the blow was supposed to have been struck by this big auctioneer's hammer, and that the prosecution had at first expected —and been ready not to resist—a plea of insanity. It was all a weariness of misinterpretation.

Didn't she *know*? *She* should have judged this case; not the mechanic

minds of Sconce and the jury. . . . Muriel, four years older than herself,
had been a dumpling baby and little girl, rather jealous, never able to fight
for what she wanted. She had been scared by Farringdon, first at his
adventurous baby experiments when she was seven years old, and, as he
grew older, at his reckless tightrope walkings along wall-tops and his bad,
teasing use of frogs, mice, and spiders against herself. She had been demon-
stratively fond of their father, glutinous in her embraces and always
unwelcome. She had then disliked Letitia, thinking *her* the favoured child.
But this phase was short-lived; they had never quarrelled; and as the lives
of their parents grew more and more wretched affection had increased.
It had continued ever since. Timid, good-natured, loving, and unambitious,
Muriel bore all their mother's cruelty because of two things. First, as was
evident, because service to the tyrant would provide for her own old age;
second, as was less evident, because the softness of her nature doomed her
to slavery.

Monty's cross-examination of the inspector had begun. It was brief.
It was right. Letitia saw the Judge give him one glance of great respect.
Whatever else happened, this old man on the bench had shown that he
appreciated quality in others. That was the grand thing about good men.
They could esteem their rivals. 'What time did you first see the accused?
If in fact, as we know she did, she spent the day in London and caught the
4.30 train back to Willowhaven, would she reach the town at a quarter-to-
six? Did you examine the hammer for finger-prints and find any prints
except those of the deceased? When you say the accused spoke hysterically
of her own guilt, did it occur to you to think that she was blaming herself
only for having left her mother alone in the house? What steps did you
take to find out if her story that a strange man or strange men had called
at the house was true?'

Then the doctor: 'How long had the deceased been dead when you
examined her? Was there more than one wound on deceased's head?
Did you notice the colour of her hair? Did you examine the hammer?
What colour was the hair on the hammer? Were you afterwards shown the
bedpost? Do you agree that there is human blood and hair on that? What
colour is it? Would you say it was impossible for the injury to the dead
woman to be caused by a very heavy fall against the bedpost? Did you
examine the accused? Had she at any time any injury to her head? No
bruises? No bloodstains? Did you form the impression that her state of
mind was incompatible with the shock of finding her mother dead?'

Monty's own speech was as simple as his questions. He did not raise
his beautiful voice, but spoke throughout as if he talked to each member
of the jury separately. He used hardly any gesture. His sincerity was so
obvious that the silence of the Court was unbroken throughout.

'The accused,' he said, 'has lived with her mother all her life. As Mrs
Reynolds grew older, the accused looked after her, managed the house,
did all the cooking and shopping, and was a devoted nurse. You have been
told by a neighbour—the neighbour to whom the accused turned when she
found her mother dead—that the two ladies were "peculiar", that strange
noises were heard in the house, violent shouting, and the like—I shall call

the charwoman, Mrs Pepperkin, to explain that Mrs Reynolds made all those noises, including the violent knockings; and that the accused, so far from joining in what Mrs Burge described as "orgies", would be quietly busy in the kitchen while they continued. Mrs Reynolds was quite sane; but when she was bored she grew rather boisterous.

'The accused will tell you that she had for a long time disliked the thought that her mother's money should all be kept in the house. It was obviously dangerous that it should be kept there; but Mrs Reynolds distrusted banks. However, the accused decided to safeguard this money by putting it, on her mother's behalf, in the bank. On the morning of the day we are dealing with, she took it all round to the Willowhaven branch of the Southern Bank and left it there. It's been suggested that she stole the money. She did not mean to steal it. She took none of it. Though she was given a cheque book she didn't once use it during the day she then spent in London. She hasn't used any of it. It was her mother's. That day in London was an escape for her. A rare escape from exacting work at home. She played truant. Wouldn't *you* sometimes like to do that? She didn't do it callously, or with an easy conscience—as she showed later on when she blamed herself so severely for what had happened—but instead of returning home to her mother whom she had left having her breakfast in bed, she caught a train which brought her to London a little before lunch-time. She had decided to call on her nephew, at his rooms in London; and she *did* call on him. He will tell you that he took her to lunch, and to a cinema, and then put her on the 4.30 train back to Willowhaven.

'Inspector Blackburn told you that the accused gave him a rambling account of her doings in London, and that she said she had spent the day alone. It's quite true that she said this. She knew that her nephew was sailing the next morning for the United States. She decided, wrongly, that it would be improper to do or say anything that would prevent his journey. But you must remember that it hadn't been suggested at that time that she would be charged with her mother's murder. We have brought the young man back from America, by cabling him (he sailed back immediately; and has been in England for just three days); and he will tell you how the day was spent. If you accept the prosecution's estimate of the time that passed between Mrs Reynolds's death and the doctor's examination, and if you accept Mr Julian Boldero's account of his aunt's visit, you will see that the charge against her is ridiculous.

'However, I'm now going to suggest to you that Mrs Boldero was not murdered at all . . .'

ii

Muriel, sitting in the dock, felt quite crushed by the size of the Court, and the buzz of noise. She could hardly raise her head, because everybody seemed to be looking at her. If she peeped in any direction, she was faced with frightening round eyes which said 'You . . . you . . .' The sound, which she alone heard, was very menacing. If it hadn't been that Letty was there, and so *sure*, Muriel felt that she must have begun to scream in fright, as she had done when she was a little girl.

At first she was too frightened to look at the Judge. She thought that *he* would be staring at her. But he wasn't doing anything of the kind. He was a gentleman. But that horrid man with the big chin and the scraping voice looked at her. He hated her. He told such *untruths*. Why did he do it? 'Oh! Oh!' She gave little secret cries of protest, which nobody heard except the wardress who sat behind her in the dock. They were cries forced from her by the cruelties of this bitter man. . . . When once she remembered that she would have, later on, to answer his questions, she grew faint.

She still could not understand what they thought she had done. But her courage, which had been sinking steadily throughout the days of solitude, now rested solely on three people, on Letitia, on Monty, on darling Julian. Her toes felt very cold. It was unkind of them to keep her here. She would rather hide now, and be told afterwards what they'd decided to do with her.

Decided. Muriel felt cold all over. She slipped forward in her chair; but recovered before anybody except Letitia and the Judge had seen how near she was to fainting.

'It is my submission,' grated Sconce, 'that the accused grew tired of waiting for her mother's money. She invented this story of a man coming to the house. *What* man? Where *is* he? Has anybody even seen him? Is the defence going to produce him? Of course not. He never existed. She appropriated the money. She struck her mother. She waited, walked about the town, came back to the house, pretended to discover her mother's body. . . . '

'Horrible man! *Horrible* man!' said Muriel to herself. 'His chin goes up and down like a ventriloquist's dummy.' She shut her eyes to hide it, and the lids of her eyes were stinging. She remembered the ventriloquist at the seaside when she was a little girl. She had made Letty hold her hand at every crossing: Letty hadn't wanted to do it; but she had insisted. . . . The voice, crark-crark-crark, went on. It went on and on and on; and against her will she listened to it with dreadful fascination. With her eyes shut she saw Mother's room; and Mother coming up the stairs, slowly, slowly, making no sound at all as she always did, hoping to catch Muriel idling; and the big unmade bed, and Mother lying on the floor in ghastly stillness as she had been that night, with her black skirt spread wide and her face grey and stretched and the eyes staring in accusation. . . .

Muriel was choking. *Had* she done it? *Had* she? She had longed, often, for Mother's death. She had—not hated, but been afraid of Mother. *Could* she, somehow, not ever of course meaning to, but in a dream; could she possibly have brought herself, when Mother had threatened her, as she was always threatening her . . .

Crark-crark. 'It will be said that the only finger-prints on the mallet are those of deceased. Gentlemen, when Inspector Blackburn was questioning accused she was still wearing black woollen gloves. . . .'

Ah! They would think she had done it. They wouldn't *know* she hadn't. They would take all he said as true. Monty wouldn't be able . . . Monty was . . . He couldn't save her. This man's voice would creak its way into their souls. He would frighten her. She wouldn't know what she was saying. They would hang her——

With her heart thudding like drums in a funeral march, Muriel opened her eyes. She looked piteously at Letitia. Letitia gave her a little nod, and a smile. . . . Letty! Letty! *She* wasn't afraid! *She* didn't believe! *She* was confident! Although Muriel still breathed very fast, the beating of her heart was less loud. She felt the back of the chair once again behind her shoulders. Nobody except themselves and the Judge knew of that loving exchange, or of the passing of strength from Letitia to Muriel. Nobody but the Judge could tell that from this moment Muriel heard the voice of Mr Sconce without terror.

iii

Terror revived when she was made to leave her chair and go to the witness-box. Her steps were so slow that the wardress supported her with an arm, and such women as were among the observers were divided between thinking it a shame that she should be tormented and thinking that guilt had never been more clearly expressed. She was now much nearer to the Judge and to a light which made his eyes seem to her to glitter as if it shone from within. She thought: He'll see if I don't tell the truth! But indeed she had no longer any reason for *not* telling the truth.

It made it easier for her that Monty should be the one to ask her about all she had done. She had always liked Monty, though she couldn't, of course, say that they had ever been friends. She had wondered if Letty were as nervous of him as she was; but, if she was, she never showed it. Letty never showed her feelings. People thought her cold.

'Yes, Monty,' Muriel said once, not realising that she had done so, but causing a murmur of amusement in Court. She could not understand what the noise was. She was looking at Monty very earnestly, trying to do her best, because, of course. he had been *very* kind and patient with her, even when he . . . when she . . . She had been thinking, naturally, of dear Julian, and the darling boy's career, not wanting him to be *mixed up* in anything unpleasant. . . .

'Did you ever raise your hand to your mother? Did you ever handle the mallet?'

'Of *course* not. No!'

And then Crark-crark-crark! The horrid man began. He twisted what she said; he kept coming back to the most disagreeable details of Mother's death, which made her shiver; he once, because she was confused, raised his voice and struck the air with his papers. But help was at hand.

'No, no, Mr Sconce. You really mustn't *bully* the witness,' sighed the Judge. 'She's given you the answer once. *She doesn't remember.*'

'As your ludship pleases.' Oh, he was different, then! Muriel saw a brilliant light, a light of understanding. She said to the Judge, in a clear voice:

'I don't know *why* he should hate me, my Lord.'

Mr Sconce, hearing the general titter, reddened under his great frown. 'I really . . . You say you spent some time in the kitchen before going upstairs. You say you were afraid to go upstairs. Why *should* you be afraid?'

'I'd been naughty,' explained Muriel. 'I'd left her alone all day.'

'But the post mortem examination showed that she had eaten a very hearty lunch not more than an hour before her death. Who cooked that lunch? I suggest that *you* cooked that lunch. Come, didn't you share with your mother a bottle of Pommard?'

'I never drink anything but water. It doesn't suit.'

'Then she drank it all?'

'I couldn't tell you. You forget I was in London.'

'My submission is that you never went to London. That after banking the money you went home, prepared the lunch——'

'My nephew will tell you what I had for lunch, in London——'

'Your story to the police was that you saw nobody in London. You now say that was a lie. Was it a lie?'

Muriel's face grew very hot indeed.

'Yes, it was. The only purposeful lie I've ever told in my life. Except to Mother.'

'But then you've never been charged with homicide before, have you? I suggest that your whole story is a tissue of lies, that you never left Willow-haven; that the story of meeting your nephew is quite imaginary——'

Now Muriel was fired at last. Her cheeks flamed anew. She stood up on the tips of her toes. She turned in wrath upon Mr Sconce, and in a loud voice cried:

'How *dare* you say my nephew tells lies. It's impertinent! How *dare* you!'

'Oh, no, no, no!' cried the Judge. And Monty was on his feet, too, looking quite startled. Muriel, conscious of wrong-doing, let the angry tears roll down her cheeks.

iv

Nevertheless, of course, it was Julian's evidence which ended the case against Muriel. Letitia, seeing him stand facing his father, knew that it was bound to do so. She knew that there could be no gainsaying his sincerity. In the eyes of all present, including Sconce, he was clothed with the prestige of Monty's reputation as an honourable man. There was as strong a prejudice in his favour as there was prejudice against an obscure little stout woman who stood to benefit by an old lady's death. Moreover Julian, in the witness box, had no nerves. He had known judges and counsel all his life. He had been many times in the Courts with his father. He had committed no crime, and was suspected of committing no crime. On the contrary, he had crossed an ocean in order to be present.

So absorbed had Letitia been in him, and so proud of the way in which he dealt with Sconce, that she had not noticed a movement of heads among the jury. But as Sconce waved him down from the witness box she was aware of a curious impatience in the Court. Everybody was staring in one direction. It was not at Muriel. It was at the jury. Then Letitia saw that the lank-cheeked man with the spoonbill nose was standing up. He seemed to wish to speak. The Judge, at last aware of him from the remotenesses of Everest, allowed him to speak.

'My Lord,' said the man. 'The jury ask me to say that unless your lordship directs otherwise they feel there's no need to go on with the case. They're convinced that the lady didn't do anything to cause her mother's death, and a mistake's been made . . .'

There was a little illegitimate clapping from the crowded spectators which was savagely shushed into silence. There was a curious pause, as if a large mill wheel had ceased to revolve.

'I may say I entirely agree,' said the little Judge.

Mr Sconce jumped up. He had been shaking his head at various people who were near him. He was adopting to them the hostile attitude which he had adopted to Muriel. He was very angry.

'My lud,' said he, like a chorus of frogs. 'In view of the corroboration as to the accused's movements, corroboration which we on this side of the Court unreservedly accept . . .'

Muriel, sitting in her chair in the dock, grew smaller and smaller. Her head came forward, dropping so that her chin was resting upon her breast. She could hear nothing. She was crying, with the tears streaming down her red cheeks and causing them to swell alarmingly. She felt the wardress raising her to her feet, saw everybody nodding and smiling, and as she stumbled down from the dock groped her way into Letitia's arms.

Eighteen

THE PATTERN

i

SURVEYING THE TABLE that night at dinner, Letitia saw her family entirely assembled for the first time for months. Monty faced her, austerely happy. Beside him, a plump, huddled black bundle, rather tremulous, but timidly smiling at them all in turn, like a newly-made orphan among benevolent giants, was Muriel. Beside Muriel was Mark, full of restrained energy. Across the table, Julian sat discreetly between Stephanie and Christine, Christine (all quick confidence) being upon Letitia's right. Ruth flitted from one to the other, as sedate as ever, her prim little mouth pursed into the perfect semblance of a rosebud. Letitia herself, at the verge of exhaustion, was sustained and invigorated by thankfulness for the day's issue.

She had been amusedly present at the meeting of Julian and Stephanie in the study, had seen his first dark constraint and Stephanie's recoil, and had then—in her heart—marvellingly praised the delightful impulsiveness with which Stephanie stepped forward and kissed him. There had been no coquetry in the action, but a self-confidence which could mean one thing only—that Stephanie felt quite securely in love with Mark for at least another year. Julian, ready to turn sardonically away, was forced thenceforward into acceptance of the old fraternal relation. With this difference: that his power to disconcert was ended for ever. Knowing his humiliation, he nevertheless responded with smiling coolness; thus pridefully baffling Christine, whose obvious irony was as malicious as her tenderness for Julian allowed.

'Should *I* have been as wise or as quick?' thought Letitia. 'Or as idiotic as Stephanie was a month ago?' She knew, even as she exchanged a secret message of accord with her daughter-in-law, that in spite of love and respect for Mark her instinct would have been all for Julian. But Stephanie knew her need of a steadier will than Julian's. As for Julian, he was still laughingly arrogant at his triumph in Court. It had been he who stopped the case. Never mind that the triumph had been largely fortuitous: it was personal enough to carry him through this encounter with a lost beloved. Defeated here, *there* he had been glorious. So as Mark could and did talk well about his Stephanie-aided political campaigning in the North, all were happy.

'Though *why* anybody should try to resuscitate Liberalism in these days passes my understanding,' answered Christine, with the object of creating healthy annoyance.

'And why Chris should use her understanding as a final test of wisdom remains to be seen,' observed Mark, calmly.

'She's egotistically young,' said Stephanie, seizing the opportunity given by a crowd to repay many a jeer of Christine's.

'Compromise is the enemy of Progress!' murmured Christine. 'Ecrasez l'Infame!'

'By all means let's perpetuate bigotry!' said Mark. 'Fratricide's grand fun!'

Letitia saw Muriel timidly peeping from one to the other, floating on the banter, and overjoyed that her darling Julian took no part in it. If he had done so, she would have been alarmed in case it became serious. Dear Julian! They were *all* so kind and unaffected. What a very handsome young woman Mark had married. Was she a *little* difficult?

'Are *you* a politician, Auntie?' demanded Christine.

'I? Oh, no. I really . . .' Muriel huddled herself together in humble amusement. 'That would be *very* . . .' Letitia saw the trembling hand seize a little piece of bread and crumble it. 'I really couldn't say I was *anything*!'

Monty said:

'Auntie Muriel's like Chris. She's got a vantage-point outside party; she derides them all.'

'No, no!' Muriel laughed in joy at being teased. 'I really can't tell one from the other.'

'Nor can Chris,' said Mark. 'That adds wings to her contempt.'

Yet Chris, thought Letitia, was the only one of them all who in the past few weeks had given her unalloyed happiness. Was *that* strain to come later? Why should it ever do so? She smiled at Christine's unruffled white brow, and thought how pretty she was, and wondered who had given her the jade necklace which she was wearing tonight for the first time since her birthday party, and was glad when she realised how much closer they were than they had ever been. She wasn't afraid of her daughter. Or *for* her daughter.

'Chris is all right,' she suddenly exclaimed. 'Chris is splendid. She can be a Communist or a Single Taxer or a Home Ruler for Kensington, for all I care.'

'As a matter of fact——' began Christine, with terrible condescending patience. She was not allowed to finish her sentence. Everybody laughed. Even Aunt Muriel laughed, her face growing as red as a beetroot as she choked into her handkerchief. Even Christine herself laughed, giving Letitia a little glance of pretended disgust at such levity, but not in the least resenting what had been said of her.

Nobody was very critical this evening, thought Letitia. All, happy in the family circle, were liberal. No doubt the Ugly Duchess could have drawn a moral from that for the world as a whole.

ii

Not long after dinner, Letitia rescued Muriel from the others and took her up to her bedroom. It was beautifully warm there, and a cheerful fire burned in the grate. Lovely gleams from it caught the faces of the pictures and the knobs of the chest of drawers, so that there were dancing lights everywhere.

'Oh, dear,' sighed Muriel, sinking to the bed. 'Isn't this delicious! I can't believe it. I feel I'm dreaming.'

'Well, you're dreaming,' Letitia told her. 'A long, happy dream. You shall have a long night in bed.'

'Oh! Not *too* long! I'm used to getting up early. I had to, you know. Mother used to wake up——' She shuddered. Everything flooded back into her mind. She listened instinctively for the hammer. She heard her mother's screams. She heard the rasping voice of Mr Sconce. She was shut into a room from which there was no escape. 'Letty! Letty!' she suddenly screamed in horror. 'Save me!'

Letitia sat down beside her and held her hand.

'You shall get up when you like. Go downstairs to the study. Anywhere. *Anywhere*. Go out. You're free. This door shall be left ajar. Monty and I are in the next room——'

The horror had passed. Muriel, flaccidly huddled again, had resumed humility.

'Oh, I shouldn't dare. With Monty. He's so . . . I'm really *nothing*, you know.'

'We'll see,' said Letitia. 'Try and think of happy things. What you'll do, and——'

'Letty, you know I *oughtn't* to have thought; but I've done it. Well, aren't I wicked! I *should* like to live—well, in London. . . . Not *near* you; I don't mean that. I don't want to be a nuisance. I'm so afraid of troubling anybody. But so that I could look at the shops. I've always *longed* to do that. Bond Street and Regent Street, and Oxford Street . . .' Her voice faded into a luxurious sigh. 'So *immense*!'

'You shall look at the shops,' said Letitia, 'in all those streets.'

'Lovely! *Isn't* it lovely! But, Letty, there's something. Something . . . Do you think people . . . will . . . *mind* me?' The ruddy face, recently so much paler, was a darker red. 'I know *you* . . . and the dear children . . .' Muriel's head was down. She took small flying peeps at Letitia, as rapid as those of a bird. 'But *others*.'

'In a fortnight they'll have forgotten you exist!' replied Letitia.

'But I was nearly hanged.'

'No, darling.'

'Wasn't I?' It was childlike. 'I thought I was. When I heard that raspy voice this morning I felt sure I should be. He made me sound so *awful* that I almost . . . gave up hope . . . Only you, sitting there so calm, kept me from fainting with fright.'

So calm! Letitia could smile now. She murmured:

'He was a goose.'

'Was he? Of course you could tell. I couldn't. I haven't . . . Well, not *very* bright, d'you think? Or *not*?'

'Quite bright.'

'Oh. I've often wondered. Monty was so splendid; he . . . And darling Julian——'

'Bed!' cried Letitia. 'Or you'll talk all night. Shall I help you to undress?'

'Oh, no!' Muriel jumped up. 'The idea! I'm quite . . . Besides, you wouldn't understand all my . . . gadgets. My tapes and buttons and hooks and eyes. *Very* out of date, I expect. But then *Willowhaven* . . . And no money, you know. I only had what *you* sent me.'

Letitia left her to undress herself; and when, later, she returned to the room she found Muriel fast asleep, breathing heavily. A curious coarsely-knitted white woollen tippet was about her shoulders, over the high collar of a pink flannelette nightgown which was edged with cheap lace. Asleep and at peace, she looked like a cherub.

iii

Christine waylaid Letitia as she went down the stairs. They continued the journey arm in arm.

'Is she off? Poor old thing. You're not thinking of having her to live here permanently, are you?' It was ruthless; not unkind. The application of realism to a matter of sentiment.

Letitia took her daughter's arm.

'No, she—and you—wouldn't be happy. She wants a place of her own.'

'She's no fool, you know. Was she good in Court?'

'She thundered at Mr Sconce when he tried to prejudice the jury beforehand against Julian. But in the dock she looked maddeningly abject. You'd have wanted to sit her upright.'

'Julian was good, wasn't he? Daddy says "first rate". They're getting
on splendidly tonight. Have never seen so much in each other before. Of
course, Julian's as distrustful as a cat.'

'I sometimes wonder if it's because he came *between* Mark and you.'

'Ah, that's psycho-pathology. Out of my line. Mother, was it *serious*
between him and Stephanie? She's a bitch, you know.'

'D'you know, oddly enough, if you mean a woman who, having got
one man, looks round for another, I don't think she *is*. She doesn't *manage*
herself very well. But she's as loyal as you are, and she *knows* Mark's
essential to her—as a better half.'

'Oh, he's that, all right. What about Julian? Nothing to say? One of
your "secrets", and a dark one. Well, you've had a lot on your hands,
lately. Still have, I suppose, with poor old Auntie Constance; but *at home*
not so much?'

'Almost nothing,' agreed Letitia, with a smiling, teasing glance.

They had long ago reached the foot of the stairs, but they were still
arm in arm, like débutantes at a ball. Christine gave her mother's elbow a
jolt.

'We'll find you something complicated,' she said. 'There's me. And
Auntie Muriel's future. And Mark's offspring——'

Letitia felt a stirring of alarm.

'Are these threats based on information? Or hypotheses?'

'Oh, hypotheses,' cried Christine, airily. 'Pure hypotheses. But
inevitable, of course. I'm sure, darling, you'll be equal to them.'

iv

The last scene of the day was with Monty, after the children had gone
to bed and they were alone together, in peace, in his study. As once before,
Letitia was sitting in one of the arm-chairs, with a table lamp as the room's
sole illumination, while Monty stood before the fire, with his back to the
sinking glow. Monty said:

'It's been a good day, hasn't it, Letty. A long one. I expect you're tired
out.'

'I've gone past that. I'm wide awake. It's been very exciting.'

'Too near to be easy, eh? Yes, I'm glad it's over. We were lucky:
their case hadn't been anything like properly prepared. Sconce is a dull
man and he'd taken the police and medical evidence as conclusive. . . .
That was curious about the meal your mother had had. So obviously a
slap-up meal. Not the sort the old lady would get herself if she were alone.
It wouldn't have been easy to account for it. It's Farringdon who offers
the explanation. If I hadn't been sure of Julian, I should have had to press
Muriel strongly about him. Tried to *force* a disclosure. Fortunately, it
wasn't necessary. Something's happened that fixes my mind on Farringdon.
Child's telephoned, since we got back to London, saying his shipping-office
inquiries have had a result. It seems that, four days after Muriel's arrest,
a small ship—I think a Dutch ship—left England for North Africa. She

sank in a storm, with all hands. She carried a few passengers, among them a Mr and Mrs F. Sebastian Reynolds. . . . Does that seem to you conclusive?'

Letitia did not move. Shock, dates, intuitions about Farringdon and Muriel flew together into a blur of sensation. It was long before she could speak. At last:

'Oh, yes; quite conclusive. You'll have to tell the police, I suppose?'

'I think so. I'll see Child.'

Letitia, clearer in thought, said to herself: So, after all, Farringdon was a villain. No, a coward. Poor Farringdon! That adventurous boy, gay and handsome and fluent—on the wall in the sunshine, pretending for fun to loose his footing; and this stupid end to his life. . . . She said to Monty:

'I've had a wretched time, thinking of Mother and Farringdon—all mine, you know; and realising what *I'd* let you in for.'

'You?' Monty smiled. After a moment his smile broadened so that it became quite boyish. 'Of course it's been a wretched time for you. I've known it; but I don't agree that it was so for the rest of us. And even for you there are compensations. Look at this, for example.' He took a letter from his pocket-book, and Letitia recognised the handwriting of Mrs Boldero, senior. Her heart sank; but soon she, too, smiled as she returned the letter. It read:

'All fortune attend you in your *Case* tomorrow, dear boy. The sister sounds *worthless*. The mother was *worse* than worthless. The brother a mere *waif*. All the more credit to *Letitia*, who in spite of her *appalling* upbringing has made you a *worthy wife*, and who now stands revealed as a woman of *sterling* courage. *Nay, heroism.* I have not always loved her. I now love her *dearly*.

MOTHER.'

'So you needn't really worry, I think. Mother's faulty; but not without judgement. Her "I have not *always* loved her" is an understatement; but see how that understatement adds lustre to the last sentence. *Most* handsome.' He put the letter away. 'I congratulate you.'

Letitia still looked grave.

'I feel we all lead such *muddled* lives,' she said. 'Not even selfish. As if we were moles, busily scratching our blind way in darkness; never getting anywhere. But I do . . .'

Monty waited for the end of the sentence. It did not come.

'You *do*?' he asked.

'I forget. I can't pretend to have a philosophy of life—apart from the Ten Commandments. I'm in as much of a daily muddle as anybody else. I can't *see*. But when I think of Muriel, and Constance, and Gabriel, whom I really loved towards the end of his life, and Farringdon . . .'

'Not to mention Mark and Julian, I suppose,' drily suggested Monty.

With a glance as expressive as his own, Letitia answered:

'All with so *much* good, or possible good, and so little happiness——'

'And *you* can't cure it?' asked Monty. 'That's your real trouble, isn't it.'

'I'm thinking of them, not as typical, but as people in a world full of pretentious cures for humanity that don't touch human nature. Evil lies in character.'

'No, you're not thinking of the world,' said Monty, stooping—as her head was lowered—to kiss her hair. 'You're wondering why on earth you haven't been able to help them more. You're dissatisfied with yourself. You don't see yourself as others see you. Therefore you don't know how you affect others. Very few of us do.'

'In a way, that's what I mean. Going along, following our noses, on our own stupid little errands. Taking no account of the way we affect others. And being tumbled head over heels, like beetles in a field, by the unexpected interference in our own lives of the general movement of life, or some such dreadful accident as this of Mother, of Muriel. The general movement's beyond our control; but our contributory responsibility for it's enormous——'

'Moles and beetles,' said Monty, reflectively. 'I couldn't agree to call you either a mole or a beetle.'

'I want some derogatory term,' said Letitia. 'Perhaps you can suggest one?'

'What about "pessimist"? You're infected by the pessimism of the children. You, and they, have gone away from simplicity. You're now trying to intellectualise the heart, which can't be done. I admit that we all need better brains, for collective wisdom. But don't, I beg you, darling, underrate what you've *got*, what you *do*. It may not be a philosophy of life; but it's an unexcogitated philosophy of conduct. In fact, the loving-kindness of a good woman——'

'A woman without character.'

'With great character. These others are deficient in character. The boys will develop it; the rest can't or couldn't. They've had this or that quality in Gabriel's case a sort of genius; but none of them have been strong enough to be *good*. You are. You're strong enough to love other people better than yourself. You've given us all happiness. You understand us all——'

'By Jove, I wish I did.'

'At any rate, we think you do,' cried Monty, laughing. 'So, as we go about our burrowing (as you gloomily call it) we feel twice the men we really are, because we know you love us, and will approve our good actions and would disapprove any base or spiteful thing we might otherwise have done. It's a great service you do us——'

'How small!' said Letitia.

'Ah, you want to be a hundred women! If every woman felt—and acted —as you do, we should have a better world. No, Letty, don't end up as a pessimist. Count your blessings—there are four of us—and your good deeds, which are innumerable. And be happy.'

'I *am* happy,' declared Letitia, stoutly.

'Isn't that what I'm saying?' asked Monty.